TIDINGS *of* PEACE

Books by Tracie Peterson

Controlling Interests
Entangled
Framed
A Slender Thread
Tidings of Peace

WESTWARD CHRONICLES

A Shelter of Hope
Hidden in a Whisper
A Veiled Reflection

RIBBONS OF STEEL*

Distant Dreams
A Hope Beyond
A Promise for Tomorrow

RIBBONS WEST*

Westward the Dream
Separate Roads
Ties That Bind

SHANNON SAGA†

City of Angels

YUKON QUEST

Treasures of the North

*with Judith Pella   †with James Scott Bell

TRACIE PETERSON

TIDINGS *of* PEACE

BETHANY HOUSE PUBLISHERS

Minneapolis, Minnesota

Published by Bethany House Publishers
A Ministry of Bethany Fellowship International
11400 Hampshire Avenue South
Bloomington, Minnesota 55438
www.bethanyhouse.com

Printed in the United States of America by
Bethany Press International, Bloomington, Minnesota 55438

Library of Congress Cataloging-in-Publication Data

Peterson, Tracie.
   Tidings of peace / by Tracie Peterson.
      p. cm.
   ISBN 0-7642-2291-0
   1. World War, 1939–1945—Fiction. 2. Religious fiction, American. 3. War
stories, American. I. Title.
   PS3566.E7717 T54 2000
   813'.54—dc21

                                                  00-010525

DEDICATION

To the memory of my Great Uncle John who gave his life in war that others might be free, and to all those who have served their country in times of war and peace—who gave of themselves with honor and dignity that America might continue to know liberty and prosperity.

To you I say a grateful and humble thank-you.

TRACIE PETERSON is an award-winning speaker and writer who has authored over thirty-five books, both historical and contemporary fiction. Her latest book, *A Slender Thread*, is a compelling family saga. Tracie and her family make their home in Kansas.

Visit Tracie's Web site at: http://members.aol.com/tjpbooks

CONTENTS

COMING
H🦋ME

CHAPTER 1

San Francisco, December 1942

David knew better than to open the blackout curtains. He likened it to a game of cat and mouse, a nightly ritual he played with the local air-raid patrol, but tonight was different. The charm of the game faded, and now David wanted nothing more than a last glimpse of the shrouded, silent city. The stage—his life—awaited his performance, the final act.

He and Kenny had often talked about coming to San Francisco. He supposed that was why he was here now instead of back in Chicago where he'd been born, raised, and left to fend for himself. Kenny had said San Francisco looked like a jumping kind of place. The kind of place that could have used a good preacher like Kenny, David thought regretfully.

He almost smiled. Kenny would have enjoyed the view from the two-dollar-a-night, run-down hotel. Beyond the serenity of the third floor, David thought of San Francisco as a vast Mecca of obscurity. Like Chicago, it was a town big enough to lose yourself in. But unlike Chicago, San Francisco draped itself in a charm and grace that reminded David of those higher-class women he'd waited on in Weinberg's Shoe Store before the war.

The slightest movement on the street below caught David's attention. It was odd how after two weeks in the hotel, David had come to know the movements and routines of most everyone in the area. The action below was none other than Mrs. Mac-something walking her prized Scottish terrier. She always waited until nine o'clock to walk the dog. David glanced at his watch but couldn't make out much in the moonlight. He didn't have to see the hands to know that it was nine on the dot. The air-raid Gestapo, as David referred to them, would soon be passing through to make certain no bit of light could be seen from the sad little coastal hotel. Mrs. Mac-something never seemed to mind their chiding that she should be indoors hiding from the enemy rather than walking her dog.

Letting the curtains fall back into place, David switched on the table lamp and instantly locked his gaze on the revolver sitting rather casually atop the dirty bedside table. There, amidst a stale cup of coffee, a flashlight, and two sticks of chewing gum, the revolver seemed to beckon him with a haunting lure.

Swallowing the lump in his throat, David tried to pretend he no longer cared about the idea of using a gun. He hadn't used a gun in the war. He hadn't had to. Forced to join the military or go to prison for a long list of violations, David had chosen what he figured to be the easiest way out. He'd joined the navy.

The job had been pretty easy too. He'd eventually been assigned a job as machinist mate, and his supervisor, a chief petty officer with a heart of gold, was Kenneth Bennett. Kenny was the only person in the world to have ever given David the time of day. Kenny had cared about David in a way that no other human being ever had. Even David's mother and aunt, the only relatives he'd ever known, had been sadly remiss in this area. His mother, a down-on-her-luck woman of Jewish descent, had found herself a victim of both the depression and a wayward husband. And because of both, she had been forced into a life that no one wanted to talk about. The last time David had seen her she was drunk, and his aunt, a stocky, stern-faced matron named Miriam, had screamed insults and damnation upon her until his mother had cowered into a corner of their filthy hovel. While David's mother cried bitterly, Miriam had loaded up his clothes and, grabbing him possessively, yanked his undersized, nine-year-old frame toward the door.

"You'll never see him again," Miriam had stated firmly to Deborah Cohen. "You don't deserve the boy."

David remembered crying for his mother, but Miriam had slapped his arms as he reached out to break free and return to the crumpled form of the sobbing woman. Miriam had rattled off heated words in a mixture of Yiddish and heavily accented English, all the while forcing him out the door and down the rickety steps of the only home he had ever known. And Miriam had been right. His mother had never seen him again because that night she had died, succumbing to her alcoholism and broken heart.

Miriam hadn't lasted long after that herself. Fixed in her staunch religious beliefs, Miriam had forced David to attend synagogue and *yeshiva*, where he was completely humiliated to realize he had no knowledge of his family's heritage. Ostracized by most and bullied by others, David had learned quickly that the Talmud was of little help to him, but his fists seemed quite capable of getting his point across. When Miriam died three years after that hideous scene with his mother, David realized he was on his own.

Just as he was now.

He crossed the room and sank onto the lumpy mattress. Cradling his useless left arm, he grimaced as pain shot through him. He took a deep but ragged breath. The pain made him feel like crying, but he saw it as a pointless exercise. It wouldn't end the pain. Only the gun could do that.

He would have preferred sleeping pills or even pain pills, but the doctor at the hospital had worried about David's mental state, and while he couldn't keep him on any longer for rehabilitation, he could limit the medication he doled out to David. David could come in every three days to receive another allotment of medication, but that was it.

David had thought of simply saving up his pain pills. He could take them all at once in a grandiose exit. It would be simple and painless. He could almost pretend to himself, and thus maybe fool his Maker as well, that he wasn't really committing suicide at all, but simply had taken an accidental overdose of medication.

But saving the pills had been impossible. Every time David went more than six hours without them, the pain was too intense. Maybe it was all in his head, maybe not. It seemed strange that almost a year to the date he had received his injuries, the pain was as bad as ever.

He picked up the revolver with his right hand and settled it onto his lap while he opened the cylinder. The loaded cylinder seemed to reassure him that there could be no other choice. He closed it again without ceremony.

"Kenny," he said, glancing toward the ceiling, "I know this isn't what you'd want me to do, but you have to understand." He felt tears come to his eyes and angrily refused to wipe them as they trickled down his cheeks.

Someone down the hall switched on a radio and the faint melody of Christmas carols filled the silence. Kenny had loved Christmas. He'd told David over and over how much fun Christmas had been in his hometown of Longview. He'd made David promise that as soon as they could get leave together, they'd go to Longview and spend time with Kenny's family. If they could make it for Christmas, so much the better.

"Deck the halls with boughs of holly. . . ."

Though the melody was faint, he instantly thought of Kenny and the wonderful description of holiday festivities he'd given David.

"*First, my mother and sisters go all out to decorate the house,*" Kenny had told him. "*I know you probably think me a little old to enjoy such things, but I'm just a big kid at heart,*" his superior had confided.

"*The whole place will smell like the heart of a Washington forest. My mom will hang fir boughs off the mantel and down the banister, then Pop will go out and cut down the biggest pine tree he can fit in the house.*" Kenny's eyes had actually lit up at the memory. David had felt more jealous of those memories than of anything else he'd ever known or seen.

Stretching out on the bed, mindful of the revolver, David ignored the pain in his nerve-damaged arm and instead forced himself to think back on all that Kenny had related.

"*We have a piano in the front room and my mom plays the most beautiful music you'd ever want to hear. Why, I believe she could get music out of a turnip,*" Kenny had joked.

David easily remembered his own comment. "*I thought that was supposed to be blood.*"

Shaking his head, Chief Petty Officer Bennett had laughed like a schoolboy. "*Not my mom. She'd want something more productive than blood. Of course, given the state of the world and the fact that America is bound to go to war anytime now, blood might just be the most productive thing after all.*"

That thought brought back the ugliness and sorrow of the days that followed. David shook his head as if to force the memories to leave him, but they wouldn't go away. They never had. Not by means of the sleeping pills or pain medication, not even the strongest drink.

December 7 was firmly etched in his memory. Every detail. Every horrible moment. Even the ones David hadn't actually witnessed were there in his imagination. He tried to forget. God knew—if there was a God—how hard he had tried to exorcise the scenes in his head.

The USS *Arizona* had been his home with Kenny and thousands of other sailors. His life had been good under Kenny's guidance. Oh, he had still managed to get into his fair share of scrapes, and more than once he'd insisted on having things his own way, usually with the help of his fists. But just as faithfully his supervisor had bailed him out of trouble. He had become Bennett's pet project, and while at first David saw this as only an opportunity to abuse Kenny's concern, the man's steadfast kindness had caused him to begin thinking twice about his actions.

That's why it hurt so much to realize he'd never again be able to see Kenny. To tell him he was sorry for sneaking off in the middle of the night to party and carouse the Honolulu hot spots. And he had been sorry. In fact, ever since meeting up with Kenny, David had suddenly found himself to have a conscience. And in the wee hours of December 7, 1941, his conscience had been bothering him something fierce. When he'd finally used up all the cash he had on hand and exhausted any hope of free drinks from the house or his buddies, David had made his way back to the *Arizona* in a stolen jeep.

Kenny would understand. He would somehow cover for David's stupidity and keep him out of any real trouble. Kenny would even pray, usually while holding David's head over the toilet while he got sick from his escapades.

David opened his eyes and refused to remember anything more. He lifted the gun and drew a deep breath. If there was any mercy in this life, it would all be over in a matter of seconds.

"You made me a promise."

For a moment, David nearly jumped up from the bed. He could have sworn he'd just heard Kenny's voice.

He glanced down at the gun. He would have to hurry. He was losing his nerve. Pain or no pain, it took a special mind-set to do a job like this, and if David remembered even one more detail of his friendship with Kenny, there was no guaranteeing he'd be able to go through with this.

"You promised."

David sat up, his right hand shaking as he struggled to control the gun. "I know I promised to go home with you, but you're at the bottom of Battleship Row. You aren't even home with your folks," David shouted to the room. If Kenny really was trying to talk to him, he wanted to clear his conscience.

Silence was all that came back to him. Kenny was dead. There were no voices outside the guilty accusations and disappointed suggestions in his own head. Even in this, his final act of life, David was again failing his good friend.

He thought of how important family and home had been to Kenny. He thought of Kenny's love of God and how special Christmas was to this tall, lanky man with an infectious joy of life. When David had been around Kenny, he could almost believe that life could be good. That something positive could happen and that David could be something other than the loser he'd always been.

I can kill myself in Longview just the same as San Francisco, he reasoned. *I can go and meet Kenny's folks, tell them I was a friend, and then go on my way. What's a few more days of pain, if it means that I keep my promise to Kenny? It's the only promise I'll ever be able to keep.*

He looked at the gun, then replaced it on the table. "It's not because I'm chicken," he told the revolver. "You'll get your chance at me. Just like everybody else."

The Christmas season helped to take the edge off the worry and concern caused by the country being at war. Longview's citizens were no different than those anywhere else. Their sons and fathers, brothers and uncles, friends and acquaintances, were off fighting a war that had rapidly spread to engulf the entire world. And while their loved ones were away, those left behind rationed supplies, took up jobs in defense plants, and longed for the days when the world would once again make sense.

Longview itself wasn't all that old, as towns went. Positioned along the Columbia River in Washington state, the tiny town had thrived because of the dream its citizens had for success. Birthed in the prosperity of the twenties, the thirties had dealt Longview a difficult blow—as it had most of the country. Wages declined, jobs were lost, and businesses closed down, but the spirit of the people lived on in strength.

Ruth Bennett had witnessed it for herself. Having lived in the area all of her life, Ruth knew well the fighting drive of its people. Neighbors cared about one another and looked in from time to time to make sure things were all right. Doors were seldom locked and children played in the streets until well after dark.

Faith Church, where Ruth and her family attended, had kept faithful watch over its little flock. Through famine or fortune, the church family had grown at a steady, if not miraculous, rate. People were drawn in by the love and genuine concern they found within the doors of the church. But not only that, people were amazed to find that this love and concern followed people home after Sunday and Wednesday night worship services. These were more than "Sunday-go-meeting" Christians. These were people who practiced what they preached and saw to it that they cared not only for their own but for their community as well. More than one "food pounding" had kept a family from going hungry, and weekly potlucks throughout the tumultuous thirties had allowed every family to have at least one decent meal a week.

Now the forties stretched before them in an ominous shroud of suffering and death. Life had picked up its pace, almost to a maddening speed, but Longview would do its part for its boys in uniform. Nothing was too much if it meant bringing them home alive. And if they couldn't bring them home alive, as was often painfully the case, they mourned them alongside the families.

At forty-four, Ruth Bennett was very much an active woman. She'd given birth to five children and had buried three. The most recent, her eldest, was the reason for the gold star in her window. Funny, she could remember as a child working hard for a gold star in memory class at school. Ruth had thought there to be nothing more grand than a gold star, but now she wished she had anything but that emblem in her window.

Gold meant death. Her Kenny was dead.

She glanced up at the living room window from the front porch steps. The banner reminded her that Kenny would never come home again. The star might have said, "Well done, you have given your best," but in her heart Ruth felt only pain where Kenny's memories lived.

"Ruthie! Yoo-hoo!"

Ruth looked up and smiled tolerantly. Mrs. Mendelson was making her way toward the Bennetts' front gate. "Hello, Mrs. Mendelson. How are you today?"

"Oh, I'm doing quite well, deary. I just wanted to bring you this fruitcake and wish you merry for the holidays. I'm going to Seattle tomorrow," she said cheerily, "and I couldn't go without making sure you had some holiday treats from me."

"How kind of you. A fine treat indeed," Ruth declared with a smile. Mrs. Mendelson made the worst fruitcake of anyone in the entire community, but the woman was nearly eighty years old and it brought her such delight that Ruth would never have said otherwise.

"My daughter sent me money for the bus!" Mrs. Mendelson proudly declared. "She wants me to spend Christmas and New Year's up there."

Ruth nodded. "I think that's wonderful, Mrs. Mendelson. Of course, we shall miss you while you're gone. I know you'll be missed at church, especially in the choir."

The old woman beamed. "Well, I was once the most sought-after soprano in Westfield, where I grew up."

Ruth had heard these stories a thousand times if she'd heard them once. It was the reason she mentioned the choir in the first place. The old woman had few laurels to live on, but the choir, her fruitcake, and her beloved family were her crowning jewels.

"Oh dear," Mrs. Mendelson said, hearing the four o'clock whistle blow down at the river dock. "I must hurry. I'll talk to you when I get back." She pulled her coat tight with one hand and gave a little wave with the other. "You have a merry Christmas, Ruthie!"

"I will, Mrs. Mendelson. You do the same."

Ruth watched as the old woman toddled off to her small two-story house. Such a sweet old woman! Shaking her head, Ruth glanced down at the fruitcake and made her way into her own house. She could already imagine the comments from her family.

As if on cue, Helen, the baby of the family at thirteen, stuck her head out of the kitchen as Ruthie came through the front door. "I saw you with Mrs. Mendelson. That can only mean she's given you another fruitcake."

"What are you complaining about?" Rachel declared. The eldest Bennett daughter pulled on an apron as their mother entered the kitchen. "You've only had to eat them for thirteen years. I've been suffering through them for nineteen."

"Now, girls," Ruth said, smiling, "she means well and it gives her pleasure."

"I remember Pop said that even Joe Bloom's pigs wouldn't touch the stuff," Helen declared with a giggle.

"Nevertheless, we shall honor the kindness," Ruth replied. She placed the cake on the counter and hurried out of her coat.

Rachel Bennett watched her mother with a deep sense of admiration. There was no other woman in the world Rachel respected as much as she did her mother. Leaving the kitchen, Rachel pulled a hanger from the closet. "Here, let me," she said. "You should warm up by the stove."

Ruth kissed her daughter on the cheek, then turned to see what Helen was up to. Rachel put the coat in the closet and quietly joined the others in the kitchen. She listened as Helen gave an animated speech about her desire to obtain her very own radio.

"It would make the perfect Christmas gift," Helen hinted.

Rachel turned away, smiling. Helen had been trying to talk her parents into buying her a radio for the past year. Drawing a large yellow glass bowl from the cupboard, Rachel began sifting flour while Helen continued her plea. Christmas gifts were the last thing on Rachel's mind, however. Instead, she thought of the war and of Kenny and how lonely it was without him. Of course, he'd been gone from the house for some time, but there were always the letters. And those, coupled with a strong bond of sibling love—a bond even miles of ocean couldn't break—had given Rachel and Kenny an ongoing relationship that only strengthened. With Kenny's death, the letters had come to an end, but not the bond of love between them.

"Is that the front door?" Ruth questioned.

Rachel put aside her memories to listen. She nodded. "I think so."

Ruth frowned. "Perhaps Mrs. Mendelson forgot to tell me something."

"Maybe she's brought us another cake," Helen offered. She gave her reddish brown pigtails a toss over her shoulder before putting her attention back on the biscuits she was helping to make.

"I'll go check, Mother," Rachel said, putting aside the sifter.

"If it's Mrs. Mendelson, don't let her in," Helen declared.

"Helen, that's not nice," Ruth replied.

"Well, then," Helen replied mischievously, "just don't let her fruitcake in."

Rachel could hear her mother's and sister's shared giggles all the way through the house. It was good to hear laughter after so many months of sorrow. The Bennett house was gradually settling back into a routine.

Brushing a bit of flour from her apron, Rachel opened the door, fully expecting to find their fiesty little neighbor. Instead, she found a dark-haired young man standing on the porch. He held his hat in his hands, and behind him a small suitcase rested near the steps. His expression teetered between confusion and panic.

"Yes? May I help you?" Rachel asked softly. No doubt he was peddling something and was simply new at the job.

"Miss, you don't know me, but I knew Kenny."

Rachel felt the familiar tightening in her chest. Anytime she heard her brother's name spoken, she felt herself washed anew with sadness. The pastor had said it would pass in time. Grandpa Bennett had said the same. He had experienced the death of children in their infancy, as well as the loss of his beloved wife. He had firmly told them that while they would always feel the loss, the deep sadness would fade in time. Rachel prayed it might be true.

"You knew Kenny?" she questioned. Then with a smile she added, "How nice. Won't you come inside? I'm sure my mother and father would love to meet you."

"I don't want to impose. I just came up this way because I made Kenny a promise. He wanted me to see Longview, and he especially wanted me to meet his folks."

Rachel felt the sadness fade and a sensation of familiarity replaced it. She could very nearly hear the lines of Kenny's letters running through her memory as she stared into the face of this stranger. "Are you David?" Her tone was one of hope.

The young man looked positively stunned. "Yes. How did you know?"

"Oh my!" Rachel could only manage to say.

By this time her mother had come to see who Rachel had taken up a conversation with. "Who is it, Rachel?"

Rachel turned to her mother. "It's David. Kenny's friend from the ship!" She turned to see the same expression of amazement on her mother's face that she imagined marked her own.

"Oh, David!" Ruth declared, throwing open the screen door. "Why, you just grab up that bag of yours and come inside out of the cold."

He shook his head and sputtered for words. "I . . . uh . . . uh . . ."

"We thought perhaps you had died at Pearl Harbor. No one seemed to be able to give us any information," Ruth continued.

"I don't understand," David replied. "Information about what?"

"Why, about you," Ruth replied matter-of-factly. "Now, don't argue with me. Kenny told us so much about you. He thought the world of you, you know."

Rachel could see by the expression on the young man's face that he didn't believe her mother. Stepping back to give him more room,

Rachel watched in silence. My, but he was handsome. Kenny had failed to mention that. Then with a smile, Rachel almost giggled aloud at the thought of Kenny sharing such a thought with his sister.

"Come on," Ruth encouraged. "Bring your things and come warm up inside. We have a fire going just around the corner."

David smiled nervously. "Does the mantel have pine boughs decorating it? Pine boughs and red bows?"

Ruth looked at him rather oddly and even Rachel was surprised by the question. "Why, yes, it does. I suppose Kenny told you all about Christmas in the Bennett house. We don't have the tree yet, but that's because Marion, Kenny's Dad, hasn't found the perfect one."

"It has to be big enough to reach the ceiling," David recited, obviously from memories Kenny had shared, "but there has to be room for the star."

Rachel read the longing in his tone. He seemed nothing like the outlandish character her brother had written her about.

Ruth laughed. "That's right. Please come inside," she said again. This time she let her own longing be heard, and Rachel clearly understood her mother's need.

"Yes!" Rachel said, rather embarrassed by her own enthusiasm. "It would be so wonderful if you would spend some time with us."

David looked at both women as though they had somehow gone daffy, then shrugged and went back for his suitcase. Lifting it rather slowly, he turned and again stated, "I don't want to impose."

"Nonsense," Ruth said, settling the matter. She reached out and motioned David into the house.

Rachel eased away from the door to let them pass. In a moment that lasted only a heartbeat, David's eyes met hers. Something inside Rachel stirred to life for the first time. Her heart nearly broke for the lost look in his eyes. Oh, Kenny had been right. This one was truly wasting away. Life had evidently treated him very poorly.

She closed the door and glanced upward with a smile. It was almost as if Kenny himself had sent them a special Christmas gift. It was almost as good as having Kenny home once again.

David Cohen felt an overwhelming urge to bolt and run from the Bennett house. He'd never experienced such kindness, and it made him most uncomfortable. Surely these people were merely putting on an act for his benefit. They couldn't really want him around. Of course, if Kenny had only mentioned the briefest details of their friendship, then he could understand. They couldn't possibly know how he had hurt Kenny time and again by lying and sneaking around. They couldn't know everything and still want him here.

But as the evening wore on and supper was served, David found Kenny's sisters, Helen and Rachel, and his dad, Marion, and grandfather George most cordial. They were every bit as enthusiastic about his visit as Ruth had been. With a spirit of true interest they asked him questions and showed concern over his injuries, but never once revealed any pity or disdain.

They laughed and told stories of Kenny and Christmases gone by. David found himself caught up in the conversation, even sharing memories Kenny had related to him while they were in the navy together. The family seemed moved by this, especially Ruth, who would dab at her eyes whenever David told of something particularly meaningful.

Supper had been marvelous in spite of the limitations put on them by rationing. Mrs. Bennett had prepared a marvelous chicken stew, and David had never known anything that had tasted quite so good.

"That was wonderful," he told Ruth as she shooed everyone to the living room.

"Thank you, David. I'm so pleased you enjoyed it."

"Good thing you didn't serve him any of Mrs. Mendelson's fruitcake," Helen threw in with a giggle.

"Now, Helen, that's not very nice." Ruth spoke in a reprimanding tone, but nevertheless there was a smile on her face.

Helen bestowed an impish grin on David before flipping her pigtails and heading for the stairs. "I have to go memorize my lines for the Christmas play. If you decide to cut the cake, don't worry about saving me any."

Ruth laughed at this, as did Grandpa Bennett and Marion. Only Rachel refrained, and David felt certain that was because she'd failed to hear what her sister had said. Rachel seemed like something out of a dream to David. She carried herself with a kind of grace and quietness that made her appear almost elegant—regal. Here she was in a simple cotton dress, nothing at all elaborate, and yet she was clearly the most beautiful woman David had ever known. He watched her as she crossed the room to pull the drapes, seemingly caught up in her own thoughts. How come Kenny had never told him just how lovely his sister was? Suddenly unnerved by his thoughts, David searched frantically for something to say.

"That . . . ah . . . that chicken stew . . . well, it was just about the best food I've ever had," David said. He bowed his head, refusing to look at Rachel for fear she'd read his thoughts.

"It helps that we raise our own chickens," Marion Bennett said, plopping into his favorite chair by the fire. "We took to raising a lot of our own stuff once rationing kicked in. I'm just glad we're old farm and logging people. We know how to get by. Rachel, darlin', don't worry about switchin' on the program," Mr. Bennett said as his eldest daughter moved toward the radio. "Let's hear more from Mr. Cohen."

David looked nervously at each of the Bennetts. "You can just call me David," he finally managed to say.

"Well, then, David, tell us about your injury," Marion suggested, not at all appearing concerned with prying into David's personal life. "We didn't hear much after learning about Kenny. I figure you must have been wounded at Pearl on the *Arizona*, but how did you manage to get yourself to safety?"

David felt the color leave his face. He imagined that the others could watch it visibly drop from healthy fleshy hues to a stark, pasty white. "I don't remember a whole lot. In fact, I . . . I—"

"Never mind with that," Ruth interjected. She picked up a ball of yarn and two knitting needles and sat herself down to work. "David would probably feel better if we left off with remembering the battle. Maybe you menfolk can discuss it later on, but for now, why don't you just sit down over here by me, David. You can tell us about your plans for the future."

David nodded, and while Marion and George looked a bit disappointed, the women of the Bennett household looked quite relieved. He took a seat on the sofa beside Mrs. Bennett and cleared his throat hesitantly. "I can't really say I have any plans for the future. I'll have to stick close to the doctors for a while, I guess, but otherwise . . ." He let the sentence trail off into obscurity, just as he planned to do for himself once he left the Bennett household.

"Why don't you stick around with us until you make up your mind," Ruth said, glancing quickly to her husband. "Would that suit you, Marion?"

"I think it would be fine having Kenny's friend stay on," he agreed.

"I couldn't," David protested, catching a veiled glance from Rachel. She seemed to be watching him with the most amazing blue eyes.

"It's no imposition, if that's what you're worried about," Ruth declared, her knitting needles clacking rhythmically. "At least stay with us through Christmas. Kenny's old room is empty. You might enjoy it there."

"I know I would," David began.

"Then it's settled," Ruth replied. She put her knitting aside. "In fact, I'll just show you upstairs right now. You look a little tired, and here we are gabbing your leg off."

She got up from the sofa and smoothed her apron. Her slightly plump frame and warm expression made her a most appealing woman in David's eyes—the kind of woman that David would have loved to have hugged. Not because of anything romantic, but in the sense of one seeking solace, of one seeking a home. He could tell just by looking at her, by watching her interact with her family, that this was a woman in whose arms you could find rest and a sense of belonging.

Without protesting, David bid the family good-night and followed Ruth to the stairs. They took the stairs slowly, and David knew instinctively that Ruth had done this for his benefit. The stair rail was on the left-hand side, and David had no way of holding on. Even this simple act endeared her to him. Was this what it was like to have a mother who cared? One who considered each child's need and made provision for it?

At the top landing, she turned down the little hallway and pointed. "That's where Marion and I sleep. Over there's the girls' room and this is Grandpa's," she said, motioning to the left. "That leaves just this one. Kenny's." She turned the handle on the door to the right. "I had Marion bring your suitcase up here earlier. I had hoped to convince you to stay." She turned on the light and smiled. "I'm so glad you've come to us."

David knew without question that she meant every word. She

really was happy to have him there. "I'm glad I came too," he said, hardly even aware of the pain in his arm.

Ruth walked over to the desk and turned on a lamp, while David did a silent inventory. Kenny had described this room a hundred times. There was the window, now draped in heavy blackout material, where Kenny had tried to sneak out and instead managed to break his arm falling from the roof. He had been trying to join his friends for a bit of midnight fun when his plans went awry. There was the bookcase where all of his favorite books were still waiting for their owner's return. There was his baseball glove and bat. It almost seemed that the memories invoked were his own. David wanted only to take it all in, to remember everything about Kenny, to feel that he could somehow bring him back.

When he glanced back at Ruth, he found her doing the same thing. She was seeking a sense of Kenny's presence, just as he was.

"I know he's with the good Lord," she said softly. "But I miss him so much. Sometimes I just come here and sit on his bed and touch his things. It makes me feel close to him again. I guess that sounds silly. I mean, with Kenny joining the navy, it wasn't like he was here all the time. But he came home on leave and he wrote often. I guess I just always counted on him coming home—someday." She gave him a knowing look and sighed. "I know it may sound selfish, but I hope you'll stay for Christmas. I haven't told anyone, but I've really dreaded facing it. I mean, last year we were still in shock. We were hopeful that Kenny would be found alive in one of the area hospitals. We clung to that hope—we even hung Kenny's stocking just like we'd always done." She wiped at her tears, not at all ashamed to have shed them.

"Now we know he's gone. We know he won't be found."

She looked beyond David toward the window. He couldn't help but wonder what she saw there. Did she try to imagine Kenny standing there happy and alive? That's how it was for David, so surely she might also be the same.

"I'm sorry," she finally said, breaking the silence. "I just hope you'll stay."

David wasn't at all prepared when she came to him and kissed his forehead. It was nearly his undoing. He could abide her tears, but her touch . . . No one had touched him in years. No one except those who sought to harm him, or in the case of Kenny, who would help him after he'd had too much to drink. But this touch of tenderness—a compassion that joined him to this woman like a mother to a son—was something he'd never had.

"Good night, David. If you need anything at all, please come get me. There's fresh water there in the pitcher and a clean glass if you should get thirsty. It gets cold in the night, so I put a couple of extra blankets on the bed. Just kick them down if you get too warm." She gave him a motherly pat on the arm. "We're so glad to have you here."

David bit his lip and looked away. He waited to let out his breath until Ruth had departed the room, closing the door behind her. Suddenly he felt nine years old again. He felt all the longing and pain of a motherless child resurface. He wanted to run to the door, to beg her to come back. He wanted to curl up beside her and let her sing him lullabies and promise him that the monster who lived under the bed would not hurt him.

He touched his hand to the closed door as if to somehow connect himself to her. She had said she was glad to have him here. She had asked him to stay.

"You wouldn't be so happy to have me here if you knew the truth about me," David said in a hoarse, tight voice. "You wouldn't want me here if you knew all the things I've done."

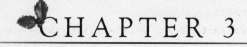

CHAPTER 3

"We'd better get down to the flower shop," Ruth told Rachel after supper concluded the following evening. "David, would you like to walk with us? It's not too cold outside and the evening looks to be pleasant." Rachel seemed to watch him with hopefulness—or was that just his imagination?

"I suppose I could," he replied, pushing back from the table.

"Helen, you take care of the dishes so that your father can get out back and work on the car," Ruth ordered in her gentle way. "Marion, we shouldn't be all that long."

"I'm sure you'll be done before I will," the man muttered. "Can't figure out what's wrong with that rattletrap, but I'm not bested yet. Bob's coming over to lend a hand. We ought to be able to figure it out betwixt the two of us."

Ruth grinned and leaned toward David. "Bob is the neighbor across the alley. He's half deaf and Marion's eyes aren't what they used to be. It should prove for an interesting time."

David couldn't help but smile. He'd smiled more in the last two days than he had in the last three years. It was easy to be happy with the Bennetts. When Rachel suddenly appeared at his side offering him his coat, however, David's smile faded. Her beauty intimidated him. Such sweetness. Such innocence. Her powder blue eyes were wide with anticipation, and he could tell that she had placed more than a casual interest in him. Maybe it was just his connection to Kenny, but maybe . . .

Stop fooling yourself, David. She couldn't possibly care about someone like you. You're no good. You don't even have two good arms.

He frowned and took the coat, then noticed that her expression had changed to one of hurt and confusion. He realized she had taken his frown for disapproval.

"It's just my arm," he assured her quickly, not willing to let her feel bad.

She nodded. "I'm sorry that it causes you so much trouble. Can the doctors do anything to help?"

"They give me medication," he said. "That helps some." His gaze fixed on her compassionate expression. Maybe she really did care. It was with this thought that David suddenly realized that Rachel's hand lingered atop his own. His heart skipped a beat and he swallowed the lump in his throat. *She does care.*

"Well, if you two are ready," Ruth declared as she pulled on her scarf, "we'd best get to it."

David followed the women outdoors and listened to their animated conversation about Christmas and the little town of Longview. He struggled to put his air of self-confidence back into place.

"We just had the Reynolds Metal plant come to town," Ruth told David as they enjoyed the brisk walk. "It was looked at as a godsend because jobs were so scarce during the depression. Now there's plenty of work for everybody."

"They even wanted me to work there," Rachel chimed in. "But Pop doesn't like the idea of ladies working in factories."

"It's all right for women to work," Ruth countered. "It is for the war effort, after all. Your father merely thinks you can be more help at the flower shop. The nursery requires a great deal of upkeep, and the vegetable and fruit plants grown there will help the war cause as much as working in a factory."

"I didn't know you had a nursery," David said, enjoying the casual conversation. "Kenny never said anything."

"Kenny never knew," Ruth said matter-of-factly. "The shop came under our care early this year."

"I suppose flowers and vegetables are better to work with than machinery and metal," Rachel replied. "A bunch of my friends have even gone up to Seattle to build bombers for the war," she said almost wistfully.

Secretly David was glad she hadn't been allowed to venture off. He would never have gotten a chance to meet her if she'd taken up residency in Seattle. He cast a quick sidelong glance at Rachel, amazed at the way her face seemed to radiate such joy and peace, even in the midst of telling a tale where she wasn't allowed to have her own way.

She seemed a reasonable and responsible young woman, so different from the women he'd known all of his life.

"You know what your father would say to that," Ruth said with a teasing smile.

"Boy, do I ever," Rachel replied, not sounding in the least bit angry. "'Rachel Bennett,'" she said, lowering her voice to mimic her father, "'what in the world would you want to do a fool thing like that for? Suckers are born every minute. Don't want it said that any daughter of mine is a sucker.'"

Rachel and Ruth chuckled, then Ruth added, "He just doesn't want to see you hurt. He believes strongly that the war will be over soon."

"Don't count on it," David said more gruffly than he'd intended.

Ruth stopped and looked at him oddly. "Why would you say that, David?"

His voice revealed his bitterness. "I just wouldn't count on it. Those dirty Japs aren't going to give up until they've killed us all."

"David, I know you've been through a great deal," Ruth said sympathetically, "but we don't talk like that in our family."

From anyone else, David would have taken that as an invitation to fight. Instead, as he caught her expression and Rachel's, he felt embarrassed. "I'm sorry, but with Pearl Harbor and all . . . well, never mind . . . I shouldn't have talked like that in front of you ladies."

They turned at the next street corner, passing a group of children who were caught up in an evening game of tag. Their gleeful laughter and animated expressions proved to him that life indeed went on as usual. David envied their innocence. It was almost as if they had no idea that the world was at war. That people were suffering and dying.

"I heard you comment about your arm," Ruth said, changing the subject. "What do the doctors say about your recovery?"

David shook his head. "They say there won't be one. Not a real recovery, anyway."

"What do you mean?" Her question was one of concern, not intrusion.

"The nerves are damaged. They can't do anything for me. I've gone through several surgeries and more rehabilitation than I care to remember. This is about as good as it gets."

"And the pain?"

He shrugged. "They have no way of knowing. They're hopeful that the pain will fade in time. They're hopeful new discoveries in medicine will help them to help me, but I don't have their sense of optimism."

"Just remember, David, with God, all things are possible."

She sounded just like Kenny, so natural and at ease. Kenny would have told him the same thing if he'd been able to.

Rachel reached over to touch David's good arm. "We'll keep praying for your recovery, and if not a full healing, then we'll ask God to show you what His plans are for your life."

David looked into her face, almost mesmerized by the tiny puffs of steam coming from her lips as she spoke. "I don't think God would even care to hear prayers about me," he murmured.

She smiled and it wove a spell over him that left David weak in the knees. "God cares, David."

That was it. That was all she said and yet David felt it was his undoing. A stir of emotions nearly brought tears to his eyes. *Oh, Rachel,* he thought, *I wish that could be true, but God knows who I am and what I've done. He knows I deserve this and worse.*

"Well, here we are!" Ruth announced, pulling a key from her coat pocket.

David looked up to see the orderly storefront. Overhead the sign read Akimoto Nursery. Confused, David looked to Ruth for some explanation while Rachel took up the key from her mother and unlocked the door.

"I'll go see to the greenhouses," Rachel told her mother, not even noticing David's discomfort. She gave him one more brief smile before entering the nursery.

Ruth seemed to understand, however, and waited until her daughter had gone. "The Akimotos are dear friends. They were sent to an internment camp when President Roosevelt gave the order earlier this year. This property is all they have. This is their home and their business," she explained.

"They're Japanese," David said, knowing full well the look of disgust on his face matched his tone.

"They are *Nisei*, David. Americans. Their parents emigrated here long before the war and they were both born in California."

"They're dirty, low-down . . ." He paused in order to keep from cursing. "They're responsible for bombing Pearl just as sure as if they'd dropped the bombs and flown the planes themselves." He felt the anger surge inside. He knew he was acting completely out of line, but he couldn't believe what he was hearing.

Ruth was undaunted. "Kenny and William Akimoto were best friends. They went to school together. Kenny was William's best man when he married Sarah. Both William and Sarah Akimoto are as American as you or I."

David began to shake, the fury inside more than he could deal with. "No!" he exclaimed. "You can't be serious. You can't care what happens to them. They didn't care what happened to Kenny—to the rest of us." He wanted to scream and shake the woman, but most of all he wanted to run away. And that seemed to be the easiest solution. Without thought for how Ruth would feel, David turned on his heel and ran from the storefront. The sound of the bombs were in his ears, the planes strafing, the screams and cries of the wounded. It was a madness that never seemed to leave him, and now Ruth Bennett, the woman he thought of as a comforting presence, was only making the nightmare worse.

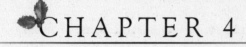

CHAPTER 4

The nights that followed David's outburst were filled with hideous visions of that morning so long ago. It seemed amazing that one moment in time could so forever change a man—a country. But December 7 had done that and more. To David, who had taken life pretty much as it was dished out, the event came as a final blow of failure.

He should have been on the USS *Arizona* with the rest of his shipmates. He should have been in the same watery grave that many of his companions now shared, but he'd taken life into his own hands.

David tried not to think about that morning. In fact, he had a hard time remembering many of the details that involved his own circumstances. He remembered one of the first bars he'd made his way into the night before, but he couldn't remember the last one. He'd passed out somewhere along the way and when he'd regained consciousness it was nearly seven-forty-five in the morning. He remembered that clearly, for some odd reason. Because it was Sunday morning he knew security would be more relaxed. They would have asked for his liberty card the night before, but coming back to catch the launch to take him to the *Arizona*, he doubted he'd get more than a perfunctory wave through.

He'd stolen a jeep, but he didn't exactly remember that. Someone had told him about it when trying to describe what had happened to him. The kind but stern-faced nurse had related the only information she'd been able to piece together. David had taken the jeep, but in the madness that became the morning, no one really faulted him for this mistake.

David had nearly reached the docks when the sky began to drone with the sound of aircraft. No one gave it much thought. David himself, suffering a terrible state of mind somewhere between intoxication and hangover, had only one goal in mind. He had to reach the *Arizona*. He had to find a way to sneak himself back on board and back to his station, or better yet, his berth, before he could be found absent without leave.

Kenny would know he was missing. Kenny had taken it upon himself to be David's mentor and point of accountability. David had abused it sorely, but Kenny was gracious and forgiving, striving instead to teach David in a gentleness of spirit rather than anger.

When the first explosions echoed across the water, David had nearly wrecked the jeep. In what became a rather surreal arena, David found his world completely altered. Bombs exploded in vivid bursts of flame. Billowing smoke rolled off the ships in the harbor and the docks. Soon it was almost impossible to see.

The noise built to an incredible crescendo. It was the noise David most remembered. The mass chaos had a sound like nothing he'd ever known. People screamed out in terror, aircraft roared overhead, bombs, cannons, and bullets offered a cacophony all their own. It was madness, pure and simple. There was no other word for it. Somehow America had gone to war, neglecting to let David in on the details.

When a Zero swooped low, barreling down from the sky, guns annihilating anything in their paths, David swerved to avoid being hit and lost control of the jeep. Flipping it upside down, David had still hoped to make it to safety as he crawled out from under the vehicle, but then an explosion rocked the very foundations of the earth and David knew nothing more. At least for a time.

Soon enough, David regained consciousness and the insanity returned. Someone had placed him on a litter, but they'd left him alongside another man—a man whose entire body lay blackened and burned, a man who no longer had even the slightest indication of life. Barely able to turn his head, David found another dead man on his left. The vision blurred before his eyes as he heard someone yell, "Forget about the dead, we can't help them now! Just get the litter."

Even in his corrupted state of consciousness, David knew they were talking about him and the men who lay beside him. Preservation gave him strength to call out. The word was garbled, slurred, and tasted of blood, but David nevertheless forced it from between his lips as the man came to move him from the litter.

"Help!"

In real life they had come to his aid, but in his nightmares they never did. Instead, David fought with imaginary demons, and rather than be taken to the sterile hospital bed where he could be cared for, David found himself wandering the docks of Pearl.

His imagination was far worse than anything life could have dealt him. He saw men dead or dying—bodies floating in the water, bodies lying on the ground around him. But worse still, he saw the dead come back to life to accuse him. He tried to get to the *Arizona*—to Kenny—but the ship was gone.

They've made it out of the harbor, he would tell himself, but then he would see the truth of it. The *Arizona* had been sunk with most of its crew trapped within. In his nightmare he would attempt to right the wrong. As was often the case in dreams, David had a superhuman strength that allowed him to move bodies and debris in an effortless fashion, but it was never enough. With the *Arizona* underwater, David knew the only way to help was to jump into the water as well, and this was what he did. But it never helped. Truth be told, it only heightened the nightmare.

The hideous macabre vision of what he found there was something David had never even shared with his doctors. The faces of his buddies and shipmates, terror-stricken in desperation, loomed before him night after night after night. David could feel them reach out to him for help. He could feel himself being pulled down deeper into the waters. He needed air! He couldn't breathe.

Coming awake in a heavy sweat, David always gasped for air as though it might well be his last breath. The beat of his heart pounded in his ear. He tasted the burning bile in his throat.

Throwing off the covers, David got out of bed and went to the window. Pushing the blackout curtain aside, he realized morning had come. Still shaking, he splashed water on his face and took several deep breaths. The doctors had told him to imagine himself somewhere pleasant—someplace he had been and found enjoyable. They had promised it would help. But instead of imagining some pleasant respite, David had actually made a pilgrimage. The stories Kenny told had left him with a desire to know a place like Longview for himself. The family Kenny had loved left David with visions of being a part of such a unit. But now that he was here, and for all the love and warmth he had found among Kenny's own people, David knew the doctors had lied. Pastoral settings and gentle people did not erase the hideous nightmares from the past. The monster still lurked beneath the bed, in the closet, behind the door. And that monster wanted David.

Ruth and Rachel both glanced up when David came into the room. It was nearly noon, but they made no comment of his tardy state. Rachel couldn't help but notice the gaunt, almost haunted expression on David's face. She'd heard his cries in the night and knew he was suffering from nightmares, but what she didn't know was how to help. She'd wanted to go to him, to wake him from the horror and promise him that life would be better, but instead she'd remained safe in her own bed and prayed. It seemed the very best she could offer this troubled soul. Prayer, and perhaps her heart.

"Sorry, I guess I overslept," he apologized, not willing to meet their eyes.

"Are you hungry?" Ruth asked in her sweet, motherly fashion.

David nodded. "But I wouldn't want to be any trouble."

"No trouble," Ruth replied. "I'm just fixing lunch. Do you like ham and beans? I mean, I know you're Jewish, and I wouldn't want to—"

"It's not a problem," David said quickly to reassure her. "I don't worry about such things."

She smiled. "Good. I have that and corn bread. Marion won't be here. He's got the day off and has gone to find us a Christmas tree. Helen is off to church to practice for the Christmas play. So it will just be the three of us.

"Rachel and I are baking cookies," Ruth told him as she motioned him to the dining room table. "We've managed to get rather innovative with our cooking now that rationing places such limits on us. Marion is hopeful that it'll be nothing more than a temporary condition, but we all agree that if it helps the boys overseas, it's the least we can do.

"I need to tend to the oven," she said after placing a steaming bowl of beans in front of him. "Rachel will share lunch with you and see to anything you need."

Rachel smiled shyly and nodded. "That is, if you don't mind having my company."

David shook his head and seemed to be searching for something to say. Rachel took pity on him and interjected her own thoughts. "Good. Just let me grab the corn bread."

She fairly danced into the kitchen, catching a quick look at herself in the glass of the china cupboard. She'd worked with extra care on her hair, having pinned her rather unruly mass with bobby pins the night before. She knew her mother had noticed the sudden change but was relieved to have the situation overlooked. Helen, on the other hand, had teased her unmercifully and Rachel had actually worried that her little sister's comments and laughter might have been overheard by David.

Bringing a plate with the corn bread, Rachel found that her mother had already seen to putting another bowl of beans on the table. David looked up and, as if realizing his manners, stood quickly and pulled out Rachel's chair for her.

"Thank you," she murmured. She could feel the fire in her cheeks and knew she was blushing. *How silly he'll think me.* She tried to compose herself before looking up. "Would you like me to offer grace?" she questioned, knowing full well from Kenny's letters that David probably had no idea how to pray. David nodded and bowed his head.

Rachel cleared her throat nervously. "Father, we thank you for the bounty you have given. We ask your blessings on our home and on our country. We ask that you would watch over our friends in service overseas and our friends here at home. We also ask a special blessing on our friends the Akimotos. Amen."

Rachel looked at David and smiled before passing him the plate of corn bread. "Mom makes the best corn bread. I'm sure you'll love it."

David took a piece, but the expression on his face was very troubled. Rachel couldn't help but ask why. "Is something wrong?"

He looked down at the bowl of beans as if ashamed to look her in the face. "I don't understand your attitude toward the Akimotos. How can you care what happens to them?" He looked up and the pain in his eyes caused Rachel to choose her words very carefully.

"I know you've been through so much, David. I can't know the exact experience, but Kenny often wrote to tell me of the atmosphere and edginess of living in Hawaii prior to the bombing. I guess my defense, if it must be that," she said softly, "is that I know the hearts of William and Sarah. I know they loved my brother as much as I did." Tears came to her eyes and she looked away. "I know William would have taken Kenny's place that day if he could have."

David put his hand on hers, and the coldness of it startled her. He seemed so void of life. Almost as if the pain and bad memories had snuffed out the very fire of his existence. Rachel felt drawn to him and looked up to see an apology in his expression.

"I'm sorry that I've upset you. That wasn't my intention. I'm sorry, too, for behaving so badly. I don't want to be the cause of your tears."

Rachel nodded. "My tears are born of my own pain—it's nothing you've done."

The moment seemed to linger and extend long past their original intent. Rachel sat very happily with David's hand on hers, and despite its earlier coldness, Rachel could now feel a warmth to his touch.

"Oh, Marion's home!" Ruth called from the kitchen, breaking the spell. "You should see the tree he's wrestling down from the truck." She came into the dining room, drying her hands on her apron. "I don't know why he didn't park out front on the street. Now he's going to have to drag that thing all the way around to the front."

Rachel pulled her hand away and sampled her mother's beans. She collected her thoughts and gave David a smile. "You will help us decorate it, won't you?"

David felt amazed at what had transpired between him and Rachel. He found himself tempted to tell her everything—to explain himself and his betrayal of Kenny and then to run as far away as his legs could carry.

Instead, he was now expected to join in the festivities and put aside his heart and fears. There was a first time for everything—even decorating Christmas trees. So he pushed away from the table and followed the women into the living room. His thoughts were momentarily lost in the vision of Rachel in a plum-colored dress with a pinafore apron of bleached flour sacks. She had taken extra care with her hair that morning—funny that he should notice something like that. She'd rolled and pinned her long chestnut hair back from her face and curled the ends. The style suited her nicely.

She turned and caught him watching her and blushed furiously. David felt awkward in having been caught.

"Well, here's the tree to beat them all!" Marion announced as he forced the evergreen beast through the front door.

Instantly the scent of pine filled the air. David had thought the boughs on the mantel to have been strong, but the tree's aroma permeated everything in the room.

"Help me put it in this," Ruth told Rachel as she pulled a good-sized metal bucket from behind the couch. Between the three of them they finally managed to secure the tree.

"Rachel, the sand for the bucket is out on the porch," Ruth instructed.

"Can I help?" David asked as Rachel went for the door.

"Sure," she said almost shyly. "I'd like that."

David followed her out and found another bucket, this one filled with sand, waiting for their attention. "If you want to get the door," David said, reaching down for the handle, "I can bring this." Rachel said nothing but did as he asked.

David brought the bucket into the house and waited for Ruth to further direct him.

"Just put it down over here, David," she called. "Marion is securing the tree with some rope."

David could see this for himself as Mr. Bennett was now on his knees, half concealed by the thick branches of the Christmas tree. Depositing the bucket nearby, David stepped back and waited for further instruction. After another fifteen minutes of adjustments and filling the bucket with sand, everyone stepped back to observe Marion's find.

It was just as David had imagined. The tree went nearly to the ceiling. He didn't know how Mr. Bennett had gauged it so close. Perhaps years of repetition had enabled him to know exactly how high was too high, how wide was too wide.

"Well, it looks just perfect, Marion!" Ruth declared. "I think it's the nicest tree we've ever had." She glanced over at David and Rachel. "If you two aren't busy with anything else, why don't you go up to the attic and bring down the ornaments."

Rachel nodded and said, "Come on, David. This is the fun part."

David shrugged and let Rachel lead him upstairs. He was curious as to what she was doing when she opened the door to her own room. As if understanding his confusion, Rachel smiled.

"You have to get to the attic through our room. Actually, it's just a storage area and a place for the pipes and wires, but it holds quite a bit."

David nodded and stepped into the decidedly feminine bedroom. It wasn't at all a pretentious room, but rather a very useful and practical place. A sewing machine stood in one corner, a stack of material placed in a neat and orderly fashion beside it. One bed, with its narrow iron frame, filled the opposite corner. Topped with a colorful, no doubt homemade quilt, it brightened the room and gave it a cheerful nature. Its twin was positioned at the bottom to form an L shape and give the girls the maximum amount of room. Around him on shelves were books, and bits and pieces of collected treasures.

"David?" Rachel called him out of his observation. "Is something wrong?"

He offered her a lopsided smile. "Wrong? No. I was just looking things over. I've never been in a girl's—I mean a lady's bedroom before."

Rachel blushed again and headed for a miniature door on the far wall. "You'll have to duck your head to get inside, but once you're in, the room opens up."

David followed her into the musty, dark room. "Is there a light in here?"

"Just leave the door open," she called back to him. "I'll open the shutters and then we'll have light from the window."

David waited, letting his eyes adjust to the darkness. He hated the feeling that washed over him. He felt momentarily trapped and rubbed his left arm to ward off the dull ache. In a moment his fears were pushed aside, however, as Rachel opened the window and light flooded the narrow room.

"We keep the Christmas things over here," she announced. "We'll have to sort through them and decide what we want to take down. Last year . . ." She paused and was momentarily unable to speak.

David felt her sorrow. "It's all right," he murmured, unable to think of anything else to say.

She knelt down beside a trunk. "We put up the tree last year, but by the time we took it down, we knew for sure about Kenny. Pop just kind of gave everything a toss up here, and I don't think any of us ever thought to come up and straighten it out." She wiped away a tear and opened the trunk.

"We can do that now," David said, uncomfortable with her emotions. He found it impossible to focus on her sentiment and keep any reasoning in his own head. Helping her lift the trunk and place it on a small table, he dusted the top before unfastening the latches.

"We've been collecting these things for years," she said offhandedly.

David could see the truth in that. Homemade decorations, as well as a couple of store-bought ones, were found within the trunk.

"See this one?" Rachel said, holding up a little snowman. "I made it at school when I was ten years old. And this one," she said, putting the snowman aside and retrieving a tiny stable scene, "was carved by Grandpa Bennett. He's quite an artist when it comes to whittling wood."

David could see for himself the craftsmanship. He could instantly tell the various figures—Joseph, Mary, and the baby Jesus. Christmas was a holiday that made its way even into the homes of Jewish families—not in celebration, but rather out of simple overwhelming attention. Stores rarely had Hanukkah sales, but they always showed their Christmas spirit.

Then, holding up a tiny silk and wood lantern, Rachel smiled. "This might seem a strange ornament, but the Akimotos gave it to my parents when they first moved to town. William was just a little boy and his father, Yoshimi Akimoto, gave this to my father as a gesture of goodwill."

"Too bad they didn't remember that goodwill at Pearl," David muttered and turned away.

"You truly hate all Japanese?" Rachel asked softly.

"Yes," he stated matter-of-factly. "And you should too. They killed your brother. They bombed us in the peacefulness of a Sunday morning." He felt his anger push aside any residual feelings of Yuletide warmth.

"Mother said you felt this way. She told us to avoid discussing anything, but . . . ." Rachel seemed to struggle with what she wanted to say next.

"Go ahead," David encouraged. "I'm not afraid to talk about it if that's what you're worried about. I'm a big boy. I can take whatever life dishes out, and I can certainly handle anything you throw at me."

Rachel winced and he immediately regretted his tone. They'd just experienced such a tender moment at lunch. How could he throw that away in his anger at the Japanese? It was one thing to be mad at the enemy, but she didn't deserve his rage.

"Look, I'm sorry. I didn't mean to take it out on you. I didn't even mean to lose my temper the other night at the shop. I just can't understand how you can be so forgiving of a people who did this horrible thing. You weren't there. The only effect it had on you is Kenny will never come home."

"I suppose you're right," she said, lowering her gaze. "Losing Kenny was so painful. He was so happy—so full of life. No one thought he would die. At least I never thought he would die." Her voice broke with emotion before she turned back to the ornaments. "We can carry this trunk downstairs. There are a couple of other boxes, but I can handle them."

David couldn't leave things like this between them. He ignored the trembling he felt inside and reached out to touch her shoulder. "I really am sorry."

Rachel turned, and there were tears in her eyes. "I've just never known anyone who hated something or someone so much."

"Then you're lucky," David said, dropping his hold.

"Can't you at least forgive people for being of the same race and nation? The Akimotos are good people. They were the first ones here to help Mom deal with the news. They cried with her, and William was so angry he threatened to go join up and see all the armies of the enemy defeated. He probably would have, but Sarah was already expecting their second baby."

David could only stare at her blankly. Her words shot all sorts of holes in his defense of a hatred he'd carried around with him for well over a year. "Their people killed your brother—my friend."

"*We* are their people, David," she replied softly. Glancing up at him, she shook her head. "I'm sorry that you can't see the truth."

"Your truth, maybe. Not mine."

"I can understand that you're angry," she said, trying hard to regain control of her emotions. She toyed with the ornaments for a moment before closing the trunk lid. "Kenny told us you were well on your way to becoming a great boxer. He figured you would probably be able to make a career of it after the war. Now here you are a wounded war hero. I can see why my feeble attempt at explaining our feelings for friends would sound silly."

"I'm no hero." David felt his chest tighten. There was no way to explain his statement without revealing all of his ugly secrets. He chose the easy way out instead. As usual. "I'm surprised Kenny told you about the boxing."

She nodded. "He said you were very good."

David closed his eyes and pushed the memories aside. "It was Kenny's attempt to redirect my aggression and give me some respectability. I'm afraid it was misdirected." He steadied himself and looked at her again. A shaft of light fell across the room and highlighted her hair. Why did she have to be so pretty—so sweet and vulnerable?

Uncomfortable with the silence, he grabbed for the trunk handle. "I'll take this downstairs."

"Are you sure it's not too heavy?" she questioned.

"I may have a bum arm," he told her, "but there's still plenty of strength left in me." He wondered if there was any truth in that statement. Somehow, he wasn't at all convinced.

CHAPTER 5

David refused to accompany the family to church the following morning. He told Ruth it was because of the way his arm felt, and in truth that was partly the reason. He needed to see a doctor and have his medication refilled. Funny, he thought, he hadn't needed the pain pills nearly as often. What normally would have lasted him no more than three days had taken him through the week.

Ruth had accepted his excuse, but she surprised David when she returned an hour later. He was sitting quietly beside the fire when she opened the door and came into the house. A light dusting of snow melted atop her wool coat and scarf.

"I didn't like the idea of you being alone," she said softly in explanation.

David wondered for a moment if she was worried that he might run off with the family silver. Then smiling to himself, he realized that in their simplicity of life, they had no silver. There was truly nothing here of any real value to steal. The things that were valuable were intangible, and no thief would ever be able to snatch them away.

"I'm glad you came back," he said, realizing he meant the words. "I wanted to apologize to you for how I acted last week at the flower shop."

Ruth hung up her coat and closed the closet door. She turned and smiled with such a look of love that David knew beyond any doubt she had already forgiven him.

"I'm sorry I didn't warn you ahead of time. I presumed upon your feelings, and I'm the one who should apologize."

David shook his head. "I just reacted and the thoughts that went through my head weren't at all the kind I can share with you."

Ruth took a seat opposite him in a ladder-backed straight chair. "Why not?"

"It's just too awful to imagine. I wouldn't wish it on my worst enemy."

"Not even the Japanese?"

He looked at her hard. "Okay, so I would wish it on them. After all, they caused it."

"David, you can't blame an entire race for the actions of a few. You also can't continue to carry such hatred bottled up inside or it will destroy you."

"You don't understand," he said, looking away.

"I don't understand?" she questioned. "I don't understand that this war has taken the life of my only son?" Her words forced him to look at her. "I don't understand that hundreds of thousands of men have already died in Europe and now they've killed or will kill just as many in the South Pacific? I'm not stupid, David."

He began to stammer. "I . . . you aren't . . . I never said . . ."

"I know you didn't call me stupid," she replied softly, "but you think me rather naïve in my devotion to the Akimotos. You think it senseless that a community would work to keep a family from losing their home and business, especially when that family is descended from the enemy. But, David, you must understand that there are many Japanese in this country, and most have clearly aligned themselves with America. Do you know why they did that, David?" He shook his head. "They did that because they are Americans."

He started to comment, but she held up her hand to still him. "Please hear me out." He nodded and she continued. "You and Kenny were good friends. The best of friends, as I understand it. Kenny took an instant liking to you from the first time you were put under his command. I remember the letters telling us of the potential he saw in you."

David tried to conceal his surprise, but apparently his expression betrayed him.

"That's right," Ruth stated, "Kenny saw great potential in you. But not only that, he genuinely liked you."

"He was like a brother to me," David admitted.

"And you would have done anything for him, wouldn't you?"

"I wish I could have died in his place."

Ruth smiled and nodded. "I believe you. Now I wish you would believe me when I say one country does not speak for the entirety of its citizens. Neither do the actions of one member of a particular race speak or act for the entirety of the country."

"Japan seems pretty united over this. Haven't you seen any of the news reels? Those people want us dead."

"You're only seeing what they want you to see," Ruth chided. She got up and went to the china cupboard in the dining room. When she returned, she held out a framed picture of an elderly couple.

David took the picture and looked at it for a moment. "Who are they?"

"My parents. They emigrated to this country in 1897. I was born the following year."

He handed the photograph back but had no idea why she had shown it to him. Seeming to understand, Ruth sat down beside him and gazed for a moment at the picture. "My family loved this country more than anything. My father was so happy to be here in America—to see his children born and raised as Americans."

"I don't understand," David finally said.

Ruth smiled and nodded. "They were German, David. I'm full-blooded German and the first of our family to be born in America. As far as ancestries go, Kenny was half German."

David shook his head. "What does this have to do with my hating the Japanese?"

"Do you hate us as well? Do you hate Kenny and me? Rachel and Helen?"

"Why should I?" David asked, his tone clearly betraying his irritation.

"Our people in Germany are killing your people, the Jews," she said softly. "Our German relatives are at war with the Americans."

"It isn't the same."

"Isn't it?"

David shook his head. "No. I don't see it that way."

"Why, because we can hide our identity and the Nisei can't?"

"It just isn't the same. Your family has been nothing but kind to me."

"And the Akimotos have been nothing but kind to me. They were the first to come see me when we heard about Pearl Harbor. They waited day after day, along with us, for some news of Kenny. They mourned with us when that news came and they remained supportive of our family right up until the day they were taken away to the internment camp." She paused and placed the photograph on the side table before turning to take hold of David's right hand. "David, you can't bear this anger and bitterness much longer. It's eating you up inside. People are people. There are bad and good ones in every group. Even so, hatred only destroys the hater."

He frowned and looked at his hands. The left one useless, the right one balled into a fist. "I've had a lifetime of training," he said in a barely audible voice. "It isn't that easy to let go of what you know best."

"I know."

He shook his head and met her eyes. "No, you don't. You don't know how awful I've been. You don't know how I've failed. If you knew the real me, you'd never even want me in this house. I can barely stand to stay in Kenny's room for the guilt I feel." He kept shaking his head. "At first it was a comfort to feel that close to Kenny. I mean, it might be hard to imagine caring about your superior officer that way, but Kenny was a brother to me. He cared when no one else cared."

"I know," Ruth said again.

David could see the understanding in her eyes, but his heart told him it was impossible. His mind condemned him—accused him both honestly and falsely. She couldn't understand.

"David, if I know my Kenny, I know he shared the gospel with you. I know he would have told you how Jesus came to earth to die for your sins and mine. No matter what you've done—no matter how well you think you've concealed the truth—Jesus knows." She smiled and squeezed his hand. "And better yet, He loves you just the same."

"He can't," David replied. "He can't know everything and still love me. I'm a lost cause."

"He specializes in lost causes, David. He leaves the flock of ninety-nine safe and secure in the pen and goes after that one lost sheep—that one lost cause. His love for you will heal your hurt, David. You can trust His love. You can trust mine too."

"You wouldn't say that if you knew the truth about me," David said, hanging his head. She couldn't love him. He was unlovable.

Rachel knew that her mother had come back early from church to be with David. She knew her mother's concern for their sad visitor. Rachel wished she could have been the one to come back and stay with David, but she knew how that would have looked to the congregation. Not only that, but she also knew her mother was aware of her feelings for David.

Walking home from church, in order to give herself some quiet time alone, Rachel tried to better understand those feelings for herself. She tried not to label it with words, but in truth she had fallen in love with David Cohen. There was no other explanation for the way she felt, and yet it didn't surprise her. Truth be told, Rachel had felt a fondness for David ever since Kenny's first letter about him. He was a rascal—a rogue—and yet Kenny had seen something special in him and so had Rachel. Her bond to Kenny had perhaps bolstered her ability to see good in his friend, but so too had her confidence in her older brother's keen discernment.

Glancing toward the latticework clouds, Rachel wondered if Kenny could look down from heaven to see her. Could he know what she was going through right now—that she had fallen in love with his friend?

"Ken, I wish you were here. I'd talk this all through with you if you were," Rachel said softly. "I know you'd understand. You loved him too. He was like a brother to you, and even though he caused you all kinds of grief, you knew it wasn't personal. You knew there was value in this man, and so do I."

Rachel shoved her gloved hands into her worn coat pockets and drew a couple of deep breaths. "How do I do this, God? How do I help David to look beyond his anger and bitterness? How do I help him to heal?" She fixed her gaze down the lane ahead and continued walking. Surely God would give her the answers she needed. Surely He would show her what to do.

Curlicue lines of smoke rose from every house along the street, with exception to Mrs. Mendelson's house. The old woman was such a dear, Rachel thought. Year after year she gave her best, and even if her best was the dreaded fruitcake, Rachel loved her elderly neighbor. She could fondly remember days when Mrs. Mendelson and Grandma Bennett had sat on the porch together, talking of days gone by. There was always some story to tell, some memory to draw upon.

Pausing at Mrs. Mendelson's front gate for just a moment, Rachel couldn't help but smile as she remembered a story the old woman had told. That was it! That was her answer. Mrs. Mendelson had told of her brother's deep heartache when his family had been lost at sea while crossing the Atlantic to join him in America. The man had been devastated, nearly suicidal, as Rachel recalled from the account. Yet Rachel also remembered that Mrs. Mendelson's brother had gone on to do great things in the field of medical research. She couldn't say exactly what it was he had accomplished, but she remembered Mrs. Mendelson's great pride in telling how he would never have brought about the knowledge and helped so many people if he'd given up on life to die with his family.

"How did you help him?" Rachel remembered asking as they sat quilting one winter's day.

"We loved him through it," Mrs. Mendelson had answered so matter-of-factly, and Grandma Bennett had nodded knowingly.

Rachel had been but a child, and the wisdom was not totally captured by her innocent heart. But now as a young woman who had endured the pain of loss, Rachel knew the truth of it. Wasn't that how they had dealt with Kenny's death? Wasn't that what her mother had tried to show her all along?

Rachel smiled and looked heavenward. "We'll love him through it, Lord. That's how we'll help him."

Picking up her pace, Rachel nearly burst through the front door of her house. She found David seated in a contemplative mood before the fireplace.

"You look half frozen," Ruth said, coming into the hallway as Rachel was hanging up her coat. "Why didn't you ride home with your father and sister?"

Rachel shivered, feeling the cold for the first time. "I needed the walk." She took off her hat and carefully placed it on the closet shelf.

Her mother nodded knowingly. "Well, lunch is nearly ready. Why don't you keep David company while Helen and I finish it up?" She winked at her daughter, and Rachel felt the cold begin to fade. Her mother did know how she felt.

David nodded as Rachel held her hands out to the fire. "You look cold."

"I'm all right," Rachel replied. "I enjoyed my walk, but now I intend to enjoy this fire."

"Do you want me to put some more wood on?" he asked softly.

Rachel pulled up the ottoman and sat down close to the hearth. "No, it's just fine. How's your arm? Is the cold still bothering it?"

David looked away, seeming uncomfortable. "It's better."

"I'm glad. It's my prayer that you can be free of your pain."

He met her gaze, and the look on his face told Rachel that he fully understood the intent of her words.

"I doubt that can ever be the case."

"Don't doubt God, David. You may not have had a chance to know Him very well all these years, but He knows you and He loves you." Rachel felt a boldness come over her. "He cares about you, and we care too."

"Maybe you wouldn't care if you knew me like God does," David said in an almost sarcastic tone. He looked into the fire, shaking his head. "If He really knows everything, then I doubt He can care that much."

"And if I can prove you wrong?"

He studied the fire in silence for several moments before returning his gaze to her face. "What are you saying?"

Rachel shrugged. "I'm just asking what you might do or say if I could prove you wrong."

"I don't know how you could possibly do that."

Rachel stood up and grabbed his hand. "Come with me."

He eyed her curiously and got to his feet. "What is this all about?"

"I think you know very well what this is all about. I want to prove something to you."

Gently, she tightened her grip on his hand. "Come on," she encouraged. She headed for the stairs. "I have something that I think will help."

Rachel could tell by the look on David's face that he didn't believe her. In fact, she could tell by his expression that he couldn't even begin to comprehend what she was about. But as if led by God's hand, which she was sure had become the case, Rachel moved up the stairs in confidence.

"You wait in Kenny's room," she instructed when they reached the top landing. "I need to get something."

He nodded and moved in the direction of the room while Rachel went to her own bedroom. When she returned she extended the small white box she'd retrieved from under her bed.

"What's this?" he asked, completely confused.

"Letters," she replied. "Kenny's letters home from about the time you joined him until two days before the bombing."

David looked at the box, then took it from her. "What does this have to do with me?"

"Plenty," she said smiling. "They're mostly about you."

"What?" He looked at the box again. "Me? Why me?"

She laughed. "Kenny felt God had put the two of you together for a reason. I want you to read those letters, David. I want you to see what Kenny saw—what he shared with us. Then I want to resume this conversation."

David seemed barely able to draw breath. "Why? What more is there to say?"

"Read those letters first, and then ask me that question."

CHAPTER 6

David's hand shook furiously as he reached to take off the lid of the shoe box. Why had Rachel done this? What was it that she intended for him to see? The lump in his throat refused to be put down.

He peered in the box and saw the accumulation of letters. Kenny's letters. What would it be like to see Kenny's heart and soul on the lines of hastily written notes home? Would it ring true? Would the real Kenny shine out from the thin airmail paper?

Bathed in silence, the room gave David a moment of uneasiness. It almost seemed he had come into a tomb—and in some ways perhaps he had. This shrine to Kenny's memory had obviously been left to offer comfort to the family. It had done the same for David at first, but now it seemed more haunting. He could almost feel Kenny's insistence that David strive toward something more than hatred and death. No doubt the letters would confirm this sensation.

Taking a seat at Kenny's desk, David could only look at the letters in apprehension and fear. Rachel had been confident they would change things for him. She had said they would prove something. She had said they would prove him wrong. But wrong about what? David shuddered. Now he felt even more the intruder than when he'd first shown up at the house. How could he go through these letters—letters that Kenny had never believed would ever be shared with David? Yet Rachel found them important enough to share. She had insisted he read them and then come back to her with his doubts and questions and longings.

Picking up the first letter, David noted the date was nearly two and a half years prior to the date of Kenny's death. It was just about the time David was facing a judge in Chicago. A judge whose idea of justice was to give David the choice of either going to jail for his thievery or joining the military. David had chosen the latter and that was how he met Kenny.

Dear sis,

Thanks for the box of goodies. Never tasted anything so good in my life as your oatmeal cookies. Mom sure trained you right. You're going to make a good wife someday. Tell Dad thanks so much for setting me up with my own subscription to the Longview Daily News. *It's like having a little bit of home here on board the ship. Sometimes it's the little things that keep a guy going.*

David read on, seeing Kenny's thoughts on the ship and way the navy did business. Kenny praised his superior officers and spoke of the good men he had working under his command. He talked of men David knew by name—dead men. Men entombed inside the *Arizona* at the bottom of Battleship Row, along with Kenny. He could see their faces, laughing, joking—forever young—gone in a moment that even now seemed too heinous to be real.

Shaking off his gloom, David went on to the next letter dated several weeks later than the first. Kenny told of a storm they'd ridden out while on maneuvers. He spoke of the fierce waves making everyone seasick but added that the battleship itself made out in great order.

I have a new man under my command. He's a wiry fellow, kind of on the small side. His name is David Cohen. He's a machinist mate and pretty quick to learn. That aside, I've never seen a fellow with a heavier load to carry. He's pretty angry all the time. Be sure to add him to your prayer list, sis. I've tried to be friendly with the man, but he's hurting and I can tell he doesn't want any part of our camaraderie. He acts all tough and sometimes even ugly, but I have a feeling it's because life's dealt him some powerful blows. My superiors tell me that David came to us as a matter of the courts. In other words, he was given the choice of jail or military service. I don't know what he did to get here, but I hope I can make a difference in his life. Pray that God will show me how to deal best with him.

David felt a tug at his heart. To see the evidence that someone knew and understood his misery was almost more than he could bear. How could it be that even upon their first meeting, Kenny knew that David was using his anger and tough nature to cover up his painful past?

Letter after letter, Kenny shared with Rachel all the details of his life aboard the USS *Arizona*. Staunchly proud to be given an assignment on board a battleship—the backbone of the navy—his purpose seemed to bring him great joy. He liked navy life, and although he worried that America couldn't remain forever neutral from the war, he felt confident in the military powers around him. He felt even more confident in God's power. Kenny's words bore witness to the faith he lived from day to day.

> *David has displayed a new talent, another letter shared. He got into a scrap last week and low and behold began fighting his way out. He's a natural at boxing, probably picked it up in Chicago. I wouldn't be surprised if he was formally trained. His size doesn't deter him from victory either. In fact, David has seemed to learn to use his size as his best weapon. Smart man. "Ingenuity born of necessity," as Grandma would say.*
>
> *I did like you said and showed David some extra kindness yesterday. He doesn't always seem too happy with his new life here on board, so I managed to swing some liberty for him. He seemed happy about it, but he didn't come back on time and that put me in a fix. I covered for him, don't know that I did him any favors, but when he did show up, I talked to him long and hard about his responsibilities. Don't know if he took it to heart or not. I can see what Dad meant about it not always being much fun to be the man in charge.*

David remembered the incident quite well. He'd thought Chief Petty Officer Bennett to be one big sucker. He couldn't figure the man out. He had been certain that Kenny was up to something but could never really catch a clue as to what he had planned for David. When Kenny encouraged David to pursue boxing, complimenting him on his natural talent and taking a real interest in getting David properly trained, David had balked. Kenny wanted to get him involved with the ship's boxing team, but David had thought he was mocking him.

> *Dear sis,*
>
> *Don't feel much like writing. I've been praying real hard about some of the men on board. The primary form of entertainment on liberty seems to come with gambling, drinking, and women. David was brought back to the ship by Shore Patrol after taking a weekend liberty. He was in bad shape. He'd been drinking and appar-*

ently had gotten himself into a fight. My guess is that several men jumped him, robbed him, and then beat him. He'll be all right, but it really discouraged me. I don't know why men like David seek their solace in drink.

Rachel, I know you'd tell me to read the psalms, and I've been doing that, but sometimes I just feel that I'm not making any difference in this world. I really see potential in David. He's a good man. Even though he often goes AWOL, he never deserts. Something keeps bringing him back. I just can't figure out what it is he needs. It would be easy to write him off, but I can't. He's got a great sense of humor and a good head on his shoulders. Why can't he see what he's doing to himself?

David's left arm began throbbing. He tried to ignore it, but it seemed to build with each of the incriminating letters. It was all there. His entire life after coming on board the USS *Arizona* had been shared in a brief but meaningful account with Rachel and probably the others. He could only imagine what Rachel must have written back to her brother. She probably told him that time would make things better and that Kenny shouldn't give up. Wasn't that the kind of woman she'd proven herself to be, even over the last few days?

David looked at the remaining letters. Apprehension squeezed the air out of his lungs. He wanted to know the contents, but at the same time his own vivid memories of the days he'd been with Kenny caused him to hold back. He needed a moment to think through what he'd just read. He had known Kenny cared, but he never knew the hours Kenny must have stewed and fretted and prayed for David's well-being.

No one had ever cared about him until Kenny. As a child, his mother had ignored him in favor of men who could give her some trinket or bit of cash. They were her meal tickets, and in making them so, they became his meal tickets as well. His aunt had certainly never cared about him. Not in any personal sense of the word. She'd only come after him to get back at his mother. His spinster aunt was jealous of her younger sister. That was all. She hadn't provided him a home, but rather gave him a roof over his head and put food in his mouth.

The rabbi had seen him as a lost cause from day one, and the people in the neighborhood merely complained about David picking fights with their children. Never mind that he'd been defending his mother's honor, what little there was of it. Never mind that those other children were usually twice David's size. David was to blame.

He drew a deep breath and went back to the letters. He had to know the truth. He wanted to know. He wanted to see if Kenny had shared everything. He didn't have long to wonder. The letters dating from the summer before the war were filled with details about how hard Kenny was trying to share God's love with David. David fought back the urge to throw the letters across the room, when he reached the one written just two days before Pearl Harbor had met its fate.

> *Dear sis,*
>
> *We're pretty busy, but I wanted to drop you a line. I know I've said this before, but I'll say it again. Hawaii is so very different from California, and especially Washington. It's very exotic and the people are of so many different backgrounds. I took some liberty and went sight-seeing. Wasn't sure I'd get another chance very soon.*

David let the letter fall to the desk. He felt as though he'd been gut punched. He remembered Kenny's enthusiasm after returning from that trip. David could boast a clear understanding of the many bars in Honolulu, but even his generous support of those sights could not match Kenny's excitement about Hawaii.

He left the letter on the desk but glanced down, scanning the lines as Kenny explained the things he'd done. His eagerness to share the foreign setting with his sister burst off the paper in a vividness of color and detail.

> *Rachel, you'd love the flowers here. I asked if they thought you could get any of these to grow in Washington state, but nobody seems to think it would work. The colors are about the brightest you could ever imagine. I don't know what they call them, but there are these tall, waxy-looking plants with bright red and yellow blossoms. Of course, the food is pretty unusual here as well. I tried a regular Hawaiian feast. They call it a luau, and I mean to tell you, you've never seen the likes. Reminds me of those Sunday potlucks we used to have, except it was all laid out to even look pretty. Mom would have loved it.*

I wanted to let you know I've been feeling better about David. He continues to lie to me and also to defy my position of authority, but I keep praying for him. I know you're praying too, and that means so much. I know what you mean about him being such a likeable guy in spite of his flaws. I just know if you ever had a chance to meet him, and maybe I'll talk him into coming home with me so you can, that you'd like him.

I know I need to talk to him and figure I'll do that tomorrow, or maybe I'll let him have the weekend and talk to him Monday. He needs to understand that he has a job to do and that people are going to suffer if he doesn't pull his own weight. I can't seem to get this across to him. I've asked God to teach him the value of friendship, particularly our friendship. I'd like to say I see a big difference in David from the time he first joined us, but I can't. Still, I know God put us together for a reason. I like David. I like him a lot. He's a decent fellow when he's not hiding behind all that rage. If we can ever work it out, I'll bring him home on leave. I know you could probably do wonders to boost his self-esteem.

Well, looks like I'd better sign off. There's not much time to get this in the mail. I love you all and will be mailing your Christmas presents tomorrow. Think tropical and Hawaiian. Love you, sis, and thanks for the letters.

Kenny

David stared at the letter for a long time afterward. The handwriting blurred and his eyes refused to focus. Kenny had never been one to waste words. He thought of the lecture he'd escaped by sneaking off the ship that Saturday evening in December. Kenny had probably come looking for him, or maybe as the letter suggested, Kenny had decided to wait until Monday.

Guilt consumed him. Kenny's memory rose up to condemn David's lackadaisical attitude.

"Everybody wants to have a good time now and then," Kenny had admonished, *"but we have a job to do. You let me down, David."* The words had been laughed off by David when Kenny had delivered them on another occasion of his insubordination. No doubt similar words would have been spoken had the Japanese not interfered with their lives.

David put the letters back into the box and, after wrestling with the string for several minutes, decided to leave it sitting on top of the box. Rachel would understand that he'd been unable to retie the package.

He stretched out on Kenny's bed and stared up at the ceiling for a long time. *I got my punishment*, he thought. *I'm crippled now and I have to live with the memories of what I've done.* "Isn't that enough?" he questioned aloud.

The last thing he expected was a knock at the door, but that's what he got. Jumping off the bed and cradling his aching arm, David went to the door and opened it.

Ruth stood there, a look of knowing on her face. "I'm going to the cemetery and I wondered if you'd like to walk with me. I want to put some flowers on Kenny's grave."

David knew his look betrayed his confusion. Kenny was entombed at the bottom of Pearl. Ruth seemed to understand perfectly.

"We bought Kenny a small marker. We wanted to have something we could go and visit. Somewhere we could honor him. Would you like to come with me?"

David nodded. "Sure."

She smiled. "Rachel told me she'd given you a project, so I didn't call you for lunch. I've brought you a sandwich, but if you'd rather eat something hot before we go, I can wait."

David met her compassionate eyes and felt the anger in his heart subside. Funny, she had a way of disarming him with nothing more than a glance. "No, the sandwich will be fine. Let's go."

The walk to the cemetery wasn't all that far. David ate his sandwich while Ruth carried the potted plants. He'd tried to take hold of one, but she'd insisted he eat first. With the last crumbs brushed from the front of his coat, Ruth handed him one of the plants without saying a word. They all seemed to just take his injury into consideration and it never was made to be a big issue. They simply accepted him as he was and worked with him.

"We put up Kenny's marker next to his grandma Bennett's grave," she explained. "I thought we could decorate both graves."

Overhead, the gunmetal gray skies threatened snow or rain. Kenny had said they couldn't ever predict whether they'd get snow or not. It was a funny climate, he had told David. Most folks thought just because they were quite a ways up north that they'd automatically have white Christmases, but David remembered Kenny saying that snow often missed them altogether.

Ruth smiled. "We have quite a beautiful park here. A nice lake and lots of grass and trees. Makes for a pleasant enough time when we aren't being deluged with rain." As if on cue, a light sprinkling began to fall. Mrs. Bennett laughed pleasantly. "See what I mean?"

"Ruth!" a woman called out. David looked up to find the woman advancing on them with two young girls at her side. The girls couldn't have been more than three or four years of age, and they clung to their mother and peered out from behind her coat as they hurried to keep up.

"Have you heard the news? The Rolands are quarantined. Measles."

Ruth nodded. "I heard that at church. We'll have to cook up something and take it over."

"Poor Margaret. That woman has had so much to endure. First her oldest daughter, Mary Ann, goes off to Seattle like she did, and now this. She's probably beside herself. I'll bet every one of those six kids comes down with measles before it's over. She probably won't see herself out in public until well after the new year."

"Could be," Ruth replied. "I'll have the sewing circle figure out how we can best help."

The woman nodded, then looked David over as if to ascertain his identity. David tipped his hat awkwardly. He'd never had much in the way of manners, but he desperately wanted to be polite for Ruth's sake.

"Is this Kenny's friend?" the woman asked. "The hero of the *Arizona*?" Her animated voice wasn't in the least muffled by the heaviness of the air. "Oh, I read all about him in the paper. You must be so proud."

Ruth smiled. "Natalie Bishop, this is David Cohen. David was indeed Kenny's friend from the *Arizona*."

The woman's expression changed from curiosity to horror as she noticed his left arm hanging rather useless at his side. "Oh, I'm so sorry for what you had to go through. Terrible thing! Just terrible. Oh my." She fidgeted with her coat and stammered on. "Well. . . I think it's . . . well, just fine that you can be here for the holidays. Kenny was so well liked. He . . . well . . ." her voice trailed off.

David could see the woman's discomfort growing by the minute. He had no idea why she should suddenly be so upset, but Ruth appeared to understand.

"It's all right, Natalie. David and I have been catching up on Kenny and old times. You needn't worry that you've opened a can of worms." This appeared to calm the younger woman, who at this point merely nodded.

"Oh," Ruth continued, "I've been meaning to thank you and your mother for that wonderful grape jam you sent over. I don't know when we've enjoyed anything more. Did you manage to get the rest of your apples put into sauce?"

"Yes," Natalie said with a smile. "Mother has always had a way with putting up fruit. I was worried with the rationing and all, but she managed to convince the Ration Board to allow her enough sugar for home canning. It ought to help a great deal to see us through the winter, rationing or no rationing."

"We were blessed as well," Ruth replied. "The walls of the basement are lined and we feel very much as though God has smiled down on us."

The sprinkles of rain gradually became a bit more heavy. Natalie looked heavenward and shook her head. "I've got to get these girls home and out of the cold, or next thing I know, they'll have the measles too."

Ruth nodded. "I'll see you Wednesday night at church."

David tipped his hat again and waited until the woman hurried off down the sidewalk before asking Ruth if she'd rather turn back for home. His arm hurt him something fierce, but he wasn't about to let on.

"No, let's go ahead and deliver these," she replied. "The cemetery is just up the ways and we won't stay long."

The rain stopped, but the dampness remained. David had always thought of graveyards as rather cold and ominous, but with Ruth at his side it didn't seem quite so bad. She spoke in a lighthearted tone of how glad she was that Marion had thought of putting up a stone and how it was nice to have some way to honor Kenny.

They walked a little ways past a black wrought iron gate that merely stated the word CEMETERY. The wet dead grass soaked David's shoes, but he tried not to notice. After all, they were here for Kenny.

"Here we are." Ruth bent down and cleared away a few dried leaves. "We can put this one here on Grandma Bennett's grave," she said as she placed the potted plant atop the marker. "And we can put the other one on Kenny's stone." She stood back up and pointed.

David caught sight of the stone not three feet away. He stepped solemnly to the grave and placed the plant beside the marker, not willing to cover up his best and only friend's name. He stood staring silently for several moments before Ruth joined him and spoke.

"Rachel told me she gave you her letters. I trust you read them," she said. He nodded but refused to look at her. "Good," she continued in her soft way. "I know she wanted you to see that we knew all about you, David. I hope you understand why. Kenny shared his feelings quite openly, and even when he was home on leave, he told us that he hoped one day you would understand his concern for you and that you would come here with him."

David glanced up ever so slightly. "I can't believe you still want to have me around when you know what I was like. What I'm still like." He looked back down at the ground.

"But we do want you to stay. I love having you here because you were Kenny's friend, but also because I've enjoyed your company. I care about you, David, and I know the others feel the same. Especially Rachel."

"I don't see how you can say that."

"David, nobody is perfect. You've had more than your fair share of knocks in life, but only you can make a change for the better. You said that Jesus couldn't possibly know about the things you'd done and still love you. Rachel gave you those letters to prove that it is possible."

He lifted his head and looked into her face. Her eyes were brimming with tears, but she wouldn't back down. "I've come to love you as a son, David. From the moment I saw you standing on our front porch, I could see what Kenny saw in you. The need, the sorrow, the longing, but also the potential, the spirit, the strength."

"I'm not strong," he said in a barely audible whisper.

"You're here," Ruth replied, "and I think that speaks for itself. The fact is, I knew all about what you had done to Kenny, the times you had disappointed him. I knew you had a scandalous past and that you had a penchant for fighting your way in and out of trouble. But it doesn't matter. You have to see that, and in seeing that, maybe you can realize that it doesn't matter to Jesus either."

"God can't be too worried about a loser like me," David declared. "Otherwise I would have died that day with my shipmates. Instead, I have to live with the guilt that I'm here and they're gone."

"I'd say you've just proven your own point," Ruth said very gently. She put her hand on his arm and squeezed it ever so gently. "If God had been through with you, you wouldn't be here."

David looked hard at the woman for a moment. She firmly believed what she'd just said. Kenny had believed it, too, and frequently had said as much. Could they possibly be right? Could there even be the remotest chance that God could forgive David and wipe away his sins?

"I don't know what to believe," David finally said, looking away.

"I know," Ruth said, patting his arm before turning to go. "Just know that I'm here for you. We all are. Flowers on a grave make us feel better, but we can honor Kenny most by helping each other. Just remember that."

He watched her walk back down the path to the front gate. He wanted to stay behind and think of what she'd said, but at the same time he wanted to run after her. He wanted to run to her, calling her name—calling her Mother.

CHAPTER 7

"Hurry up, Helen, or you're going to be late," Rachel called up the stairs. She knew her sister had an affinity for waiting until the last minute to make herself ready for any given event.

"I'm coming!" Helen yelled back down. "I'm trying to fix my hair."

"Angels don't need to worry about their hair," Rachel replied in an exasperated tone.

She glanced over to where David stood by the door. He had agreed to go with them to the Christmas play at church. Secretly she was glad for a number of reasons. Folks at church had been hounding them since David's arrival to bring him around for introductions. Then there was the whole situation of folks wanting to honor a war hero and feel like they were doing their part for the war effort. Besides this, however, Rachel wanted so much to pick up the conversation where her mother had left off. She wanted to help David in whatever way would bring him to real happiness, and she was finally ready to show him how she felt about him.

"Would you and David like to walk on up to the church?" Ruth asked, seeming to understand her daughter's need.

Rachel looked to David hopefully. "Would that be all right? Or would the weather be too hard on your arm?"

"I wouldn't want you to get too cold," David offered. He opened the door and frowned. "Besides, it's raining again."

"I suppose we can wait for everyone in the car," Rachel replied. "Helen may well take another half hour at this rate."

"Well, she'd best not, or we'll never get there on time," Ruth stated. "You two go ahead to the car. I'll rally up Grandpa and Marion and together we'll drag Helen along, if necessary." She smiled good-naturedly.

Rachel buttoned her coat and secured her black felt hat. "I'm taking an extra blanket for the car," she commented, reaching back into the closet for an old wool blanket. She led the way to the Model A Ford and let David open the back door.

Sliding to the middle, Rachel waited until David climbed in to spread the blanket across their laps. "We need to talk," she said without giving herself time to rethink the moment.

David closed the door and, in the soft glow of porch and street lights, offered Rachel a surprised look at her nearness. "We do?" he said in a tone that suggested she'd unnerved him.

"Yes," she replied, shifting in the seat. "I have to say a few things before the others come." He nodded very slowly but said nothing. "I know Mom talked to you about the letters, but I wanted to talk to you also. You see, I know all about you, and in spite of your past and the trouble you've had, I care about you."

"I know," David barely whispered.

"No, I don't think you do," Rachel replied. This caused him to raise his head and meet her eyes. "I've fallen in love with you, David." Her voice softened and some of the boldness faded. "I don't know how you feel about that, but it's the truth."

He reached up to touch her cheek, his eyes filled with wonder. "How can you just tell me something like that?"

"Because it's how I feel and I'm afraid if I don't tell you, you might leave before I get another chance." She trembled at his touch and leaned forward ever so slightly. She knew he would kiss her and she wanted nothing more.

He stroked her cheek, then moved to touch her hair before putting his hand to the back of her neck. Pulling her to him, David kissed her slowly, gently. Rachel felt her heart beating so rapidly that it nearly took away her breath. She wrapped her arms around his neck, and when the kiss ended, she merely rested her head against his shoulder. She loved him. Pure and simple.

Except it wasn't so simple. She pulled away and drew a deep breath. "My only problem is that you don't walk with God. I can't consider marriage to someone who isn't a Christian."

"Marriage?" he said, his voice cracking. "You'd marry me?"

She shook her head. "Not unless we felt the same way about God. I can deal with anything else—your anger at the Japanese, your past—

but your future has to be His or I can't be a part of it. And," she added, knowing that it must be said, "you can't do it just to marry me. It has to be a choice from your heart. I'll know the difference."

He looked at her for a moment, then reached out to touch her face again. "You'd really want a life with a cripple like me?"

"You're only as crippled as you want to be, David."

There was no time for anything else to be said. Helen burst into the car, her long hair dancing in curls around her shoulders and down her back.

"We're here!" Helen declared, sliding into the middle of the front seat. "Fear not!" she declared, spreading her arms wide. This had become her well-known opening line for the play.

The rest of the family piled into the old Model A Ford, laughing at the icy rain and the gaiety of the evening. No one, save perhaps Ruth, had any idea what had transpired between Rachel and David. Rachel wouldn't have been at all surprised had her mother known her exact intentions, but if she did, she'd said nothing to Rachel on the matter. Rachel appreciated the fact that her mother trusted her judgment. And why shouldn't she? It was Ruth and Marion's good upbringing that had given Rachel a strong foundation of faith. She'd never let that go.

"The Christmas play is the event of the season," Ruth told David. "We always have such fun. The kids put on the play and the church has refreshments. Oh, speaking of which," Ruth said, glancing around her, "I forgot the cookies."

"No, you didn't," Marion announced, pointing to Grandpa Bennett, who was wedging himself into the seat beside Rachel. "Pop has them."

Ruth sighed and eased back into the seat. "Thanks, Pop."

"Don't tear my costume!" Helen declared to her father. She found herself snuggled in between her father and mother in the front, fighting hard to keep her white gown from being wrinkled and caught up as her father shifted gears.

The single wiper cleared away the icy rain while the engine chugged faithfully along, compliments of Marion and Bob's ingenuity.

"We should sing!" Ruth declared, and before anyone could comment, she began a rousing chorus of "Jingle Bells."

Helen joined in, as did Grandpa and Marion. Rachel sang quietly, but it wasn't heartfelt. She held a deep gladness for the season in spite of Kenny's absence, but her mind continued with a preoccupation of David. Had she said too much? Would he turn away from her now? She prayed the evening might be pleasant for him in spite of her declaration. *Don't let it be too tiring for him, Lord.*

He'd just gone to the doctor the day before, and while the doctor had prescribed more medication, she knew David dealt daily with pain. Pain could be quite exhausting—Rachel knew that very well.

"Here we are," Marion said, pulling the Ford up to the front steps of the church. "You go ahead inside, and I'll get parked and join you. Save me a seat!"

They scrambled from the car and up the steps of Faith Church just as the rain began to fall in earnest. Ruth paused long enough to take the cookies from Grandpa Bennett before ducking inside to greet her friends, while Rachel remained supportively at David's side.

"Mrs. Bennett, it's so nice to see you here on this less-than-perfect evening," Pastor Gray said as they entered the building. The roly-poly pastor bobbed his balding head up and down as he shook her free hand. It was as if the actions of his hand dictated those of his head.

"We wouldn't miss it," Ruth said, smiling. "And how is Mrs. Gray? I heard she had caught a cold."

"Nothing to worry about," the man assured. "She's here tonight. Ever ready to take on her job at the piano. But thank you for asking."

Helen quickly hurried downstairs to prepare for the play. Rachel leaned over to her mother. "I can take these downstairs for you."

Ruth became instantly aware of a growing crowd. She felt David press in behind her. She turned and smiled. "No, I'll handle it. You stay here and introduce David." She gave his shoulder a gentle pat. "They're coming to greet the hero of Pearl Harbor," she said softly. "You're important to them, David. You and so many others are the reason they are working so hard, doing without. Remember that." He nodded.

"Ruthie, is this that young man you told us about?" a sweet-faced older woman questioned.

"Yes, this is the man. I'll let Rachel do the introductions while I get these goodies to the kitchen." She spoke for the benefit of everyone who had gathered to meet their houseguest. She added, "He isn't used to so many people. He's been recuperating from his wounds, mostly seeing just doctors and nurses, so go easy on him." With that she took her leave and Rachel took over.

Rachel threw David what she hoped was an encouraging glance. "This is Kenny's good friend from the ship, David Cohen."

"Well, we're proud to have you here," the older woman said, reaching a hand out to shake with David. "I'm Ginny Williams. My son joined up with the Army Air Corp just this year. I'm glad to get to meet you."

David murmured thanks and was soon inundated with names and faces from congregation members. When her father came through the front door, shaking the rain from his hat and coat, Rachel felt a sense of relief. He would no doubt see to it that they made their way into the sanctuary and save their socializing for the party after the play.

True to form, he did just that. Marion Bennett paused only long enough to hang up his coat, as well as David's and Rachel's, then doffed his hat and suggested they find a seat.

"Looks like it will be a full house tonight," Ruth said, sliding into the pew beside her husband.

"Looks like half the town has turned out," Rachel's father replied. "Some probably came for the play and some to catch a glimpse at David."

He gave David a wink, but Rachel felt him tense in the seat beside her. She started to lean over and ask him why, but Pastor Gray made his way to the front of the church and a hush followed.

"Let us pray and give thanks for the season," he began.

All heads bowed in unison, with exception to one. Rachel couldn't help but note that David was uncertain what he should do. She squeezed David's hand reassuringly, then closed her eyes.

"Oh, great and merciful God, we ask for a speedy end to the war and the safety of our boys. We ask that here, in the season celebrating the birth of your Son, Jesus, you would touch the hearts of all, blessing them with the assurance that you are in control. And that no matter what heartache we might have to face, you alone are just and righteous—thy will be done. Amen."

Without much introduction, the Christmas play sprung to life. Mrs. Gray played familiar Christmas songs while a ten-year-old Mary walked faithfully beside a rather disgruntled twelve-year-old Joseph.

It appeared Joseph wasn't all that excited about playing the role, but because the eldest Roland boy had gotten the measles, he had been forced to fill in.

The shepherds, complete with paper beards, dish towel-covered heads, and strange pillowcase sheep, took over the next scene. They sang with childlike strength.

"'Silent night, holy night. All is calm. All is bright.'"

They drew a breath between each phrase and shouted the words to make certain the world could hear their declaration.

As they finished, Helen appeared on stage. She had been given a paper halo supported awkwardly with wire. It was a little bent on one side, but it nevertheless signified that this white-robed child was indeed an angelic being.

"'Fear not!'" Helen declared. "'For, behold, I bring you good tidings of great joy, which shall be to all people.'"

One of the shepherds began to fidget and tugged at his beard, while the youngest, no more than three years of age, began to wander around Helen as if in awe of her celestial appearance.

The congregation chuckled softly as Helen continued to deliver her lines, eventually having to pick up the shepherd and hold him so that he could inspect her halo. By this time, several additional angels appeared. Some were dressed in white like Helen, but others had decorated paper streamers affixed to their street clothes. And everyone had a wire halo.

While the angels sang, Mary and Joseph and a wooden manger were positioned on the side of the stage. The shepherd began to protest Helen's grip, and so she put him down, only to see that he wasn't going to be very cooperative. He continued to wander around even while the other shepherds were trying to deliver their lines. Rachel found it all pleasantly amusing, for she could remember a time when Helen herself had been the one stirring up trouble, snooping around while the play went on in her oblivion.

Helen tried to herd the little shepherd toward the manger scene, where he was supposed to say his only line, but he wasn't very interested at this point. More laughter erupted from the congregation, and this seemed to please the boy immensely. So much so, in fact, that he began to jump around and do a little dance. Probably the only time dancing had been allowed in Faith Church.

Helen, in complete exasperation, took hold of the boy and pushed him toward the manger. "Go see Jesus," she told him in a whisper, which seemed to echo throughout the church.

The boy howled in protest, but eventually something near the manger caught his eye and he left his one-man-show aspirations behind and shouted, "I want to see Jesus!"

Rachel laughed until tears were streaming down her cheeks. Even David was laughing, and this gave her hope that he could somehow find joy in his sadly tumultuous life. Maybe he would even come to the place where he would say those very words for himself. *I want to see Jesus!* How Rachel prayed that might be true.

And then the play was over and the actors had taken their bows. The children were released to join their parents, and the entire congregation made its way downstairs for fellowship and refreshments.

Rachel remained close to David, sensing his need for her protection, while her father and grandpa wandered off to talk with the other men of the church.

A group of ladies crowded around and introduced themselves to David. Rachel knew he would have rather run from the room, but she looped her arm through his good one and suggested they make their way to the refreshment table.

"You'll enjoy this, I promise," she said smiling.

David let her lead and seemed to perk up a bit when he found Ruth behind the table helping to serve.

"Oh, David, you have to try this," Ruth declared, pouring him a glass of punch. "I made it myself. In fact, it's my own recipe."

"She's not a bit proud of the fact that everyone here at Faith Church has declared it the best punch in all of Washington," Rachel added.

David took a sip and smiled. "I'd say it's the best punch I've ever tasted, anywhere."

"High praise indeed," Marion stated, joining them.

David filled a plate with food, as did Marion and Rachel, and together the three of them made their way to one of the many tables. Laughing and chatting about the town and the season, David seemed to relax. Rachel prayed that the demons would leave him, that God would replace his fear and hurt with hope and peace. What better Christmas present could either of them ask for?

"We love our baseball," Ginny Williams told David. "We have a great rivalry with the town of Kelso."

"You call that a town?" someone muttered and laughter erupted.

"My father once took me to see Satchel Paige pitch an exhibition game right here in our ball park," another woman declared. "I was the biggest tomboy in all of Longview, and Satchel Paige was just the bee's knees."

Rachel laughed and noted that David took real interest. "Satchel Paige was here?" he questioned.

"He sure was," the woman said as her husband came and plopped a chubby baby in her arms. "I must have been about fifteen, but I can remember it like it was yesterday. I thought surely the man would be ten feet tall. Instead, there he was, just about the same size as my dad. He came out carrying a satchel, all battered and black. He put it down on the mound and took out his pitching mitt. I'm telling you, you could have heard a pin drop."

Everyone who had experienced the moment agreed in a murmuring of affirmation. Rachel could see that David found their stories fascinating, and even when the conversation turned to comments about how they hoped he would stay on in Longview, Rachel couldn't denote any of his previous apprehension. Things went fairly well, in fact, until Natalie Bishop strolled over with her father.

"Mr. Cohen, this is my father, Max Campbell. He's been wanting to meet you ever since he read the article in the paper."

Max Campbell, a broad-shouldered logger turned factory worker, pumped David's arm enthusiastically. "Good to meet you, son. It's not often I get to shake the hand of an honest-to-goodness hero."

Rachel saw David's face pale. There was no way to graciously remove him from the attention, and yet at the same time she wondered if this attention wasn't exactly what David needed.

"I'd like it if you'd come over to the plant and speak to the boys. Give them a pep talk about what they're doing for the war effort. Seeing you there and hearing about Pearl Harbor . . . well, I know they'd get up a steam and really put out the work."

"I don't think I'd be very good at something like that," David said shyly.

"Nonsense!" the man declared rather gruffly. "I'm telling you it would work wonders. You just come on over on Monday. Marion can show you the way."

David appeared at a loss for words, and yet Rachel felt compelled to keep her mouth shut. Funny, she always counted on God to give her words to speak, and when He didn't, she found it almost impossible to believe that He would want her to remain silent.

The party lingered for another hour or so until the food was gone and the children began to grow cranky. Rachel watched David struggle into his coat as they prepared to leave. He was determined and strong. That was what had brought him this far, she thought. She could only pray it would be enough to take him to that place where he'd find peace for his soul.

Even though the trip home wasn't all that far, the icy rain left them all chilled to the bone. "What say I make up a pot of cocoa?" Ruth suggested. "Marion, you could build up the fire just a bit and we could unthaw before going to bed."

"Sounds good to me," her husband agreed.

Soon the family was settled around a blazing fire, with the melody of Christmas carols playing softly on the radio. Even David appeared completely content. Ruth brought a tray with steaming mugs of the rare treat. It might have cost her extra sugar, but Rachel knew her mother would find somewhere else to skimp. A special moment like this required a special refreshment.

With everyone served, Ruth took up her own mug and proposed a toast. "I know we aren't usually the kind of folks to take on such airs, but I'd like us to take a minute to remember Kenny. He would have loved tonight. He would have laughed with us and sang and probably eaten more than anyone there."

"To be sure," Grandpa Bennett chuckled. "Kenny would say, 'Enough with the grief.' He would tell us it was time to move on— to let go of his death and remember his life."

Marion nodded and lifted his mug high. "To the best son a man could have."

"To the best brother," Rachel declared, her heart blazing with a wealth of emotions.

Helen echoed her and added, "And to the best baseball player Longview ever had. If we just had a hitter like him next summer, we wouldn't have any trouble beating Kelso." They all smiled and nodded.

"To a fine grandson who is sorely missed," Grandpa Bennett added.

Ruth looked to David and waited for his toast. David stood and held out his cup. "To a good friend—the best friend a man could ever have."

Ruth nodded and raised her mug to David's, and one by one the others joined them there in the middle. "To Kenny," Ruth murmured.

"To Kenny," they called in unison.

CHAPTER 8

The holiday season grew in a fervor of carolers and baked goods. David felt overwhelmed by the reception of those congregation members who stopped by from time to time to bid him a warmer welcome. He'd been given gifts of cookies, socks, books, and cards with a dollar—sometimes two—and always the warmest wishes that he might stay on in Longview.

Often in the evenings, Ruth would sit down at the piano and play Christmas songs for the family. Rachel and Helen loved to sing, and even Marion and Grandpa Bennett appreciated the music and often joined in. They were the family Kenny had described, right down to Rachel's sweet voice and Helen's tomboyish escapades.

Rachel's voice wasn't the only thing sweet about her. Her spirit had won him over and convinced him that her words of love were sincere. Not even once had she tried to get him alone since the night of the play. She knew he needed time to adjust his thinking, to decide what to do with his life and his heart. And he knew she was right— that she would know the truth about his decision. It had to be for the right reasons.

David sat contemplating this very thing one morning when Ruth appeared, boxes in hand, to announce that she planned to pack up Kenny's belongings.

"It's time to put things away. I'd like it, and so would Marion," she had said, "if you would pick out a couple of things for yourself. I know Kenny would want you to have something of his."

David had no idea what piece or pieces might be important to the family, so he had asked Ruth for help in choosing. By the time the morning had passed, David found himself the owner of three books, two sets of cuff links, one fishing pole, and a Bible. It wasn't the same thick black book David had seen Kenny read night after night on board the *Arizona*; instead, it was a new Bible that Ruth and Marion had planned to send Kenny the previous Christmas.

Even now David wasn't at all sure what he would do with it. He didn't know what he would do with any of the things Ruth had given him. His previous plans for ending his life came back to haunt him. Somehow it had been easier to consider suicide when he didn't have anything to worry about. Now he had these things and these people who cared, and suddenly life had become very complicated.

"David?" Rachel called to him from outside the bedroom.

Putting the Bible aside, David opened the door. He looked into the face of an angel and felt his heart beat a little faster. She smiled at him and it lit up the entire room.

"I have to go downtown for some shopping. Would you like to go with me?"

David grabbed his cardigan and negotiated the left sleeve awkwardly. Rachel immediately stepped in and helped him, never speaking a word. Her act of kindness came naturally and unplanned, and yet it was hard for David to take help.

He put aside his feelings of protest and smiled. "Let's go!"

They paused only long enough for hats and coats and for David to sample Ruth's newest batch of honey oatmeal cookies before heading outside.

The day appeared surprisingly clear and sunny. After nearly a week of gray clouds and rain, David thought he could definitely stand a bit of sun. Rachel lifted her face to the skies as if drinking in the rays. They weren't very warm, David decided, but they nevertheless did something to lift the spirits.

"So what are you shopping for?" David questioned. He really wanted to ask her if she still felt the same about him or if she'd changed her mind. After all, maybe she would tire of waiting for him to come to terms with the past and his future.

"Mother wants me to pick up a few things for her, but besides that, I have a couple of last-minute presents to buy."

Hearing the word *present*, David realized he hadn't even thought of Christmas gifts for the Bennett family. He reasoned that he'd never bought Christmas gifts and so it wasn't like it should be a natural thought to him, but at the same time he felt compelled to do something nice for his host and hostess.

"I'd like to get your folks something," David said softly. He hoped by mentioning the idea, Rachel might be able to steer him in the right direction. "Do you think that would be all right?"

Rachel's pace never slowed as she guided them across the street. "I think it would be swell. Mom could use new embroidery thread or a scarf and she absolutely adores candy. She has a fierce sweet tooth, but with rationing and such, candy is pretty expensive. Pop is harder to buy for. He doesn't have too many needs. He likes listening to the radio and eating." She grinned at David. "Makes it kind of hard to buy for him. Of course, he'd probably love you forever if you found a way to get him some new tires for the Ford."

They laughed and it made David feel good. Everyone in the Bennett family had a good sense of humor. Maybe that's why adversity never seemed to hold them down for long.

Sobering just a bit, David asked, "What did you get your father—surely not something for the Ford?" He let the smile linger on his lips.

"Helen and I traded preserves for some material. Dad's getting two new work shirts and some handkerchiefs from us."

David nodded. "Sounds good. What about Helen and Grandpa Bennett? Is there some little thing that would please them?"

Rachel tucked her clutch bag under her arm and pointed to a small shop. "There's all sorts of things in the Simpsons' store. You could probably find Grandpa a new muffler or pipe, and Helen would be positively delighted with anything to read. She's a tomboy at heart, so adventure is her main interest. Simpsons' carries quite a few books. I could show you what she's read and what she hasn't."

"That sounds easy enough."

She looked at him for a moment and David could have sworn there was a hint of anticipation in her expression. Was she waiting for him to say something more? Perhaps to ask what she herself might like for Christmas? He wanted to ask that question, but on the other hand, he felt much too inadequate to bring the subject to light. It was safe and easy to discuss the rest of the family, but his feelings for Rachel confused him. No, it was better left unspoken. Should he start to speak of how he felt about her, he very well might say things he wasn't ready to say.

David let Rachel lead the way to the shop. Someone had placed a string of bells on the inside handle. The melodic sound caused the other customers to look up as David and Rachel entered the store. David thought the sound rather pleasant and festive—maybe there was something to this holiday celebration.

"Why, hello, Rachel," a kindly matron declared. "I see you've brought us the war hero."

David cringed inwardly but remained stoic. Rachel appeared undaunted. "We've come to shop for Christmas, Mrs. Simpson."

The woman smiled. "Wonderful! I'm so glad. How are you, Mr. Cohen? I doubt you remember me, but I was at the church fellowship after the play."

David nodded. "Nice to meet you."

"Well, let me show you around. What did you have in mind for gifts?"

"Do you have boxes of candy?" he asked, remembering Rachel's suggestion for her mother.

"We have some very nice boxes. A little pricey, but the contents are heavenly."

David thought of the money he'd managed to put together. He'd brought every cent with him. "Let's see them."

He busied himself with the selections, settling on candy for Ruth, a copy of *David Copperfield* for Helen, a plaid wool muffler for Grandpa Bennett, and a special just-in-from-Seattle set of wrapped cheeses for Marion.

"While you finish up with Mrs. Simpson," Rachel told him, "I'm going to run next door. I need to talk to the Vandercamps about the greenhouse." She bit her lip momentarily. David sensed her discomfort at having mentioned the Akimotos' livelihood.

"Oh, Rachel, tell your mama to bring me by a couple more poinsettias. Those other two pots sold so quickly it took my breath away."

"I'll tell her," Rachel replied. She flashed David an apologetic look, then added, "I'll be right back."

As soon as the bells had jingled in declaration of her departure, David turned conspiratorially to Mrs. Simpson. He felt his pulse pick up a bit. Nervously he shifted from one foot to the other. "What should I get Rachel for Christmas?"

Mrs. Simpson smiled, reached on the back shelf behind the counter, and grabbed a small bottle of perfume. "She's always admired this scent. I know she'd love it."

David nodded. "I'll take it too."

He paid for the purchases and waited while Mrs. Simpson sacked them in such a way that they would remain hidden from view. "Thank you," he said, taking the sack in his good arm.

"You come anytime, Mr. Cohen. We're mighty glad to have you here. Mrs. Bennett told us what a good friend you were to Kenny. He was one of a kind."

"He sure was," David agreed.

He managed the door without spilling the sack out onto the floor, then waited outside for Rachel. He noticed the hardware store next door and figured that was where Rachel had gone, but he wasn't in a hurry to rejoin her. Sitting down on a bench outside the Simpsons' shop, David struggled with his thoughts.

A lifetime of anger and bitterness seemed to come up against a new and most curious roadblock: love. Ruth Bennett had shown him such loving compassion, as had the others. Her love disarmed his anger and made him feel almost silly for his bitter thoughts. Ruth had lost her only son, yet she felt confident that God was still worth worshiping and honoring. Not only that, but she felt that there was no good reason for assessing blame and punishment. She wanted the war ended before other mothers' sons were killed. She had told him that all sides stood to lose their hope for a productive tomorrow as they killed off the children of today.

He then thought of the Akimotos and their bond to the Bennett family. He could remember Kenny talking about his friend Willie, but he'd never heard a last name associated with the first. David had never even guessed that Willie might be of a Japanese lineage. It had never been an issue.

The longer David sat and thought about it, the more he had to face the truth. He wasn't nearly so mad at the act of war dealt Pearl Harbor. They had known it was a possibility. Hadn't they stepped up security in some areas? Weren't they admonished to be watchful? No, if the truth were told, David wasn't half as mad at the Japanese as he was himself. He was the one who had deserted in the middle of the night. He was the one who had betrayed Kenny's trust.

But it was easy to blame it all on the Japanese. Being at war with the Japanese even made it acceptable to feel that way. David could well remember the posters put up around various places in San Francisco.

The hospital had been full of them. Perhaps someone had thought them a morale booster. *Slap the Jap! Stay on the Job Until Every Murdering Jap Is Wiped Out! Remember Pearl Harbor! Bomb Tokyo With Your Extra Change—Buy War Bonds!*

It was all there. The encouragement to avenge and hate. The country had enemies, and those enemies had to be stopped. If hatred fueled the battle, so what? If it got the job done and saw the enemy defeated, why not allow, even promote, it? It shouldn't be so appalling to suggest that the Japanese in America were dangerous. Even if they were citizens, they could switch loyalties—anyone could.

He thought of Rachel and her declaration to him on the night of the Christmas play. He'd feared he might feel uncomfortable around her after that announcement, but nothing could be further from the truth. If anything, he felt just that much more comfortable. She had made it clear to him that he wasn't a cripple in her eyes. That she loved him as a person in spite of knowing the truth about him. That God could love him too. Was that true? Could it really be possible?

"Are you ready?" Rachel questioned.

David glanced up and realized she had probably been standing there for several minutes. He got to his feet slowly. "Sorry, I was just thinking."

"What about?"

"Christmas secrets." She smiled. He saw the package in her arm and offered to carry it, but she shook her head.

"Now tell me what you were thinking about."

"It's not so easy," David began. "I've had a great deal to think about since coming to Longview. I guess it's all just catching up with me. I've been thinking about what you said—how you feel about me, even though you know the truth. But there's something you don't know."

She shifted her package and seemed to consider his words thoughtfully. "Well, let's head back for home and you do the talking."

They crossed the street at a slow, almost leisurely pace and finally David spoke. "I'm not a war hero. I was at Pearl Harbor, that much is true. But I should have been on the *Arizona*. I should be there still, but I left the night before and went drinking." He refused to look at her, focusing instead on the sidewalk ahead. "I had duty that weekend and didn't have permission to be gone. I knew I'd have to face

Kenny when I came back. I did him wrong and there are no two ways about it."

She said nothing and David grew increasingly tense. Perhaps this was too much to expect anyone to accept. He'd always figured on telling Ruth first, but somehow it seemed right to explain himself to Rachel.

"I don't remember everything about that morning. There are bits and pieces, and frankly a good deal of it is probably more imagination than truthful recollection. I wrecked a jeep—a jeep I'd stolen prior to the bombing and it was while trying to escape that wreckage that I fell victim to shrapnel and a concussion from a nearby bomb explosion." He stopped and turned toward her. She stopped as well and looked at him with huge, sympathetic eyes. "Do you understand what I'm saying? I'm not a hero. I'm not even worthy of being here."

"Only God can give life and only God can take it," she said. "If God had wanted you to die at Pearl Harbor, He had ample opportunity to allow it. You're here for a reason, David. I think you're here for several reasons, my own selfish one included, but maybe even more you're here because God knew Mama needed someone to help her deal with Kenny's death. She's been so strong—so brave. She saw the rest of us through the ordeal and always stood fast. She's helped other mothers with their losses but always kept her heart guarded. She needed you, David. Not because you were or weren't a war hero. She needed you because you both loved Kenny, and because of that, you could help each other lay him to rest."

"Why not find that help with your father or you?" David questioned. "You loved him too. Your father was no doubt just as devastated in losing his only son."

Rachel nodded. "Yes, that's true. We tried to help Mama, but she's always taken it upon herself to be the backbone of this family. There was no way she was going to stand by and let someone else take that position. She made it through those awful months by helping us cope with the truth. She knew Pop needed someone he could count on—and that someone was her."

"I still don't think I understand."

Rachel smiled and continued walking. "You may not like to hear this, but I think my mother sees a lot of herself in you."

"That's impossible. There isn't a hateful bone in that woman's body," David said, keeping pace beside Rachel.

"Don't be so sure. She isn't perfect and she'd be the first one to tell you that. She knows that people like the Akimotos had nothing to do with Kenny's death, but she knows there are people who had plenty to do with it."

They were nearly back to the house, yet David felt that there was so much he didn't understand. "If she were like me, she'd show it. There'd be too much anger and hate to keep it inside."

"She doesn't keep it inside," Rachel said matter-of-factly. "She gives it on a daily, even hourly, basis to God. She told me there was nothing else that could come anywhere near to equaling the productiveness of that single act. It doesn't mean she doesn't have her moments, David. It just means she's found a way to handle her feelings." They paused at the porch and Rachel reached out to halt David. "There's something else—something our mother has always said, even well before Pearl Harbor."

"What's that?"

"Hatred only causes the pain to be more intense. Love eases pain." The look on her face magnified the love in her voice. "I hope my love will help ease your pain . . . but if not mine, then I know God's love will."

He thought of his arm and how much better he'd felt ever since coming to Longview. Maybe love did ease pain. Maybe just being around love had the power to heal. Then David looked deep into Rachel's eyes and in his heart he knew she was right. The answer to all his problems was so close at hand, he could nearly touch it. He opened his mouth to say that he didn't know what to do, but Rachel had already turned to go into the house. *Show me*, David thought. *Show me what to do.*

CHAPTER 9

Early on Christmas Eve day, David felt compelled to visit the cemetery. He slipped out of the house well before breakfast and made his way in the growing light of predawn. He knew it probably made no sense to anyone else, but he wanted to go there and apologize. He wanted to come clean with Kenny, and then maybe, just maybe, he could come clean with everything else.

What he didn't expect was to find Grandpa Bennett already in attendance. The old man stood in the silent chill of the December morning, hat in hand, murmuring words that David couldn't quite make out.

The sight of the old man touched David's heart. He'd had very few men in his life. Perhaps that was why Kenny had meant so much to him. What had started out as nothing more than a relationship of subordination to a superior had grown in a most compelling manner into friendship.

"I thought I heard someone," Grandpa Bennett said, turning to where David had stopped. Uncertain what to say, David only nodded and stepped forward.

The old man put his hat back on his head and sized David up for a moment. "I know you."

"Of course you do." David wondered if the cold weather had somehow affected the older man's mind.

George Bennett smiled tolerantly. "No, I know you. I know you because at one time I was exactly who you are."

David felt none of the old fear of being found out. Hadn't he already confessed his actions to Rachel? Hadn't Kenny's letters home proven that the entire family knew David's secrets? The gentleness of truth that came from Grandpa Bennett left David without worry or fear.

"You might find it hard to believe," George Bennett continued, "but I was once just as lost and angry. I thought the whole world was my enemy. We weren't even at war as a country, but I was at war with everyone."

David knew that feeling well. He had always thought it a means of protecting himself from further hurt. *If I hate them first, they can't disappoint me when they hate me in return. If I hurt them first, they can't hurt me.* These thoughts had been his constant companions throughout his youth.

"I didn't want Marion to court Ruth. I didn't want them to marry," the older man said flatly. "Ruth's family were strangers. Their ways and religious notions troubled me. I didn't care for foreigners. My family had been in this country since just about as far back as the *Mayflower*. I felt we were the only ones who truly belonged in America, not some Johnny-come-lately who saw the prosperity of the land and decided to make his fortune. My people were here when there was nothing to offer but hard work. I was mighty proud of that lineage."

David had never heard anyone talk in such a manner. It made him suddenly mindful that his own heritage had certainly not started in America. His people were Jewish. He knew very little about where they'd come from, but their ancestry spoke for itself and many had been the time he'd suffered for that very thing.

"My wife thought me an ungrateful snob when Ruth's family showed up and offered their friendship. When Marion and Ruth fell in love and it became very clear that they had marriage in mind, I did everything in my power to put an end to it." David couldn't help shaking his head and Grandpa Bennett smiled. "Kind of surprises you, eh?"

David smiled back. "I guess so. I would never know from the way Ruth treats you that there was ever any trouble."

"Before I gave up having things my way, standing on my own merits and those of my lineage, I wasn't a good man. I deserved Ruth's anger and bitterness, I deserved her mistrust and suspicions, but you know what I got instead? I got her kindness and love and I also found peace with her Savior."

"How did that all come about?" David asked, realizing he really wanted to know.

George Bennett squared his shoulders and walked to where Kenny's marker lay. The poinsettia had withstood the weather quite well.

"One day, not but three weeks before Marion and Ruth were to be married, I went to see Ruth and her father. I had hoped to talk her out of the marriage and to put some sense in her father's head. When I rode up, Ruth was the only one home. Seemed the little ones were still at school and her mother and father had gone to bring them and a few supplies home from town.

"She greeted me warmly and offered to see to my horse, and when I refused and told her I just wanted to talk to her and her father, she merely nodded. I gave her my fiercest look and harshest voice," he remembered with a laugh, "and that little gal just stood her ground."

David could well imagine. He smiled at the image in his head. "What happened next?" he asked eagerly.

George looked up and shook his head. "She told me her father would be back in about half an hour but that she'd be happy to hear me out. First, however, she wanted to ask me a favor. Imagine that. Here I'd come to destroy this young woman's dreams and she wanted to ask me a favor. I eyed her kind of suspicious-like and asked her what she wanted, and she told me. She wanted only to be able to speak her mind first."

"And did you let her?" David questioned.

The old man shrugged. "I didn't see any harm in it. Especially since what I wanted to say to her, I really wanted to say to both her and her father. So I granted her permission to speak. Best and worst thing I could have done," he said, and the amusement in his voice was clear.

"So what did she say?"

George looked back at Kenny's marker. "She said, 'Mr. Bennett, I love your son. He means more to me than anyone in the world. I think if I had to, I'd even be willing to die for him.' I kind of laughed that off, thinking her a silly female with all her silly notions, but she didn't leave it there. She told me that her love for Marion paled in comparison to God's love for me. She shared the plan of salvation with me without even hesitating. She told me I was a sinner—that we were all sinners. That without repenting and accepting Jesus as my Savior, I was hopelessly lost and would spend eternity paying for my mistake."

David shivered and came closer to where Grandpa Bennett stood. "And what did you say?" He felt the pull at his own spirit. Kenny had tried on more than one occasion to share the plan of salvation with David. Kenny had hoped after leaving the navy to become a preacher, but while he was in the navy he saw no reason to let opportunities pass him by.

"I wanted to say a lot of things, but you know, I couldn't. I opened my mouth to condemn that little gal, but nothing came out. And in my silence, she continued. She told me God knew how I felt and that He knew everything I'd ever done. She told me He knew those things for everybody and because of it, He'd sent Jesus to die on a cross—a sacrifice for those sins.

"I didn't want to hear such nonsense, but I couldn't leave. I'd given my word that she could have her say, but more than that, I felt as though my boots were nailed to the front porch steps where I stood. There we were, me six foot two and two hundred pounds and her a good foot shorter and half my weight. But in all my days I've never seen a stronger, more dynamic person as that little gal. She was the kind of person you'd want in your corner. The kind of woman you just knew would stand by her man and her family no matter what storms they had to weather. She wasn't afraid—not of me, anyway, and I had my doubts that she was afraid of anything. Until this."

He looked down at the headstone and shook his head. "Kenny's death made her question a lot of things. Things like how God would keep you from bad if you trusted in Him. Or that if you prayed hard enough, you'd get whatever you asked for. She had to accept that bad and good happened even when you prayed. And on the other side of that fact, she had to decide for herself that God was still a loving and merciful Father."

"It's hard to believe that," David admitted.

"Sure is," George replied. "David, on that day so long ago, I knelt beside Ruth and gave my heart to Jesus. Suddenly all my pitiful efforts to be an upstanding man, a good father, a loving husband—it all just passed away in the void of my life without God. You have that void too. I can see it in your eyes. And I think that in your heart, in the depths of your soul, you know what it is you're seeking. I guess I just want to ask, are you ready to come home?"

David couldn't stop the tears that came to his eyes. His entire body began to shake. He could only nod. All the pretenses were gone, stripped away by this old man's humble confession.

George Bennett knelt down on the ground beside Kenny's marker. He reached up a hand to David. The time had come to stop fighting and lying. It was time to lay his painful life upon the altar and let Jesus heal his hurt. It was time to come home.

Ruth put breakfast on the table, then went upstairs to finish packing the last of Kenny's belongings. Carrying the final box of items to the storage room, Ruth could not deny the sorrow she felt. She went back to the room, now nearly void of her son's presence, and felt an overwhelming wave of emotion wash over her.

Blinking back tears, she sat on his bed and ran her hand over the quilt top. She'd made this quilt for him when he was ten years old. It had all his favorite colors—greens and blues and purples. She remembered his surprise at the gift and his pleasure at her efforts. He had hugged her hard, nearly squeezing the air from her.

She remembered other things as well. The feel of his hand in hers, so soft and warm. So alive. She remembered his voice, often yelling at her from some part of the house. She had chided him for all his hollering. How she wished she could hear him just once more. She wouldn't mind him banging the screen door or forgetting to put the milk back in the icebox. She wouldn't scold him when he teased his sisters or complain when he forgot to put his dirty clothes in the wash basket.

Tears streamed down her face. The image of Kenny in a cold, watery grave made her hurt in such a powerful way. She knew his soul was in heaven, but her mother's heart wanted to tend to his body as well. She had been the one to wash him and dress him for bed when he was young. She had been the one to dress his scrapes and cuts. She had held his hand as the doctor set his broken arm, but now she couldn't even bury him properly.

"Why, God?" she questioned. "Why Kenny? He loved you so. He had so much to live for."

For the first time since Kenny's death, Ruth was aware of her anger. It startled her at first, and then it broke her heart. How could she be angry at God? He had been her mainstay. He had been her only hope. People like David got angry at God, not her.

"Ruth?" Her husband's voice made her feel even worse. He would see her crying and know that she was sad. She had tried so hard to keep her pain from him.

She dried her eyes with her apron as Marion came into the room. He looked at her for a moment and then at the room. Nodding, he came to sit beside her. He put his arms around her and pulled her close. The tears fell anew and Ruth felt her strength give out.

"I'm so sorry," she whispered.

"Sorry for missing Kenny?" he questioned.

"No, I'm sorry for crying in front of you. It just sort of came on me."

"Ruthie Bennett, I'm your husband," he said in a tone that suggested chastisement. "If you can't cry in front of me, what good am I?"

Her shoulders shook as she sobbed. "I wanted to be strong for you. I know how much this hurt you."

He lifted her chin gently and gazed into her eyes. "Ruth, we're one. When you hurt, I hurt. I've seen this coming for a long time now. You had to deal with being so angry."

"I don't want to be angry."

"But you are. You're angry at me for not being able to keep bad things from happening to our son. You're angry at Kenny for dying, and you're angry at God for taking him away from you."

She nodded because he was right. She could see it now. "He's really gone," she cried. "I just kept hoping it was a mistake. I kept praying he would come back home. Then David showed up and I knew Kenny was gone forever."

"No," Marion said, touching her cheek lightly. "Not forever . . . just for a time."

Ruth knew the truth in his statement. Maybe it only felt like forever because she had loved him so very much. Maybe it felt like forever because she was tired of battling this with her own strength.

"I'm sorry if I took this out on you, Marion. Here I thought I was being so brave and helpful."

"You were all of that and more," her husband assured. "God understands how you feel, Ruth. He knows what it is to sacrifice a son for a greater cause."

She nodded and drew a deep breath. "But He's God," she smiled ever so slightly. "He can handle anything."

Marion wiped away her tears. "Yes, He can, including this. You don't have to bear this alone, Ruthie."

She knew he was right and in that moment her pain began to subside just a bit. More importantly, the anger seemed to drain away.

"David needs us." She offered nothing more than that simple statement, but it was enough.

Marion nodded in understanding. "I think we should ask him to stay for as long as he likes."

"Not as a replacement for Kenny," she said, knowing that she had seen him as such when he'd first arrived.

"No," Marion agreed. "We're going to do this for David." He offered her a hint of a grin. "And for Rachel, too, if I don't miss my guess."

Ruth hugged her husband close and felt her strength returning. Healing in full would take time, just as Grandpa Bennett had suggested, but pain was not so fierce in the face of true love.

Later that morning, Ruth made her way to the flower shop. She wanted to make sure that everything would be all right for a couple of days. She didn't plan to come back until after Christmas and hoped that by taking care of things now, she could have a nice leisurely time later. Just as she reached the shop, however, she stopped. To her surprise, David waited on the bench outside the door. It was as if he had expected her to come.

"Hello, David," she said.

He smiled and seemed more at ease than she'd ever seen him. "I figured," he began, "that it was time for me to put aside my anger. I'd like to see life like you do. Instead of just black and white, I want to see it in all its colors and contrasts and know that each and every one has a purpose and reason for being here."

She felt her heart leap for joy and knew that God had dealt with both of them that day. She reached out and took hold of his hand. "Maybe we can help each other," she said softly and led him toward the door.

CHAPTER 10

Spending Christmas Eve night in a merriment of feasting and song, David found the hardness of his heart begin to soften. By the time they sat down to open gifts, David knew that the prayer he'd prayed with Grandpa Bennett had forever changed his outlook on life. There were still questions, still a great deal of anger, but now he knew where to take it.

"Here, the last present is for you," Helen said.

David smiled and took the gift. "Well, thank you, but you certainly shouldn't have gotten me anything more. The gloves and scarf were more than enough." He looked around the room at the Bennetts. How he wished he could express his gratitude. Not just for the material things they'd given, but for the emotional and spiritual as well. They'd already given him a reason to go on with life. They'd shared their home and their hospitality, but most of all they'd given huge doses of unconditional love.

"It isn't anything big," Ruth said, "but we wanted you to have it. We have something else to give you, but it can wait until you unwrap that one."

David raised a brow, then smiled. "This family is just full of surprises." He unwrapped the package and opened the box. Inside, he found a brown leather scrapbook. Opening the pages, he found pictures of Kenny and the Bennetts. His eyes teared up and unashamed he looked up to meet Ruth's motherly smile.

"It's a family album," she explained. "We realize that you have no family, and I guess in our own way, we're volunteering ourselves to be one for you."

"That's right," Marion stated, nodding in complete agreement. "We'd like you to stay on, David. We want you to consider this your home for as long as you like."

"That's our real gift," Ruth said softly. "We aren't trying to replace Kenny, so don't even think it. We know nothing and no one could ever do that. But we care about you, David. We want to stay beside you as a family and help you in your future."

David wiped at his tears, feeling no embarrassment. "No one has ever cared about me like this," he admitted. He glanced to where Rachel and Helen sat, their faces offering the same compassionate expression as their mother's. He looked to Ruth and Marion, and finally to Grandpa Bennett. Such a wise old man.

"Yesterday I asked Jesus into my heart—to live inside me," David said. "It seemed the right thing to do." Glancing at the open scrapbook and a picture of Kenny in full dress uniform, he felt an overwhelming peace. Kenny's love had worked. But not just Kenny's. The Bennetts saw David as worth something when no one else had been able to see it. And because of that—because of them—David was able to see that Jesus felt the same way.

He looked up and realized beyond any doubt that he was exactly where he belonged. "This seems like the right thing too. I'd like to stay," he said, meeting Ruth's gaze.

A joyous celebration warmed the house the next morning, and amid presents from the night before and laughter, David Cohen knew what it was to be at peace.

"Come with me," Rachel whispered in his ear sometime later.

She grinned at him mischievously, and David finally knew his heart where she was concerned. "I'd follow you anywhere," he replied, getting to his feet.

"Now, don't you two be gone long," Ruth said as she headed for the kitchen. "I've got a great Christmas breakfast planned and I don't want it going cold."

Rachel let David help her with her coat. "We'll only be a minute, Mom," she called back.

David grabbed his own coat and followed Rachel onto the front porch. He wasn't at all sure what she would say or do, but he knew what his intentions were. He loved this woman and he had to make certain that she knew how he felt.

David awkwardly pulled on his coat and, without bothering to button it, walked to where Rachel leaned against the railing. Reaching out, he pulled her close and gently turned her to face him. "I want to tell you something."

"I know."

He stared into her blue eyes for just a heartbeat before adding, "I love you."

She nodded. "I know that too. But I'm glad to hear you say it. In fact, I'll be glad to hear you say it over and over and over for the rest of my life."

He laughed. "Is that a proposal, Miss Bennett?"

She nodded and smiled, then wrapped her arms around him, embracing him as he'd always hoped she would. With her lips only inches away from his, she breathed the words, "I love you, David. Now and forever."

He had come to Longview to fulfill a promise and instead found the hope of a new promise that would give him a reason for living. "Merry Christmas, Rachel."

Their lips touched for the briefest of kisses. "Merry Christmas, David," she breathed, then leaned into his kiss once more—only this time, there was nothing brief about it.

David sighed and let the newness of her love wash over him. This love—and the love and peace he found in Christ—saturated his heart and soothed away the emptiness and pain of a lost man without a single hope. He had truly come home.

REMEMBER ME

CHAPTER 1

South Pacific, December 1942

The sun-drenched warmth of salt air against his body and face might have been pleasant in another time and place. After all, men were freezing their tails off in the Aleutians, and the tropics offered glorious sun and lush vegetation. But none of that seemed important or interesting at the moment. Fighting for his life, First Lieutenant Erik Anderson twisted violently from the risers of his parachute. Suspended some five thousand feet above the earth, with a canopy of jungle green rushing up at him faster than he cared to imagine, Erik didn't feel at all interested in the lure of the tropics.

Five minutes ago he'd been caught up in the dogfight of his life with a Japanese Zero. Four minutes ago he'd plastered the Zero with .50-caliber rounds. And three minutes ago, as the Zero belched smoke and accepted the earthly limitations given the plane, the pilot had managed to make a desperate head-on pass. A lucky hit from the Zero's 20mm cannon exploded in the engine of the F4F that Erik piloted. Even the tough Grumman Wildcat couldn't withstand the damage.

Erik had no choice but to jump out of his damaged plane and pray in his cynical fashion that his chute would deploy. He'd "got the one that got him," but there were no witnesses to the dogfight. No one could step forward and give credit to Erik for his kill. His first kill. Probably his first real act of heroism for the war effort.

The emerald green brilliance below him grew ever closer and Erik found he had no way to maneuver himself out of the range of the trees. He felt lucky to even be reaching land. He'd never been one to listen very faithfully to his flight briefings when it came to details about the surrounding areas. The Solomons might well have over nine hundred different islands, but all Erik really knew was his plane had now become a permanent part of the Pacific Ocean and he was about to land only God knew where.

Looking to the cloudless sky, he murmured, "Hope you'll remember I'm down here." His faith in God, seemingly strong at home when things had been easy, had been shaken from his first moment in uniform.

Heading ever closer to the trees, Erik caught a momentary glimmer of a silvery ribbon. A river, he figured. Or at least a creek. He did remember from his training that rivers and creeks often connected to paths, which would in turn lead to some form of civilization—although Erik doubted there was any form of civilization on this island. It looked completed deserted.

"Looks can be deceiving, old man," he told himself. He strained his eyes against the leafy growth beneath him. Trees, trees, and more trees.

"Better than being lunch for the sharks," he said, trying hard to look for silver linings. His mother had always said that God wouldn't give you more than you could handle. He was trusting that to be true.

Erik had little time to comment on anything else. The chute wasn't slowing him down as much as he would have liked, and now he faced the jungle tops with a sense of trepidation. This just hadn't been his week. Or month. Or year.

His boots hit the branches first and after that it was a rhythmic beating of palm fronds, vines, and various other branches against his body, tearing at his clothes and skin, reaching gnarled fingers to poke and prod him like some ancient backwoods doctor. At this rate, his body would be pulverized before the chute finally managed to snag a branch.

Feeling the tension in his groin and shoulders as the harness and straps reached their limits, Erik found himself momentarily halted before being snapped back up a short distance only to be dropped down again. When he finally came to a halt, he closed his eyes and waited a moment before moving. He wanted to make sure he'd really come to a stop and that he was still in one piece—that he wasn't dead.

"I'm alive," he said, almost gasping for breath. He hadn't realized he'd been holding his breath until just that moment.

For a few minutes his head seemed to spin while he awaited the return of blood to his brain. Slowly he opened his eyes and began to move rather gingerly, testing his body for damage. His legs moved easily—too easily. Glancing down, he quickly ascertained why. The ground was still well below him. At least he hoped that was ground down there, somewhere. The darkness and intricate weave of the jungle vegetation made it impossible to see much of anything.

Seeing overhead where the chute had caught itself up in the rain forest canopy, Erik realized he'd dropped into quite a predicament. If only it were raining, his day might be complete.

"Well, if this just isn't a plum dandy way to end a day of fighting. A fellow can't even have a minute to revel in his glory." He twisted against the chute rather violently before realizing that if he were to free the thing, he might yet meet his death from the long-distance plunge.

"Well, what am I supposed to do?" he wondered aloud. He had little to go by. No one had ever really instructed him on how to free himself from such an adventure. He had a jungle kit consisting of survival gear. Maybe that would give him some ideas.

He tried to work the kit free, only then noticing that he'd cut his hand pretty badly. No telling where he'd done it. He wiped the blood against his flight suit and continued trying to free his supplies.

Hanging in the air was beginning to lose its charm. Erik managed to slip the jungle kit loose, but just as he opened the pack, movement at his side caused him to freeze. Glancing over, trying hard to be nonchalant about the entire matter, Erik let out a yelp at the sight of a slithering tree boa.

With the yelp went the jungle kit. Flashing out against the green foliage, the articles rained down on the land below, not giving so much as a sound when they reached the bottom. *If* they reached the bottom. For all Erik knew, he might as well have been suspended over a bottomless cavern or a swamp.

The boa seemed concerned with neither Erik nor the jungle kit. It simply slithered off to some unknown destination. Erik really didn't care so long as the thing kept moving away from him.

Calming his nerves, Erik tried to analyze the situation as best he could. The only reasonable solution seemed to be that he somehow get loose of the chute and climb down the nearest tree. Having been quite a tree climber as a boy, Erik assumed the matter could be done without too much difficulty.

"Maybe it has been a good five or six years since I did any serious climbing," he said to no one but himself, "but I bet I can still handle it."

He thought of his mother back in Longview, Washington. A regular member of Faith Church and a devout woman of God, Lena Anderson would have told him that God could handle it. And maybe He could—if He were listening. Erik only allowed himself a small moment of guilt as he realized how negative he'd become. He had grown up in church and knew God for himself. He'd accepted Jesus as his Savior when he was a boy of thirteen. But somehow the last few months had done more to tear at his faith than the preceding twenty years of life.

His first disappointment had been in finding himself stationed at Guadalcanal or "The Canal," as the marines called it, where everything ran on a shoestring. Not only that, but his first few weeks there had consisted of a constant barrage of enemy fire at night and a military game of "Get 'em before they get you" during the day. It held no charm and did absolutely nothing to endear the South Pacific to him.

His second disappointment was a seeming lack of concern or interest from the folks back home. He'd had so few letters or packages from home that his despair had grown into a lurking, shadowy monster of doubt. They didn't care. They didn't even know he existed. He'd left Longview and then Washington and then the continental United States. It was as if he'd simply disappeared, and once out of sight, he was definitely out of mind.

But surely Mary Ann remembered him. He smiled and his tension seemed to ease a bit. He thought of her angelic face, eyes as blue as the waters he'd just flown over, and a sweet innocence that made him want her for the mother of his children.

"I'll write to you every day," she had told him when they'd shared a private moment before his departure. The church had sponsored a going-away party for several of their young men, and Erik had been among their numbers.

"I'll think of you day and night," she promised. *"I just wish you didn't have to go."*

"It's my duty," Erik had assured her, but now he could only wonder if he'd done the right thing. Here he was hanging from a tree in the South Pacific, and Mary Ann was somewhere in Seattle—probably at the mercy of those wolves in sheep's clothing who were left at home running things.

"No sense feeling sorry for yourself," he said, but the image of Mary Ann's sweet face refused to fade from his thoughts. "I have to be strong and remain focused on my task. I have to come home to you in one piece."

Erik gave a slight bounce against the chute straps. They held fast. Maybe, he reasoned, he could swing back and forth and grab on to that fairly smooth barked trunk to his left. Like a five-year-old at the park, he swung his legs forward in an overexaggerated manner and let the chips fall where they would.

The chute didn't so much as budge. It was wedged in good and tight and, for reasons that seemed to elude understanding, even the silk seemed firmly resistant to tearing.

He caught the trunk on his third good swing. Hugging the tree like the lifeline it was, Erik managed to get ahold of his knife and saw through the shroud lines of his parachute. The fluttering in his stomach gave rise to a nervous notion that maybe he was making a mistake. Like an umbilical cord being cut, Erik realized his security was now in his own ability to survive. But then again, he was a marine.

God is your light and your salvation, son, whispered the memory of his mother's words.

"Let it be so," Erik prayed.

The sounds of the jungle permeated the vegetation. Somewhere to his right came the unmistakable scolding of an irritated bird. Obviously distressed by Erik's appearance in their territory, a number of birds joined in the chorus. And there were other noises—trees rustling, tapping sounds, rubbing and scraping sounds. The place was alive with its own kind of music. Erik just hadn't bothered to hear it until now. His own rapidly beating heart, the rushing blood against his eardrums, had been all that he could focus on. But now as his breathing evened and his heartbeat relaxed a bit, Erik became more than a little aware that he had landed in the midst of an entirely new world.

His descent proved less than eventful, and when at last Erik put his feet back on the spongy yet solid ground of the island, he let out a huge sigh of relief. Training told him to sit down and take stock of the situation and figure out where he was. Looking around, he shook his head.

"I'm in a jungle. Somewhere in the Pacific. Okay, so that's resolved."

He laughed as he recalled his next issue of training. Stay with the aircraft because it's big and easily spotted. "Well, that might work—if the plane wasn't under hundreds of feet of ocean." He paused. "So much for training."

Wiping the sweat from his neck, Erik surveyed the area for his survival kit. It was nowhere to be seen. The thick vegetation and overgrowth of the undisturbed jungle refused to give up its secrets. It became a strange game of hide-and-seek and Erik didn't stand a chance.

On his hands and knees, he felt his way through some of the mossy terrain, but when something moved under his touch, Erik began to realize he might very well be in more danger than he thought. Jumping to his feet, he reached for the reassurance of his .45 revolver. At least he had managed to hang on to it. There were six rounds chambered and another six in reserve. Certainly not enough ammunition to fight a one-man war, but maybe enough to keep him alive while he searched for some form of rescue.

Besides this, he had his knife. Together, the two could double as tools and weapons. Surely it was enough to keep him going. It had to be. There wasn't anything else to rely on.

"Erik Anderson, you know full well that you can always rely on God," he heard his mother chide.

Nodding, he felt his spirits lift only marginally. "Yes, ma'am," he said as if his mother were at his side. He glanced around at the creeping, crawling, oozing charm of the jungle and laughed out loud. "But I can't exactly sit here and wait for a lightning bolt from heaven."

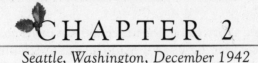

CHAPTER 2
Seattle, Washington, December 1942

"Isn't Ray just swell!" Mary Ann Roland declared as she paraded through the shared boarding room with a new pair of stockings. "I can't believe he just gave these to us for free."

Ellen Anderson eyed her friend suspiciously. "Maybe they aren't for free. Did you ever stop to think that Ray Blasingham might very well have a price in mind? You need to be careful, Mary Ann."

"Oh, you're just worried I'll fall for him and leave your brother Erik at the altar," she said in a teasing tone. She knew, however, that Ellen did worry about such things. "I adore Erik and I would never do anything to hurt him." She plopped onto the bed, still admiring the stockings. "Besides, I've told Erik about Ray, and I've told Ray about Erik. I think Ray realizes how much I miss Erik. He's just trying to be nice to us."

Ellen shook her head. "Don't count on that."

Mary Ann put the hose aside. "You said yourself that there was nothing wrong with having a little fun. Why, we only started going to those dances with Ray because you said we were doing our part for the war by keeping morale up."

"I don't have a problem with letting Ray act as an escort to the two of us," Ellen admitted. She toyed with her brown hair before pinning it into a neat bun. "I just have a problem with us taking gifts from him. Ray is your foreman, after all. You let it get around that the boss is paying you extra favors and you'll lose every friend you have." She secured a hairnet over the bun, then walked to the bed she shared with Mary Ann. Housing was so short, they were lucky to even have a bed to share. "You'd better get a move on or we'll be late for work."

"I'm sure Mr. Boeing would understand." Nevertheless, she'd never been late to work and didn't intend to start now. She tucked the stockings into her dresser drawer, gave them one last look of longing, then left them to await her return. Surely Ellen was wrong about Ray and the situation causing problems. He was just a nice man who knew how lonely she was. Besides, he had that whole problem with his one leg being shorter than the other and not being able to get into the war. He'd told her how sad it made him to watch his buddies go off to war and not be able to join them. It had just about broken Mary Ann's heart. She knew how hard it had been on her uncle Morris not to be able to go to the Great War. Why, Mama said it had been the undoing of Uncle Morris and that he'd taken to drinking and bootlegging after that. Mary Ann surely didn't want to see something like that happen to Ray, and if she could help to keep his spirits up, then she just knew it was the Christian thing to do.

"Mama would surely have a fit if she caught sight of me wearing trousers in public," Ellen said, studying her figure in the vanity mirror. "I told her there was no sense in wearing a dress to work. I said, 'Mama, even if I work in the office, I still find myself out on the plant floor for a good portion of the day.' But you know her. She worries about such things. Doesn't think it's proper for a young lady to go doing a man's job."

"I know. My mama worries too. If we didn't need the money so badly, she'd have never let me come clear to Seattle to work."

Ellen looked at Mary Ann sympathetically. "There are lots of things to worry about these days. War is such a frightening thing. Here we are on the western coast and such an easy target for the Japanese. I keep telling myself that Erik has it much worse than we do, but he is a man and maybe he doesn't get as scared as we do."

"Sometimes I just don't know what to do," Mary Ann admitted. "I know Mama's back home with six kids to raise in that three-bedroom house, and with Daddy passing away three years ago, I'm the only one old enough to make money to keep them all eating. Sometimes that's what really scares me. What if something happens to them—or to me?"

"Nothing's going to happen. You have to keep your chin up and look for the rainbow. We're going to be just fine. Besides, your brother is just about old enough to start working full time. He's never cared much for school anyway. Once he's able to bring in some money, you'll be able to ease back a bit."

Mary Ann clung to the hope in those words. "I'm sure you're right."

They skipped their chance at a real breakfast and instead grabbed pieces of toast off Mrs. Neal's sideboard. At one end the faithful boardinghouse mistress had breakfast set up, and at the other end were lunches for the Boeing workers to take on their way out the door. Usually it wasn't all that great of a spread, but it was better than having to find your own grub and plan for the day.

Mary Ann whistled a tune as she and Ellen made their way to their main mode of transportation—bicycles. Every day, rain or shine—and of late it was more rain than shine—they made their way to the Seattle Boeing plant. Lucky for them the boardinghouse wasn't that far away, but the ride usually set the tone for the day to come. Once, Mary Ann had been pelted by icy rain and nearly run over by a plant transport all at once. The rest of the day had gone downhill from there. Another time, the sun had been shining, the air was crisp and cool, and everyone had been pleasant and courteous as they made their way to work. Mary Ann had received a promotion that day and a raise in pay.

She didn't count herself as superstitious, however. Her mama had said a smile would do just as much to make things better as a frown would do to make them worse. Sometimes you just had to make up your mind to have a good day.

But the best days had been with Erik. She had loved him for almost forever. He was everything she had wanted in a husband, and when he'd proposed she had been the happiest woman in the world. Even now she could feel his arm around her waist, smell the heady scent of his cologne, and almost hear him whisper his love for her.

"You've got that look again," Ellen said as they moved their bikes out into the morning traffic.

She smiled shyly. "I was just thinking about Erik, that's all."

"I've been thinking a lot about him lately." Ellen's tone betrayed her worry. "Mom says he hasn't written to say he got our packages or anything. I don't like to borrow trouble—"

"Then don't!" Mary Ann hurried to interject. "Don't say anything bad. Let's just keep remembering that God will watch over him and things will be all right."

Ellen pulled up alongside her, pedaling in the same even pacing.

"I'm not trying to suggest that God won't watch over him, I'm just worried."

"We have to believe the best."

Ellen laughed. "I wish I could have your childlike faith, Mary Ann."

She frowned. "I don't think it's so childish."

"I didn't say childish, I said childlike. There's a big difference. You have no trouble believing the best about everyone. Even Ray is just a sweet man with a sad past that keeps him out of the war. Erik is safe and sound in a nice, comfortable job, and really this war isn't that big of a deal."

"Of course it's a big deal. I might have childlike faith, but I'm not that naïve," Mary Ann declared rather defensively. People were always telling her she was too naïve—too naïve to be getting married, too naïve to be living in a big city. It was always something, and she was bound and determined to prove them wrong. The only real problem was that Mary Ann knew they weren't far from the truth. She was naïve. Life in a small town with good parents and strong moral values had lent itself to her never having to worry much about the seedier side of life. Marriage to Erik would give her the same liberty. The only problem was, she wasn't in her small town anymore, and Erik was thousands of miles away.

They rode the rest of the way in silence. Traffic remained light and the constant flow of walkers seemed to limit themselves mostly to the sidewalks. Mary Ann determined in her heart to have a good day as they reached the plant parking area. With a smile, she waved as Ellen went her way to the offices, and Mary Ann made her way to the plant floor.

Mary Ann worked with the B-17 production, primarily the bombardier's nose cone. She had once tried to explain her job to her mother, but the idea of her daughter working in war factory production so far from home only gave her mother worry. Her little girl might well be twenty years old and doing her part for the family and the war effort, but it grieved her to see her baby so completely separated from her care.

Mary Ann felt only a small twinge of guilt as she parked her bicycle. Remembering her mother's disappointment over her lack of visits home, Mary Ann was determined to take an armful of presents for the kids and be home for Christmas. The only problem was in how to accomplish it. The expense of the bus or the train was almost more than Mary Ann could see sense in paying. And that was if a ticket could be purchased in the first place. Leaving her bicycle and making a promise not to think about such gloomy things until later that day, Mary Ann put a smile on her face and headed for work.

"Hi ya, doll," Ray said as she entered the plant. "Ya know, you sure look swell in that uniform."

Pulling off her coat, Mary Ann thought the work shirt and baggy uniform pants did little to enhance her tall, slender figure, but she smiled. "Thanks, Ray. You sure know how to make a lady feel better."

Ray began to sing like Frank Sinatra, who just happened to be one of Mary Ann's favorite singers. Pretending he had a microphone in hand, he dipped ever so slightly to the right and crooned, "'She's a doll with the face of an angel. . . .'"

Laughter and giggles erupted as several of Mary Ann's co-workers came in behind her.

"Hello, ladies!" Ray greeted them warmly. "What a swell job I have. I feel like I'm working with beauty queens on the boardwalk in Atlantic City. Gorgeous women to the right, incredibly beautiful ones to the left."

More giggles filled the air, and even Mary Ann smiled. Ray was such a sweet guy. He knew how to appeal to a girl's heart, either singularly or in a group. And although some of the girls said he was as slick as the oil they eventually pumped into those finished B-17s, Mary Ann just knew he was sincere and genuine with his attentions. *He's just a nice guy*, she thought.

Mary Ann had tried to point out to Ellen and to Erik that Ray didn't mean anything by his innuendoes and gifts. It was simply his job to up production, and he would do that by whatever means he saw necessary. If a gal found herself getting a little needed attention when she went to work in the morning, what in the world was wrong with that? After all, they had those uniformed war heroes come and speak to the plant from time to time. The men were always inspired to hear other men talk about the war. Besides, Erik had never written back to say anything more on the matter, so Mary Ann figured he believed the best about the man as well. Ellen would surely come around in time.

"So are you and Ellen going with me on Friday night?" Ray questioned, coming up from behind Mary Ann.

She nodded. "As far as I know. Ellen seems excited about the idea," Mary Ann lied. Ellen wasn't in the least bit excited, but she didn't want to hurt Ray's feelings.

"Great! It's not too late for me to get a buddy to go along with us. Ellen might even fall in love," Ray said, then lowering his voice, he added, "You know—double date."

Mary Ann looked around rather nervously. No one seemed to pay them the slightest bit of attention, but still she felt uncomfortable. "I don't think it would be a good idea to call it a date. After all, I'm engaged."

"Sure, doll face. Half the country is. I wasn't proposing," he said, laughing. "I was just suggesting you might like a little extra attention. I know it's hard on you gals to be without your guys." He sobered a bit. "It's hard on me too. You know how much I'd love to be out there fighting the enemy and helping to win this war."

Mary Ann felt a wave of sympathy wash over her. "Oh, Ray, you're doing an important job here. You mustn't be so hard on yourself." She glanced at her watch. "Look, I'd better get to my station. Ellen and I will be ready when you come on Friday. Seven o'clock, right?"

"Seven and heaven!" Ray declared. "'Cause I'll be in heaven for sure when I'm with two of the prettiest angels in all of Washington." He made a clicking sound and pointed his finger like a gun. Winking, he popped a piece of gum in his mouth and danced off down the plant floor.

His shorter leg didn't seem to interfere with his dancing, Mary Ann observed. Shaking her head, she laughed as he made an exaggerated bow to one of her other co-workers. He certainly had a way about him.

"Morning, Ellen."

Ellen hung up her coat and murmured, "Morning, Mr. Chandler."

"I put a stack of invoices on your desk. We're going to have to get right to those this morning."

"No problem. I stayed late last night and typed up those letters you needed. You'll find them in your office," she said, taking a seat at her rather disorganized desk. It seemed the war never allowed for her to get caught up even for a moment. Staring at the mess in silence, she couldn't help worrying about Mary Ann and Ray. Why couldn't she understand that men like Ray were bad news?

"You seem a little preoccupied this morning," Chris Chandler said. He came to stand by her desk and smiled. "Anything I can help with?"

Ellen looked up at the older man and shook her head. He was a great boss. Good family man too. He was the kind of man Ellen hoped to someday meet and fall in love with. Stable, Christian, kind, and intelligent. That didn't seem like too much to ask for.

"It'll work itself out," she assured him.

He didn't appear convinced and pulled up a chair. "Ellen, I try to be a good supervisor to my people. If the workers are happy and well cared for, they produce better work. But even more than that, I know it's what God would have me to do. Now, why don't you tell me what's eating at you?"

Ellen felt a wave of relief wash over her. She needed someone to talk to, why not let it be Mr. Chandler? "I guess I'm worried about my roommate."

"Mary Ann Roland, right?"

"Right. You see, she's engaged to my brother, and we came here to Seattle to help with the war effort. My brother is a marine pilot somewhere in the Pacific."

"I know several of the boys from our church who ended up in the Pacific."

"Well, we haven't heard much from Erik since October. Mom's pretty worried. I suppose the good thing is there haven't been any telegrams to suggest he's anything but safe."

"That is good. You shouldn't worry too much. They try to be good with mail delivery, but there is a war on." He smiled and touched her shoulder gently.

He always came across fatherly in his concern. It amazed Ellen. Anytime Ray touched her she felt like taking a bath, but when Chris Chandler touched her it seemed comforting.

"It's more than that." She found herself opening up. "I'm worried about Mary Ann. She's a good girl from a good family. But she's totally overwhelmed by life in the big city. When we first arrived she was one of the shyest, most reserved people I knew. And while it's not that she isn't still rather shy, it's just that she wants so much to believe the best about everyone. She believes that everyone is telling her the gospel truth and that no one would ever have an ulterior motive. Now, what with Ray's interest—"

"Ray Blasingham?" Chandler cut in, coming back around the desk.

Ellen noted the anger in his tone. "Yes. Do you know much about him?"

"Too much. Ray's been the source of many problems for me. Nothing can ever be proven, but he's been brought to my attention more than once. Has he done something that I should know about?"

"Not really," Ellen replied. "It's just that he's definitely a smooth operator. He's friendly—too friendly, in fact. He's always giving the girls gifts and offering them nights out on the town. He's been nice enough about it, but he just makes me uncomfortable. I'm afraid that someone like Mary Ann, someone who is needy and lonely because her guy is off to war, will fall for one of his lines."

Chris nodded. "No doubt they will—probably have." He leaned down on the desk. "Look, if he does something and you can prove it, come to me. Ray's good at his job here, but I want to protect my girls. I want to run a tight ship with quality people, and we don't need—how did you put it?—'smooth operators.'"

"I appreciate your saying so, Mr. Chandler. I suppose I'll just keep praying about it and keep going with Mary Ann when she accepts Ray's invitations."

"If she's engaged to your brother, why is she so eager to accept?"

Ellen shrugged. "My guess is that she's bought in to all his sob stories. He's told her about being turned away when he volunteered for the service. Apparently he has one leg shorter than the other."

Chris shook his head. "That's a line for sure. I've never seen anything that would suggest any truth in that. I do know that his father has connections and money, and it wouldn't surprise me any if his stay from military service isn't connected to that. In fact, it's probably why my superiors have tolerated his Romeo advances and overactive affections."

"So he wasn't 4-F?" Ellen asked in disbelief.

"Oh, that very well might be what the record showed, but I doubt if there is any truth in it."

"Well, that just makes me even more committed to not leaving her alone with the guy."

"That's probably best," her boss agreed.

Ellen felt only marginally better. At least she knew that someone else had his eye on Ray Blasingham. "Thanks, Mr. Chandler."

"I'll be praying about it," he added as he headed to his office. "You'd do better to do that than to sit around fretting."

Ellen smiled. "You sound like my dad," she said without worrying about whether it might offend him.

But instead of being offended, Mr. Chandler stopped and smiled. "I'd be proud to have a daughter like you, Ellen. Your folks did a good job in raising you, and you're a dynamic young woman."

Ellen felt her face grow hot. "Thank you," she said, quickly turning away to take the cover off her typewriter.

"Don't be so embarrassed by praise, Ellen. It's the light of Jesus shining through you. Just remember that. Trust in God to keep you straight and true—Mary Ann too. You can't do this on your own. No one can."

Ellen looked back to see her boss's compassionate expression. "I appreciate what you've said. Sometimes it's just nice to hear the truth confirmed."

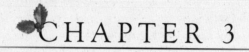

CHAPTER 3

"Mary Ann, will you marry me?" Erik Anderson asked. Reaching up, he gently brushed back golden curls from her ear, then whispered the question again.

"Oh yes!" she exclaimed in absolute delight. "I've always dreamed of the day you'd ask me that question."

He felt her gently touch his shoulder and neck, then her hands seemed to trail down to caress his chest. Something pinched at his flesh and Erik awoke with a start, only to realize that it wasn't Mary Ann's touch, but some kind of crab. In fact, several crabs had taken to crawling up his flight suit as he dozed beside a tree. Flicking them away, Erik wished fervently he could somehow recapture the dream.

Yawning, he tried to figure out what to do. He'd long ago given up trying to find the remnant of his survival gear and had headed in the direction of the river. But without a path or any working knowledge of the island, Erik tired quickly of fighting off the perils of jungle life. He hadn't intended to nap, but the tension of the day and all the events that had brought him to this place had taken their toll.

Glancing around, Erik found himself faced with a real dilemma. In the thick undergrowth of the jungle and the high canopy of trees overhead, he had no idea which direction to go in. The river had been to the south of where he'd landed, but now he wasn't really all that sure which way that was.

"I'm no Boy Scout," he said, laughing at his own stupidity. He pulled out a blue ball cap and snugged it down on his head. It was then that he got the idea to put a notch in the trunk of the tree, just a little mark to let him know he'd been there. *That way,* he figured, *if I go in circles I'll see the mark and be able to set myself straight.*

He reached up to mark the tree trunk and saw that his hand wound was oozing blood. It wasn't a steady flow, but it needed some attention. The best he could do was cut a strip from his already torn flight suit. Using his knife, he finished slicing through the ripped material on his right pant leg. He only took as much as he needed in order to cover the wound and tie it off tight. It seemed to work well to just cut the lower portion, leaving as much length to the pant leg as possible. When he brought the piece up for inspection, he had a complete circle. After cutting the material, he opened the strip and wrapped it around his bleeding left hand. He wasn't the best at tying a knot without the use of both hands, but between his right hand and mouth he managed to get the wound covered.

"That's not so bad," he said, eyeing his accomplishment. He sheathed the knife and looked around the area in despair. "But this is impossible. What am I supposed to do?"

Through the various shades of green, Erik couldn't make out any sign of a path or civilization. Maybe that was to his benefit, he thought. But then again, maybe not. He had no idea what kind of animals might live on this island, short of tree boas and crabs, which he'd already been introduced to. He remembered enough about his training to know that poisonous snakes abounded in the South Pacific. Boas weren't poisonous, he remembered, but it was rumored that they'd coil around you while you slept and squeeze the life right out of you. It didn't sound like a friendship he wanted to cultivate.

A strange noise came from overhead. It almost sounded like some kind of music, but then the sound changed and with it came the unmistakable droplets of rain. With the steady increase of the rain, the sound changed again and soon a heavy shower filtered down through the lush, leafy ceiling to soak Erik to the bone.

"Great! Just what I needed." He pulled down his hat and tried to keep a positive outlook. Perhaps the rain would drive the inhabitants of the island into hiding. Be they four-footed or two, Erik was fairly certain he wouldn't want to run into either one. So many of the Solomons had been invaded and taken over by the Japanese that he could only pray that this island had gone unnoticed. But then there was the worry that if the Japanese had left this island alone, there would be a reason for it. Perhaps it was already inhabited by headhunters. Or maybe there was no fresh water. With a sigh, Erik tried to pray.

"I know you're there, Lord," he whispered, "but it doesn't feel like you're here. I could sure use a break and a real sense of direction. I need to find water and food and hopefully a way off this island and back to my unit. If you could just see your way to helping me, I'd be much obliged."

Hearing a noise somewhere to the left, Erik felt for the reassurance of the .45 under his arm. "Oh, and please don't let there be any headhunters on this island. Amen."

The noise came again and this time Erik decided it was time to move on. Nobody was getting his head without a fight. He pushed aside some vine growth and looked past for some sign of a path. There was none. The only thing he could do was push through the jungle and hope for the best. It was a fairly small island, at least from what he remembered while coming down on top of it, but now it suddenly seemed massive.

Deciding to stop feeling sorry for himself, Erik pressed on. He sidestepped and manhandled branches and vines, flowering bushes and long-stemmed plants that seemed to be all leaf and nothing more. The rain let up for a moment, then increased for a time and then stopped altogether. He paused and listened from time to time, hoping to hear the rush of water or the sound of animals. What he didn't want to hear was the sound of voices, but after about twenty minutes of negotiating through the humid dampness of the rain forest, that was exactly what he got.

With water and sweat dripping from his face, Erik stood stone still and listened to what he had been certain was a human voice. Silence met his unspoken question and for a moment Erik wondered if he'd imagined the entire thing. Then it came again. Only this time a chorus of other voices followed. *Natives*, he thought warily. *Maybe headhunters or cannibals.* He swallowed hard and tried to reason a logical course of action. His reasoning failed him, however, as two native children with warm brown skin and dark, tightly curled hair came bounding through the brush, laughing and squealing. Obviously they were entertaining themselves in some sort of tag game. When they caught sight of Erik, however, they screamed in terror and immediately turned to run the other way.

Erik, having no idea if he was about to encounter an angry head-hunting father, ran in the opposite direction. *Guess that answers the question as to whether or not the island is inhabited*, he thought. At least they weren't Japanese. Of course, that didn't mean they weren't working for the Japanese. Erik remembered hearing stories of missionaries to the area who had met with untimely deaths at the hands of just such folks.

When he thought he couldn't run another step, if indeed running constituted inching your way through the tangle of jungle while being slowly beaten to death by the plant life, Erik paused to regain his breath. The rain had started to fall again, although this time it wasn't as heavy. Erik was dying of thirst, and rain didn't seem to be such a culprit anymore. He held his mouth open and lifted it toward the sky, but it didn't do much to satisfy his thirst. He looked around for any sign of water, but short of seeing the glistening way it ran on huge elephant-ear-shaped leaves, there were no creeks or pools that beckoned to him.

It dawned on Erik that he might use one of the large leaves to funnel water into his mouth. He didn't even stop to think if the water might be contaminated with some sort of poison by the leaf until he'd already sampled the moisture. It didn't taste bad, however, so he cupped the leaf and let it gather rain until there was enough for a good swallow.

With a sigh of relief, he let the leaf fall back into place. It snapped into form without any visible sign that Erik had ever disturbed its slumber. Looking behind him, Erik could see that this was pretty much the way the rest of the area was as well. It was hard to see any sign that he had ever even passed that way.

Feeling depleted of energy and hope, Erik realized a growing weakness. He'd contracted malaria right after arriving at Guadalcanal, and now he could count on having a spell at least once a month. The signs were upon him now, even though he tried to deny it. He'd denied those feelings when he'd climbed into his Wildcat to go to battle with the Japanese. Fellows flew in worse shape than he had been that morning. No sense in making a big deal out of a few aches and pains. Now, however, the buzzing in his ears and intense headache made Erik gravely concerned. There was no place to get help here. He had to suffer through this bout on his own. Suddenly Erik didn't feel at all hopeful. If he succumbed to a bout of malaria, he would be helpless. It was the final straw.

This isn't fair, God, he grumbled inwardly so as not to make any noise. *I've had nothing but trouble since I've come into this war.*

He thought back over the last few months. He hated his assignment in the South Pacific, when he had figured to be flying in the war over Europe. He hated the tropics, much preferring his Longview home and the not-so-distant snowcapped mountains. The men he had to work with were arrogant risk takers who seemed to live only for the moment. And added to all of that, he hadn't received a bit of mail since finally being stationed at the Canal.

Erik continued his internal prayer. *Nobody at home sees fit to write me. Nobody on earth cares that it's nearly Christmas and I'm stuck in this tropical rat maze. And I'm beginning to wonder if you care, either.* He felt awashed with guilt for his doubt. The guilt caused him to push on through the vegetation. He had to keep his wits about him.

He thought of Christmas and how much he enjoyed cold weather. He liked going north from Longview. North to the mountains and the snow. He liked just walking in the snow, hearing the way it crunched under his feet. This forest floor crunched under his feet as well, and frankly, he didn't want to know half the time what it was he was crunching. He'd already seen bugs that were big enough to saddle and ride, and no doubt there were plenty of them underfoot.

"You can eat bugs if you get hungry enough," one of his commanding officers had mentioned. "Not all that appealing in thought, but they'll keep you alive in a pinch."

Erik grimaced. A person could do a lot of things in a pinch, he agreed, but he wasn't feeling compelled to cry "uncle" just yet. He'd save the beetle platter for later—for when he'd exhausted the possibility of any other means of nourishment.

Thinking of food made him think of home. His mother could cook up a storm with little more than a pinch of flour, a couple of eggs, and a bit of this and that. Marshall, his older brother, had always said that he wouldn't get married until he could find a woman who could cook like their mom. Marshall had never gotten married. Marshall had died at Midway Island, performing his tasks as a gunnery sergeant right up until a Japanese bullet stopped his heart.

Thinking of Marshall came as a worse grief than anything else. Erik had worshiped the ground his older brother had walked on. He had been the reason Erik had learned to fly and subsequently the reason he'd joined the marines. Marshall was nearly ten years older and had lavished most of his pay back on his family. Erik had always wanted to be a pilot—ever since seeing his first plane, an old beat-up Curtis Jenny biplane. Marshall thought it a grand scheme even though their parents were more cautious. They had finally conceded defeat when Marshall agreed to pay for the lessons, and they had seemed proud when Erik had flown his first solo at seventeen.

Marshall's love of the marines had sent Erik down to enlist almost the minute after he'd graduated from high school. Again his parents were cautious and worried over his choice, but Marshall had sent a letter home praising the choice. Erik had lived on that praise all the way through boot camp and beyond.

Devastated to know that Marshall could no longer praise or frown upon any of his choices, Erik felt a weight of responsibility settle on his shoulders. The war had taken his brother, and now it was trying to take him too.

Well, I'm not giving in that easily. I'm a marine like my brother before me, he thought with a bit of restored determination.

He marched onward, thinking of his brother, his parents, and anything else that could keep him focused on beating the odds. Mary Ann came to rest in the center of his thoughts. She hadn't wanted to say good-bye and she hadn't wanted him going off to war without marrying her first. He'd given her his word that they'd marry whenever he could get leave home, but he wanted her to be sure in his absence that he was the right man for her.

He already knew that she was the gal for him. Tall and leggy, she was as pretty as she was smart. Mary Ann Roland was the pick of the bunch. Her blond curls had attracted him even when they were been children. Her twinkling blue eyes and winning smile had pulled him out of many a gloomy mood.

Mary Ann had taught him to dance, to work algebra, and to laugh at himself. Funny, he couldn't seem to figure out how to do that just now. Mary Ann would say that life was a game and that he'd just landed into a new adventure. Mary Ann would find a way to laugh at this.

He smiled. He liked that about her. She knew how to see the positive in most everything. She could be rather naïve about life, but she was nevertheless looking at it from an optimistic view. She balanced his pessimism quite nicely.

"Ah, Mary, wish you were here now," he said in a whisper. Then he shook his head. "No, I wish I were there. I wish this war were over and done with and victory won. I wish I could be there to decorate the Christmas tree, and I wish I could walk in the snow with you by my side." He shuddered from the chill that washed over his body. The malaria made itself more evident with each passing hour.

Looking overhead, Erik realized the rain had stopped. But instead of leaving the air refreshed and clean, it felt as though someone had smothered him in wet wool blankets. His flight suit stuck to him uncomfortably and his skin fairly crawled.

Gradually the light began to fade. He glanced at his watch. Surprisingly it appeared to still work, but the crystal was fogged over, making it difficult to make out the time. As best he could tell, it was nearly six o'clock, and Erik wondered how long it would be before he'd be completely without light. He pressed on and found himself in a small clearing. Staring overhead, he was amazed to see how dark it had gotten. Evening was approaching and in the already darkened jungle, Erik knew he'd have no hope of finding anything even remotely resembling a path.

I guess I'd better get settled somewhere. He spied a mossy patch of ground near the base of a tree that must have been fifteen feet in diameter. It looked like a good place to hold up. Well, at least as good as anything he'd seen so far. He eased onto the ground and put his back up against the tree.

This seemed to be the best choice, and he pulled the brim of his cap down low over his eyes and prayed that sleep would come quickly. He could hardly stand his own company when he ventured into self-pity. He knew his family cared about him. Something probably just came up that kept them from writing. But even as he thought of this, he knew he'd rather they not care than that something be wrong at home. He couldn't bear the idea of something happening to his mom or dad or any of his siblings. There had been rumors of the West Coast being bombed, even invaded, by the Japanese. Even though these stories had been deemed "scuttlebutt" by his superiors, Erik worried that this was the real reason he'd not received any mail.

Just as he began to doze off, Erik had visions of Mary Ann. He could see her dancing and laughing—only she wasn't dancing with him. Ray Blasingham's name had appeared more than once in her earlier letters. She talked in her sweet way of how sorry she felt for this man. How he'd watched his buddies go off to war, only to be left behind because of a bad leg. It couldn't be too bad, however, as she had also told him of going to dances with Ray. She and Ellen seemed to believe the man worthy of their concern, and while Erik tried not to be jealous, he couldn't help himself. The letters showed her life without him, and that was nearly unbearable.

Then the letters had stopped coming altogether, and Erik found that even worse. He couldn't help but wonder if Ray had replaced him in Mary Ann's life. Maybe giving her time to decide if Erik was the right man for her had been a mistake. Maybe he should have married her before heading to his duties elsewhere.

The sensation of someone touching his leg caused Erik to go stiff. He thought of the crabs and started to flick them away, but it didn't feel the same. Surely his imagination was just playing tricks on him. But the feeling came again and this time it was unmistakable. Something was crawling across his leg. Pushing back his cap and squinting in the fading light, Erik saw the culprit was a yellow-and-black banded snake that slithered its way across his right ankle and left boot. For a moment, he felt a rising panic, then as the snake moved off into the brush, Erik realized there was little he could do about the situation. He was the intruder in their world. He had no shelter, no means to take himself to a haven of protection. He was stuck right where he was until something better came along.

Somehow this resolve helped him to relax. The worst that could happen would be that something or someone would decide to dine on him. Frankly, in his weary state of mind, with the malaria taking a stronger hold on his system, Erik decided it wasn't worth expending his energy on such thoughts. If he perished in his sleep, so be it. At least he wouldn't have to eat bugs.

CHAPTER 4

"Are you girls sure you want to go home?" Ray questioned as Mary Ann and Ellen slipped out of the front seat of the '39 Chevy.

"Ray, it's nearly midnight," Ellen said like an admonishing mother. "We have to be at work bright and early tomorrow. 'Don't you know there's a war on?'" She laughed at the cliché phrase.

Mary Ann yawned and nodded. "We're already back a lot later than Mrs. Neal will like. We'll have to sneak in as it is."

Ray leaned back against the seat and shrugged. "Well, if that's the way you want it, guess I can't argue with the two of you."

Mary Ann smiled. "Thanks for the evening, Ray. We had a lot of fun."

Ellen nodded. "Yes, thanks. We'll see you tomorrow." She took hold of Mary Ann's arm and added, "If we can wake up on time." She closed the car door and pushed Mary Ann forward. "I swear, he'd follow us into the house if we invited him."

"He's just trying to keep our spirits up," Mary Ann said defensively. "I told him how we hadn't heard anything from Erik in a while. He was so sweet. I started to cry and he offered me his handkerchief. He even put his arm around me and told me it would be all right. He's just a swell kind of guy who cares about the people he works with."

"He's dangerous," Ellen said, slipping her key in the front door lock.

They crept through the house silently without turning on a single light. They'd only come home this late on two other occasions, and both times they'd made the mistake of turning on a lamp in order to see their way upstairs. Both times they'd awakened their landlady, who was none too happy about the hours they were keeping. There was even an underlying threat that perhaps Mrs. Neal would have to ask the girls to leave if they couldn't be in at a decent hour.

Once they were safely inside their room, Mary Ann switched on the light and yawned. "Honestly, Ellen, you need to stop seeing the worst in people. Here it is nearly Christmas. Where's your spirit of love?"

"I have a great deal of love for my family and close friends," Ellen replied defensively. "I just think there's a chance that Ray is more than he appears, and that makes him dangerous."

"I don't see that Ray is any more dangerous than your Mr. Chandler. I seem to recall that he put an arm around you last week when you broke down and cried."

"He's different. He's a Christian and old enough to be my father."

"Oh, and that makes it all right? A lot of people can say they are one thing or another. Talk about naïve." Mary Ann seldom raised her voice to Ellen and now, realizing she had done so at such a late hour, she immediately apologized. "Sorry. I just don't see that there's that much of a difference."

"Mr. Chandler clearly lives by Christian standards. I trust him to keep proper boundaries. When you cried in Ray's arms, you told me yourself that you felt almost unfaithful for letting him comfort you. Isn't that true?"

Mary Ann thought back to that moment and couldn't deny that Ray had made her feel awkward. It wasn't the fact that he'd given her a handkerchief or even that he held her while she cried, it was more the *way* he held her. He'd pulled her very close and stroked her arm and massaged her neck and shoulders while she'd tried to regain her composure. At one point he was whispering in her ear, and the entire situation became very uncomfortable.

"Well," Mary Ann finally admitted, "it's just that I've been with Erik so long. Being around any other man, especially having one touch me like that, is just . . . well . . . he was just being nice."

Ellen shook her head. "Listen to yourself. You're making excuses for him. He's too free with his hands, if you ask me. While we were dancing tonight, he kept touching my hair."

Mary Ann looked away. Ray had touched her hair as well. He'd also rubbed the small of her back and tried whispering again in her ear. "Well, if you're worried about it, don't go next time." She couldn't believe she'd just snapped at Ellen that way, but she wasn't about to apologize. Exhaustion washed over her in waves, and she didn't have the time or energy for a big confrontation. She hated feeling stupid and yet that's what this conversation was making her feel. Stupid.

"If I don't go along, you can't very well go alone," Ellen reminded her.

"Why not? I'm not doing anything wrong. Ray's my supervisor, nothing more. He's a nice guy who's trying hard to keep everyone's spirits up. I think he's doing a swell job. I mean, the poor man was rejected by the draft board for having a bad leg. He's heartbroken because he can't serve his country. Here it is Christmas, and all his buddies are overseas. He's all alone and you have no compassion for him." Mary Ann approached Ellen in an almost pleading tone. She wanted very much to salve her conscience and just once feel that she had handled a matter with wisdom. "You heard him talk tonight."

"I heard him," Ellen said, her voice sounding a bit skeptical. She came to Mary Ann and gently touched her arm. "I'm not accusing you of anything. Please understand that. I just worry about you. Erik would never forgive me if I let something happen to you—especially if I had the power to stop it."

"Is that why you go with us? Just to keep something from happening?" Mary Ann felt a sudden surge of indignity. "You're just like everyone else. You think me incapable of making good judgments. I'm not a child. I'm not stupid. Just what do you think I might do?"

"It isn't you I'm worried about," Ellen replied.

Mary Ann jerked away. With hands on hips she accused her friend. "Are you just spying on me for Erik? Is that it?"

"Do I need to?" Ellen questioned.

"What kind of friend are you?"

"I hope I'm the good kind that helps a friend see things for what they are. Especially when that friend might be headed into dangerous waters."

"If that's the case, you must think I'm drowning."

Ellen shook her head. "I trust you, Mary Ann, but I don't trust Ray. There have been rumors about him."

"Rumors? Didn't your mama raise you to ignore rumors?" Mary Ann hated arguing with Ellen, especially when her friend's words hinged on so much truth. Ray could be a bit much, Mary Ann had to admit, but she wasn't about to give Ellen further means to accuse her.

Ellen appeared to be thinking over her words. "I care about what happens to you. I know you're worried about Erik and I know you're lonely. I also know that you've been doing some soul-searching over the last couple of years. God cares about your well-being and so do I."

Mary Ann's anger abated. She was never one for harboring ill feelings for long. "I know you do. I know God cares about me as well. I'm trying to be the person He wants me to be, and that includes offering compassion to a man who seems so sad—so left behind. Haven't you ever felt that way, Ellen? My uncle Morris felt that way and it drove him to the bottle. It broke my mama's heart. If I can help keep another soul from going down that same path, shouldn't I at least try? I mean, you know that Ray used to drink all the time when we first started going with him to the dances. I told him about my uncle and how it worried me that he could ruin his life too. He was so touched that I cared. He admitted he was seeking solace in the bottle. And you know very well that he doesn't drink at all now."

"Well, I have to admit you're right about that. I haven't seen him take a single drink at any of the dances," Ellen replied. "Maybe I am being a bit hard on him, but I still don't care for the way he flirts and seems to have to be touching all the women."

"He's just lonely, Ellen," Mary Ann said, slipping off her clothes. A cold draft touched her skin, making her teeth chatter uncontrollably as she hurried into her nightgown. "We just need to keep being friends with everyone," Mary Ann suggested, "and pray for all of them. Ray included."

"Maybe Ray in particular," Ellen murmured and finished changing her own clothes.

Mary Ann climbed into bed and snuggled down into the covers. The argument between her and Ellen faded into thoughts of Erik. She conjured his image to mind, remembering him not in his uniform, but rather his Sunday suit and tie. He was so handsome with his sandy brown hair all slicked back and his grayish blue eyes shining with love for only her. Wrapping her arms around her, Mary Ann hugged herself tightly and tried to pretend it was Erik's arms that held her.

I miss you so much, she thought silently. *If only we could have married before you left. But you were so worried that I'd be rushing into the decision because of the war. Oh, Erik, nothing could be further from the truth. I've loved you for so long. How could I not want to be your wife and spend the rest of my life with you?*

"Good night," Ellen said as she turned out the light. "Did you remember to set your alarm? I have to go in early tomorrow, so I won't be able to make sure you're up and ready."

Mary Ann yawned. "I set it. I'll be fine. Just wake me when you leave."

Mary Ann felt Ellen's gentle nudge. "Come on, sleepyhead. I need to get going and you said to wake you."

"Let me sleep," Mary Ann moaned. It just couldn't be time to get up. Surely there was some mistake. She rolled over to catch sight of the alarm clock and moaned again.

"I still have an hour," she murmured.

"I know. Just make sure you don't turn off your alarm," Ellen chided.

"I won't. I promise."

Ellen grabbed up her things and headed for the door. "Guess I'll see you at the plant."

Mary Ann mumbled good-bye, then pulled the covers up over her head. She'd just rest for a few more minutes and then she'd get up. Surely there was no harm in that.

But when Mary Ann did wake up, more than a few minutes had passed. She looked at the clock in disbelief and then looked at it again.

"It can't be nine-thirty!" she declared, throwing off the covers.

The icy chill of the room caused her to shiver. She hurried into her uniform and prayed that the clock was wrong. Racing against time, she threw her hair into a haphazard knot at the nape of her neck, grabbed a hair net, and pinned it on loosely. Her head pounded furiously with the pulsing rhythm of her heart. She was going to be in for it for sure—tardiness was not very well accepted. Absenteeism was looked upon as treasonous.

When she finally reached the plant, Mary Ann was still mulling over the events of the night before in her mind. She felt guilty for her defense of Ray, especially when Ellen had been right about the way he'd made her feel. She'd have to talk to him about not being so physical. She could only hope it wouldn't hurt his feelings.

"Miss Rolands, you're late," a voice growled out.

Mary Ann cringed. Sam Johnston wasn't exactly the understanding kind. As one of the plant's area supervisors, Sam took special pride in policing the plant for any kind of violation.

"I know I'm late," Mary Ann said, trying hard not to sound scared.

"Can't have it, Miss Rolands. There's a war on and this is the kind of thing that the enemy thrives on. You might as well be putting bullets in our boys yourself."

Mary Ann looked at the man in disbelief. "I have a fiancé in this war," she said, tears coming to her eyes. "You have no right to suggest—"

"I think we'll take this up with management and see if your employment is even needed," Johnston said, eyeing her severely.

"What's happening here, Sam?" Ray questioned as he came onto the scene.

"Miss Rolands seems to think she can wander in here anytime she likes. I don't think we need employees like that."

"Calm down, Sam," Ray said, slapping the older man on the back. "Miss Rolands was running an errand for me. No problem here."

Sam gave the briefest look of disbelief, then muttered, "Well, if that's how it is." He stalked off in the direction of his own department, leaving Mary Ann to breathe a sigh of relief.

"Oh, thanks, Ray. I didn't hear the alarm and Ellen didn't wake me up."

"No problem, doll face," Ray said, giving her a suggestive grin. "But you owe me now."

Mary Ann swallowed hard. Her stomach did a nervous flip. "I owe you?" The words came out in a croaking kind of tone.

"Yeah, that's right," he said, moving closer. "See, I just saved you from losing your job and having to go back to that little no-nothing town of yours. I think you're special, you know. I wouldn't have done it for just anyone."

"Well, you know I'm grateful."

"Yeah, I knew you would be," Ray replied.

His oily smoothness caused Mary Ann to back up a pace. "Well,

I am. I won't let it happen again."

Ray backed her against the wall. "So how are we going to resolve this?"

Tension twisted Mary Ann's stomach into knots, and she shook her head. "I don't know what you mean."

He smiled and lowered his voice. "I just figure we can find a way for you to give me a proper thank-you."

"I don't know what you mean," she repeated.

Ray stepped back and studied her for a moment. "I'll let you know what I mean when you go dancing with me tomorrow night. I'll pick you up at seven-thirty sharp." He clicked his tongue and pointed his finger at her in his characteristic nature. "Wear the red dress—it's my favorite."

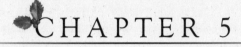

CHAPTER 5

The rumbling sound of Erik's stomach reminded him that he'd not eaten in over seventy-two hours. Weak and wracked with pain, Erik pressed through the jungle in hopes of finding something to eat. No matter which way he turned, however, neither food nor the river availed itself to the tired marine.

"God, this is starting to be pretty annoying," he muttered quietly. He had started talking out loud again out of sheer rebellion to the maddening silence. His concern over making noise and thus attracting attention to the enemy didn't seem so dire this morning, and Erik needed his voice for company or he'd go mad.

Erik had created for himself a new kind of one-on-one relationship with the Almighty. He'd been in church all of his life and had accepted that God had a plan for him, but this was different. Born out of necessity and a feeling that perhaps this had been the only way God could get his attention, Erik figured the sooner he paid attention, maybe the sooner God would deliver him out of this mess. God seemed to want something from him. Maybe it was just affirmation of Erik's devotion. Maybe it was something else. But here in the island jungles of the South Pacific, Erik knew God was his only hope.

Sweeping the ground in front of him with a walking stick, Erik suddenly stood still as he heard the unmistakable sound of rustling in the brush. A grunting, snorting kind of sound followed, and immediate visions of food began to dance in Erik's head.

Creeping ever so cautiously ahead, Erik was certain the sound had to be coming from somewhere to his right. Perhaps if he circled the area quietly, he could get a feel for where the animal was—and what it was. He figured it to be a wild pig, but since he'd already been wrong on so many other counts, Erik wasn't taking a chance. For all he knew it could be some sort of hideous island monster that would just as soon eat him as be eaten. No sense in getting himself killed, Erik reasoned.

In a tiny clearing of the brush, Erik could see that his instincts had served him properly—this time. A wild sow with several piglets stood nosing at something on the ground. Her snorting and sniffing seemed to echo in the heavy air around Erik. It was a beautiful sound.

Holding the walking stick up like a club, Erik figured if he could just whack the creature over the head, he might be able to stun it long enough to catch hold so he could slit its throat. The last thing he wanted to do was shoot the animal and possibly bring the attention of the natives and maybe Japanese down on his head. He watched the sow for a moment longer, trying to decide how best to sneak up on her. She appeared completely oblivious to his presence. He could already taste roasted pork in his mouth—never mind that he had no matches or means to cook the pig.

Somehow, much to his own surprise, Erik managed to get within three feet of the beast. The little ones seemed far more interested in nursing than in concerning themselves with anything else, and by the time Erik made a lunge for the collective group, all four of the piglets had returned to their mother's side. The introduction of a human being to the group, however, was not received in a welcoming manner. Squealing in terror, the piglets ran in circles around the mother pig, while Erik held on for dear life to the back right leg of the sow.

Why did I go after the sow? he wondered as the pig grunted in protest and began thrashing back and forth. She was twice as big as he'd originally thought and none too happy about his intrusion. Taking off in the direction of her piglets, the sow squealed and carried on, dragging Erik with her as she went.

Erik didn't know whether to let go or not, but soon he had no choice. The pig managed to scramble over a fallen log, but Erik wasn't so lucky. Smashing up against the obstacle, he hit his head hard and let go of the pig.

Hunger refused to keep him down. Erik knew he'd seen little else that interested him half so much as that pig and her babies. He got to his feet and pulled out the .45. He might make quite a racket, but at least he'd have food.

"I'll teach that sow to mess with a marine," he muttered.

Racing after the sow, Erik maneuvered through the vegetation in record time. Slapped and beaten by the brush, Erik hardly paid it any attention. He could hear the pig snorting and squealing up ahead and he had to stay on her path.

But just as he managed to regain his position, Erik heard the unmistakable sound of voices. There seemed to be several people and they were apparently quite interested in something. Erik reasoned they'd probably heard the commotion he'd caused and were now coming to seek out the source of the noise.

With a deep sense of frustration, Erik watched the backside of the sow disappear into the brush. He had no choice but to seek cover and hope he could hide himself away from the natives until they passed by. As quietly as he could, Erik crawled backward into a heavily overgrown collection of flowering vegetation. His thought was that the different colors, including those of the bright scarlet flowers, would help to keep him from being visible.

The stench from the plant life around him, combined with the constant process of decay on the jungle floor, did nothing to ease Erik's already queasy stomach. He fought waves of bile that threatened to push their way up his throat. He'd already endured the dry heaves earlier that morning, and the last thing he wanted to do was suffer another round.

He heard the voices grow louder and listened, straining to understand the language. He tried to make out the words, but they were garbled and rapidly spoken. Soon, however, the voices faded as the natives moved off in a different direction. Erik waited for the better part of an hour before crawling out from his hiding place. His head spun violently as he stood. He knew he was fighting a losing battle as the malaria took hold of him.

"If I can just make it through the next few hours," he told himself softly. "Just hang on."

He pressed forward, only now realizing he'd lost his walking stick. He thought of trying to retrace his steps, then laughed at the folly of that idea. He had no idea where his previous steps were, much less where he might head now.

A light rain began to fall, as was the routine most every afternoon. Erik bore the inconvenience as best he could. He knew there was no getting away from the rain, and the more he grumbled about it, the harder it seemed to fall. Turning up his collar, he tried to think of something more pleasant.

He imagined his mother standing over the stove in the kitchen. She made a beef stew with gravy thick enough to stand a spoon in. His mouth watered. Maybe it wasn't a good idea to think of home. But home was all he wanted to think about. Home and the people he'd left behind.

Oh, Mary Ann, he thought, dreaming of the only girl who had ever stirred his heart. *I need you. Please remember me. Please don't let someone else steal you away from me.*

Thinking of home and Mary Ann came as a bittersweet incentive to keep moving. He worried about those he'd left behind. Worried that in his absence from civilization and news of what was happening, the West Coast of America might well have met with a terrible fate. He couldn't stomach the idea of not knowing. His commanding officers had told him rumors were the best way to defeat a man and that all rumors of the homefront should be ignored. He had admonished the men to write home and let the letters coming back be the proof of their family's safety.

But those letters had never come. Erik had written when he could manage to get time between missions. He'd written to everyone at home and nothing had come back in return. He had a nagging feeling that maybe they couldn't write him. Maybe something had happened in those festive weeks before Christmas and now those he cared most about were injured or even prisoners of war.

Then again, maybe that Ray guy had found a way into Mary Ann's heart. Maybe he had charmed her with trinkets and outings. After all, he was there. Ray was flesh and blood; Erik was only words on pages, a picture on her nightstand, a ring on her hand.

"You're borrowing trouble again," he chided himself. The rain poured down in earnest now, drenching him to the bone. He never felt dry anymore, just various stages of wetness. The first thing he planned to do when he got back to civilization—and that certainly didn't mean Guadalcanal—was dry off. He longed for dry socks, dry underwear, dry anything.

He remembered a summer walk in the rain with Mary Ann. They'd both laughed and enjoyed the feel of the water against their faces. They had taken refuge under a tree, holding each other close and waiting in perfect contentment for the rain to pass. Now Erik doubted he'd ever want to take another walk in the rain, even with Mary Ann.

A noise caught his attention. It was muffled and almost non-existent, but something made Erik take note. He paused, listened again, and waited. His heart pounded in his ears, but even against that rapid beat, Erik made out the unmistakable squeal of a piglet. The thing sounded scared. Maybe it had lost its way and had managed to get separated from the rest of its family. Maybe God was sending him supper.

Erik walked toward the sound, mindful of tangling vines and fallen logs. No sense in falling again. His head still smarted from where he'd hit it earlier. Rubbing it gently with the back of his hand, Erik tried to concentrate.

He walked upon the piglet almost without realizing it. In fact, he'd nearly stepped on the poor thing, so stunning it that the animal froze in place. Erik quickly picked up the baby pig. That was all it took to press the piglet into action. Squealing for all it was worth, the animal thrashed against Erik's hold.

"This little piggy is coming to dinner," he said, still not having a clue as to how he was going to eat the thing.

The unexpected sound of rustling in the brush caused Erik to fall silent. Not so the pig. Erik tucked him under his arm, wishing he knew how to silence the little guy. He thought to take off running, just in case the natives had returned after hearing the noise. No sense in having to share his find.

He'd taken no more than two steps, however, when the mother pig, complete with three of her babies, burst from the lush green camouflage to charge right at Erik.

"Ahh!" Erik let out his own yell before taking off at a maddening pace to avoid the angry mother. The piglet under his arm squealed and bellowed while fighting against Erik's hold. It brought to mind visions of his high school days when he played football with a less-active pigskin.

Snap! A branch smacked against Erik's face, nearly breaking his nose. But this was no time to stop and feel sorry for himself, and Erik knew his only chance for maintaining his newly found supper was to keep running.

The sow kept after him in dedicated pursuit. Erik had taken her baby, and she wasn't giving it up without a fight. Snorting and squealing encouragement to the piglet, the mother continued after them faithfully.

Erik thought about turning around to confront the sow with his gun, but to do so he'd have to put the piglet down, and that would rather defeat the purpose. Still, he didn't have the energy to keep it up much longer. The jungle around him was already swimming in his vision, and there was a roar in his ears that blended with the chorus of pig protests.

"God," he panted, "I could use some help here."

He fell in the slippery undergrowth and lost his hold on the piglet. The beast flew out from under his arm while a steady stream of water rushed over him from the jungle floor. Somehow he'd managed to land himself in an impromptu creek.

There was no time for further consideration, however. The sow bore down on him in her displeasure. Apparently it wasn't enough that Erik had let the piglet go, even if it wasn't what he'd intended. This sow figured to teach him a lesson about messing with her family.

Barely getting to his feet before the angry animal reached him, Erik followed the rapidly building flow of water. Soon he was so caught up in the stream that it washed his feet out from under him. Sliding downward, Erik felt the earth go out from under him. He looked back to the ground only long enough to note that there was no longer any ground to look at. He couldn't stop himself from plunging right over the side of the muddy cliff. As he fell, Erik noted the churning water below him. Well, at least he'd found the river.

CHAPTER 6

"I don't feel like dancing tonight," Ellen told Mary Ann emphatically. "I'm sick. I've caught cold and all I want to do is rest."

Dread settled over Mary Ann. "You have to go with me. I promised Ray."

"Well, unpromise him. I'm not leaving this house."

Mary Ann reached over to touch her friend's forehead. "You don't have a fever."

"I don't need a fever to feel sick," Ellen said. She paused long enough to blow her nose before adding, "I just can't go with you. Why not stay home tonight?"

"Because I promised, and I don't think Ray's going to take the news very well if I go back on my word."

Ellen looked at her rather suspiciously. "Has he done something to make you feel that you have to go with him?"

"Not exactly," Mary Ann lied. "It's just important to him, that's all. Look, I promise if you go tonight, I'll make it clear to Ray that we can't go to any more functions for the rest of the week. Please, Ellen."

Her pleading did the trick. Ellen sighed and pushed out of the overstuffed chair. "Okay, okay. I won't have a minute's peace around here if I don't just get up and go. What are you wearing?"

Mary Ann felt a new surge of guilt wash over her. "My red dress."

Ray seemed a bit surprised when Mary Ann and Ellen both came out of the boardinghouse. He said nothing, however, as he reached over to open the car door for them. It wasn't Ray's style to get out and properly help a woman into the car. This irritated Ellen to no end and she told Mary Ann this on regular occasions. Mary Ann, on the other hand, kept trying to explain to Ellen that perhaps it caused problems for his bad leg. Ellen had not been persuaded, and even Mary Ann had to admit it was a rather lame excuse.

"You gals sure look sweet tonight," Ray said.

"We can't make this a late night," Ellen told him right up front. "Mary needs some sleep and I have a cold."

"Sure you wouldn't rather stay home?" Ray questioned. "I don't want to be the reason for seeing you miss work."

"We'd both be better off staying home," Ellen replied, "but Mary Ann insisted and here we are. Might as well give it a whirl."

Ray settled back against the seat and eased the Chevy into traffic. "I promise you won't regret it. We'll have us a swell time—you'll see."

They reached the dance just as an entire shipload of sailors, it seemed, converged on the place. The men were more than a little happy to have some liberty in town and instantly took up the company of any woman they could latch on to. Mary Ann found herself swept away before Ray could even protest. She glanced over her shoulder to give a helpless shrug as Ellen met the same fate and was danced off in a different direction. Ray didn't appear at all happy with the results.

Mary Ann danced with one sailor after another, listening to their stories of boot camp and the adventures to come. She felt sorry for them and yet she couldn't express that. She knew they were excited about this strange rite of passage and yet she sensed in most of them a cautious amount of fear. They were going off to war with no idea of when or if they would ever return. Dancing to the slow, almost mournful strains of a love song, Mary Ann couldn't help but think of Erik. How she longed for him to be home. To be here with her now.

Erik had been a poor dancer all of his life, but Mary Ann had taught him how to dance with her, and when they were in each other's arms, Erik danced like he'd been doing it forever. That was only one of the reasons Mary Ann knew they were suited to each other. Erik couldn't dance to save his soul with any of the other girls. He clomped around, stepping on their feet, turning them the wrong direction and completely exhausting them before the song ever came to an end. She smiled at the memory. The ladies had been happy to leave Erik to her care, and that was just as Mary Ann wanted it.

"Well, doll, ya wanna dance another?" the tall sailor asked her as the music ended.

"She's promised me the next one, bud, so cut on out," Ray declared.

The sailor glared down at the man. "How come you ain't in uniform?"

Ray put his arm around Mary Ann and led her away. "Somebody has to stay at home and keep our gals happy." He pulled Mary Ann into his arms and held her tight. "I never thought I'd get a chance to dance with you at all. We'll have to remember this place and avoid it next time."

"I don't know," Mary Ann said innocently, "I think it's kind of nice."

"Too crowded. Those sailor boys think they own the world. Well, they don't own you."

"Neither do you," Mary Ann replied without thinking. She surprised herself with the uncharacteristic comment and quickly looked away.

Ray raised a questioning brow. "Oh? And who saved your sweet little smile when Sam Johnston intended to see you canned?"

"That doesn't mean you own me," Mary Ann replied, trying hard to sound nonchalant about the matter. She didn't want a confrontation, and she didn't want to hurt Ray's feelings.

"Don't go getting all riled up, angel. You know you're my best gal," Ray said, pulling her closer. "I was glad to come to the rescue. I wouldn't want to see anything happen to you." He rubbed the small of her back, pressing her closer.

Mary Ann tried to push away, but Ray would have no part of it. Clucking at her like a scolding mother, he leaned down to whisper against her ear. "We have a lot in common, you and me. You're lonely. I'm lonely."

"I'm engaged." The statement did nothing to dampen Ray's enthusiasm.

"To a guy who's far away. A guy who may never come back to you. Do you suppose he's spending his nights pining for you? Grow up a little, sweetheart. He's having the time of his life. It's the uniform, you know. Does it every time."

"Erik isn't like that," Mary Ann said with a smile. "He's true blue."

"Sure he is, doll. Sure he is."

The song ended and Mary Ann felt Ray tighten his grip. "I want to dance another."

"I need a break. I want something to drink and I want to sit down for a minute," Mary Ann replied.

Ellen came up about that time, sniffing and sneezing. "I'm going back to the house. Some friends have offered to take me. You go ahead and have a good time."

Mary Ann realized just how bad Ellen looked and felt guilty for having dragged her along. "That's all right, Ellen. I'll go back with you. You'll need someone to take care of you."

"No, stay. I know this meant a lot to you," Ellen said, shaking her head. "I'll be all right once I get a hot bath and get into bed." She started to go, then turned back. "Ray, you'll look out for her, won't you? You won't let anything happen to her?"

"Cross my heart," he said, beaming Ellen a smile.

Despite his sincerity, Mary Ann sensed that she would have to be careful. Something didn't feel right, and while she couldn't exactly explain it, she felt almost certain that she was in trouble. *Well, you got yourself into this, you can just get yourself out of it,* Mary Ann reasoned. *Nobody made me take up with Ray Blasingham, and Erik even warned me about guys like him. If I'd listened to Erik and Ellen, I wouldn't be in this predicament. I'm just as silly and simpleminded as everyone thinks, and I need to grow up and stand up for myself.*

"Ready to dance, doll?" Ray questioned as he swung her into the lively steps of the jitterbug.

The music picked up to accommodate the peppy dance, and Mary Ann couldn't help but lose herself in her worried thoughts. She had to figure out a way to make it clear to Ray that she wasn't interested in anything more than friendship, but that was easier said than done.

She thought of praying, and before she knew it she was silently pleading to know what to do. *God, I suppose I'm just going to have to figure this out for myself, but it would be awfully nice if you could give me a hint of what I'm supposed to do.*

Ray danced her to exhaustion and all the while Mary Ann worried about the close of the evening. When the clock struck nine, she was certain she'd have at least another hour, maybe two, in order to figure out what was to be done, but this wasn't to be the case. The bandleader thanked the crowd for coming and announced that the dance was over.

Ray whistled a tune as he helped Mary Ann into her coat. He pulled his own jacket on and popped his hat on as they stepped from the building. "Look there, the stars are winking down at us. It's one good side to the blackout. It's a perfect night to do some star gazing. How about it?"

"No, Ray," Mary Ann said firmly. "I have to get home and check on Ellen. Besides, I still have to work tomorrow. I need my rest. And you ought to save the gasoline. There's a war on, you know." She tried to sound more lighthearted.

"With my rations, I can get all the gas I want, you know that. I'm in essential war production." He winked. "And in my book, this is essential."

"Well, getting a good night's sleep is essential in mine."

He said nothing but surprised her as he helped her into the car before going around to the driver's side. Fumbling with his keys, he appeared preoccupied and Mary Ann silently breathed a sigh of relief. Maybe he'd taken her "no" as the final word. She could only hope that was the case.

They drove in silence for about a mile. Mary Ann hugged the far side of the seat, almost clinging to the passenger-side door. It was uncharacteristic of her to act so silly, but she couldn't help feeling nervous. Then, when Ray pulled the car over and parked on the side of the road nearly a mile from the boardinghouse, Mary Ann's nerves began to tingle.

"What's the matter?" she asked him, trying not to sound accusatory.

"I just can't fight what I'm feeling for you," Ray said quite seriously. He lost the smooth character charm and seemed to gain a sense of genuineness that Mary Ann had never known. "I know you have your boyfriend, but, Mary Ann, I've fallen in love with you. That's never happened to me before."

Mary Ann felt her cheeks grow hot. "I didn't know you felt like this."

"I didn't either—well, not exactly," Ray said, looking out the front window. "I didn't plan on falling in love. It just sort of crept up on me. Then tonight, watching you dance with those other men, seeing them in uniform preparing to defend the country . . . well, I just sort of lost my way."

"I don't understand."

Ray nodded. "It's hard on a guy not to be able to go to war with his buddies. It's the kind of rejection you don't get over real easy. Maybe you never do. I struck out at the draft board and now I'm striking out with you."

"But, Ray, I'm with Erik. I plan to marry him," she said softly. Her heart went out to Ray. He seemed so lost and lonely. "Erik is a good man and so are you. You'll find someone else."

He shook his head. "Don't think I'll count on that," he said, lowering his head. "Nobody wants a failure."

Mary Ann reached out to touch his shoulder. Gone was her earlier trepidation. "You aren't a failure. You're one of the best workers Boeing has. Someone has to stay stateside and build planes and supply equipment. That's just as admirable as Erik going off to fly against the enemy."

"You're just saying that," Ray said, refusing to look her in the eye.

"No, I'm not. I mean it." Mary Ann leaned forward. "You have to see that you're valuable for who you are. That the job you're doing is important."

"You're good to say that," he said, leaning back against the seat. He stared up at the roof of the car. "I want to believe that, but . . . well . . . it's just hard. I don't have anyone—no friends, no family. And now I've given my heart to the one girl who can never be mine."

"I'm sorry, Ray. I didn't know that was how you felt or I wouldn't have gone dancing with you. I didn't mean to lead you on."

Ray shook his head and reached up to touch her cheek. Mary Ann was so lost in her sympathy for the man that she didn't even think to recoil. "You didn't lead me on. I led myself on. I dared to believe I was worth having a girl like you."

"But you are, Ray. You're a good man. Someday you'll find a woman out there who will adore you. You'll fall in love with her and it will be far better than anything you could have had with me."

"I hope you're right," he said, still fingering her cheek.

"I know I am. I just wish I could make you feel better. I do appreciate what you did for me—keeping me from getting fired and all."

He sighed and the look on his face nearly broke Mary Ann's heart. "I always dreamed of sitting under the stars like this with you. Of kissing you in the moonlight." He leaned forward. "Couldn't you give me just one kiss? Something I could take away with me until I find that girl you believe is out there."

Mary Ann didn't like the idea of letting Ray kiss her. Something inside her screamed in protest, but even as it did, she found herself nodding. "Sure, Ray. One kiss."

He moved toward her hesitantly. "Are you sure? I don't want you angry at me."

"I'm sure," she hesitantly said, trying to fight back the growing sensation that she was in danger.

Ray put his hand at the back of her head and pulled her toward him. "You won't be sorry," he whispered as his other arm went around her shoulder and his lips came down hard on her own.

It was the manner in which he spoke that caused Mary Ann to grow even more uncomfortable. She was already sorry and now, with Ray's kiss growing more ardent, more needful, Mary Ann realized she'd made a terrible mistake.

She pushed at him, but he refused to be put aside. Mary Ann twisted violently, knowing that Ray intended to have much more from her than a simple kiss.

Fighting for all she was worth, Mary Ann felt sickened as Ray gave a low, guttural laugh. He had planned this all out. He had worked on her sympathy until he had her exactly where he wanted her. His ability to woo her in such a way was far more frightening than the smooth moves he'd made as a playboy foreman.

"Relax, baby," he said as he barely took his lips from hers, "I promise you'll have a good time. Haven't I always shown you a good time?"

He started to kiss her again, but Mary Ann bit his lip instead.

"Why, you little . . ." He grabbed her wrists and pulled her back. "You want it rough, is that it?"

"Get away from me!" Mary Ann demanded as she reached for the door. "You have no right."

She was desperate to get out of the car, but Ray seemed to fully understand her intentions. He grabbed her knee and held her in place with one hand while he ran his free hand along her thigh.

"You want to keep your job, don't you? Being nice to me is the way to get that done. Otherwise, I'm afraid I'll have to agree with old Sam." He said the words matter-of-factly, then shrugged as if there simply wasn't any other choice.

Mary Ann gathered her strength and slapped him hard across the face. She took his moment of surprise as her cue to exit the car. Running as fast as her weakened legs would carry her, Mary Ann ducked down an alley and prayed as she went. She heard Ray start up the car.

"Please, God, I didn't know what I was doing. I need your help. Please don't let Ray catch me." She had no idea if Ray would follow her down the alleyway or not, but she kept pushing herself to run faster. If she could just reach the street, she'd have a better chance of losing him.

It wasn't any time at all before she heard the car in the alley behind her. He was following her. This wasn't over as far as he was concerned. Apparently no one denied Ray Blasingham and got away with it. Mary Ann felt a painful stitch in her side but knew she couldn't stop. He'd catch her and when he did, he'd make her pay for what she'd done—for the way she'd humiliated him and rejected his advances. It was no longer a matter of whether or not she'd keep her job—no doubt she'd already lost that—now she worried that if she didn't escape him, Ray Blasingham might very well get exactly what he wanted.

With one final burst of energy, Mary Ann ran for the opening in the alleyway. The street was just ahead and already she could see other people walking back and forth along the sidewalk. Once she reached that place, she told herself, she would be safe from Ray. At least for the moment.

She reached the street, surprising several uniformed sailors and their dates. Unable to stop before she'd entered the main thoroughfare, however, Mary Ann found herself with a bigger obstacle to hurdle. Bearing down on her with no hope of stopping, a delivery truck was even now skidding and squealing in protest as the driver tried to avoid an accident. Stunned, Mary Ann could only stand frozen in place.

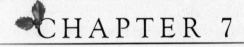

CHAPTER 7

Although Erik knew it was impossible, the river actually felt drier than the jungle. The calm waters were almost soothing in their warmth. Had he not been hurting so much from the fall and weakened from the malaria, Erik might have just floated indefinitely.

He gave no mind to what else might also be swimming in the river that day. Banged up, scratched, and growing seriously weary of the battle, Erik thought only of survival. He forced himself to the riverbank and fell onto the ground in complete exhaustion. He shook so hard he could barely manage to sit up. All he wanted to do was sleep in a dry bed without things slithering or crawling or biting at him in the interim.

Scratching furiously at his arm, Erik saw that his hands and arms were broken out in a strange red blistering rash.

"Great! What else can go wrong?"

He knew he shouldn't have asked the question, but it came from his lips without considering all the possibilities. Hours later, after wandering downstream for some distance, Erik remembered the question.

"It's nearly Christmas," he said, grumbling. "It doesn't feel like Christmas. It doesn't look like Christmas." He stumbled forward, nearly losing his footing. "Does anybody care?" he yelled.

He began a running conversation with himself. "Nobody cares about Christmas and nobody cares about me. I'm just out here by myself having the time of my life." He waded into the water when a mangrove, the only tree he recognized besides palms, edged the water and made it impossible to follow the bank with any success.

"Smelly things!" he shouted at the tree as though it could somehow understand. "Stupid, smelly jungle. You won't feed me—you won't help me." He battled the mangrove roots and found himself in waist-deep water. "But you will try to drown me. If it isn't the rain, it's this river."

He thought of the irony. How he'd longed to find the river and now he longed to be rid of it. "But I'm looking for a path!" he declared, slapping at the shoreline brush. "We can't have a path in a decent place. Nooooo. We can't fight the war in a decent place. No, sir, we have to go to the pits of hell and fight. We have to go someplace where they don't even grow things that are recognizable so you know whether or not you can eat them!" What he wouldn't give for a simple Washington apple tree.

He climbed back up on the banks and shook his head. He looked upstream from where he'd just come, then downstream. Nothing, not even the territory he'd just passed over, looked familiar.

"*Semper Fidelis*," he muttered. "Always faithful. A marine is always faithful." He continued working his way downstream, alternating between fighting the vegetation and talking to it. Pausing beside another mangrove, he questioned, "What about you? Are you always faithful?" He was starting to feel punchy, almost like he'd had too much to drink. His head seemed to be pulsating with a jungle rhythm all its own.

His thoughts were coming in loosely connected visions. "Are you being faithful, Mary Ann? Did you get rid of that no-account Ray What's-his-name?" Erik shook his head, trying to clear his vision. His arm itched furiously, burning and nagging at him, demanding his attention. He scratched. His mother always told him not to scratch when he'd managed to get into poison ivy. But this time he was scratching. If his mother couldn't even write him a Christmas card, why shouldn't he scratch?

"I'm scratching for everyone," he said, giving his arms a good going-over. "You can all sit at home and forget about me. Don't remember me. Don't worry about Erik Anderson. I'm a marine. I'm Semper Fi!" He stumbled over his own feet and crashed to the ground below. Mud oozed up, coating the front of his flight suit. "Now I'm a mud marine!" he declared, laughing at his own little joke. Sick and weary, he rolled onto his back. "I wish I were a mud marine. At least then I'd have a pack full of rations."

Glancing overhead, Erik felt serious despair begin to settle over him. Maybe it was just the malaria or maybe it was the fact that he'd had nothing to eat in days, but he couldn't help but think back to Job in the Bible. It was suggested to Job that he curse God and die. Erik began to wonder if maybe that was the answer.

He sat up and tried to regain his composure. It was then that he spotted the leeches firmly attached to his right ankle. He pulled at one of the slimy creatures, but it didn't want to come off. Yanking it, Erik couldn't help but wonder if he'd just done something very stupid. His vision blurred and he wiped at his eyes. Then, without warning, a clear and concise declaration rose up from somewhere deep in the heart of his soul. "I'm not going to make it."

He gave in to the misery. "I've tried, Lord," he said weakly. He picked at the leeches, not knowing exactly what to do to rid himself of them. "I can't go on. Hate me if you will, but kill me off and let it be done with. This slow torture is driving me mad."

The birds overhead cackled and called in mocking fashion. Perhaps they had come to accuse him or, as Job's friends did, to make helpful suggestions about where he must have gone wrong.

Falling back against the wet soil, Erik knew there was very little fight left in him. He didn't really want to die, but there didn't appear to be many other options. His stomach churned, and a piercing pain caused him to double up. With this came a wave of nausea that sent him into a round of dry heaves. There was just no end to his misery.

Panting for breath as the nausea seemed to pass, Erik rolled to his side and forced himself to sit up. Sometimes life was just too much to understand. Marshall had died only months earlier defending Midway Island, and now Erik would die having been shot down defending the Solomons. Up until a year ago, he'd had no idea where any of these places even were, much less that they needed defending. But until December 7 of the previous year, few had envisioned the American military having any reason to concern themselves with those islands. Wake was a stopping-off place for trans-Pacific flights of the China Clipper, while Midway, a barely heard of outpost, took the northern route of the same. Neither seemed the kind of place a boy from Longview, Washington, should even wonder about.

"*Think of the world you're seeing, men!*" his commanding officer had boasted. "*Few people will ever experience all that you will in the next few months.*"

"Thank God for that," Erik said aloud, only the words sounded

like moans. He squinted and tried to see what might be down the
river. His vision blurred, however, and he buried his face in his
hands.

"Okay, okay. I give up. Do you hear me, God? I give up. You can
kill me now. I give you permission. Not that you needed it." He
pressed his hands against his temples to ease the pain. "My mom's
going to be awfully disappointed. She didn't want me to follow in
Marshall's footsteps. Said that one son was more than enough to give
any country."

Erik tried to fight the dizziness that he knew would soon claim
his conscious mind. He wouldn't stand a chance of defending himself if he passed out. Not that he had much of a chance anyway, but
at least he had the .45. He patted the holster reassuringly. A wave of
reasoning came with this act. _Stop feeling sorry for yourself. Act like a
man._

"I'm a marine," he said, rolling and pushing himself up on his
hands and knees. "Death before . . . dishonor." He fell sideways and
landed hard against the ground.

Noise came from the brush behind him. Erik reached for his
revolver and pulled it from the holster. Clutching it as tightly as he
could manage with his shaking hands, Erik licked his dry lips and
tried again to sit up.

Voices sounded and without warning, Erik found himself surrounded by several dark-skinned native men. He looked at each one,
barely able to focus. The one closest to him stepped even closer.

"_Watkaen nem blong iufala nao?_" the man questioned, leaning
down. He noticed the gun and added, "No shoot."

Erik could understand the latter words, but the first held no
meaning for him.

"_Iufala save toktok languis blong Solomon?_" another man asked.

Erik heard the words _toktok, languis,_ and _Solomon._ Were they asking him if he could speak their language? "Do you speak English?"
he asked, barely able to keep his shaky hold on the gun.

"_Ya, toktok plante. You see._" The man grinned at him, and Erik
could see that his teeth were nearly black. The apparition was unlike
anything Erik could have dreamed up.

Having no more strength, Erik began to sway. _God, if you're
listening to me at all, please help me._ The native reached out to catch

Erik before he lost consciousness. The man nodded and said something more, but nothing made sense. Blue skies and green trees swirled around the dark faces that now stared down over him.

"I'm sorry, Mom," Erik muttered and gave up the fight. "I didn't mean to scratch."

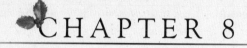

CHAPTER 8

Mary Ann could still see the delivery truck bearing down on her. In spite of a quick-thinking sailor who pushed her out of the way in the nick of time, and in spite of her determination to keep the details of the previous evening from Ellen, the images and feelings refused to be shaken. There was no haven of rest for Mary Ann. If she lingered at the boardinghouse and rode to work with Ellen, the truth might come out about Ray. Yet coming to work early, as she had, meant the possibility of having to deal with Ray all over again.

She couldn't win. She knew Ray would probably want to talk to her—if not fire her. Dread left her almost unable to function. How could she deal with this situation and not expose her own stupidity? She didn't want to discuss the matter with Ray and neither did she want to talk to Ellen. That left her with only one choice.

Swallowing hard, Mary Ann tried to settle her nerves with a quick unspoken prayer. *God, I don't know where I went wrong. I was just trying to be nice to him. To believe the best about him. I felt sorry for his loneliness and disappointment. I wasn't trying to be wanton or a flirt.*

I'm a fool, God. I know that. She trembled as she peered out of the ladies' rest room. Workers were coming in at a steady stream now and she felt safer. Ray wouldn't pull anything with so many watchful eyes keeping track. He might corner her to talk, but at least he wouldn't put his hands on her, and given the hour, he wouldn't have much time to talk to her either.

She crept out of her sanctuary and glanced out onto the plant floor. No one seemed to notice her arrival. She cautiously walked to her area, fully prepared to do battle in whatever manner presented itself, but instead of Ray, she found Ellen waiting for her.

"I was so worried about you," Ellen told her. "You didn't come in until late and then when I got up this morning you were already gone. Are you okay?"

Mary Ann knew that if she looked Ellen in the eye, she would probably start to cry. She had to remain composed. "I'm fine. I didn't want to bother you."

"You aren't a bother to me," Ellen said softly. "Look, we've got a few minutes. I want you to come with me."

"I better stick around. You know I was late the other day. They aren't going to like it if I'm not here working when it's time to start."

"I'm not going to keep you that long," Ellen replied, taking hold of her arm.

"Ow," Mary Ann yelped. She hadn't realized how sore her bruised arms had become. The obvious hand-shaped bruises, compliments of Ray's insistent hold on her, weren't going to be easy to explain.

"What happened to you?" Ellen questioned, inspecting Mary Ann's wrist.

"Nothing." Mary Ann was barely able to croak out the word.

"This doesn't look like 'nothing.'" Ellen pulled Mary Ann toward the rest room.

"Really, I'm fine."

Ellen wouldn't listen and Mary Ann knew she'd have no other choice but to tell her everything that had happened. Tears began to stream down her cheeks. It was all so embarrassing. Ellen had warned her and now Mary Ann would have to humble herself and admit that Ellen's concerns had been justified.

Surprisingly, the ladies' room was empty. Ellen practically pushed Mary Ann inside and demanded to know all the details.

"Oh, Ellen, I feel so stupid. I'm just as dense as everyone thinks I am."

"What are you talking about? What happened?"

"Ray got out of hand," Mary Ann admitted. "He got fresh and I decided to walk home. He grabbed me and tried to keep me in the car, but I fought him off and left." She buried her face in her hands and sobbed. "I didn't want you to know. I feel so stupid."

Ellen put her arm around Mary Ann's shoulders. "You aren't stupid, Mary. You were just too trusting."

"Maybe at first," Mary Ann said, lifting her head. "I just wanted to be nice. But after a while, even I sensed there could be a problem.

You told me not to keep encouraging Ray." Ellen looked surprised but said nothing. "I thought he was a nice enough guy. I really thought I could handle it."

"And you did," Ellen replied with a reassuring smile.

"Oh, Ellen, I don't know what to do. I just can't stand the idea of seeing him again."

"Well, I know what we're going to do," Ellen told her. "We're going to talk to my boss. Mr. Chandler knows all about Ray. Apparently there have been other times—other girls. Mr. Chandler wants to do something to put an end to it."

Ten minutes later they sat in chairs in front of Chris Chandler's desk. Mary Ann couldn't keep her hands from shaking, even as he offered her a cup of coffee.

"I know this kind of thing is hard," he told Mary Ann gently, "but I'm afraid I need to know what happened."

Mary Ann nodded. "Ray invited Ellen and me to a dance. We went, but Ellen's head cold was making her feel bad, so she wanted to go home. She got a ride home with friends, and I stayed at the dance with Ray. When it was time to go, Ray and I headed home."

"Then what happened?"

Mary Ann took a sip of the hot coffee. She hated even remembering the events of the evening. "I thought at first he was being a little fresh, but then he started talking about how bad he felt that his buddies had gone off to war and he was left behind. He was saying all these things and I . . . well . . . I . . ."

"You felt sorry for him?" Mr. Chandler questioned.

Ellen patted Mary Ann's hand reassuringly. "That's nothing to be ashamed of."

"I did feel sorry for him. He said he'd fallen in love with me and that even though he knew I was taken, he couldn't help the way he felt. He kept saying things like that and I didn't know what to do or say."

"How did you get the bruises?" Mr. Chandler questioned.

Mary Ann shrugged. "I guess when he grabbed hold of me to keep me from leaving. I know he held on to me pretty tight."

"Is that all?"

"No," Mary Ann admitted. She hated confessing the part about the kiss, but figured if she was going to do it right, she had to tell them everything. "He talked me into letting him have a kiss." She shook her head and looked down at the cup of coffee in her hand. "I know it was stupid. I feel like ten kinds of a fool, but I felt sorry for him. He asked me to give him something to hope for until the right woman came along. I never should have let him kiss me—I know that—I knew it then."

"Miss Roland, you needn't be too hard on yourself. Men like Ray Blasingham have a way of enticing young women and then demanding more from them than they should give. He's a real wolf when it comes to working with the ladies. I've heard rumors for months now and wondered how I could put a stop to it, but I never had any proof. Until now." He turned to Ellen. "Miss Anderson, I want you to send a runner to bring Mr. Blasingham to my office."

Ellen nodded and got to her feet. Mary Ann felt panic-stricken. "I don't want to deal with him!"

Mr. Chandler looked at her sympathetically. The older man had an obvious compassion for her fear. "You don't need to be afraid. He's not going to be able to hurt you anymore. If you're afraid about your job—stop worrying. I'm not one of those people who band together with management or one of the 'good old boys' who sticks with his own gender. This has to be stopped. I run a tight ship here, Miss Roland. My convictions are that men and women should conduct themselves in an orderly fashion in keeping with God's Word. I know Mr. Blasingham will see little merit in Scripture, but it doesn't matter. What he's done is offensive even outside of my faith."

"I know, but I'm as much to blame," Mary Ann replied. "I went to the dances and I took his gifts. He probably thinks I led him on."

"Even if that were true, it's no excuse. Given what you've said, you made it clear to Mr. Blasingham that you were engaged and not interested in anything more than friendship. If he chose to read more into it than that, it isn't your fault."

"I wouldn't even have gone to the dance last night if Ray hadn't threatened my job."

"What are you saying?" Chandler asked, leaning forward.

"I overslept one morning and when I came in, Sam Johnston caught me and started to give me what-for. Ray interceded and then made it clear that I owed him. He said he could have let Sam fire me."

Chris Chandler showed the first outward signs of anger. Mary

Ann saw his face redden slightly as his eyes narrowed. "He forced you to go to the dance or lose your job?"

Mary Ann nodded. "It didn't seem like such a big deal to go to the dance because we'd been to so many others. But he said I owed him and that made me uncomfortable. I didn't know exactly what he meant by it, but I figured it wouldn't be anything on the up-and-up."

Just then Ellen returned. A strange expression caused both Chandler and Mary Ann to take note.

"What is it?" Chris Chandler asked.

Ellen shook her head. "You aren't going to believe this. Well, then again, maybe you will. Ray and his superior, Mr. Guffy, will be here in a moment."

"Why Guffy?" Chandler questioned.

"That's the amazing part. Apparently a huge scandal has broken down at the local draft board. Mr. Guffy's secretary is a friend of mine and she managed to tell me that apparently Ray has been taking an undeserved deferment. He wasn't rejected as 4-F at all. He's been listed as deferred from military service as a special-skilled, essential war worker."

Chandler pounded his fists against the desk. "I knew it! I just knew something like this was going on."

Mary Ann took a deep breath and shook her head. He'd lied about it all. Every word of it. He'd arranged to skip out on the war, to avoid risking his life, while her Erik honorably served, even after losing a brother. The idea enraged her.

They waited in silence for Ray and Mr. Guffy to show up. Mary Ann nervously toyed with the mug of coffee, wondering how he would handle the confrontation in addition to this latest news about the deferment.

It wasn't long before Adam Guffy knocked on the door. "Chris, I heard you needed to see us." A pale-faced Ray followed the man into the room, his head hung low and shoulders bent.

Mary Ann wondered how Mr. Chandler would handle the situation. Would she have to tell all those embarrassing things again?

"Adam, we have a bit of a problem. It seems Mr. Blasingham took some liberties with Miss Roland last evening."

"His problems are a lot worse than that. Mr. Blasingham has been caught red-handed as part of a draft board scandal. Seems our boy here has taken an illegal deferment." Ray refused to look up and Mary Ann was glad. She didn't want to see his face. "And, as I understand it," Guffy continued, "he's going to be in for a world of hurt. Seems he has a friend on the board who allowed Ray to be listed as having specialized and vital skills for Boeing. When his number came up, a little money changed hands and Ray's deferment was issued."

"Well, I guess that does create quite a problem for Mr. Blasingham," Chris Chandler declared. "I was going to suggest transferring him to our Wichita plant, but now I see his transfer is going to be much more distant."

"To say the least," Guffy replied. "I have no idea what will be done with him, but the authorities are on their way to pick him up, even as we speak."

Chris looked at Mary Ann and smiled. "I told you this would work out. Looks like God had a plan all along, eh?"

Mary Ann nodded. "Thank you," she whispered.

"So now, with Mr. Blasingham leaving our plant, you should feel safe to return to the job you perform so well."

Mary Ann felt a sense of relief wash over her. She knew what she wanted and in simply recognizing that fact, she felt as though she were on her way to having it. "I appreciate your confidence in me, but I'm afraid that won't be possible. I'm going home," she stated. "I'm going back to Longview." She smiled at Ellen. "I'm going back to get my life in order and wait for my husband-to-be. I'm certain God will give me a job back home in which I can help my family, but I'm just as certain that He's sending me back to where I belong."

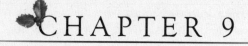# CHAPTER 9

Erik woke to feel something warm and gooey being rubbed all over his body. He couldn't remember where he was or what he was supposed to be doing. In his mind he ran through an entire universe of ideas. Was he sick? Was he late for something? Did someone need him to be doing something? He couldn't focus. He couldn't think. There was pain in his left leg, but he couldn't think of why. Someone urged him to swallow as they lifted a bowl to his lips. Warm, meat-flavored broth trickled down his throat. It tasted strange but wonderful. He tried to acknowledge this but felt hopelessly lost in a fog. Finally he gave up and went back to sleep.

The next time he woke, Erik felt a gentle rubbing sensation on his legs. Something warned him that perhaps he should play dead. For some reason the image of wild animals hung in his thoughts, but he couldn't figure out why. Was he camping out? He tried hard to open his eyes, but the sensation of being dragged down into a deep, warm pool of water caused him to give up his fight. It wasn't at all unpleasant to simply float away. Again something warm was ladled into his mouth. He accepted the offering but knew it was senseless to try and speak.

Eventually conscious thought and reasoning returned to Erik. He opened his eyes and found himself lying on a woven mat inside a grassy framed hut. His head and leg ached but not nearly as badly as he had remembered them hurting. He looked around the room hoping to identify something that could tell him where he was and why. The dirt floor and sparse furnishings did little to encourage him.

Little by little he remembered parachuting onto the island. His memory came back in gradual pieces; small but meaningful pictures presented him with a better understanding. He was a marine. He had parachuted onto the island after a dogfight and now he was being held captive by . . . whom?

He struggled to sit up, then glanced down at his body. He'd been stripped of his flight suit and other clothing and now had nothing more than a thin piece of material draped across his midsection. It wasn't much comfort. His hands and arms weren't nearly as blistered as he recalled them being only days before. Or had it been weeks before? How long had he been unconscious? Then he noticed his left foot and leg. His foot had been wrapped in bandages of the natives' making, while his leg, swollen and red, bore clear signs of blood poisoning in hot red streaks. Fear gripped at Erik's heart. He tried to move his leg but it hurt too much.

Hearing a bit of commotion outside the hut, Erik fell back against the mat and feigned sleep. By opening his eyes slightly, he could see a young native woman enter the hut. She carried a bowl and behind her came a man carrying two more. They knelt beside Erik and began caring for his body. Unnerved by the process, Erik started to protest.

"What are you doing?" he asked, startling both the man and the woman.

The woman jumped back, but the man merely grinned. His blackened teeth reminded Erik of a blurry image. Something he'd seen before but just couldn't place.

"*No seksek*," the man said in a reassuring tone. "You no worry."

Erik forced his muscles to comply as he sat up. "What is that?" he asked as the woman dipped her hand in the bowl, then reached hesitantly for Erik's arm.

"You *plante* sick. You no worry, *waetimani*." The man rattled on in his native language, but Erik couldn't understand a word of it. He offered Erik a bowl of something. "You drink."

Erik took the bowl and looked at the contents. It appeared to be some sort of soup. He lifted the bowl to his lips cautiously. What if they were poisoning him? He almost laughed out loud. What if they were? They could have been doing it for days. His stomach growled loudly and he figured he had nothing to lose. But as he drank the rather smelly soup, a feeling of dread came over him. What if they were just fattening him up?

The woman rubbed Erik's arm with the concoction from the bowl. It felt soothing and warm. Erik felt almost as if he were being slathered in butter. Butter? He looked at the soup bowl and then at the woman. Maybe they were cannibals and this was their way of preparing him for the food pot!

He jerked his arm away and shook his head. "Leave me alone!"

The man smiled again. "You no worry."

"I'm worrying plenty," Erik replied. "Where am I and who are you?"

"*Mi Kobu*," the man answered. "You sick, but you *moabetta*."

"Better?" Erik questioned.

The man nodded. "*Ya, moabetta*."

Erik sighed. "My name is Erik Anderson. My foot hurts. What happened?"

"You *blong keeng?*"

Erik thought he understood and it gave him a bit of encouragement. "Do I belong to the king?"

"*Ya*," the man nodded enthusiastically.

"No," Erik said, shaking his head. "I'm an American."

The man grinned and kept nodding. "Yankee Doodle."

Erik actually laughed. "Yes. Yankee Doodle and apple pie." He relaxed as the woman kept applying her medicine. "Where am I? I need to get to a radio so that I can return to my unit."

"*Mi no savay*," the man said, shrugging.

"Savvy?" Erik questioned. He tried to reason what the man meant.

Outside the hut came the sound of singing. Erik was almost startled by the music. It almost sounded familiar. He strained his memory for some clue, but nothing came to mind. The music continued and it sounded as though children were the ones doing the singing. Erik wondered how he might question the man about it but realized quickly enough that the singing was really unimportant. What mattered was getting back to civilization.

"Do you have a radio?" Erik tried again.

"*Redio?*"

"Yes," Erik said, excited by the possibility that the man understood.

"*Wan redio longwe.*"

Erik thought he caught the meaning. "Long way to radio?"

"Ya," the man replied. *"Plenta longwe.* You sick."

"Yes, I know, but I need to get to the radio. I need medical attention for my leg." He pointed to his injured foot and leg as if to emphasize the matter.

The man spoke to the woman in their rapid-fire way. Erik hoped the man was arranging to somehow get him to wherever the radio might be. The woman wiped her hands and picked up the bowl she'd carried. Without a word she exited the hut, leaving Erik and the man alone.

Erik tried to remember what the man had called himself. Patting his own chest, Erik spoke his name. "Me, Erik Anderson." Then he reached up and touched the native's chest. "You?"

"Kobu," the man replied.

"Kobu." Erik nodded in understanding.

The man grinned and touched Erik's chest. "Areek."

"Close enough."

The woman returned and said something to the man before stepping back out of the hut. As soon as she had gone, another man entered. He was followed by two more men, and Erik began to grow fearful of what they had planned for him. Struggling, he sat up to face his new visitors.

The three men came to his side and sat down. The two younger helped the older man and waited until he was seated before joining the group. Erik studied the man. His gray hair had been cut close to his head, while thick eyebrows accentuated his dark, foreboding eyes. The stern expression on the man's face left Erik feeling rather ill at ease, but at the same time his clothing, which constituted nothing more than a wrapping of cloth around his waist, made Erik want to laugh. The material itself was the culprit. It looked more like something that should have hung from a kitchen window. Tiny red apples and vining greenery decorated the otherwise white background. It seemed very inappropriate for a man who obviously was someone of importance.

"You no English?" the man finally questioned.

"No," Erik admitted. "I'm American."

"You *soldia*—you fight?"

"I'm a marine pilot," Erik explained. He held out his arms and made a motorlike sound.

The man nodded and spoke to his companions. One man got up and left rather quickly.

"I *bigman*. I *misinare* friend," the older man continued.

He said a great deal more, but it was only the first part that Erik thought he understood. The man apparently had spent time with missionaries and was a person of some importance. As if to confirm this, the man looked to his companion, who produced a bag from around his waist. The older man opened the bag and brought out several articles.

The first item was a necklace. At the end of the rather simple silver chain was a medallion of sorts. He handed the piece to Erik.

Erik read, "'Native Chieftain, by order of King George V.'"

The man nodded and handed Erik the next article. The olive drab C-ration tin rattled a bit when Erik took hold. Looking inside he saw bottle caps from a variety of soda drinks and beers. Erik looked up, uncertain as to what he should think or relate. The chief seemed unconcerned. He took the tin back almost ceremonially and handed it to the other native. In the process the man handed the chief a cloth-wrapped article. The chief very meticulously unwrapped the piece and presented it to Erik for inspection.

Erik eyed the piece, a pin with a rusting clasp. The words *Remember Pearl Harbor* were spelled out in red, white, and blue. Some of the paint had chipped away, but Erik felt a sense of connecting with home. Between the bottle caps, ration tin, and now this pin, he felt a glimmer of hope that he might once again be found. That someone might remember him and come searching. *Remember Pearl Harbor. Remember Me.*

Feeling a sense of exhaustion wash over him, Erik eased back onto the mat. The older man grunted several words, then packing up the things they had brought, he turned back to Erik.

"*Iumi ma go-go-on.*" The man got to his feet with the help of the younger man.

Erik nodded. He longed for his strength to return so that he might at least feel capable of dealing with these men. While the pin had given him hope, it had also reminded him of how far away from home he really was. Feeling despair from the memory and the illness, Erik closed his eyes and began to pray.

I don't know what to say, God. But I'm lost and alone, and I desperately need you to help me. Forgive me for being so stubborn. I thought I could take care of myself, but I'm starting to see just how incapable I am. Here it is almost Christmas . . . Then again, maybe Christmas had already passed him by. He had no idea what the date might be. He seriously doubted these natives even worried about such things.

He heard the rain begin to fall. In the dry confines of the hut, the rain sounded almost comforting. The noise lulled him to sleep, and as he passed into a state of dreams, Erik again heard familiar singing. What was that song? The tune seemed like one he knew, but he just couldn't place it. God, he prayed, *just give me a sign. Please just show me that I haven't pushed you too far away. That my stubbornness hasn't caused you to desert me. Please, Father—just a sign to let me know you remember me.*

Erik was roused from his sleep by the same native who had first communicated with him. How long had he slept? What day was it? Blurry-eyed, Erik sat up and tried to clear the cobwebs from his mind. He felt remarkably better and very hungry.

"Areek," the man said, grinning from ear to ear.

Erik nodded. "And you're Kobu," he remembered.

"Ya, me Kobu." The man went to the door of the hut and brought a stack of folded articles. Erik immediately recognized the items as his uniform and underclothes. "You make dressed."

Erik eyed him suspiciously as he took hold of the clothes. "You want me to get dressed? Why?"

Kobu nodded, not understanding that Erik was questioning him. Erik tried again. "Why do you want me to put this on?"

"No worry," the man said. "You make dressed." Kobu made a rather hurried exit from the hut, leaving Erik to wonder what was happening.

Deciding he'd rather face his fate in his own clothes, Erik quickly dressed. He felt surprisingly good. The rash on his hands and arms had faded, no doubt thanks to the ointment he'd been bathed in. His bruises and scrapes had healed up rather nicely, and even his foot didn't seem to hurt quite so badly, although the frightening red streaks were still evident on his leg. Apparently these people knew something of medicine—at least jungle medicine. Perhaps he wasn't in quite as much danger as he had presumed.

As Erik secured his belt, Kobu returned, bringing with him Erik's boots and a bundled cloth. Placing these things at Erik's feet, Kobu smiled again. "*Blong* you."

"Yes, but I can't stand on this foot and I know I'll never get the boot over the bandage," he said as if the man could understand everything he said.

"You no worry," he said. He went to the door and came back with a litter and three other men. "We carry you."

Erik didn't know what else to do. Nodding in agreement he pulled on the one boot and laced it tight. Next, he opened the bundle. His knife, gun, holster, and extra rounds were neatly awaiting his attention. Apparently these natives saw him as no threat. Maybe he'd do well to think of them in the same way.

Erik secured his gun and holster, then attached the sheathed knife and extra rounds to his belt. For whatever it was worth, he was dressed and ready. Picking up his spare boot, he looked to Kobu for help as to what he should do next.

Kobu spoke to his companions while motioning at Erik. Apparently something of great importance was happening and they were already running late. Erik was helped onto the litter, and without so much as a word, the men hoisted him into the air and out the door.

It was the first time Erik had been outside of the hut since coming to the village. There were many other grass huts representing other families and all of these ran in a semicircle around a large center clearing. In the middle a big tank, the type used for watering livestock, had been positioned. Erik had no idea where the tank must have come from but it looked to hold water.

Kobu lead them past the tank and clearing and through a narrow path between two huts. Directly in front of them another clearing opened before them. Here an assembly of natives lined up on either side of a long, festive-looking arrangement of food. Grass mats had been spread on the ground between them, and pots and bowls of every kind were filled and placed in preparation of a great feast.

The chief who'd spoken to Erik earlier sat at the head of the table, surrounded by several important-looking men. He motioned to Kobu, and Erik found himself and the litter settled into position beside this gathering. Still uncertain as to what was happening, Erik did as he was instructed. With a shaky weakness washing over him and leaving him in a cold sweat, Erik sat up. His foot throbbed painfully. He supposed he must have hurt it when he fell into the river.

The chief clapped his hands and without further warning, a group of children appeared from the brush. They sang a rousing chorus, giggling and laughing as they went. Erik appreciated the fun they appeared to be having and for the first time in a long time he smiled.

Then to Erik's amazement, while the kids continued to sing, several adult men came in a procession bearing an ornate wooden cross. The cross was intricately carved with images of sharks and people. Erik watched as they secured the piece into a hole in the ground. Rocks were positioned around the wooden base to keep the cross firmly in place. Next came a group of women. Erik blushed and glanced away. The women weren't wearing anything from the waist up. The only thing they had to cover their breasts, in fact, were multiple necklaces. The women danced and sang, and Erik felt compelled to watch only when Kobu nudged him and motioned toward the group. While they danced, several men tied palm fronds all over the cross. When this had been finished, the women pulled strands of shell and coral from around their necks and used them to decorate the palm fronds.

After this was completed the women took their places beside the others. Erik was completely fascinated by the festivities. He found himself caught up in the moment, and when the children began to sing the unmistakable melody of "Silent Night," Erik began to see the celebration for what it was. They were celebrating Christmas! They'd brought out the cross of Christ and decorated it as if it were a Christmas tree.

Before he could say anything to Kobu to confirm this, a processional of several native men brought an ornate box and laid it at the feet of the chief. The box looked to be wood, inlaid with gold. The men sat down and a hush fell over the crowd as the chief reached to open the box.

With great awe and reverence the people watched. Erik felt a sense of elation as the man drew out a black book. Holding it up, Erik easily recognized the book. A Bible. Erik wanted to laugh and cry at the same time. God had sent him a sign. There could be no doubting it.

God did remember him! God had heard him!

The chief looked to Erik and nodded. Then to Erik's surprise he handed Erik the Bible. "You read."

Erik looked at the group of eager faces, then returned his glance at the chief. "You want me to read?"

"Ya," the man said in a clipped tone. "You read us Krismas, Jisas, *nabawan pikinini blong God*."

Erik understood. He didn't know how, but he understood. They wanted him to read about Jesus. They wanted him to read the Christmas story. He nodded and smiled. Turning the pages to the second chapter of Luke, he cleared his throat.

"'And it came to pass in those days, that there went out a decree from Caesar Augustus, that all the world should be taxed.'" The familiar words warmed Erik's heart. God cared. He really cared. He'd not only given Erik a sign, He'd given him Christmas as well.

He continued reading, wondering if the people understood. They smiled and nodded and all Erik could imagine was that someone before him had shared these same words and traditions. They had taken what they had to work with and had created their own Christmas celebration to honor God's Son.

He concluded the reading, then handed the Bible back to the chief. "Merry Christmas," Erik said with a smile.

The chief nodded and the children began to sing again. This time Erik recognized the song and began to sing with them. "'Adeste Fideles, laeti triumphantes . . . '" *Oh come, all ye faithful, joyful and triumphant.* A feeling of pure joy and hope coursed through Erik's soul as the song ended and the feasting began.

"G'day, mate. Semper Fi, Yank," came the unmistakable sound of an Australian accent.

Erik looked up to see a white man making his way into the camp. Several natives accompanied him and quickly left his side to take their place at the makeshift table.

"You're a sight for sore eyes," Erik said, realizing his rescue had come.

"I'm a coast watcher. I'm always on the lookout for lost souls." The blond-haired man pushed back his hat and grinned. "I've been lookin' for ya since that dogfight two weeks ago."

Erik looked at the man in surprise. "You saw my dogfight?"

"Aye. It was somethin' else. I figured ya to be a goner, then I saw the chute open. Knew ya had to be here someplace. The chief fetched me over. After ya eat, we can head back."

"Do you have a radio to contact someone for me?" Erik asked.

"Better 'an that," the man replied. "I have the boat to take ya to Brisbane. They'll fix ya up proper-like and then send ya back into the war." He grinned at Erik. "We'll just tell everyone ya've been on holiday."

Erik laughed at this. "I don't know that I'd call it that, but I'm happy to go wherever you'll take me."

"Then eat up, fella. We'll head out after the party's over."

Erik nodded and accepted a bowl from Kobu. He smiled at the man and thanked him. Then without even thinking about it, he raised his bowl to heaven. "Thank you, God. Thank you for remembering me and thank you for sending your Son. Merry Christmas."

The natives mimicked him in raising their bowls. Perhaps they thought this to be some strange Christmas tradition from America. Either way, it connected them to one another—to Erik. They were brothers and sisters who gathered at a birthday party for the King of Kings.

CHAPTER 10

Mary Ann shivered as she brought in the last of the applewood for the fireplace. Her favorite apple tree had died from blight nearly a year ago and her brother had chopped it up for wood the spring before. The aroma it sent off was one that Mary Ann found particularly pleasing. It reminded her of happier days—of being courted by Erik and sitting in the front room holding his hand and gazing into the flames.

She hurried to stoke up the fire. Her siblings had come down with measles and it was important to keep the house warm. The knock at the front door did little to pull her focus from the task at hand. The doctor was due to come check up on the children, so no doubt that would be him now. She tossed a couple of logs on the fire, then dusted her hands and went to the door.

"Ellen!" she exclaimed. "I didn't think you were still in town."

"I know," Ellen replied and the animation in her tone told Mary Ann that something very good had happened.

"What is it? Have you heard something from Erik? Has he written?"

Ellen smiled and waved a telegram. "Even better."

"Better?"

She nodded as Mary Ann opened the screen door to allow Ellen inside. "What could be better?" Her heart pounded as she bit her lower lip.

"Read it for yourself," Ellen said, handing her the telegram.

Mary Ann glanced down at the words on the tape. "Erik's coming home?" She felt faint and reached for the only thing close by. Ellen.

Ellen put a supportive arm around her and met her gaze. She nodded. "He's coming home. He was injured, but he's all right.

160

Mother hasn't been able to find out much more than that. Oh, Mary Ann! Isn't this the best news of the new year?"

Mary Ann felt tears come to her eyes. "The very best. It's like all my finest wishes coming true at once." She looked at the paper again. "He's coming home. My Erik is coming home!"

Lounging in the Brisbane hospital dayroom, Erik was still trying to come to terms with the news he'd been given. The terrible infection in his foot, brought on by a compound fracture, was not responding well to the medication available. He was being sent back to the States for more intense therapy away from the Tropics. The thought of being discharged from active duty still came as a tremendous surprise. Somehow he'd always figured to be in this war for the duration.

The doctor had assured him they'd get word back to his family in America and let them know he had been found and was headed home. Erik longed for their company and looked forward to seeing Mary Ann—to holding her and kissing her. But even as those thoughts came to bolster his spirits, Erik couldn't help but worry that Mary Ann no longer cared. She seemed so distant. So very far away. Had she remained faithful—did she still love him?

"Lieutenant Anderson! Lieutenant Erik Anderson!" came the call.

"Yes!" Erik replied, waving from his seat.

An older man came forward, limping as he did and dragging behind him a huge duffel bag. "You Anderson?"

"I am," Erik replied.

"This is yours," the man said. He gave the duffel a powerful swing forward and landed the bag at Erik's feet.

"What's in it?" Erik asked curiously.

"Mail," the man replied. "You were harder to find than ice water in the desert. Mail kept coming and stacking up for you and we had no clue where to send it. For some reason, the marines just lost track of you."

Erik shook his head. "But how . . . why would it end up here?"

"Mail from the States goes to Hawaii and then Australia. We send it out from here to the boys all across the South Pacific. We just lost you in the shuffle."

Erik tore at the strings that tied the bag shut. It was like having his own private Christmas morning. There inside the bag were packages and letters in such abundance that Erik immediately felt guilty for every negative thought he'd ever had about his family. For the first time since his ordeal had begun, Erik felt his eyes mist with tears.

Lovingly he picked up a letter and easily recognized his mother's handwriting. Next he took up one from Mary Ann and then one from his sister Ellen. Laughing, he recognized letters from church members and neighbors, as well as additional missives from his loved ones. They had remembered him—they had been faithful.

He looked up at the man, not in the leastwise embarrassed by his tears. "Thank you. Thank you so much. I thought they had forgotten me."

The man put his hand on Erik's shoulder. "Merry Christmas, Lieutenant."

Erik smiled. "You too, and thanks."

He opened a letter with Mary Ann's return address.

My dearest love,

You consume my thoughts and I can't help but wonder when we might next meet again. My heart is so full of love for you. . . .

He could read no more as the tears blurred his vision. He sighed. The disappointment of being injured and sent home was overcome with a longing for the woman who was to become his wife.

He looked at his treasure of letters from home and knew that nothing could have made him feel more festive. Christmas had passed without snow or his mother's home cooking. The new year had come without a sweetheart's kiss or tender embrace, but this just might turn out to be one of his favorite memories of the holiday season. Something had changed inside his heart, and this time he truly knew why he was celebrating.

SHADOW *of* HIS WINGS

CHAPTER 1

Longview, Washington, December 1943

With a gentle winter rain falling outside and a well-laid fire on the hearth, Melody Thompson attempted to decorate the Christmas tree, while Ginny Williams settled down to string cranberries. The radio offered a variety of holiday songs and the day promised to be good for staying inside, drinking something hot, and reading a good book. If only her husband and Ginny's son could be on hand, Melody thought, the day might well have been perfect.

Ginny sighed and stuck a needle through a rather tough cranberry. Melody knew her mind was far away. Ginny's son, John, was somewhere in England flying bombers for the war effort, and her dear husband had passed on to his reward two years earlier. Melody thought her a very brave but very lonely woman.

Ginny smiled from across the room, and Melody couldn't help but feel warmed at her caring expression. Ginny had taken her in as a favor to her son. Melody was married to John's good friend and co-pilot, Collin Thompson. The two men had trained together in California and it was there that Collin had fallen in love with sixteen-year-old Melody. It was also there that their love led to Melody getting pregnant and to both rushing into a wartime marriage that neither had planned on.

Melody's parents had been enraged when they'd learned of her condition. Highly religious people, they proclaimed Melody had disgraced the family in a most unforgivable way. They'd kicked her out of their home in spite of the fact that she and Collin quietly married. They were ashamed of her and it grieved Melody sorely. She knew she'd done wrong, but her folks had always said that God could forgive a person when they were truly repentant. And Melody was truly repentant. She had never intended to get caught up in her whirlwind romance with the dashing pilot. She had never intended to become romantically involved with any soldier. But Collin had a way about him.

She smiled as she thought of him and tried to reach past her ever-expanding stomach to hang a ceramic cherub on the tree. Collin held her heart in his hand almost from the start. He had winked at her one morning as she worked collecting scrap paper and from that moment on, Melody had been captivated by the handsome stranger.

Falling in love had been easy. It had been just as easy to say yes to Collin's proposal and to find herself in his arms sharing a passionate kiss and whispered promises for their future.

Her courtship, however, was bittersweet with the memory that she'd not remained pure as she'd always planned. She grieved over her thoughtless choice that night and when she knew for sure she was carrying Collin's baby, the wedding was rapidly stepped up. Even so, her parents had been harsh and cruel. Her father had voiced threats of physical violence. Her mother had cried until she was sick.

Knowing her folks were highly respected religious pillars in the community had made Melody feel even worse. Once the talk started circulating, her father was asked to either put Melody away from them or resign his position as an elder in the church. One simple act, one sinful choice, had caused everything to change. Consequences were strict masters.

"The tree is looking a little bare on the top half," Ginny teased. "But don't you go worrying none. I'll help you out as soon as I get these stubborn berries strung."

Melody laughed lightly and stepped back. "It does look a little strange."

"Never you mind. Although it's good to hear you laugh," Ginny said before focusing back on her work.

Melody had been so discouraged over her parents' rejection. A part of her understood the stand they'd made, but a part of her didn't. If they served a God who truly forgave, then why, after Melody had apologized and married, did they continue to act as though she didn't exist?

It was almost her undoing when Collin announced that his unit was leaving for the war. Terror had struck a deep nerve in Melody, who was not only shut out of the relationships she'd held all of her life, but now she would have no husband to care for her either. John had been the one to save the day for them both by suggesting Melody stay with his widowed mother.

Ginny Williams had been understanding and kind. She listened to their story and agreed that what they had done was wrong. Collin had bristled at her chiding, but Melody found herself easily drawn to the older woman. Ginny wasn't simply pointing a finger and harboring disgust, she openly offered forgiveness or at least assurance that God had forgiven them. After Collin and John said their goodbyes and Melody moved into John's old room, the love she found in Ginny's care was all that would get her through the coming days.

There were goods days and bad. Long nights that seemed to never end tormented Melody the most. The first few weeks had been given over to crying herself to sleep each night, and sometimes even waking up in the night to cry some more. She missed her folks and she missed her husband. She harbored the fear that she might never see any of them again and she worried for her future and that of her child's.

"You're going to grieve yourself to death," Ginny had admonished the girl months ago. And Ginny knew well how that could be.

Two years earlier, John had told Melody, Ginny had been the happiest woman in the world. Life was pretty routine in Longview in spite of the war raging in Europe. America was cautiously being neutral on the side of the Allies, yet life went on in a fairly normal routine. John had just graduated college the previous May, and Ginny and her husband, Harold, had proudly announced his accomplishment to the world. He was the first Williams to attend college, much less graduate. That same summer, John had completed his pilot's training and hoped very much to begin working in commercial air service.

But that winter the Japanese had attacked Pearl Harbor and not two weeks after that, Ginny's beloved Harold had suffered a heart attack at work and had died on the spot. Ginny had been inconsolable. Harold and John were her life, and now an important part of her life was gone.

Melody finished with the last ornament and turned to see Ginny wipe away a tear. Today was the anniversary of Harold's death. Two years had passed, and yet Ginny had told her it seemed like yesterday.

"*I can't count the number of times I'll glance at the clock and think, 'Two more hours until Harold is home.' 'Wonder what Harold would like for supper?' 'Wonder how Harold's day went,'*" Ginny had told her that morning. Melody could only pray she'd not find herself up against the same painful experience. She dreaded any sight of the local telegraph deliveryman.

"There!" Ginny declared and got up with the string of red berries. "I'm glad to have that finished." She went to the tree and adjusted the cranberries along the branches.

"What do you think?" Melody questioned, turning from the tree with a hand to her back.

She moved a couple of ornaments around to balance out the top, then stood back. "It looks just lovely, Melody," Ginny remarked. "I'm so glad you're here to help with it."

"I don't think I'm that much help," she said with a frown. "I can hardly reach the tree because of the baby."

Ginny laughed. "Well, it won't be long now. Doc Ketterman says it could be any day."

Melody's frown deepened and she turned away to prevent Ginny from seeing her discomfort. Having this baby terrified her. With Collin so far away and her own parents refusing to have anything to do with her, Melody felt very much alone. What if something went wrong?

Ginny walked to where Melody stood and put her hands on the young girl's shoulders. "It will be all right. You'll see. Remember, I used to be a nurse. Plus, I've had two babies."

"Yes, but you lost one," Melody said, turning to meet Ginny's gaze. "What if my baby dies?"

Ginny nodded. "Things do happen. My little girl had the umbilical cord wrapped around her neck. Nobody could have known that. We have no guarantees that life will be easy, Melody, but God is good."

The girl shook her head. "I don't know if I can see Him that way anymore. Look at how my folks have acted. I know I did wrong, but I asked them to forgive me. I asked God, too, but they told me He couldn't forgive what I did."

"Melody, I'd be the last one to tell you not to listen to your folks, but in this case, I know they're wrong. If a person repents and seeks

God's forgiveness, it will be given. You did make a mistake. You gave in when you should have remained pure. But it happens. More often than you'd know. Still, there are consequences for your actions and you're enduring those even now. It doesn't mean God can't forgive you and it doesn't mean this baby is a punishment. You married your baby's father and now you have your whole life ahead of you."

"But what if something happens?" Melody questioned.

Melody was surprised that she'd found the courage to ask that question. She had positively refused to speak aloud anything negative since first coming to live with Ginny the previous June. Even when Ginny had made comments about worrying over John and Collin, Melody refused to admit her own concerns. It was almost as if she worried that should she voice her fears, it might well give fuel to bring them about.

Ginny opened her arms to embrace Melody, and she eagerly stepped into Ginny's embrace.

"Melody, no matter what happens, you must remember that God loves you, and I love you too. I always wanted a daughter, and when mine died I felt so grieved and saddened by the loss. My daughter would have been just two years older than you, and I like to think she would have been pretty and sweet like you."

Melody hugged Ginny tight. "She would have been smarter than me. Oh, Ginny, I don't know why I did what I did. I just felt so happy to be with Collin. He was so sweet and compassionate. He made me feel happy and loved, and when he kissed me I knew I wanted to spend the rest of my life with him." A sob broke her voice. "But now he's fighting in the war and he may not come back. I can't bear it. I just can't bear it."

Her shoulders quivered as she cried against Ginny's neck. "I'm so scared, Ginny."

"I know, sweetheart. But you don't have to be."

Melody shook her head and pulled away. The tears streamed down her face. "I just don't see God as loving me anymore. And even if He did, if He's what my folks think He is, I'm not sure I want to love Him."

Ginny nodded. "Listen to me, Melody. God is everything good and perfect and true. The Bible tells us that He is love. The Bible also says that we have but to come to Him and confess our sins and He will be faithful to forgive them. Your folks are good people, with good intentions. They feel so strongly about this because they love you." Melody started to turn away, but Ginny put out her hand and stopped her. "Child, just because you and your folks have had this disagreement, don't stop loving them and caring about them. I can guarantee you, as a mother, I never stopped caring about and loving John, even when he was being a bit of a pistol. He's my child, just as this baby you're carrying will be your child . . . just as we are God's children. Mistakes and misunderstandings do not take that love away."

"My folks are different. You don't know them," Melody said, wiping at her tears. "They chose the church over me. They told me I was a sinner."

Ginny nodded. "We all are."

"They told me I was lost and going to hell."

"Without Jesus to save us, we'd all be headed there."

"They told me God couldn't forgive me."

"Well, my Bible says that He can," Ginny smiled. "I think they're just speaking out of their pain."

"Their pain?" Melody questioned. "What do they know of pain?"

"I'm sure that given everything that's happened, they know plenty about it. Give them time, Melody. Have you ever written to let them know where you are?"

She shook her head. "No. They don't deserve to know. They told me if I ever came home they'd see me driven out of town. You know that—I told you how hateful they were."

"I know what you've told me, but I would think now that so much time has passed, they are probably wishing things had not gone that way. They probably regret their choices and decisions."

Melody looked down at her rounded belly and gave it a gentle rub. "I'd like to think that what you say is true. We were always so close. I have three little sisters and I have no idea how they are or what they are doing."

"You could always write them a letter if you're afraid of talking to them face-to-face."

"I doubt they'd read it," Melody replied.

"Well, you'll never know unless you try it."

The girl nodded. "I think I'm going to go lie down. I'm feeling pretty tired."

"That sounds like a good idea," Ginny said. "Maybe things won't seem so bad after you get a little rest."

Days later, Ginny felt confident that Melody was considering her idea of writing home. She'd found several wadded-up pieces of writing paper in Melody's wastebasket, and while she didn't intrude to see if they were letters started to her folks, Ginny figured they probably were.

Another thing Ginny was confident about was that Melody was going to deliver any day now. The baby had dropped, a sure sign that he or she was getting into position for the birthing process. Then, too, there was the little cleaning frenzy that Melody had launched into the day before. Ginny remembered her own pregnancies and how important it had seemed during those last few days to get everything in order. Why, she had been cleaning the nursery for John's arrival the very second her water broke.

It had already been agreed upon that Melody would deliver the baby at home. Ginny had helped with hundreds of births, and Melody was so leery of strangers that it just made sense. Doc Ketterman would come and do the actual delivery, but Ginny would be there for assisting and helping afterward.

Ginny liked the idea of having a new life come into her home. She had been secretly glad when John had presented the idea of taking on Melody and helping her in her situation. Ginny would never have admitted her loneliness to John, especially with him heading off to war. The thought of spending all her time alone in the family house had nearly driven her to sell it off and move back east to live with her sister. Melody had given her a reason to stay.

Now with the war reports being so grim and worrisome, Ginny was especially glad that the two women had each other to lean on for comfort and encouragement. She knew things would be difficult for her son. As the pilot of a B-17 bomber, he had told his mother what would be expected of him. Ginny had appreciated his honesty, but at the same time she almost wished she didn't know what his job was. She had no way of knowing when he was sitting safely in England or when he was risking his life over occupied portions of Europe. It could often be maddening and yet at the same time Ginny knew there was nothing positive to be gained by worrying.

"*Worry just kills hope,*" her Harold used to say. "*And hope is all we have when things seem darkest.*"

Ginny smiled and looked out the kitchen window to the backyard, where Harold's shed stood. She could almost see him there chopping wood just outside the door. He would look up and wave and sometimes he would make a motion like he was drinking a cup of coffee. Ginny knew that was his way of asking her to put on a pot so that he could come inside and warm up.

An icy rain had been falling since before dawn, but Ginny could still make out the woodpile beyond the frosted window. Harold had always seen to it that there was plenty of wood for the fireplace; now Ginny relied on the Bennett family for help in that area. Marion Bennett and his war-wounded son-in-law, David, would come down and see to her needs every couple of weeks. All of her church family had been good about helping her out. She would have expected no less, however. That was what family was for. If Marion had died instead of Harold, Ginny knew her husband would have been the first to sign up for offering help to the Bennett family. That was the way they did business in this small town.

Glancing at the clock, Ginny saw that it was nearly time to start breakfast. Soon Melody would be waking up and they would face Christmas Eve together. The vision of Harold faded, but the warmth of his memory burrowed deep into Ginny's heart. It still hurt so much to be without him.

"I miss him, Lord," she whispered, bowing her head. "I know you have a perfect plan. But I miss my Harold."

"Ginny!"

Melody's terrified scream pierced the otherwise silent morning. Forgetting her prayer, Ginny felt her heart race as she hurried to John's old bedroom. Standing in a puddle of water, doubled over from the pain of her labor, Melody could barely choke out her words.

"It's the baby!"

CHAPTER 2

Somewhere over the Pas de Calais, France, December 24, 1943

"So, Deac, this is a milk run, eh?" Collin "Digger" Thompson yelled over the commotion of the moment.

John Williams looked at his co-pilot only briefly and fought against the heavy vibration of the B-17's yoke. The aircraft lurched as a flak burst detonated nearby. The formation of B-17s sliced through the skies at an altitude of twenty thousand feet as they traveled en masse to return home to their base in England.

Coming back from their no-ball mission near the Pas de Calais in France, the B-17 crew members were feeling less than festive on this Christmas Eve. The enthusiasm they'd had earlier in the morning for the "milk run" had faded in light of the heavy flak they were now facing. This was supposed to be nothing more than a simple bombing raid. A routine trip that would tack one more mission to their needed twenty-five missions before they could go home.

Digger tried not to think about home as he concentrated on helping to keep the plane in formation. The plane, *Circuit Rider*, was a very capable B-17F and their home away from home. Nicknamed as most planes were, *Circuit Rider* had been christened with the nose art of a horseback-riding preacher, Bible in one hand, six-shooter in the other, and the reins in his teeth. Added to this, the saddlebags were stuffed with bombs. Bombs to teach Hitler a lesson. Bombs to put an end to the war.

And just as the plane had been nicknamed, so too had most every crew member. John was "Deacon"—so called because of his love of the Scriptures and his faithful attendance to church whenever he was able to go to services. The men had first called him Deacon as a sort of teasing insult. Digger himself had started it. He'd tried over and over to get John to lighten up and have some fun. But as time went on and the crew grew more familiar with one another, John became a symbolic anchor for them all. Deacon was the one who could pray and get results. Deacon knew just the right words to say when the worst things happened. The name suited the man, just as *Circuit Rider* suited the plane. Digger had to smile. If John had had his way, they probably would have dropped Bibles instead of bombs.

Digger's own nickname was born out of a previous occupation of helping to dig graves with his grandfather. As the groundskeeper for the local cemetery, Digger's grandfather had shoveled out graves until into his sixties. He'd be there still, Digger mused, had he not rolled the tractor over on top of him. The accident, now five years past, had come as a shock to the family. Digger's grandfather had been driving tractors for even longer than he'd been digging graves. It seemed a senseless accident and had angered Digger as an even more senseless death.

"*It was just his time,*" Digger's mother had said. "*God has called him home.*"

The idea of God robbing a sixteen-year-old boy of his idol and only father figure didn't sit right with Collin. He thought God harsh, unjust, and unkind. And then Collin went one step further and decided not to think of God at all.

"Tail to Pilot, *Stormy Weather* just took a hit!" The call came over the plane's intercom system and jerked Digger out of his morose thoughts.

"Roger, Tail," John replied, touching his hand to his throat mic. "How bad is it, Del?"

"They're on fire, Deacon!" The usually cocky eighteen-year-old sounded rather frantic. "They're dropping out of formation and there they go!"

"Pilot to Navigator, mark the time of *Stormy Weather*'s loss."

There was no time for the navigator to reply, however. Another burst of flak exploded somewhere to the left of the plane. Pieces of hot metal tore through *Circuit Rider* like soft butter. Digger and Deacon both jumped at the spray of crystallized glass from the instrument panel as it showered the cockpit.

"You okay?" Deacon questioned his co-pilot. He glanced quickly at the man to reassure himself that he was still alive.

"I'm fine!" Digger exclaimed, taking visual assessment of the control panel.

"All stations check in, report damage," Deacon called over the intercom.

"Bombardier, check, clear" came the first confirmation from the crew.

Digger heard Deacon give a sharp intake of breath. "I'm hit, Digger," Deacon said as the rest of the crew began reporting.

Digger's face contorted before settling on what he knew was an expression of disbelief. "Where? How bad?" His gaze ran up and down the full length of his captain before settling back on Deacon's face. He didn't see blood and yet knew Deacon wasn't the type to jump to conclusions.

But Deacon had no chance to answer, nor to assess his wound. Something out the left window caught his attention.

"Dig, number two engine's on fire. Kill the power and feather the prop! Hit the fire extinguishers."

Digger quickly went into action, his mind still on Deacon's injury. "Top Turret, check. Hey, Captain, number two is smoking!"

"Roger that, Top Turret," Deacon replied.

"Engine two, off. Feathering two. Fire extinguishers, on," Digger announced as he went through the procedure.

The number two engine coughed and sputtered before dying. Deacon cast a quick glance out the window, and Digger strained to see the results of his actions. Like an oversized rendition of a child's whirligig, the propeller continued to turn as it met the onrushing air. *Circuit Rider* began to shake fiercely, causing Deacon to grip the yoke even harder.

"Radio compartment, check, no damage here, sir."

"Left Waist Gunner, check. I'm clear."

"Right Waist Gunner, check."

"Ball Turret, check, undamaged."

"Tail Gunner, check, A-OK here."

"No go, Deac, number two isn't feathering. It's windmilling!" Digger said as he repeated the procedure for feathering.

The plane's vibrations were an increasing worry. Digger knew the news wasn't what Deacon wanted to hear.

"Okay, Digger, let's increase throttle to number one and decrease to three and four. We're starting to crab," he commanded as he fought to keep the B-17 from its sidewise pull. "I'll see if I can trim us up."

His words came through rattling teeth as he looked to the aileron tab control on the floor panel to his left.

Touching his throat mic, he said, "Pilot to Radio. Pilot to Radio."

"Radio here, sir." The reply was crisp and concise.

"Call the lead ship, advise them of our situation and tell them we're dropping out of formation. We can't keep up."

The windmilling prop continued to reduce the *Circuit Rider*'s speed, and Digger could see for himself that the formation was already pulling away at a noticeable rate of speed. His heart dropped and his adrenaline increased. There was safety in numbers as everyone on the bomber knew. Their flight formation was specifically designed to benefit the group and allow the B-17 gunners to cover one another, and while far from foolproof, the formation gave them at least some security against the formidable German fighters.

"Wilco." The radio operator's voice sounded less sure.

"We'll need a course for home," Deacon said. "Pilot to Navigator. Pilot to Navigator." He waited for a moment, and when no reply came he called to the bombardier. "Pilot to Bombardier. Tex, check on Lawrence."

"Wilco" came the drawl of the Texas-born bombardier.

Suddenly an excited voice broke onto the intercom. "Ball Gunner to Pilot! Ball Gunner to Pilot!"

"Pilot here, go ahead, Ball."

"Deac, that flak burst must've put some holes in the left wing. We have a fuel leak right behind number two engine!"

"How bad?" Deacon asked. Things were quickly going from bad to worse.

"Bad enough. There's a bunch of fuel in the slipstream."

Digger shook his head. If fuel was leaking out that badly, then the hole or holes had to be large enough that they'd defeat the self-sealing fuel tanks. He tried to steady his nerves, knowing that Deacon would know what to do.

"Pilot to Top Turret."

"Top here, sir."

"Davis, start transferring fuel from the port inboard tank," Deacon commanded.

"I'm already on it" came the clipped reply.

Digger knew Davis to be a good man, but he had a chip on his shoulder big enough to land an overloaded B-17. Davis had left a good life back in the States and never let anyone forget it. He resented the war and often appeared to resent his crewmates as well. *At least he knows his job*, Digger thought, with no more time to worry about Davis's attitude.

The increased vibrations caused by the windmilling prop gave Deacon and Digger more to concentrate on than a surly crew member. If they didn't get the prop under control, it could spell real disaster for them.

"Digger, keep trying to feather number two."

"I'm on it!" Digger snapped, the frustration of the moment putting an uncharacteristic edge to his tone.

Digger had always been rather nonchalant and easygoing, even in the face of adversity. His cavalier attitude was born out of figuring he had nothing to lose in trying whatever it took to stay alive. Getting home to Melody and his soon-to-be-born child was the only thing in life worth fighting for, as far as he was concerned. But this time, faced with a seriously crippled plane, Digger worried that his main objective might be compromised by circumstances beyond his control. Fear washed over him in waves of despair.

"Bombardier to Pilot!" Tex's normal slow drawl came across the radio unusually hurried, almost panicked. "Deac, it's Matt. He's been hit bad. He's losing blood! Oh . . . I mean . . . there's a lot of blood, Deac! Somebody get down here to help me!"

Digger felt his stomach tighten. They must have taken a much bigger hit than he'd figured.

Deacon appeared to be considering the matter before replying, "Davis, slip down and help out."

"Can't, sir," he replied. "I'm still transferring fuel."

"Pilot to Radio. Pilot to Radio."

"Radio here, sir."

"Come forward and help Tex."

"Wilco."

The bombardier's frantic voice interrupted the silence again. "I didn't know he was hit! I thought he was working a problem at the table. He was slumped over. I didn't know he was hit! There's blood everywhere, Deac!"

"Pilot to Bombardier. Settle down, Tex. Smitty's on his way forward to help you," Deacon said, his voice calm and reassuring.

"Hurry, he's bleeding to death. It looks like he got hit in the throat! He's bleeding bad."

"Keep the intercom clear, Tex, that's an order!" Deacon's authority rang clear.

Digger tried to focus on the job at hand. No doubt Deacon was already praying over the matter—not that Collin thought it would do much good. He could almost hear one of Deacon's speeches about God watching over them and seeing them through. Every time there was a crisis of any sort, Deacon always resorted to a moment or two of silent or spoken prayer before he pursued the matter any further. Digger always shook his head in disbelief. Moments of trouble called for action, not hokey religious mumbo jumbo.

As worried as Digger was about the navigator and plane, he knew they had other things to consider. Luftwaffe fighters loved to look for crippled or damaged bombers they could pounce on and shoot down. To the bomber crews these were the "boogeyman," more fearsome than flak because this enemy had eyes and could see you.

Digger might not have confidence in Deacon's prayers, but he had the utmost of confidence in the man as a pilot. He refused to make it easy on the enemy. He wouldn't give up without a fight. Digger figured Deacon would fly low and make it harder on the German fighters. Attacking at lower altitudes would increase the danger. The fighters wouldn't be as likely to dive on them for fear of being unable to pull up before crashing into the ground. The fighter's loss of speed would also give Deacon's *Circuit Rider* a better chance of hitting their target.

Then, as if reading Digger's mind, Deacon announced, "If we're going home single, then let's make it harder for the boogeyman to get us. Let's take her down to the deck nice and easy. We don't want to put any more strain on number two's prop than we have to. Also, keep an eye on number one—I'm not sure but it might be damaged too."

"Wilco," Digger replied, already working to comply. "So where are you hit and how bad?"

"It's my left leg and it doesn't seem too bad. Hurts some, but I'm all right." Deacon grinned from behind the oxygen mask and added, "You could always say a prayer for me—better put one in for Matt as well."

180

Digger frowned. "I don't think God would much appreciate my talking to Him, especially seeing as how I don't believe in Him."

"I think right about now might be a good time to start."

Digger turned away and pretended to check the instrument panel. He didn't want to admit that Deacon had a good point.

"Radio to Pilot. Radio to Pilot." Smitty's voice sounded through the headset.

"Pilot here. Go ahead, Radio."

"I'm up front. Sir, Lieutenant Lawrence is hit pretty bad. Looks like a piece of shrapnel went through his throat. There's a hole in the fuselage up here big enough to put my head through." Digger marveled at the calm and businesslike sound of Smitty's voice. "I've administered morphine and Tex is holding pressure to the wound. I'm thinking the artery in the neck has been severed. I don't know what we can do."

"Is there any way to clamp off the bleeding?" Deacon called.

"I wouldn't know, sir. We can try, but every time Tex releases pressure, blood goes everywhere. As it is, the bandages are getting soaked pretty fast. The cold air seems to slow it down a little, but it's not enough to keep him from bleeding to death." He paused as if to give Deacon a moment to take in the news before adding, "Another problem, sir, his oxygen mask has been perforated—it's like a sieve. He's not getting much oxygen. I'm using the walk-around bottle, but that won't last for long. You're going to need to get us below ten thousand."

"Roger that, Smitty. We're working on it."

Digger tried not to let the news distract him. Lawrence was dying. The crew would have heard everything over the intercom and now they'd be worried. It wasn't a good way to be when your life depended on staying focused.

Digger watched as Deacon glanced out his left window. "She's still windmilling," Deacon informed.

Digger knew if they dropped altitude too quickly, the strain might well cause the propeller shaft to break. This in turn could send the propeller cartwheeling through the fuselage like a giant buzz saw. Not a good thought at all.

Glancing back at the control panel, Digger noticed something alarming. The turn bank indicator and artificial horizon were out.

Glancing upward he noted the compass had been shattered as well. Minor problems except for the fact they were needed for negotiating the undercast of clouds that stretched out below them. *Shrapnel must have hit the instrument panel*, he thought. *That's just what we need.*

"Deac, the TBI and artificial horizon are gone. Compass too. It just doesn't get any better than this, does it?"

"I'm havin' a ball!"

"Tail Gunner to Pilot! Tail Gunner to Pilot! The excited voice of the tail gunner filled Deacon's headset.

"Pilot here."

"Bogey, five o'clock high!"

"Keep an eye on him, Tail Gunner," Deacon replied.

"Maybe it's a Little Friend," Digger offered, hoping the plane was an American P-47 or perhaps a British Spitfire catching up to them to shepherd them home.

"Tail to Pilot. Make that a bandit at five o'clock high. Looks like an ME-109!"

"I guess we're about to have someone crash our party."

Digger had just about had all he could take of war and its surprises. "Maybe it's just God sending an angel to take you home," he threw out snidely.

"Or the Devil coming for you," Deacon replied.

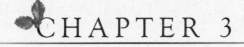

CHAPTER 3

"Oh, Ginny, this hurts so bad," Melody cried as another contraction ripped through her body. The young girl sat up in bed, grabbing her stomach. "Make it stop!"

"Now, Melody," Ginny said, reaching over to offer the girl comfort, "this is just the way it is. I can't make it stop. But soon enough this baby will be born and you'll be a proud new mommy and then you'll forget all about this pain."

Melody shook her head. "I'll never forget. I'm never having another baby!" She threw herself back against the pile of pillows and kept shaking her head from side to side.

Ginny sat down on the bed beside her. "Melody, listen to me for just a minute." Melody looked up, and Ginny wiped her face with a cool cloth before continuing. "I called Doc Ketterman and he can't get here just yet. The ice is making it too dangerous, but besides that, he's working on another patient, someone who was in a car accident and is doing pretty poorly. You and I are probably going to have to do this together. First babies generally take their time. You've not been in labor for any time at all. This could go on for some time and you need to conserve your energy."

"How long are you talking?" Melody questioned.

"I had contractions for two days when I had John," Ginny said with a smile. "Of course, my best friend had all of her babies in less than six hours. The last two were within less than half an hour of starting contractions. So you see, you can just never tell. The thing that's important is that you save your energy. The harder you fight this, the more tired out you're going to be."

"Two days?" the younger woman groaned. Tears formed in her eyes. "I can't stand it, Ginny. I'll never make it."

"Nonsense. Half of the battle is up here," she said, pointing to the girl's head. "You have to decide that you're going to give this baby every advantage. You don't have a right to be selfish anymore. You have to consider your child's needs first."

"I wish Collin were here," she sobbed. Things would be all right if only he were here.

"I wish he were too. Because if he were here, then John might be here as well. But they aren't here," Ginny added, pushing aside her worry. "So we have to do the best we can."

"I wish my mother were here," Melody said, turning her face to the pillow. Why did things have to be like this? A girl should at least have her mother nearby for an occasion like this. Maybe she should have Ginny call her. The thought intrigued Melody momentarily and took her mind off the labor. If Ginny called, then perhaps she could convince Melody's folks that they needed to forgive her and come to Longview. But just as quickly as the thought came, Melody decided against it. She could easily remember the look on her father's face and her mother's disappointment. She had broken their hearts, and as far as they were concerned, she was dead.

She cried quietly, wishing against all hope that a miracle could change her situation. That she could wake up safe and warm back home—that she could start over. She didn't want to say that she'd trade Collin and the baby, she just wished she could have had them both under different circumstances.

"Your contractions are nearly twenty minutes apart," Ginny announced, "so it'll probably be a little while before this young one makes his or her appearance."

Melody opened her eyes and turned to faced Ginny. "I'm so tired."

"I know, sweetheart. But," Ginny said with a smile, "you are getting the very best of all Christmas gifts. You will have the best of all presents to remind you of our Savior's birth."

Melody looked back at Ginny and shook her head. "I don't want to think about God. Collin says it's questionable if God even exists, and given the way my folks have acted, I'm beginning to think he's right."

Ginny was undaunted. "Melody, ever since you came to live with me, you've been making comments like that. Who do you think provided for you in your hour of need?"

"You did," Melody replied.

"No, child. God did. God put my son and your husband together. God allowed me to have the heart and compassion to care about someone in your predicament, and God caused all of us to come together in such a way that we could help one another."

"Collin says it's just dumb luck," Melody said, drying her eyes with the sleeve of her flannel nightgown. She hadn't been brought up to believe that way, but in her anger, Collin's suggestion made her feel justified in ignoring God.

"Well, I don't believe in luck, dumb or otherwise," Ginny replied. "I believe in God's divine direction. Why, even the birth of Jesus was divinely directed."

"Why do you say that?"

Ginny smiled. "Jesus was born to a family who made their home in Nazareth. They lived a long ways from the town of Bethlehem, yet that's where the Bible prophets foretold the Savior would be born. So God did a little bit of work here and there and low and behold, the ruler of the day decided he needed to count heads. He put out an order to get everyone to go back to the city that their families were originally from. Now, Joseph was from the lineage of David. You remember stories about King David, don't you?"

"The one who killed the giant?" Melody questioned.

"Exactly the same." Ginny leaned over to the nightstand and rinsed out the washcloth in cool water. Handing it to Melody, she continued. "Now, because Joseph was betrothed to Mary, he took her along as well. Can you imagine riding on the back of a donkey in your condition?"

Melody actually smiled. "I wouldn't want to ride in a *car* in my condition."

Laughing, Ginny took back the cloth after Melody wiped her face. "The point is, God wanted to fulfill prophecy. He had a plan. A divine plan for His only Son to be born in Bethlehem. He had to move in a ruler's heart and mind, and in turn this moved a nation of people into action, and all in order to bring two very special people to the place they needed to be. He had it much easier in bringing you and Collin into my life."

Melody relented and considered Ginny's words quite seriously. "If that is true, then God would also have a reason for making my parents react so heartlessly with me. I don't like to think of God being that way."

"There are all sorts of influences on folks," Ginny said. "Could be God wanted your parents to react another way and instead they turned from His will and looked to their own. Either way, I think once they calm down and see what's been done, they'll want you back in their lives again. You and Collin and this baby."

"But what if they don't?" Melody questioned soberly. The thought struck terror in her heart. She loved her parents. She loved her little sisters. And she missed them all desperately.

"I'm sure they'll come around, and until they do, you can just stay with me. Even if you have to wait until the war is over and Collin comes home, you'll have a place. I have no one else to worry over."

Melody allowed doubt to creep into her heart. She gripped Ginny's hand tightly. "But what if Collin doesn't come home?"

"We won't cross that bridge until we need to. No sense going down a path that neither of us wants to travel. No matter what happens," the older woman assured, "I will be here for you, just as I hope you will be here for me."

"Ohhh!" Melody moaned. "It's starting again." She rolled to her side and drew her knees up as best she could to stave off the contraction. In her heart she wanted to pray, but fear kept her from crying out to God. Fear that He wouldn't hear her. And worse yet, fear that even if He did, He no longer cared.

Two and a half hours later, Melody was no closer to delivering her baby. Her contractions still came between fifteen and twenty minutes apart and her hope was fading.

Ginny took time away from the girl to fix herself some breakfast. She didn't feel all that hungry, but she knew it might well be a long day and an even longer night. Slicing a bit of ham, she made a sandwich. With this and a cup of coffee, Ginny sat down at the kitchen table and began to pray.

"Oh, Father, I come to you with a heavy heart," she began. Then worrying that Melody might overhear her, Ginny prayed silently. She'd been thinking about John and Collin and couldn't help but wonder if they were in some sort of jeopardy.

I don't know why I feel so worried about my boy, Lord, but he's been on my mind all day. You know how concerned I've been. I don't mean to worry and doubt that you have it all under control. I'd do well to take my own advice and give it over to you. But, Father, I just don't know what to do.

Call Mrs. Meggison.

Ginny looked around the room. The voice had seemed very audible. But there was no one else in the room. She felt a slight chilling sensation go up her spine. *Lord, are you trying to tell me to call Melody's mama?*

The silence in the room was not at all reassuring. *What did I expect?* She chuckled and said a silent thanks for the food. *If God wants me to call, He'll make it clear, even if He puts the call through himself.*

Just then the telephone rang. Ginny nearly jumped three feet into the air. Getting up quickly she answered the phone, half expecting Melody's mother to be on the other end of the line.

"Ginny, it's Ruth Bennett," the voice came.

"Ruthie," Ginny said in relief. "What can I do for you?"

"I called to see if you needed anything. The ice is really bad. Marion said everything that wasn't already closed down is shut up tight as a drum. We just wanted to make sure you and Melody had enough wood and anything else you might need."

"That's good of you, Ruthie. Truth is, I haven't paid much attention. Melody went into labor early this morning. We've been waiting to see how things progress, but so far the baby is just taking his dear sweet time."

"Better be careful about saying it's a boy," Ruth chuckled. "Girls can be just as stubborn in coming."

"Well, Melody wants a boy so badly, I guess I'd just begun to believe that's what she'd have. I tell you, if sheer willpower has anything to say over it, then she'll have a son. Say, that reminds me. How's Rachel feeling these days?"

"Oh, she's just fine. Baby isn't due for another couple of months. David is half beside himself worrying over her. I've never seen a young man more devoted. He's the best son-in-law a mother could ask for."

"I'm sure he is," Ginny replied. She'd often seen David and

Rachel Cohen at church, and it was her belief that no couple was more suited to each other. David's arm had been permanently injured when the Japanese had attacked Pearl Harbor in '41. The doctors had worked diligently with him, but David was still unable to have much use of the arm. He didn't let it stop him, however.

"Well, I guess I shouldn't keep you," Ruth said. "If you need anything, just holler. We're within walking distance and even with the ice, we'll get to you if you need us."

"Thanks, Ruthie. I appreciate your concern."

"We'll be praying for Melody," Ruth added.

"Thanks. I know we'll need all the help we can get."

Ginny hung up the telephone feeling only marginally better. She stood there looking at the wall phone for several moments. She had written down the Meggisons' California number some time ago. Surely it couldn't hurt to just call and let them know that Melody was all right. She wouldn't have to say where Melody was, but as one mother to another, Ginny couldn't help but feel that Melody's mother was probably grief-stricken. Ginny knew *she* would be—she knew she was. She had no idea where John was and would have given the world if someone would call just to let her know he was all right.

She stepped over to the kitchen counter and opened a drawer. There among the dish towels, toward the back of the drawer, Ginny had put the slip of paper with Ralph and Louise Meggison's telephone number.

"Lord, if this is your will and not just my hopeful thinking, let them answer right away. I won't call a second time if I don't get ahold of anyone this time," she promised, heading for the telephone.

Cranking the handle, Ginny rang for the operator. "Hello, Mary Beth, I need to call long distance."

She waited patiently for the long-distance operator to come on the line. Finally, when the entire matter was settled, Ginny heard the telephone ring on the other end.

"I have your number," the operator said in a singsong voice.

"Thank you," Ginny said, her heart racing as she waited to see who would answer.

"Hello?" a woman's voice sounded distant and scratchy through the lines.

"Go ahead, Longview," the operator told Ginny.

"Mrs. Meggison?" Ginny questioned.

"No, I'm sorry, the Meggisons don't live here anymore" came the reply.

Ginny's heart sank. She didn't know what to say. Apparently God didn't want her getting in touch with the family and this was His way of interceding.

"They moved a while back. Are you a friend?"

Ginny sighed. "In a roundabout way, I guess you could call me that. I'm caring for their daughter while her husband is in the service."

"Oh my!" the woman grew excited. "You have Melody there with you?"

"Yes," Ginny replied. "She's gone into labor and I figured on letting her folks know."

"Where are you?"

"Longview, Washington."

"Oh my!" the woman repeated. "I'm Melody's cousin Ann. Her folks are living in Portland now. I can give you their address and new telephone number."

Ginny felt her spirits lift. "Portland? Why, that's hardly any distance at all. They could be here in a few hours. Well, if it weren't for the ice," Ginny added.

"I know they'd love to be with her. They've been heartsick since she left. All of us have been. Their grief was so bad and their anger at the church so great, they up and moved. Melody's father came back once in all that time, hoping and praying that maybe Melody would find her way home. That's why I'm here. They didn't want to change the number or have any chance of Melody losing a single connection to them."

"I'm so blessed to hear that," Ginny admitted. "She's hurting something fierce over all of this, and I know it would do her a world of good to have them here. To have their forgiveness."

"I know you're right," Ann replied. "Please tell her I'm thinking of her, and if you'll wait just a minute, I'll get that new number for you."

While Ginny waited, she offered up a prayer of thanks. Not only did it appear God wanted her to tell Melody's folks about the baby, He'd even managed to move them close enough that if the weather cleared, they could probably be here for the birth of their first grandchild.

Ann returned and Ginny quickly jotted down the number. "Thank you so very much. I know this will be the best of Christmas gifts for Melody." She said her good-byes and went through the entire process of calling long distance once again. All the while, Ginny prayed, and when at last another female voice, this one older and less enthusiastic, sounded on the phone, Ginny hoped all would be well.

"Mrs. Meggison?" Ginny questioned.

"Yes."

"My name is Virginia Williams. You don't know me, but your daughter Melody is staying with me."

The silence on the other end of the line was soon broken by the unmistakable sound of crying. "Is she all right?" the woman struggled to ask.

Ginny felt her heart nearly break for the woman's pain. "She's doing very well. In fact, the reason I'm calling is because she's gone into labor. I thought you might like to know. I even thought you might like to be with her."

"Oh, I can't tell you what this means to me," the woman said. "I've worried so much about her. We were so harsh with her—it was the shock, you know. We never meant to hurt her. Oh, we've been so heartbroken ever since she went away. Are you sure she's all right? Can she come to the telephone?"

"She's just fine," Ginny assured, "but it would be difficult for her to come to the telephone. She's having pretty solid contractions and she's very miserable. I think it would comfort her a great deal if you were here. I called your old number, and Ann told me you were living in Portland. I'm just up the way in Longview, not so very far from Vancouver. I don't know how long she'll be laboring, but you'd be welcome here at my house anytime you choose to come."

The woman's tone perked up. "Tomorrow's Christmas!" she exclaimed. "Oh, this is the best present of all. I'll come as soon as I can. I don't know how for sure, but I'll find a way. Maybe I can get a seat on the bus."

Ginny gave the woman her address and directions for getting to her place from the bus station. "We're having trouble with ice," Ginny told her. "We don't usually get anything like this so early on, but everything is shut down tight. If you can't get here for a few days, don't worry about it. I'm sure Melody will just be excited to know you're coming."

"Oh, please don't tell her. Let it be a surprise," Mrs. Meggison suggested.

Ginny smiled. "As you like."

"Oh, thank you again, Mrs. Williams, and Merry Christmas. You've given me the only thing I really wanted—to know that my child is safe."

Ginny smiled and bid the woman good-bye. Now, if someone could just let her know that her Johnny was safe.

CHAPTER 4

After playing hide-and-seek with the German fighter, Digger was beginning to have hope that they'd eluded him. Without the proper instruments, they were asking for trouble as they dodged in and out of the clouds. Not only this, but the sun was gradually moving west and soon it would be evening.

"Pilot to Radio. Pilot to Radio. How's Matt?"

"Radio to Pilot. He's all clammy and pale, Deac. He wakes up now and then and tries to talk, but I can't make it out."

"Let me know if anything changes."

"Wilco."

"Tail Gunner to Pilot. Tail Gunner to Pilot."

"Pilot here."

"The boogeyman's back at seven o'clock!" the excited voice announced.

"Keep him away from us," Deacon replied, looking to Digger. "Guess we're not out of this yet."

"He's turning into our six—here he comes! I'm on him!" the tail gunner exclaimed.

Pilot and co-pilot exchanged a worried glance. They could only hope that the tail's twin .50s could take care of their little problem.

"He's breaking low! He's going under us! Ball Turret, get him! Get him!" The tail gunner's excited cry sounded more like the encouragement he might call to a baseball teammate during a close game than the deadly reality of their situation.

"I'm on him, he's mine!" the ball turret gunner, also known as the "Two Gun Kid," exclaimed.

The ball turret's guns fired in short, measured bursts that shook the plane in a staccato pulse.

"Ah, shoot! I missed. Not even tail feathers! My pappy would chew me out for that one for sure." The Kid's laconic Kentucky twang filled the intercom.

"Can the chatter," Deacon interrupted in his command voice. "Pilot to Crew, did we take any hits?"

"Negative" came the reply from several stations.

The 109 was going twice the speed of the crippled B-17, but Digger knew Deacon wasn't about to admit defeat.

"He might come back for a head-on pass," Deacon announced. They all knew the probability of just such an attack was likely, given that this was one of the Luftwaffe's favorite tactics.

"Pilot to Top Gunner. Davis, are you back in your turret?"

"Roger."

"Keep your eyes peeled forward. That 109 may well make a head-on pass at us."

"Roger, Deac."

They were dependent upon Davis's twin .50s should the 109 make a gunnery run at the nose. In fact, Davis's guns were the only forward guns able to bear on the target, since the bombardier was busy keeping the navigator from bleeding to death.

Digger licked his dry lips. His mouth tasted like the inside of an old boot, compliments of the oxygen mask he'd finally been able to discard. Smitty kept oranges just for such occasions, but there just wasn't time for such luxuries.

"Pilot to Radio."

"Radio here, sir."

"Smitty, have you got Matt stabilized enough that you can get back to the radio compartment?"

"You need to watch the evasive action, sir. Tex is holding his artery closed with his bare hand. He's as stable as we can get him, sir."

"Then get me a fix and a bearing home."

"Wilco."

Knowing Smitty to have the most military professionalism of anyone on the plane, Digger had faith the young man would have the problem resolved in a flash. But before he could voice this to Deacon, something attracted his attention straight ahead.

"Deac, bandit, twelve o'clock high and closing!" Digger called. The tiny black speck continued to grow as it rapidly approached the B-17.

"Get him, Davis!" Deacon ordered as the 109 became clearly visible.

Tracer rounds passed over the cockpit, making a sound that resembled hail on a tin roof as it hit the aircraft. Davis returned fire at the same time, the sound of the guns and the odor of burnt cordite filling the cockpit.

"Davis, did you get him?" Deacon called.

"I got pieces, Deac," the top gunner answered. "And I have a problem."

Deacon held his breath. They didn't need any more problems.

"Some of the 109's shells hit the turret. The turret's jammed facing nine o'clock. Can't get it to move."

"Are you okay, Davis?"

"Just some scratches on my face—nothing I can't handle."

Digger couldn't help but wonder what they would do if the 109 decided to make another forward attack without the top turret operating properly. The thought was apparently on his pilot's mind as well.

Deacon exchanged a glance with Digger. "Roger that, Davis, can you fix the turret?" he questioned.

"Negative, but I'll keep trying," Davis called back, frustration replacing his usual cocky tone.

"Right Waist to Pilot. Right Waist to Pilot."

"Go ahead, Walt."

"Deac, I saw pieces as the 109 flew by, but no smoke."

"Great," Deacon muttered. "We may have hit him, but that doesn't mean he's out of commission."

"Captain," Smitty radioed uncharacteristically informal, "we've got another problem."

"I don't want another problem," Deacon said, shaking his head.

Digger rolled his gaze skyward. "I can see those prayers of yours are really doing the job, Deac."

Deacon ignored his co-pilot's sarcasm. "God's doing His job, make sure you do yours. What's the problem, Smitty?"

"Looks like a twenty-millimeter cannon round exploded in the radio compartment. The intercom is obviously working, but the radio is out."

"Can you fix it?" Deacon questioned.

"Negative, sir. Marconi couldn't fix this set. It's in pieces."

"Maybe God could fix it," Digger suggested. "How about a special radio prayer. Do they have one of those?" He knew he wasn't being fair to Deacon, but his fears were rapidly dissolving any positive thoughts.

Deacon's face flushed red in anger, but he said nothing.

This only made Digger feel worse. He'd been a burr under Deacon's saddle ever since Melody's parents, the only other religious people Digger knew, had rejected their daughter. Deacon had tried to explain the difference between being religious and being spiritual, but Digger figured the two were identical and both were a pain.

While Deacon seemed to collect his thoughts and most likely pray, Digger looked out from the window. They needed to figure out what to do next. Because of their evasive action in and out of the clouds, Digger had no idea where England was. And without a radio or a navigator to get them a bearing, they could wander around until they ran out of gas and never come anywhere near their base.

Normally, they could have counted somewhat on visual reference and compass bearing, but looking below he found nothing but cloud cover. Were they over France? Over the Channel? He had no way of knowing, and without a radio fix they could well believe they were headed to England when in fact they were headed back to France.

"Send an angel to guide us, Lord," Deac prayed aloud.

"Amen, Deac" came the voice of the right waist gunner.

Digger had long ago learned of Walt's shared faith in Jesus. Deacon said it gave him great comfort to know that someone else was praying. *"Where two or more are gathered in my name . . ."* The old verse came to Digger's mind from childhood. He pushed it aside, but in doing so he felt even more weary. He was tired. Tired of battling the vibrating plane. Tired of hearing the announcement of one crisis after another. Just plain tired. It was Christmas Eve. He should be home listening to carols on the radio. Home with his beautiful wife.

"Angels, huh?" Digger finally said, refusing to give in to his exhaustion. "Why not just ask for winged Pegasus as well?"

Deacon took a deep breath and looked around him as if trying to make a decision. "Digger, I'm thinking we've been heading more or less in a northerly direction since we dropped formation. Even given the jinking and evasive action, we're probably north of the Pas de Calais—"

"Wait a minute, Deac. We don't know that for sure. Since we were hiding in the clouds, it's hard telling what kind of drift or turning we did. We were doing well just to keep ourselves right side up," Digger interrupted. "I'm thinking with the bum engine we've probably been pulled to the northeast. That would put us running parallel to the French coast and heading east."

"If we turn ninety degrees from our present heading," Deac said, appearing to do the calculations in his head, "and if we're traveling at a hundred and twenty knots per hour . . . ." He fell silent for a moment. "We'll know within ten minutes whether we're over England or France."

"Wait a minute, we could be over Germany for all we know. We don't know where we are. That's the point."

"Well, we have to do something," Deacon said. "And since I'm in charge, we're going to turn ninety degrees from our present heading and see what happens."

"And what are we going to do if that 109 comes back? Pray? Throw Bibles at it? We have no top gun. If that 109 makes another head-on run at us, we're in trouble."

"By my calculations, Digger, we're already in trouble. What difference will it make?"

"Well, I'd just kind of like to make it back home in one piece," Digger said.

"I think we'd all like that, Digger. I could take a vote," Deacon said, his patience obviously wearing thin, "but I'm pretty sure everyone would give me an affirmative on that one."

"You think you have all the answers, don't you?" Digger said angrily. He hated this lack of control over their circumstances. He hated feeling they were simply out there somewhere without any hope of making it back.

"No, I don't think that at all, Digger. But I know who does have the answers. And furthermore, I'm not afraid to ask for help. But you are."

"Are you talking about the kind of help like Melody's parents gave?"

Deacon looked at his co-pilot rather sympathetically. "Digger, they were just hurt and disappointed. They're only human."

"Well, I don't need their kind in my life."

"Are you going to deny Melody the right to see her folks? What about the baby? Are you going to keep the baby from his grandparents? You're all one family now. After the war, you're going to have to find a way to put this all behind you and if not through the power of God, then what?" Deacon questioned.

Digger shrugged and looked away. "Maybe I don't see it like you do. I can keep Melody happy. She won't need her folks and neither will I." He didn't really convince himself with the words and was certain he hadn't convinced Deacon.

"Maybe, maybe not. But one thing is for certain," Deacon said quite seriously, "you're going to need something."

"I know. I know. Don't preach at me." Digger's voice betrayed his exasperation. "You think I need religion."

"I think you need God."

"Same thing."

"No, Digger. It isn't. He isn't a man-made religion. God is so much more than what most religions allow Him to be. He isn't limiting like Melody's parents suggest. He can forgive sin and does so on a regular basis."

"How would you know?"

Deacon smiled. "Because He forgives me."

"I thought you were perfect. Saved and sanctified and cleansed by the blood!" Digger said as if he'd taken to a pulpit. He could hear those words from his folks and grandparents as if it were yesterday. He could remember songs they'd sung on Sunday morning with words so vivid about forgiveness and redemption.

"All of the latter, but not perfect," Deacon answered. "I'm forgiven and there is a difference."

Digger scowled and kept his focus straight ahead. "Well, let it be your difference, then. I don't see it that way now and I'm not going to see it that way later. Provided there is a later."

"Well, we don't have the luxury of waiting around here," Deacon said, deciding the time had come to execute his plan. "We're going to turn ninety degrees from our heading and see where that gets us."

"Pilot to crew. We're making a ninety-degree turn off of our current heading. Keep your eyes open for landfall and don't forget that 109 is still out there somewhere."

"Roger, Deac" came a unison chorus.

CHAPTER 5

"Melody," Ginny said rather gravely, "I think we have a problem."

The older woman had just checked the baby's progress and to her great consternation, found that the baby was breech.

"Problem?" the girl asked rather shaken. "Is the baby all right?"

Ginny tried to sound confident. "I believe so, for the time. But he's backward. He's coming bottom first and that isn't good."

"What can we do?"

Ginny heard the terror in the girl's voice. She reached up and smoothed back Melody's blond, sweat-soaked hair. "I'm going to call Doc Ketterman and see if he's been freed up to head our way. You're far enough along that I don't think we can safely move you to the hospital, even if I could get someone out in this ice. We're going to have to do what we can and trust the rest to God."

"I'm so scared, Ginny. Please don't let my baby die!" Melody began to sob uncontrollably, and Ginny knew she had to get the girl calm.

"Look, you can't give yourself over to this kind of spell. You need your energy, and crying and such is only going to wear you out. Why don't you write a letter while I go try to get ahold of the doctor," Ginny suggested. She reached over to the nightstand and pulled open the drawer. Inside she found paper and a pencil. "Write to Collin. Tell him how excited you are. Tell him how much you love him. Tell him anything."

Melody took the paper and pencil and allowed Ginny to help her onto her side. Ginny then brought a book for Melody to use for a writing surface. Seeing that the girl was as comfortable as possible, she went to make her call.

"Mary Beth," Ginny said, reaching the operator, "I need to get a call through to Doc Ketterman."

"Has the baby come yet?" the operator questioned.

"No, and it's going to be a while in coming. Looks to be breech and I need to talk to the doctor."

"Poor lamb. What a shame to go through such a time with your first baby. You know I had three children and all three were head down and easy as pie. Of course, my sister Annabelle, now, she had trouble right from the start. Poor thing had to go to bed for her entire time of confinement."

"I remember," Ginny said, trying to remain patient. "I helped deliver her babies as well as yours, if you recall."

"Of course I remember. I still have all my faculties."

The woman was clearly offended, but Ginny didn't have time to worry over such things. Mary Beth always had a penchant for discussing everyone's business and never once did it occur to her that she was being a gossip or a bore.

The phone was ringing now and Mary Beth was silent. No doubt she'd listen in on the entire conversation.

"Hello?" came the voice at the other end of the line. The weather made the connection sound nearly as poor as the long-distance call Ginny had made earlier in the day.

"This is Ginny Williams again. Could I talk to the doctor?"

"I'm afraid he's gone. He went with my pa to help old Gus Ferguson to the hospital," replied the young woman.

"I see," Ginny replied, wondering what she should do next.

"You want me to connect you to the hospital?" Mary Beth asked without waiting for another word to be spoken.

"Yes, Mary Beth," Ginny answered, "I suppose that would be the best."

But the news was not good. Doc Ketterman hadn't shown up yet and the nurse had no time to discuss much of anything with Ginny.

"It's like we've got our own private war going on," the woman told Ginny. "The ice has caused several accidents."

"I'm sure sorry to hear that," Ginny said. "I have a young woman here who is about to deliver a breech baby. I need to talk to Doc Ketterman to see what I should do."

"Can you turn the baby?" the woman questioned. "That's always best. I know you've had experience in nursing. Haven't you delivered a breech?"

"Yes, I have," Ginny replied, "but I haven't kept up much with modern medicine. I thought maybe there were new techniques—things to make it go easier."

"Not really," the woman replied. "See if you can't just push the baby back up enough to turn him. If he's stuck solid in the birthing canal, you may not have a chance to do this."

"I remember," Ginny said, none too happy. She hung up the telephone in despair. "Lord, I need you. Now more than ever, I need you."

Up until that moment, the reality of what was happening hadn't really sunk in. Now Ginny realized she was most likely going to be Melody's only help in this delivery. She went quickly to the linen closet and pulled out several towels and extra sheets. Next, she went to the back porch and pulled down the galvanized tub from the wall. She'd have to scour this out good, but then she'd be able to use it for keeping things clean—herself, Melody, and hopefully the baby.

Melody cried out and Ginny glanced quickly at the clock. The contractions were only about ten minutes apart now. There was no telling how much longer this would go on. Ginny had seen stubborn babies before and breech deliveries were always questionable.

"I'll be there in a minute, Melody. Just bite down on that washcloth I gave you," Ginny called to the girl.

"Father," she said as she scrubbed out the tub, "I feel completely inadequate to this task, but you surely know that. I'm praying that you will guide me to know what I'm to do. This poor girl is so alone right now and she's scared and hurting. Lord, please make it easy on her. Ease her mind of worry and deliver her safely of this child."

Once the tub was scoured and drying beside the sink, Ginny built a fire in the stove and began heating water. She tried to think of all the things she'd need. Scissors, string, baby blankets, towels, and water. Her mind raced with thoughts of what she'd do if things went wrong. She wasn't in any way capable of performing emergency surgery on the poor woman. If the baby refused to be born or got stuck, the outlook was grim.

She shook the thought from her head and carried the tub into Melody's room. She cleared the top of the nightstand and placed the tub there. Melody was still on her side and still trying to write her letter to Collin.

"I'm going to gather some things we'll need," Ginny told Melody. "Then I'm going to have to check the baby again."

"Please hurry," Melody said, looking up mournfully at Ginny. "I don't want to be alone." Her voice was barely a whisper.

Ginny hurried around the house, gathering everything she thought might be useful. Last of all she checked the water and found it sufficiently hot and brought it with her to pour into the tub.

"I'll be right back. I'm going to put some more water on to boil. It makes the house warmer anyway, and we just might need it in the long run."

Melody moaned. "Oh, hurry, Ginny. I feel so strange."

Ginny worried at this statement and rushed back to the kitchen to put on the water. Usually when women commented on feeling strange, they were transitioning into the stage of labor where they were ready to push. She glanced at the wall and saw that not even five minutes had passed since Melody's previous contraction. The pains were coming closer together.

Ginny steadied her nerves and rolled up her sleeves. There was no putting this off. The baby would come in its own time and she supposed Doc Ketterman would do the same.

Helping Melody to roll onto her back, Ginny went to work checking the position of the baby. The baby was wedged tight and refused to budge, even when Ginny tried her hardest to push the baby back. Melody screamed in pain as Ginny tried one more time to adjust the baby.

"I'm so sorry, child," she whispered. "This isn't very comfortable, and I know you're hurting. The thing is, if I can get the baby to turn around and come head first, it'll be much easier for both of you."

"Don't mind me," Melody said, between clenched teeth. "Do whatever you have to. Just help my baby."

"I want to help you both," Ginny said, trying to maintain a smile. "But it looks like this baby is coming bottom first and that's that."

Melody cried out in pain and grabbed for the iron railing at the head of the bed. "The baby's coming now!"

Ginny felt Melody's abdomen tighten. "Do you feel like you have to push?"

"Yes!" Melody cried. "I can't . . . I have to . . . push." Her moans gradually built to a crescendoing scream. "Make it stop!"

Ginny patted her gently. "You have to stop fighting it. This baby is coming whether you like it or not." She reached up and wiped Melody's forehead. The young woman's blue eyes pleaded with Ginny to put an end to her misery.

"I'm going to die, aren't I?" Melody said, suddenly much calmer.

"Goodness, child, every new mama thinks that," Ginny said reassuringly.

"No, this is different. Oh, I wish Collin were here. I just want to see him one more time. I just need to be with him—to know he's safe. Ginny, you will give him my letter, won't you?"

Ginny glanced to the half-written missive at the girl's side. "Not until you finish it up. You'll have a chance to write some more after the baby's born."

Melody gritted her teeth and strained against the pain that was coming much more quickly now. "I . . . won't . . . get a chance. Just . . . ahhh . . . just give it . . . to Collin."

Ginny could see that the baby was edging ever closer to birth. "It shouldn't be too long now, Melody."

"Promise me," Melody said, gasping for breath, "promise you'll take care of the baby if I die."

"Stop being so morbid," Ginny commanded. In truth she was already worried about both mother and baby and she didn't need Melody's reminder that things were far from right.

"Please, Ginny. Take care of the baby until you can talk to Collin. He'll know what to do."

Ginny grimaced as Melody pushed harder than ever to expel the baby. "Melody, there is one way you can help the baby." She remembered another breech delivery from many years ago. An older woman, a local midwife, had instructed the mother to continue pushing during the final delivery moments and not let up until the woman told her otherwise. This had seemed to help keep the woman's body from clamping down on the baby's neck and thus strangling the poor infant before a full delivery could be made.

"When the baby begins to come out, I want you to keep pushing until I tell you to stop. Do you understand me?"

Melody let go of the metal railing and pushed the hair from her face. "I think so."

"It's very important and it's one way you can really help the baby."

"I'll do whatever you tell me," she said rather weakly.

The pains were coming again and Ginny knew it wouldn't be long. She readied herself as best she could and gave up another prayer for guidance.

"Ginny," Melody managed to say, "please pray for me. Pray for my baby."

Ginny saw the girl's desperation. "I already have," she told her, reaching up to give her hand a squeeze. "You might try saying a prayer yourself."

Melody nodded. "I am, Ginny. I am. I just hope God is listening."

"He is, darling. I promise you, He is."

Just then Melody let out a cry and reached desperately to the head rail. Her scream filled the air as the contraction ripped through her body. Ginny saw that the time had come. The baby was nearly out. "Melody, listen to me. You need to push with all your might and keep pushing no matter what. Do you hear me?"

"Yes!" she gasped against the pain.

Ginny took up a towel and prepared to help the infant into the world. "Now, Melody. Push and keep pushing."

The girl gave it her all, and Ginny was proud of her for her efforts. She knew it couldn't be easy given the circumstance, but it was the only way that Ginny knew to give the baby an edge in delivery.

Reaching up, Ginny gently pulled at the baby's midsection as the shoulders began to slide forward. *Please, God,* she said as she continued to guide the infant out, *please let this baby be all right.*

But then things seemed to come to a halt. The baby seemed stuck and Ginny was hard-pressed to know what to do. Melody was no longer pushing with as much force and her body was tiring of the delivery.

"Push, Melody! Push hard," Ginny instructed, feeling the sense of urgency mount. There wasn't much time.

She saw Melody bear down, knowing that the girl was probably giving her last bit of strength to this supreme effort. Ginny pulled, worrying that she was pulling too hard but certain that if she did nothing, the baby would remain stuck in place.

Then, as if by a miracle, the baby slid free from the birth canal and into Ginny's hands. A tiny, blue-skinned baby boy lay still and unmoving. Ginny looked up to see if Melody had noticed and found that the girl had passed out. Maybe it was better this way.

Ginny quickly tied off the cord and cut it, but still the baby showed no sign of life. She remembered a time when her father had helped a ewe with a twin delivery. One of the lambs wasn't breathing when it was born, and after clearing its breathing passages, her father had taken a warm towel and rubbed the lamb vigorously.

Gently, Ginny cleared the baby's face and nose, then ran a finger in its mouth to make sure there was nothing blocking the airway. Next, she rubbed the baby's chest and backside as roughly as she dared.

"Please, little one, you must live," she whispered, trying to coax the baby boy back to life.

At first, it was just a flutter, and then the tiny chest began to move. Ginny saw this first sign of life as the most marvelous of miracles. She continued rubbing the baby and praying.

"Please, God, help this little one. Help Melody and her son!"

A cry rang out. It was the most beautiful and awe-inspiring sound Ginny had ever heard. It started as a tiny whimper and then as oxygen filled the baby's lungs, it grew louder—more sure. Soon the baby was squalling like any normal, healthy child.

"Oh, thank you, Father!" Ginny declared, hurrying to clean the baby so that she could get him wrapped in warm blankets.

She had little time to pay attention to Melody but glanced over to see that the girl was still unconscious. Ginny had paid so much attention to the baby that she hadn't even noticed the great amount of blood coming from the young mother.

"Oh no," she cried, realizing they were far from out of the woods.

CHAPTER 6

"Bombardier to Pilot."

"Pilot here. What's up, Tex?"

"I don't think Matt's going to make it. My hand's half frozen from holding his neck, but there's still bleeding."

"Just keep trying, Tex," Deacon said, catching Digger's doubtful expression. "We can't give up."

"He was awake a minute ago but he's out again."

"Just do what you can. Smitty will be coming back to help you." Deacon fought to hold the yoke while the plane shook violently as they turned and descended. Digger did what he could to help, but Deacon knew his co-pilot didn't agree with his decision.

"Radio to Pilot. Radio to Pilot."

Deacon couldn't afford to take his hands from the yoke, so he had to delay on his reply until he could master the turn. Finally they evened out. "Pilot to Radio. What's up, Smitty?"

"Matt's awake again. He's asking for you. Keeps saying something else. We're trying to understand him. He says 'Deac' clear as a bell, but I'm not sure what else."

"Try to keep him quiet. It can't be good for him to be talking," Deacon replied. He wished he could go to the man, but there was no way. Even if he could leave the responsibility of the plane to Digger, the nose was overcrowded with the three men already in position there.

This isn't how I figured to spend Christmas Eve, Lord. Deac knew the only comfort he had was in praying. He figured this would be a quick hop and then he'd be back at the base enjoying turkey and all the trimmings. The meal they'd been promised would have dispelled any belief in the fact that rations were hard to come by in England. Deacon had always eaten well, especially on flight days when they were given the best of everything. Real eggs and butter, bacon—even if it was that funny round English-style stuff. His stomach growled and he realized he was getting pretty hungry. This short hop was rapidly turning into a lengthy journey, and soon they were going to have the problem of whether or not they had enough gas to even make it back to base.

"Radio to Pilot!" The voice was animated, excited.

"Go ahead, Smitty," Deacon replied.

"He's saying pray, Deac. Matt's askin' you to pray."

"Repeat that, Radio," Deacon said, uncertain he'd understood.

"Matt wants you to pray for him. He said it as clear as a bell, then he passed out again."

Deacon smiled, and even Digger had no smart-aleck reply. "Of course I'll pray," Deacon said, touching his throat mic. "Father in heaven, I'm asking you to help us. We're in a bad way. We can't see to find our way home and we have no radio communication. Added to that, our friend Matt Lawrence is gravely wounded. He asked me to pray, so I figure that means he'd talk to you himself if he could.

"God, we know you have a plan for each man's life. We know this because the Bible tells us so. You have a plan for Matt, as well as each of the rest of us. We're trusting you for that plan. Your Word says that all we have to do to accept Jesus is to confess our sins and turn from evil. It also says that Jesus is the only way to have eternal life, so that even if our planned days here on earth are finished, we know we can go on forever in heaven with you. You know our hearts. Please hear us today and please bring us home."

"Amen" came assuring replies from all over the plane.

Deacon felt his heart fill with hope, and even though Digger remained silent, he seemed to be thoughtfully considering Deacon's words.

They flew in silence for several minutes and for the first time since they'd taken the hit, Deacon felt himself relaxing. He just knew things were going to be all right. He knew God would guide them home.

"Radio to Pilot," Smitty's voice sounded once again.

"Pilot here, go ahead, Smitty."

"Deac, I've got cloud break, but I don't think you're going to like what I see."

"What is it, Smitty?" Deacon exchanged a hesitant glance with

Digger, who in turn tried hard to see beyond the front of the plane.

"We're over water, Deac. Not just a little water either. I don't see anything but water."

Deacon felt his heart sink. They shouldn't be over water. They should be over land—over England. What was he going to do now? He'd taken a gamble with the turn, but there wasn't enough fuel to keep making those kinds of risks.

He looked at Digger and realized that his co-pilot had probably been right in assessing their position. "Well, Dig, looks like you had a better feel for it than I did," Deacon admitted. "What do you suggest we do to fix things?"

Digger seemed surprised at the apology. For a moment he sat there looking rather stunned. Finally he said, "We'd better make another ninety-degree left. If I'm right, we're over the North Sea and England is that way," he said, pointing across Deacon's field of vision.

"All right," Deacon said, realizing they were running out of time and gas. "Pilot to Crew, it looks like we're off course over the North Sea. We're going to make another turn ninety degrees to port and also bring it down under the clouds. We can't count on the skies remaining broken and we'll be better off if we need to ditch."

He looked to Digger and smiled. "Well, ready to go again?"

Digger nodded. "We're shaking pretty bad, but I think that shaft will hold. We have to give it a try." His words were rather rattled and broken as they hit a bit of turbulence.

Deacon nodded. "Let's do it, then."

The B-17 acted sluggish as they banked to the left and broke through the clouds. Below them the shadowy gray waters appeared ominous and foreboding. Deacon definitely didn't want to put down in the water—not if there was any way to avoid it. Matt would be certain to die if they did less than make it back to base, and given the cold weather and the fact that no one knew where they were, they were all certain to die from exposure if they had to take to a life raft. Worse still, Deacon was sure every man on board knew this as well as he did.

In the back of his mind, Deacon worried about the ME-109. If the fighter came back upon them, they were doomed. They could shoot from behind or the sides, but that was it. If the pilot made for another forward attack, there would be nothing they could do.

For he shall give his angels charge over thee, to keep thee in all thy ways. The verse from the psalms came to mind as Deacon leveled the vibrating plane and prayed for direction once again. *At least the wisemen had a star,* he mused. *I'd take a star, a shoreline—just about anything would do, Lord.*

Deacon thought of his mother back home in Washington. He couldn't bear the idea of her getting news that he'd died while on a mission. She'd not even recovered from the death of his father when John had gone off for training. How would she ever endure losing her only son? Then he thought of Melody and the baby. If the plane went down, Digger would die as well, and Melody would be widowed and the baby left fatherless. It just couldn't happen that way. Deacon couldn't let it happen that way.

"Top Turret to Pilot! Bandit at twelve o'clock high!"

"No," Deacon muttered. They couldn't deal with any more trouble. The speck loomed over them like an executioner preparing for the kill.

"Well, looks like we're in for it," Digger said.

Deacon tried to be optimistic. "He won't dive at us. We're too close to the water."

"We don't stand a chance." Digger looked at Deacon and shook his head. "Guess my choice wasn't any better than yours. I'm sorry."

"We aren't done yet. Don't you go quitting on me." The plane was closing fast and Deacon knew that their only hope was for a miracle.

"Pilot to Crew, keep alert. Let's not let him think we're sleeping."

"Radio to Pilot, sir, I don't think that's a 109," Smitty said in hopeful voice.

Deacon squinted his eyes and strained to make out the identity of the plane. The B-17's constant shaking was causing the muscles in his arms to ache painfully and his head throbbed from the noise and stress, but his eyes were in perfect working condition. So perfect, in fact, that before Smitty could confirm, the approaching aircraft broke to the left, revealing to Deac the graceful silhouette of a British Spitfire. The Little Friend was making a show of breaking away rather than approaching in a manner that could be perceived as a gunnery pass.

"Radio to Pilot, it's a Spitfire!"

"I see that, Radio."

Comments and exclamations of relief were offered up by the crew members, and Deacon didn't even bother to quiet them. The Spitfire shot past them, then made a wide banking turn to circle back.

"Tail to Pilot. She's coming back around."

Deacon breathed a sigh of relief. No doubt they were trying to raise the B-17 on the radio. Now they would know there was no chance of communication and hopefully Deacon could relay the need for an escort to their base.

The Spitfire closed and slowed, almost to what Deac knew would be its stalling speed. He signaled to the pilot that the radio was out and saw the man nod. Then the British pilot motioned forward using his hand to symbolize landing a plane.

Deacon nodded, patted the console, then pointed down. "Take us home," he said without bothering to touch the mic.

The Spitfire pilot seemed to fully understand and pushed ahead, picking up just enough speed to keep a reasonable distance between the two planes.

"We're going home, boys!" Deacon said over the intercom. "We've got our own personal escort back to England."

He smiled confidently and offered a silent prayer of thanks to God. They were safe now, Deac just knew it. He no longer even worried about the windmilling prop. They had outrun the boogeyman and they were going home. Home for Christmas.

The landing back at base was a rather hard one, but no one seemed to mind. Deac had worried over leaving the three men in the nose, but there was no other recourse. They couldn't move Matt without risking further bleeding. The crippled B-17 performed admirably, however, and after bouncing once and then twice, she rolled to a stop on the tarmac amidst the high-pitched sound of ambulance and fire equipment.

Before he could even think about the events that had just transpired, Deacon and his men were off the *Circuit Rider*, congratulating one another on a job well done and fussing over their wounded navigator.

Digger stood strangely quiet beside the ambulance as Deacon made one final check on Matt before the medics rushed him to the hospital. There was no way of knowing whether they could save him or not, but Deacon was hopeful.

"You seem kind of quiet for a man who just cheated death," Deacon said, slapping Digger on the back. "Come on, we've got a celebration ahead of us after debriefing."

"Aren't you going to say something about that Spitfire?" Digger questioned, taking off his leather flight helmet.

"I'm sure glad he showed up when he did," Deacon replied. "Answered prayer, if you ask me, but I know you don't hold any stock in that."

"You didn't see it, did you?" Digger said, pulling back. He studied Deacon for a moment. "You didn't see it."

"See what?" Deacon questioned, shaking his head. "I saw the Spitfire—she led us home. What are you saying, I didn't see it?"

Digger began to laugh. "I figured you'd be rubbing my nose in it for sure. But I guess I'm the only one who saw it."

"Saw what?"

"The name on the Spitfire," Digger said in disbelief. "It was there as big as the nose on your face."

Deacon shook his head again. "I didn't see it, Digger. What was it?"

"*Ipswich Angel*."

Deacon looked at his co-pilot and smiled. Walking away he said, "*Angel*, huh?"

Digger came after him. "Go ahead. Tell me how God sent us an angel to lead us home. Go ahead and tell me how God was looking out for us and how we wouldn't be here now except that He was listening to our prayers. Come on, Deac," Digger prompted. "Tell me how God answered our prayers."

"*Our* prayers?" Deacon said, stopping to look Digger in the eye. "Did you say *our* prayers?"

Digger grew red in the face and looked away. "You know what I meant. I just figured you'd want to make some comment about it—that's all. I just figured you'd want to give God the credit."

"Don't need to," Deacon said, grinning. "You just did."

"Merry Christmas, Deac," Digger said as Deacon came into the room they shared. He'd been waiting nervously for his friend to appear.

Deacon seemed surprised by the greeting. "Merry Christmas, yourself. I got the word—looks like Matt's going to be all right. They've operated and his chances look real good."

"That's the best news yet," Digger agreed. Then he grew thoughtful. "You know, Deac, I've been giving some thought to what you said."

"About what I said when?"

"When we were on the plane. You said that God was so much more than most religions allowed Him to be. You said He cared and He forgave people."

"True enough," Deacon said. Giving his hat a toss to a nearby chair, he shrugged out of his Class A coat and removed his tie. "Look, I'm tired, Digger, and I don't feel like listening to you argue your points on why God isn't who I believe He is. Can we talk about this another time?" Deac said as he eyed his bed hopefully.

Digger frowned. "I thought you'd be glad to have this conversation, Deac."

"I'm always glad to listen to your arguments against God," he said, yawning. "It only serves to make my faith grow that much stronger. It's just that right now I'm tired. I haven't slept in over twenty-four hours."

"If you remember, I haven't either," Digger replied. There was none of his usual sarcasm; instead, there was almost a worried tone to his voice. Deacon just had to listen to him. He just had to. This thing had to be done.

"So let's catch some sleep and we can argue all you want when I wake up."

"I don't want to argue, Deac."

"Okay, so we'll debate, discuss, consider, or whatever else you want to call it, after I get a chance to rest." Deac stripped out of the remaining uniform and slid into bed. "I promise. I'll let you rant and rave all you like. We'll do whatever you want—just let me sleep."

"Will you pray with me, Deac?"

Deacon had barely closed his eyes when Digger's question came. He opened his eyes quickly. "What did you say?"

Digger swallowed his pride. "I said would you pray with me? You know, when you wake up."

Leaning up on his elbow, Deacon eyed his co-pilot quite seriously. "What's this all about, Digger?"

Digger smiled sheepishly. "Well, it's like I've been trying to tell you. I've been thinking about what happened on the plane. I've been thinking about all the things you've been saying to me since we first met. I guess seeing your faith in practice when everything was going wrong that could possibly go wrong made me realize that this was something more than lip service. You have something I want, Deac. You have hope and you have a purpose and you have a friend in God." He looked to the floor and his voice broke slightly. "You're the only friend I've got, Deac. You and Melody."

Deacon swung his legs over the side of the bed and got up. "You're wrong there, Digger. You've got a friend in Jesus. He's been there all along. He's just been waiting for you to notice."

"You think He's still there?" Digger asked softly.

"I know He is, and to answer your question," Deacon said, reaching out to touch Digger's shoulder, "I would be honored to pray with you."

# CHAPTER 7

Ginny had barely tucked the baby into blankets and secured him in the bassinet that she'd brought down from the attic before Melody began to rally. She knew she had to keep the girl calm so that she could get the bleeding stopped.

"Melody, lie still, sweetheart. Everything's going to be fine," Ginny stated as she put her hand on Melody's shoulder.

"Baby," Melody murmured. "My baby . . ."

"Is just fine," Ginny replied. "You have a fine healthy boy, but you need to lie still. You're losing quite a bit of blood, and I need to see what I can do to get it stopped.

"I'm dying," Melody said before passing back into unconsciousness.

Ginny shook her head. "Not if I have anything to say about it." Just then she heard a knock on the front door and voices.

"Ginny, are you in here?"

It was Doc Ketterman. Ginny looked heavenward and breathed a sigh of relief. "Thank you, Father." She left Melody and hurried to the front of the house. "We're back here. Hurry. She's losing a lot of blood."

"Has she given birth?" the older man questioned. He shrugged out of his coat and handed it to a young woman.

"Yes. It's a boy and he wasn't breathing at first, but I revived him."

"Good job, Ginny. Let me wash up. Oh, and this is Nurse Stanford. She's come to assist us."

Ginny nodded. "Glad for the help. You can both wash up in here," she said, turning them toward the kitchen. She took their coats and hung them in the hall closet.

"I have Melody in John's old room. She delivered the baby with great difficulty."

"Breech birth, as I heard from the nurse at the hospital. That's when I decided they could handle old Gus and I'd just head on over here."

"Yes, the baby was breech. I couldn't begin to turn him, he was just wedged in there too tight. Come this way," she replied, leading them down the hall to the bedroom.

Doc Ketterman went immediately to work. He was undaunted by the bleeding and seemed to quickly assess the problem. Nurse Stanford turned her attention to the sleeping baby boy, and Ginny stood by waiting for instructions.

Within an hour everything seemed to come under control and Doc Ketterman stood back to consider the situation as a whole.

"You did a good job here, Ginny," the man said. "They both probably would have died without you. Breech deliveries are never easy."

"Then they'll be all right?" Ginny questioned, feeling herself begin to relax.

"I think they'll be just fine. You need to keep our little mother in bed for at least a week, but otherwise, I don't see too much to worry about. If she starts running a fever or starts bleeding more than she ought to be, you get in touch with me. You know what to look for."

Ginny did indeed. She didn't know why she'd let herself get so worried and distraught. Maybe it was because of Melody's connection to John and Collin. Maybe by keeping Melody and the baby alive, Ginny had somehow figured it would keep her son alive as well.

Hours after the doctor and nurse had made their way back to the hospital, Ginny brought Melody a tray of food. The girl looked so pale and small lying there in the seemingly massive double bed. Ginny's heart went out to her. "I've brought you some supper."

Melody tried to sit up, but Ginny waved her back. "Don't be straining yourself. I'll prop you up with the pillows. Doc Ketterman said you're to take it absolutely easy. No getting up and no straining yourself. You lost a lot of blood and we need to build your strength back up."

"I almost died, didn't I?" Melody questioned. Her huge saucer eyes searched Ginny's face for confirmation of her suspicions.

"You had a tough time of it," Ginny admitted, placing the tray on the nightstand. She helped Melody to sit up a bit, then eased down on the bed beside her. "I can't say I wasn't worried there a couple of times, but God knew what He was doing."

Melody nodded. "I prayed, Ginny. I really prayed. I kept hearing the Christmas music you were playing and I kept hearing that song saying, 'Glory to God in the highest.' All I could think about was that this was Christmas Eve and my baby was about to be born. I had to live and I knew I had to trust that God was still as faithful as I had thought Him to be before I made a mess of my life."

Ginny felt shaken by Melody's declaration. She patted the girl's hand, however, and tried not to show how Melody's words had affected her. "He is good, Melody. He's good and true and He loves you more than anyone on this earth. Now, I want you to start eating, and I'll go get you some milk to go along with the food. You have to drink milk to make milk, don't you know." She smiled at the petite girl and felt overwhelmed with the sense of what God had done.

It wasn't until Ginny left the room and made her way to the kitchen that she allowed herself the full impact of what Melody had told her. *"I kept hearing the Christmas music you were playing and I kept hearing that song saying, 'Glory to God in the highest,'"* Melody had said so innocently.

The only problem was, Ginny hadn't been playing the radio. There were no Christmas carols playing in the Williams' house that day, unless they were angelic praises. The thought caused Ginny to shiver. God had truly visited her house that day and He'd brought a choir of angels with Him.

Ginny smiled and looked out the kitchen window. She thought of Harold and how he must even now be enjoying such wonderful music as well. "I wish I could have heard it," she murmured. "I wish I could have heard the angels." And then she realized that in some ways she had. It had come in the cry of a newborn's first breath. Yes, she had heard angels that day and there was no sound more beautiful on earth.

She looked to the shed and smiled. Someday, hopefully soon, John would be home and it would be his form she watched at the woodpile. He would come home safe and sound—she felt confident of it. She felt sure that God was giving her that confidence as a gift.

"Merry Christmas, John," she whispered, her mother's heart overflowing with love. "Wherever you are, my darling boy, merry Christmas."

"You'd never know the weather was so bad yesterday," Ruth Bennett said as Ginny ushered her into the house on Christmas Day.

"I know, but that's how it is around these parts. Just look at that sunshine out there! What a glorious day."

"I brought you some holiday goodies. Didn't figure you had much time to bake," Ruth said, handing Ginny a basket.

"Oh my. What a treat. Indeed my baking has suffered. I even found myself missing Mrs. Mendelson's fruitcake."

"Poor dear, God rest her soul," Ruth declared with a grin. "That woman had a heart of gold, but she couldn't cook to save herself."

"Well, she's probably enjoying angelic fruitcake now," Ginny said with a laugh. "Probably standing in line with my Harold and our little daughter, eating God out of house and home."

"I'm sure my Kenny is right beside them," Ruth stated, nodding. "I like to think of them all there in heaven. No war. No pain. No sadness. What a day that will be, Ginny."

Ginny saw the tears in her friend's eyes. They were women whose lives had been lived in quietness and gentleness of spirit. They had loved their husbands and children, their neighbors and friends. They had given of themselves to their community and to their church. One day God would come to bring them home as well, but until then, they both knew without complaint that there was still work to be done.

Ginny embraced Ruth and hugged her tightly. "Merry Christmas, Ruthie. Thank you so much for all you have done for me."

Ruth held her friend just as firmly. "Merry Christmas to you and may this war end soon."

"Amen," Ginny said, her heart speaking the sentiment as a prayer. "Amen."

They laughed and dried their eyes, suddenly feeling very silly for being overcome with emotions. "Do I get a peek at the new baby?" Ruth questioned.

"I think that could be arranged. Let me go check on Melody and make certain she's up to a visitor."

"I promise I won't stay long," Ruth said, then added, "I'd probably just start crying again. I know my Rachel is a grown woman, but the idea of her giving birth to our first grandchild makes me powerful nervous."

Ginny nodded. "I can well understand. But I'm telling you, Ruth, our kids are stronger than we give them credit for. They're probably better equipped for all of this war nonsense and conflict of the day than we are. They are invincible in their own way."

"Oh, the strength of youth!"

Ginny laughed. "And the wisdom of old age. Combine them together and what a mighty force we make."

Melody was happy for the company. She proudly showed off her new son and delighted when Ruth declared there to be no finer infant in all of Longview.

"Of course, I'll have to change my opinion when my grandchild comes," she teased. "But, then, you'll understand."

"Oh, I'm sure," Melody said with a smile. "I wouldn't expect it any other way."

"What have you named him?" Ruth asked.

Ginny smiled as Melody's gaze met her own. "I'm calling him John, on account of John Williams bringing us all together. And because Ginny said that John means 'the Lord is gracious.'"

"That He is," Ruth agreed. "He was most gracious in this situation."

"He sure was," Melody agreed. "I know I grieved Him, but I know He loves me still."

Ruth looked to Ginny before handing little John back to Melody. "Never forget that love, Melody. It will see you through the darkest of hours."

"Without a doubt," Ginny countered. "And sometimes it's all you have."

Melody nodded. "I can see that now. I really can. I feel so lucky to be able to have a second chance. I'm not going to mess up this time."

Ginny laughed, surprising the other two women. "Oh, child, never say that. We all make mistakes and we all mess up. It happens even when we try our hardest to be perfect. Just do your best and trust God for the rest—that's what my mama always said."

"And her mama was very wise," Ruth said, leaning over conspiratorially to whisper in Melody's ear. "And it rubbed off on Ginny."

The words were loud enough for Ginny to catch, causing her to chuckle. "Don't know as I would say that," she replied, "but one thing's for sure, her words of wisdom made a difference in my life."

"Just like yours have in mine," Melody said, reaching for Ginny's hand. "Thank you, Ginny. Thank you so much for helping me to find my way."

CHAPTER 8

Melody looked down at her son and smiled. He nursed noisily at her breast, and all Melody could think of was how very blessed she was. He was the perfect Christmas present, and in her heart she knew Ginny was right. God had forgiven her and she was free to begin again.

Outside, Ginny had told her, the wind was cutting like a knife, but inside, Melody was warm and safe and filled with such joy that she threatened to overflow with happiness. The only thing that could possibly have made things any better was if she could have made peace with her parents and have Collin home.

But, she surmised, that would have to wait. They were in this war for the duration, so there would be no telling what part Collin would have to play until it was all over. As for her parents, Melody had finally taken Ginny's advice and tried to call them, but no one answered the telephone. It worried her slightly, but she prayed about it and gave it over to God, knowing that Ginny had been right about Him being faithful. From the time she'd been a little girl, she'd listened to her father read Bible stories to her and her sisters. She had been fascinated by the great men of God and the examples of how faith and truth always won out over evil and lies.

She touched the brown downy hair atop her baby's head and sighed. Her life had taken such a dramatic change. A little less than a year ago she had been in school without a clue of what direction her life would take. Now here she was a wife and mother. She glanced at her bedside photograph of Collin. Dark brown hair and brown eyes, a lopsided, almost mischievous grin. He had posed for the picture a couple of days before they were married, and Melody cherished the memory of a happier time.

No matter what happens, she told herself, *I will trust God. I have little John, and should anything happen to Collin, I will go on believing that God is still faithful and good.* She glanced at the photograph once again and sighed. *But please don't let anything bad happen to him, Lord.*

She finished nursing the baby and had just put him to her shoulder to burp when a knock sounded at her bedroom door.

"Come on in, Ginny. You don't have to knock."

The door opened, but instead of Ginny, Melody found her mother standing expectantly in the doorway.

"Mama!" Melody gasped in surprise.

"Oh, my sweet baby," her mother said, tears starting to pour from her eyes.

Melody realized in that moment that all had been forgiven. She held out her free hand to her mother. Mrs. Meggison came quickly to her daughter's bedside and embraced her gently.

Melody smiled and buried her face against her mother's plump form. "Oh, Mama. I've missed you so much."

Baby John cried a squeal of protest and Melody suddenly realized he was being sandwiched between the two women. Both women pulled apart and Melody's mother glanced down at the bundle with such a look of love that Melody knew everything would be all right.

"This is John, your new grandson." She lifted the baby up to her mother.

Mrs. Meggison hesitated only a moment before taking the baby in her arms. "Oh, he's lovely. He looks just like you did when you were a baby." She cooed at him before asking, "Does Collin know?"

Melody nodded, surprised that her mother even remembered Collin's name. "I think so. The Red Cross was supposed to notify him."

Then to Melody's surprise her father's tall, lanky frame filled the doorway. He had been so cruel and heartless to her. Melody stiffened momentarily, not at all sure she wanted to have his company.

"*You have to let go of the past,*" Ginny had told her. "*If you want God to forgive you, you need to forgive others as well.*"

Melody met her father's stern expression and bit her lip. He looked old and worn. Maybe even sick. She felt a bit of panic. Surely he wasn't sick. It was then that she realized that she could let go of the past. The idea of her father growing ill and dying was enough to make her long for his presence—to hug him one more time—to receive his smile of approval.

But could he approve of her now? Could he approve of his grandson?

Mrs. Meggison seemed to sense her husband's presence and turned with a smile. "You have a grandson, husband. Come and meet him. His name is John."

"A good Bible name," Melody's father said, coming a few steps into the room. "More books of the Bible are named John than any other name."

Melody smiled. "We named him after Mrs. Williams' son, John. The name means the Lord is gracious."

Her father nodded. "That it does. If we'd have ever had a boy, I would have liked to have called him John."

"Well, you could just use the name on your grandson instead. Maybe enjoy him like you would have a son," Melody said, extending the peace between them.

"I'd like that, Melody," he said, rubbing his chin for a moment. "You know, we could fix a room up for you at home. We live in Portland now and the house is plenty big."

She smiled. All was forgiven. "I think I'd like that, Papa."

Her father said nothing more, but she thought she saw a look of peace come upon him.

Melody watched as her mother took baby John to present to his grandfather. The old man studied the baby for a moment, then surprised both women by taking the infant in his arms.

"Would you mind if we prayed for him?" her father questioned. "Well . . . that is . . . if you don't mind, we could dedicate him to the Lord."

Melody choked back a sob. "I wouldn't mind at all, Papa. I very much like the idea of you praying for my son."

Her father nodded and bowed his head. "Father, we give this child to you. We commit our hearts to your ways and pledge unto you this day our promise to guide and direct this child in your paths. Give us wisdom to help him see what is right and wrong. Give us patience to deal with his mistakes and our own. And give us love, that we might be forgiving when things go wrong and that we might be a stronghold to one another when times are bad. We call him John and we present him to you, Father, with loving thanksgiving for another life safely delivered into this world. Amen."

Melody wiped away her tears and met her father's eyes. "Amen," she whispered and reached up to take back her child. As her father leaned down to deposit the infant into her arms, Melody leaned forward and kissed his cheek. "Thank you, Papa."

Her father, clearly embarrassed by the emotion of the moment, nodded and stepped away to where his wife stood watching with tears of her own.

All was well, Melody thought, and a peace settled upon her. She didn't know where Collin was, or if he was all right, but God was with her and she would continue to pray that Collin, too, might find peace with his Maker.

"Nothing is too hard for God," Ginny would say. And now, finally, Melody could believe that as well. She smiled at her parents.

"Oh, do sit down and tell me everything. How are my sisters? Where are they?" Melody questioned eagerly. She was ready to go forward with her new life and suddenly every moment was precious.

PARACHUTES
and LACE

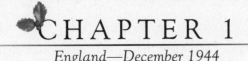

CHAPTER 1

England—December 1944

"And this must be Clara Campbell," a rather refined English-woman said as she extended her hand in welcome. The woman was impeccably dressed in a navy wool crepe suit.

"Miss Campbell, this is Mrs. Sylvia Clarke. She has agreed to sponsor our girls," Anna Nelson, supervisor of some twenty Red Cross volunteers announced. "As soon as we were able to secure the nearby hotel for your billet, Sylvia volunteered to open her home to our Red Cross ladies."

Clara Campbell, a twenty-three-year-old American Red Cross worker, couldn't get over how elegant Englishwomen sounded. Their accents suggested years of breeding and refinement, touching on a dignity that made Clara envious. Her own Washington state inflections seemed almost guttural in comparison.

"How do you do, ma'am," Clara said, reaching out to shake the older woman's hand.

"You are certainly a welcome addition to our little town," Mrs. Clarke said, smiling. "The Red Cross has done much to boost morale and keep the fighting men from feeling completely deprived of female companionship."

Clara smiled. "We do what we can."

Clara's superior, Anna Nelson, nodded. "Sometimes all it takes to make someone feel more at ease is a little conversation about home. We provide the soldiers with doughnuts and coffee and some music from the States, and then for good measure we throw in a couple of our young ladies. It helps to remind them of what they're fighting for."

The white-haired Mrs. Clarke nodded. "I'm afraid this war has been going on for so long now that many of our boys are struggling to remember that as well." She smiled at Clara. "I'm very glad the government agreed to billet you nearby. Lodging is at a premium, what with so many servicemen and military needs. If you don't mind my asking, what brought you into the service of the Red Cross, Miss Campbell?"

Clara glanced momentarily at her superior. Mrs. Nelson could sometimes act rather strangely when it came to her girls volunteering information. She believed there to be a spy behind every tree and reminded her girls constantly, "Loose lips sink ships." When the woman nodded at Clara, giving her approval, Clara relaxed a bit. Apparently Mrs. Clarke was no threat to the welfare of their men in uniform.

"I'll leave you two to chat," Anna said before slipping across the room to speak to one of Clara's co-workers.

"I signed on for the Red Cross after my fiancé shipped out with the army. He was a doctor back home and we fell in love and planned to marry. But the war came along." Clara tried not to dwell on what might have been. She had been blessed beyond measure since arriving in England. Her co-workers were remarkable women who had become instant friends. But best of all, Clara had been overjoyed to learn that her fiancé, Captain Michael Shepherd, had recently been moved to a base nearby.

"My fiancé is stationed not far from here. We are able to see each other on occasion, which has been a blessing."

"I can well imagine," Mrs. Clarke replied. "Love should never have to be interrupted by anything or anyone—certainly not by war. Although it has been often quoted that absence makes the heart grow fonder."

Clara decided immediately that she liked the older woman. Her eyes were a brilliant blue and they seemed to almost twinkle with delight as she related her best wishes to each of the girls. Sylvia Clarke maintained a gentleness of spirit, which seemed to dominate the woman's entire demeanor, and it was this that endeared her to Clara.

"It's very kind of you to offer such hospitality to us," Clara said, glancing around the room at the holiday decorations. Mrs. Clarke was apparently quite wealthy, in spite of the war, and while Clara would never have accused the woman of flaunting her life-style, she appreciated the lovely atmosphere Sylvia Clarke had arranged for the war-weary visitors.

"My home seems very empty without family here to share it," Sylvia said softly. "My son is in India, and rarely does that allow for visits home. I'm glad for the company. As I told your Miss Nelson, I want all of you to consider this your home away from home. Feel free to come over and play the piano, read books from the library, or simply come to tea."

Sylvia's attention was immediately drawn to the clock as the chimes sounded from the hall. "In fact," she said, looking to her companions, "tea is served. Won't you join me?"

Clara took a seat on a rose-colored sofa. She sat sandwiched between two of her good friends, Madeline Cooper and Darlene Keller. Both women were comrades in uniform and helped Clara, along with others, to keep the area staffed with Red Cross workers.

Clara marveled as tea was served, and the partylike atmosphere washed away all notions of a world at war. Except evidenced by the gray winter uniforms of the young women who'd been invited to tea, no other reminders of the war were allowed. Even the food—tiny cakes, delicate sandwiches, and some of the most delicious tea Clara had ever tasted—bore no reminder that England had long been rationed for even the most basic staple.

Sylvia Clarke gave no indication of where the food had come from, and no one present at the party would have dared to ask. Clara was simply grateful for the marvelous flavors and spicy aromas.

The gathering had been arranged to boost morale among the girls and to alleviate any feelings of desperation by these young women in uniform. For many days, and sometimes weeks on end, the girls were lucky to see or talk to another woman, save their own ranks. They were never so lucky as to sit in such glorious surroundings and enjoy tea and cake—at least, not without someone else sponsoring the event. Now, with Christmas coming rapidly upon them, Clara relished the charm of the manor house.

Trimmed in red and gold, Sylvia Clarke's home reminded Clara of a more peaceful time. Holly and ivy trimmed the mantel, along with gold candlestick holders and long, tapered red candles. The massive stone fireplace conjured up visions of Yule logs and nightly gatherings to sing Christmas carols and drink eggnog. At least, that was how Clara imagined it.

Back home in Longview, Clara had been in charge of decorating

Snyder's Department Store window. Her uncle Bob owned the store and let Clara come down to help her aunt Reba with the bookkeeping. Mainly it was to keep Clara from seeking employment elsewhere, because neither her mother nor father wanted their daughter working a job. Clara, however, was eager to make money. She wanted to have a nest egg set aside, especially after having lived through the hard, lean times of the depression. She'd seen her mother scrimp and do without on more occasions than Clara could count. It was this that drove her to accumulate as much money as possible. That way, when Mr. Right figured out that she was Miss Right, Clara would be ready.

One of the pleasures of the job, however, came in a rather unique side job that her uncle had given over to her when he'd found himself too busy to see to the task. Decorating Synder's store window had been a seasonal event, and the folks of Longview had rather come to expect and anticipate it just as they did the holidays. With each holiday and change of season, Synder's window was covered up, redesigned, and then unveiled. It was quite an event. When Uncle Bob couldn't see to the details because Aunt Reba had taken ill and required surgery in Seattle, Clara had been called upon to use her artistic eye to turn the empty window into something magical. After the success of that first window, Bob had been content to turn the entire matter over to Clara. He'd never received half as many compliments on his own creations and figured maybe it needed a woman's touch.

It was there, while Clara was putting in a display for June brides, that Michael had surprised her and asked her to marry him. Her Mr. Right had finally made up his mind about her. She had immediately said yes, amidst the lace and candles. And why not? She had known Michael since they were children. Even if he was seven years her senior, Clara had always thought she would marry the ambitious but good-humored Michael Shepherd. Michael, of course, hadn't even noticed Clara until many years later at a church social. Clara remembered when the six-foot-two, very serious-looking Michael had returned from college and interning in a Seattle hospital to join his parents at church. At twenty-five, he had been even more handsome than Clara had remembered. She had stared at him hard and long as he passed through the supper line, and since she was all of eighteen, Clara figured she had more reason than ever to look.

Michael had caught her staring and had given her a grin that shot straight through her heart and out her back. She held his gaze, afraid that if she looked away, he might disappear or she might very well bolt and run. But neither thing happened. Instead, when Michael reached the place where she was helping to serve apple salad, he asked Clara to join him for the meal.

"He probably just wants to see if you can get him a date with your sister Natalie," one of Clara's friends had suggested. The thought that Michael might be interested in her older sister certainly put a damper on things, but Clara put the idea aside and could hardly contain herself as she finished serving apple salad to what seemed a never-ending line of congregational members. Finally the people were served and Clara was free to be seated.

Shaking so hard she could barely hold on to her plate, Clara had joined Michael at a far table. She could only pray that he wasn't interested in Natalie, but rather had asked for her company in order to be with her—to know her better—maybe even fall in love with her as she had already done with him so very long ago.

"Clara, I don't believe you've heard a word anyone has said," Anna Nelson stated rather sharply.

"I am sorry. I'm afraid I've been a bit preoccupied," Clara offered apologetically.

"It's really quite all right," Sylvia said, waving off Mrs. Nelson's concerns. "I'm amazed at the stamina displayed by you and your co-workers. I've been quite impressed with the long hours the girls keep, standing ready to serve no matter the hour. It's a wonder they aren't all fast asleep by the fire, even if it is only four o'clock."

Clara smiled. "I considered it," she admitted mischievously. Anna frowned, but Sylvia actually chuckled. Clara continued, "You have such a lovely house, Mrs. Clarke. The Christmas decorations cause me to long for home."

"And where is home?" Sylvia questioned.

"Longview, Washington. It's a quiet little community in the northwest corner of our country. We're situated on the Columbia River just north of Oregon."

"I see. So is England very different from your homeland?" Sylvia asked.

"Actually, no," Clara replied. "There are many similarities. We have a great deal of rain and many cloudy days, and we also have a lush green landscape. We have parks and greenbelts that remind me very much of some of the English countryside. However, we also have many trees—firs and such that are harvested for lumber. Logging is big business in our neck of the woods."

Madeline and Darlene chimed in to tell of their homes in the States, while Clara noticed a photograph on the fireplace mantel. A regally gowned bride and groom peered out most seriously from a silver frame. The photograph only served to remind Clara of her latest preoccupation. Her eyes greedily took in the sight of the wedding gown before transferring her gaze to the tiny Mrs. Clarke. No, even if her gown still existed in good condition, the woman was much too small.

Clara nibbled at an egg salad sandwich, not even remembering to enjoy the rare luxury. For all that she had, the one thing Clara wanted most in the world was a wedding gown. A white gown with lace and bows and a veil and satin shoes. And she wanted those things most desperately. Michael had been privy to some inside scuttlebutt, and rumor had it that a surprise German offensive had the high command worried. The results might very well mean Michael would ship out for a more dangerous position in the war. Field doctors were dying alongside soldiers, and desperate times were calling for desperate measures.

Desperate. What a perfect word, Clara thought. It summed up the feelings in her heart—feelings that extended down to her toes and up to the top of her head. She had felt that desperation the day Michael had shipped out and she felt it now.

What if they put him on the front lines? What if he were injured or killed? She loved him so much that it hurt to even be separated for a few days. What would it be like to have him separated from her for months or years or a lifetime?

She chided herself for such gloomy thoughts. *If I continue thinking this way, I will only cry*, she told herself. Quickly, she bit into a cream-filled sponge cake. The confectionery was surprisingly bland, but there was just a hint of almond that made the entire matter completely acceptable. Clara forced her mind on the food. Michael would be fine, she told herself. After all, hadn't God brought them together here in England?

Michael had called it remarkable, but Clara had called it a miracle. She thought back to that day at the church when she'd feared Michael's affections might be intended for Natalie. Nothing could have been further from the truth. Michael had wanted to talk to her for no other reason than to get to know her better. They had talked all through dinner and then walked back to Clara's house to talk long into the evening. Finally Clara's mother had come out to shoo Michael home, but not before he had asked Clara to have dinner with him the next day.

Their courtship had been tender and sweet. Michael was a thoughtful man who, in spite of his busy schedule at the local hospital, always managed to find time to send Clara little notes or gifts. By autumn, both Michael and Clara knew they were in love.

But Pearl Harbor had upset their plans. Michael went off to train with the army and do residency in an army hospital, and Clara had stayed home trying to decide what to do. She had, at one time, considered college, but the war was making everyone do some reconsidering. She both hated and loved Michael's sense of duty. He felt that even though his experience was limited, he could offer his doctoring skills to the war. Clara couldn't help but support his decision. To suggest he do otherwise would change everything Clara loved about Michael.

It was only after seeing him off to parts unknown that Clara really considered what she should do. In time, her answer came clear. The Red Cross was looking for women to sign up for overseas duty. The pay was considerably more than Clara was making at Synder's, and the idea of busying herself with something that might well be helpful to the war efforts excited her. So for the promise of $150 a month and the experience of a lifetime, Clara signed on. It wasn't until much later, however, and learning that Michael was stationed near to her own base of operation, that Clara realized just how intricately God had staged this part of her life. It was a miracle, pure and simple.

"*We should have married in the States,*" Michael had told her when they first found each other.

"*Yes,*" Clara had agreed. "*It would have saved us all the time and trouble of trying to figure out how to go about it over here in England.*" But in truth, Clara had been acting on a promise to her mother.

"*Don't marry in haste,*" her mother had pleaded. "*Your father and*

I eloped and I have always regretted not having a real wedding with a dress and veil and flowers." The longing in her mother's voice had touched something deep inside Clara. For as far back as Clara could remember, her mother had shared her sorrow in not having at least a white wedding gown to marry in. It had set about a determination in Clara to have no less for her own wedding.

For weeks, Michael had worked feverishly with friends and acquaintances in order to receive all clearances and permission to marry. One problem after another presented itself, yet Michael was undaunted. Clara's job, he had told her, was simply to be ready for the wedding the very minute HQ gave the word. The only trouble with this was Clara's pride. She wanted a wedding gown and she felt driven to put Michael off until she had one.

But what if I wait too long? What if the dress isn't that important? But it was to Mama, she argued internally. *So what if you get your dress but have no groom? What if he dies in battle while you go running about looking for white satin?* She swallowed hard on the cake and nearly choked. Grabbing up the delicate bone china cup, she took a gulp of tea to wash down the cake.

"Are you all right, my dear?" Sylvia questioned, looking quite worried.

"Yes," Clara managed to say, coughing lightly against the back of her hand. "Sorry for the interruption."

Sylvia smiled. "I feel as though I should apologize to you. You appear quite exhausted. Perhaps you will feel more rested another time. I hope all of you young ladies will feel free to come calling. I am happy to lend a shoulder to cry on or a listening ear. That's what I'm here for."

Clara smiled. "I'm sure we'll appreciate that."

Her companions nodded in agreement while Anna Nelson replied, "We couldn't do our jobs without wonderful people like you."

"I am happy to avail myself to the cause. The war is a harsh reality that we must all deal with in our own ways. I couldn't sleep nights knowing I had offered nothing in return for all that had already been done for me."

Clara pondered the older woman's words and knew without a doubt she would like to better know Sylvia Clarke. The woman seemed completely at ease with life around her, in spite of the fact that a war was going on very nearly in her front yard.

Back at her Red Cross quarters an hour later, Clara was delighted to find a note awaiting her. With her heart racing, she opened the letter and read the brief message.

I'll be here at seven. Taking you for dinner and dancing.

Love, Michael

A squeal of delight brought the curious glances of several other women, but Clara didn't care. Soon she would be with Michael. Nothing else mattered.

CHAPTER 2

Clara thought there could be no better-looking man in all the world than her Michael. Dressed in his Class A uniform, he stood out even among his peers. At six foot two and one hundred eighty pounds, he was perfection. Clara waved from across the small entryway. She wished fervently that she might have something more alluring to wear. She had sent home most of her civilian clothes before leaving the U.S. for England, but there was always someone with something to borrow. The short notice, however, had left her with little to settle upon but her own Class A's.

"Clar, you look wonderful," Michael murmured as he leaned down to kiss her cheek.

They were cautious not to give any overly open display of affection, but it was hard. All Clara really wanted to do was throw herself into Michael's arms and kiss him, but of course that would never have been tolerated.

"So where are we off to?"

He grinned. "I've found the most remarkable pub. The food is incredible, given what they have to work with." He helped her on with her coat. "Then just down the street there's a marvelous club. Very top drawer," he said, simulating a refined British accent.

Clara laughed and looped her arm through Michael's. "And will Joe be joining us this evening?" Captain Joe Wittmer had become a regular companion for Michael and Clara. Stationed with Michael as one of the resident dentists, Joe was teased mercilessly for not being a "real" doctor.

"Joe's meeting us at the club," Michael said, maneuvering Clara through a crowd that had gathered around the front door of the ancient hotel. The Gatehouse Hotel served as billet for the Red Cross and had definitely seen better days.

"Who's he bringing?"

They hurried outside and down the steps. "Watch out for the doodlebugs!" someone called from behind them. Doodlebugs were slang for the infamous V1 bombs that assaulted England on a regular basis.

They were halfway down the street before Michael paused and pulled Clara into the shadows of a narrow walkway. "I've missed you," he whispered, drawing her snugly into his arms. The damp, cold air did nothing to discourage their affections.

Clara wrapped her arms around Michael's neck and relished the warmth of his lips against her own. How she loved this man! And then, just as quickly as he'd taken her aside, Michael was pulling Clara back down the street. His demeanor suddenly seemed more formal, almost stilted.

"I think we may be hearing something in the next day or two about our request to get married. If I get word to you, can you manage to get a day off for the wedding?"

"Michael, you know I haven't found a dress yet. I've tried, but I'm not having much luck and I really don't want to marry you in this uniform."

"Why not? I'll be marrying you in mine."

"Yes, but you look wonderful in yours. I look like a drab little nun dressed in gray and black."

"So wear your battle dress. The RAF blue is rather fetching, even if you are in pants," he teased.

Clara knew he was put off by her desire for a wedding gown, but she wanted very much to help Michael see how she felt. Slowing her pace, she implored him to understand.

"Please, Michael, you know I want to marry you. You know how much I love you. I want our wedding to be special. I want it to be something more than a rush job without heart or feeling."

"I have plenty of heart and feeling," he told her quite seriously.

She reached up and gently touched his cheek with her gloved hand. "I know you do. That's why I want the best for us. I'll find a wedding gown, and whether we have the church or the flowers or anything else, I'll marry you. Even if we have to get married in an air-raid shelter, I'll do it."

He frowned and shrugged. "I might have a lead on some parachute silk. I'm trying to trade for it."

Clara felt her hope renew. "That's wonderful. If you can get me the silk, I can make the dress. There's even a sewing machine back at the hotel and I've already gotten permission to use it."

Michael pulled her close and they began walking again. The streets were alive with other couples and hundreds of American GIs and English Tommies. There was a kind of desperation in their celebratory spirits. The soldiers and sailors, many of whom Clara had met while distributing the Red Cross's good cheer, took serious stock of their leave. Everyone knew it might well be the last leave they were given for a good long time.

"You never answered me," Clara said, trying to change the subject. "Who's Joe bringing tonight?"

"I think he's coming with Jeanine. He's certainly been talking about her a lot lately."

Clara knew her friend Jeanine Butler had been working double-time to get noticed by the rather skinny dentist. Clara didn't know what she saw in the man. To her, Joe was rather mousy and boring, but Jeanine seemed to adore him.

"Jeanine thinks he's the bees knees," Clara replied, then added conspiratorially, "What does Joe think of Jeanine?"

Michael opened his mouth to answer and gave her a sidelong glance. Seeing that she was staring at him intently he shook his head. "Oh no, you don't. You women are worse than the enemy in trying to weasel out secrets."

"How can it be a secret?" Clara asked, frustrated by Michael's sudden silence on the matter of her friend. "He's obviously interested in her or he wouldn't have asked her out."

"Well, all I'll say is that Joe thinks she looks like Greer Garson."

Clara grinned, realizing it was fairly serious when a man equated a woman to a movie star. Especially when she knew how nuts Joe Wittmer was for Greer Garson.

"You can stop smiling like a Cheshire cat," Michael said, glancing down. "That doesn't necessarily mean anything."

Clara nudged his ribs with her elbow. "You, Captain Shepherd, are either blind or completely senseless. Joe is batty for her and you know it."

"Either way, it's not my business," Michael answered. "As for your analogy, I must be without sense to let you keep putting me off simply in order for you to wear a fancy gown to our wedding."

"It doesn't have to be fancy," Clara said, hoping they wouldn't argue the point. She knew Michael felt a sense of urgency in seeing them married. When he'd first proposed back in the States, neither of them felt there was any need to rush into marriage. Even after Pearl Harbor was bombed and America officially went to war, Clara and Michael felt confident the entire matter would be quickly resolved. But as the first heartbreaking months went by, and both realized that putting an end to the war would be no easy matter, Clara and Michael had grown more desperate. Here in England it was even worse. Buzz bomb attacks and the constant knowledge that Hitler's troops were just across the Channel made for a sense of frantic discomfort. Maybe they didn't have tomorrow. Maybe they had nothing but the moment.

Clara stopped and pulled Michael to a nearby bench. She didn't want to see him so agitated with her. She sat down and waited for him to join her. "Please, darling," she said, leaning close to take hold of his hands. "I don't want to fuss and fight over this. If you absolutely put your foot down about it, we can be married the minute the papers come through. The dress is important to me, but not at the cost of your love."

He looked at her oddly for a moment, then shook his head. He squeezed her hands and brought them to his lips. "Nothing could ever make me stop loving you," he said softly. He kissed each hand, his warm breath touching the skin of her wrist where her gloves and coat sleeve had pulled away from each other. Clara shivered, but not from the cold.

"Look," he continued, "I want this wedding to be special to you. You can't have the wedding you deserve, so you should at least have the dress you desire. We'll just keep working on it, but I have to warn you, rumor has it we might not be around much longer. If the papers come through, dress or no dress, there may not be a second chance before they ship me out."

"I can't bear to think of you going into combat," Clara said, swallowing the lump in her throat. "I couldn't bear to lose you, Michael."

The gravity of the moment was ruining their evening. Luckily Michael found the good sense to move the subject away from the war. "Look, I'm starving. This pub has a warm fire and good food. Let's save this gloomy talk for later."

Clara nodded as Michael stood, drawing her with him. He sensed her reluctance and smiled. "God has plans for us, Clar. We can't worry over the details and little things like a war."

She laughed and decided Michael was right. They should simply enjoy the evening and let God worry about the rest. She walked quietly by Michael for several minutes before adding, "Do you think Jeanine looks like Greer Garson?"

The pub had been delightful, just as Michael had promised. The club, however, was so crowded that Clara thought it a waste of their time. From time to time she caught glimpses of men she thought looked familiar, then laughed to herself realizing she'd seen thousands of faces since coming to England. Serving with the Red Cross had its moments of pure exhilaration as well as despair. Sometimes, like now when they were all laughing and enjoying the moment, Clara could almost ignore the war. She thought of times when she and Jeanine and some of the others would set up position near the troops and hand out doughnuts, coffee, and hope. Even now, with the threat of air raids and gas attacks, hope was the only thing they had to get them through.

Some folks, like Clara and Michael, put their hope in what God could do—what intercession He could offer. Others put their hope in the moment—the next dance, the next drink. Everyone sought their comfort in whatever manner worked best.

"Hey ya, doll. Wanna dance?" a rather drunk navy officer questioned.

"I'm afraid my fiancée would prefer to sit this one out," Michael answered for her.

Clara didn't mind Michael stepping in to speak on her behalf. She'd had her toes stepped on too many times by drunken soldiers or sailors. Tonight, she wanted to be with Michael—to relish their few moments together.

"I can't hear myself think!" Jeanine exclaimed as she and Joe returned from their dance. She put her hands over her ears and plopped down on a chair beside Clara. "I think my ears are ringing," she shouted.

Clara studied her for a moment and nodded. She did look like Greer Garson. Her soft brown hair had been parted on the side and curled in just such a fashion to very seriously imitate the movie actress. Her Red Cross uniform didn't distract from her beauty; in fact, Clara thought for just a moment it seemed very much like they were all actors and actresses—part of a much bigger play than any of them realized.

Joe, the more quiet of the group, took his seat opposite Clara and grabbed for the soda he'd ordered prior to the dance. "I don't think I'm cut out for the night life," he said over the din.

Clara agreed. This simple dentist hardly seemed to fit the scene, even in his uniform and captain's bars. He came across as far too mild-mannered to have a war thrust upon him. Surely someone had erred in bringing him to England. He was much easier imagined in the small rural Iowa town that he boasted of living in prior to the war. Then again, Clara thought, they all were better suited to their simplistic lives back in America. Sadly, however, Clara somehow knew their lives would never again be quite that innocent or simple.

She looked at her friends and then beyond to the faces of the men and women who danced and laughed and enjoyed each other's company. Americans and English mingled freely in a sea of identifying uniforms and telltale fashions. How many of them would die in this war? How many would lose their loved ones? The hilarity and party spirit could not hide the fact that even now, friends, family, and fellow citizens were giving their lives in order for others to dance and drink and laugh.

Clara tried to shake off the feeling. *Oh, God,* she prayed, *please end this war. Please let us go home to freedom and happiness. Give us back our lives.* She felt tears threaten and knew Michael would only worry if he saw her crying. Just then the band struck up a lively dance tune, and couples moved at a jaunty pace to celebrate the moment.

"Wanna dance?" Michael questioned.

Clara nodded. Why not? There might not come another chance.

The blare of sirens permeated the fast-paced beat of the Big Band music. No one seemed to mind or pay attention to the warning. It was the second time the alert had been sounded, and for obvious reasons it only seemed to crescendo the party atmosphere inside the club. The message couldn't have been more clear. Live for today, for tomorrow we may die.

CHAPTER 3

"Are you sure about this, Tinker?" Michael asked the redheaded corporal who dogged his every step. Nicknamed Tinker because he was able to fix anything from cars to radios after he had his turn at tinkering with them, the young kid had become invaluable to Michael.

"Sure, Cap," the man said enthusiastically. "Bob over in D Company said that if you could get them a couple of bottles of champagne, they could get you parachute silk."

Michael rubbed his chin and thought for a moment. "Well, I could probably wheedle a couple of bottles out of one of the generals. I'm owed some favors. You go tell Bob it's a deal. I'll meet him later tonight just outside the officer's mess."

The buck-toothed corporal grinned and nodded. The kid wasn't all that bright, but he was a good fellow. He'd been assigned to Michael almost from the moment the doctor's feet had touched English soil, and the man was faithful to a fault.

Watching the boy—and to Michael's way of thinking, he was still a boy—amble off to deliver his message, Michael couldn't help but feel a bit guilty. He'd put the kid to work almost full time trying to scrounge up a wedding dress or parachute. The men teased Tinker for his latest escapade, but the young corporal didn't seem to mind.

Michael finished dressing and prepared for a busy day. Something was clearly afoot. The brass had been lining up for the past two days for physicals and minor treatments of this and that. Michael knew the routine. They were preparing for something big, and everyone was putting his affairs in order.

The idea made Michael nervous. He knew from overhearing more than he had a right to that things had gone terribly wrong in Belgium for the Allied troops. Weather had kept the air corps from being able to lend support to the ground troops, and what had been thought to be a simple probing assault by an already weary and worn enemy turned out to be something entirely different. News trickled back from the Front and no one cared for the obvious conclusion. The war was far from over.

The day progressed in a steady stream of minor concerns. Michael checked on his hospital patients, removing sutures and casts as needed. One young man, a fighter pilot who'd been injured when his plane had taken a round of flak, had died early that morning. Michael had known the man would die. How he made it back to base had been an absolute feat of sheer will. But once he was on the ground, the boy seemed to know he could let go. He'd gone from bad to worse, and nothing Michael did could help the boy. It was infuriating to watch these brave young men die knowing there was nothing he could do to stop it. It was nearly Christmas and everyone had been certain the war would be over by now. Germany was beat and retreating to the Rhine. *It should be over*, Michael reasoned. *Enough blood and tears have been shed for one war.*

"Sir, General Danner is here to see you."

Looking up, Michael nodded at yet another of his staff. "Send him in."

Michael stood in respect and nodded as Danner entered the examination room. "Sir, good to see you again." General Danner was an old friend of the family. He had known Michael's uncle Ralph back in the States. In fact, the two had trained together at West Point, and their lifelong friendship had benefited Michael's army duty tremendously. Michael had no doubt that his uncle Ralph and General Danner were just two of the reasons he had been given a soft assignment in England rather than a battlefront position in mainland Europe. He was also Michael's main hope for getting clearance through all the channels in order to marry Clara.

"Michael, my boy, you're looking fit!" the gruff-looking general announced.

"I might say the same of you," Michael said, grinning. "Doesn't seem like you need to be gracing my offices."

The burly man laughed. "I've got an ingrown toenail. Pesky thing but it keeps bothering me, and given the future of things, I figure I'm going to need my feet in working order."

This was Michael's first real confirmation that a move was up and coming. General Danner would never willingly divulge critical information, but he was good to share what he could.

"Let's see the toe," Michael said, reaching into a drawer to take up the necessary instruments.

Danner took a seat and quickly dropped his left boot. "It's not all that bad, just annoying, don't ya know." He pulled off his sock, rather embarrassed by the entire matter.

Michael laughed. "I've seen men with busted arms and bleeding skulls tell me the same thing. Why don't you let me do my job and I'll be the judge of whether it's bad or not."

"Well, the cure can't be anything that's going to keep me off my feet for more than forty-eight hours. I'm afraid I can't give it much more than that."

Michael examined the festering toe and tried not to show any concern for the general's comment. Forty-eight hours. Was that all they had? What did it mean? What would it mean for him?

"I hear tell we've had it pretty bad in Belgium," Michael said offhandedly as he worked. "Heard the weather was bad and the fighting worse yet. Doesn't seem fair that we can't get a break for Christmas."

"Fair's something you attend with your girl," Danner said in mock sternness. "Truth of the matter is that the enemy has no respect for God and therefore no respect for the celebration of His Son. No Christmas armistice is planned as far as I know. If anything, it will be just the opposite."

Dread coursed over Michael. He tried to focus on his work, but it was difficult. "So are we all heading over to lend a hand?"

"Well, let me just say this, I'd study up on frostbite if I were you," Danner replied. "Wish I could say something more encouraging, but that's the thing about war—doesn't much care whether the news is encouraging or not. It just takes its toll and leaves it to someone else to sort out the details."

Michael straightened and decided to play his cards with a personal touch. "Uncle Ralph sent me a note from somewhere in France. He sounded good, but like you, he doesn't see this thing going away anytime soon."

Danner nodded. "He knows the way of it. Knew it back in the

Great War, when we were still wet behind the ears. You go where you're sent, my boy." His blue eyes bored holes in Michael's hopes for remaining in England. "You go and you do your duty and give your best."

Michael smiled. "Yes, sir, and you keep your mouth shut. Uncle Ralph taught me at least that much."

"So what about the toe?"

"It's not that bad," Michael replied, realizing he'd gotten as much information as Danner was willing to share. "I've taken care of the worst of it. You'll need to soak it and keep it clean, and I'll give you an ointment to put on it. If you plan to go traipsing off in mud and wet boots, you may have more of a problem." He handed Danner some medication and shrugged. "But maybe if you pull rank and stay dry, your foot will be A-1 in about a week."

"Can't promise anything. You can't lead from the rear, you know," Danner said and pulled his sock back on. "An infantryman is only as good as his feet." He pulled on his book with a grunt and began to relace it. "You haven't asked me about your clearance papers to marry that sweet little ARC gal."

"I figured you'd tell me something when you knew something," Michael said.

"Well, I do know something," Danner said, jumping up. He reached into his coat pocket and pulled out some papers. "Here's what you've been waiting for."

Michael reached out in disbelief. "I can marry her? We can get married right away?"

"Under the circumstances, my boy, I'd say the sooner the better." The older man smiled and gave Michael a hearty slap on the back. "I guess congratulations are in order. You just let me know if there's anything else I can do for you."

Michael leaned back against the counter and suddenly remembered the champagne and the parachute silk. Without her gown of white, Clara was going to be less than enthusiastic about his news. "Say, you don't know where I could get my hands on some of the bubbly, do you? I have a bit of a problem and I can solve it easily enough with two bottles of champagne."

Michael's hopes rose as the hour for his meeting drew near. Tinker was convinced the deal would go down as planned. Clara would finally have her parachute silk, and Michael could see them quickly married before he found himself on a boat for who knew where.

He glanced at the clock and then smiled at the two bottles of champagne. Maybe whoever was making the trade had a celebration of their own planned. If he'd been a drinking man, he might have asked Danner for a third bottle. But it was probably just as well. Clara didn't drink either, and Michael knew their celebration would be just as nice without it.

"Captain Shepherd?" a voice called from the doorway. Michael looked up to find a tired-looking sergeant standing there clutching a clipboard in his left hand, saluting with his right.

"Yes?" Michael questioned, uncertain if the man needed medical attention or had come on behalf of someone else. He returned the salute and waited for the man to speak.

"General Blevins requests your presence in his quarters."

Michael nodded and cast a quick glance at the clock. Surely there would be enough time to see what General Blevins needed and still make his rendezvous with Bob in D Company. He grabbed up his hat and headed for the door.

"I can drop you off if you like, sir," the sergeant said as he followed Michael from the hospital.

"Thanks," Michael said, glancing around for the man's vehicle. "That would be swell." Michael calculated that the sergeant's offered ride would save him at least five, maybe six minutes.

They rode in silence and Michael jumped from the slowing jeep as the sergeant pulled up in front of the general's quarters. "Thanks," Michael called out, returning the man's rapid-fire salute. He bounded up the walkway and soon found himself ushered inside.

Saluting his superior, Michael awaited whatever announcement General Blevins might make. Sometimes these meetings meant supplies would be scarce, and sometimes they were warnings to let Michael know a hospital ship would soon be docking, bringing him new wounded.

"Captain, we're moving out in three hours. I'll expect you to inform your men of the move and oversee the matter personally."

Michael's lungs refused to draw air. This couldn't be happening.

Three hours? He was leaving for the Front in three hours?

"Where are we going, sir?" he managed to question.

"About twenty miles from here. The buzz bombs are making the base commanders a little nervous, and this, coupled with rumors of a new secret weapon, are causing them to push the hospital back away from the coast. It'll make for a rougher transfer of patients, and we still plan to keep a team here for emergency cases, but most of the men will be loaded off the ships and put onto ambulances and trucks and taken to the new location."

Michael felt himself breathe again. He wasn't being sent to Europe. There was still time—still hope. "I'd like to get word to my fiancée," he stated simply. The general knew all about Michael's desires to wed and had been very supportive. "General Danner brought me the proper clearance to marry her, and I haven't even had a chance to tell her."

"I understand, Captain, but I haven't the time to spare. Leave word with someone or wait until we're settled at our new location. I'll try to make it up to you once we're settled. It's important you stay with your patients and see them through this transfer. Some of your boys are probably going to have a tough time of it."

No doubt they would, Michael thought. Some of them were barely clinging to life as it was. "There are two in particular," he replied. "Private Thomas and Private Davidson. They shouldn't be moved in their condition. They came in off of a shot-up B-24. They may not make it, but if we move them I can guarantee they'll die."

"So noted," General Blevins replied. He grew thoughtful. "Look, Michael. I was completely sympathetic to your desire to get married; in fact, I still am. But you have to understand, when I helped you to push through the paper work, I figured the war to be over. The Germans were on the defensive, beating a path back to the Fatherland, and we had hopes for an end to the war by Christmas. This latest business in the Ardennes has changed all of that, however. It won't be a cakewalk now, that's for sure. I'm not so sure marrying at this time would be prudent."

"I understand, sir. I appreciate your honesty, but this is very important to me. I will pray about it."

"Well, like I said, I'll try to make this up to you. The base will be closed, but if you're still determined to do this, then I'll do what

I can to make it happen."

"Thank you, sir," Michael said, feeling only a moderate amount of encouragement.

The general dismissed Michael to head back to the hospital. In a daze, Michael realized he'd missed his seven o'clock appointment. *So much for the parachute silk*, he thought. He should have put Tinker on it. If he'd just given Tinker the champagne and left him to make the trade, things might have worked out.

There was little time to fret over the matter, however. Even now, as Michael made his way back to the hospital, trucks and transport vehicles of every kind were being lined up outside the building.

"Hey, I just heard the news," Joe Wittmer said, coming up the walkway. "We're leaving day after tomorrow."

"I'm leaving tonight," Michael declared. "Look, I need you to get word to Clara. I don't have time to call her or even write a note. Just tell her we're relocating and that I'll be in touch. Oh, and, Joe, tell her the paper work came through for us to get married." He shrugged. "I'd wanted to tell her myself, but it doesn't look like that's going to be possible for a while."

"I'll tell her," Joe promised. "One way or another, I'll get word to her."

"Thanks," Michael said, giving Joe a single pat to the arm. "I knew God would provide a way."

Clara sat opposite Sylvia Clarke and listened to the woman talk about her once-famous garden. Clara liked to imagine the glorious array of colors and vegetation. England seemed like such a lovely country and it saddened her to think that so many ancient treasures and romantic landscapes had been scarred by the enemy's bombing raids.

"I had always wanted to travel abroad," Clara commented. "I'd always wanted to see foreign lands firsthand. I'm sorry, however, to come under the circumstances and I'm sorry, too, that England has been so injured by this war. I've seen the rubble in London, and frankly, it brought tears to my eyes. Such destruction. And for it to happen to such glorious old buildings—irreplaceable architectural marvels—well, it's a grave injustice."

"Such things are happening all over Europe," Sylvia said sadly. "But, England will always be England. She is a grand old lady who wears the passage of time as one might expect. She is not without her wrinkles and scars, but a certain grace and elegance makes its place with her as well."

Clara nodded. "Oh, I agree. I didn't mean to imply otherwise. I've been so impressed with the cathedrals and abbeys. But I've been even more impressed with the people. They hold such hope and determination. I don't know that I would be able to do the same under the circumstances."

"I am certain you would," Sylvia said with a smile. "You strike me as a very determined young woman."

Clara thought of her desire for a wedding dress and nearly shared her longing with Sylvia. This woman obviously had some clout and connections. After all, she served lovely food to the girls and never seemed at a loss for tea and sugar. Perhaps Mrs. Clarke could also connect her to a wedding dress. Still, Sylvia was really a stranger, and Clara felt rather odd bringing the idea up. Perhaps another time and setting would lend itself to the discussion, but for now, Clara felt a definite need to remain silent. She'd find her dress or the means to make it. She'd not let her mother down and settle for second best.

CHAPTER 4

Clara poured another cup of coffee and smiled at the soldier in front of her. The kid couldn't have been more than sixteen, but obviously he'd fooled the army board into believing him to be older.

"So where are you from, Private Woods?" she asked.

"Kansas, ma'am." The freckle-faced boy took a doughnut from Jeanine and moved to one side in order to let his comrades in arms have their turn.

Clara smiled at the next man in line. Tall and lanky, he had a weary look on his face that suggested he'd been in the army too long. "Cup of joe?" she asked, extending a cup.

"Thanks," he said, looking up at her with eyes that suggested such misery that Clara could hardly stand it.

"You look a little down in the mouth, soldier. Better let Jeanine fix you up with a doughnut. Hey, you want to hear some Glenn Miller?"

The man shrugged. "Guess so."

He moved on by and the next G.I. lumbered up with a whistle and an appreciative smile. "You're the best-looking Red Cross gal in all of England."

Clara laughed. "I've only heard that line about four hundred times today. Tell me, Private, have you got a girl back home?" She handed him some coffee and waited for his answer.

"Nah, I've only got eyes for you. Look here," he said, reaching into his pocket. "I've even brought you a present." He put a tube of lipstick on the counter and pushed it toward her.

Clara recognized the cosmetic as one of the cheap versions many of the soldiers bought to take with them to Europe. Lipstick was often exchanged for one thing or another, and the boys seemed only too happy to load up on trinkets before heading into the combat zone.

Clara would have laughed had it not been so sad. She couldn't imagine the boys back home being caught dead or alive with women's compacts, lipstick, or nylons in their pockets. Suffice it to say, war changed things.

"I think you ought to save that for the girls across the Channel. I don't use much of the stuff and I have an easier time getting it if need be."

Jeanine cranked up Glenn Miller's "In the Mood" and slipped out the back of the Clubmobile, where they'd been serving coffee and doughnuts for over an hour. "Let's cut a rug, boys," she called and soon had no fewer than fifteen dance partners.

Clara would never get over the sight of uniformed soldiers dancing with each other, but whenever they put on the music, the results were the same. It was just another reminder of the desperate need to live every minute of every day to its fullest. They'd heard horrible rumors, frightening rumors of a German winter offensive. They knew the odds weren't always on their side and that tomorrow might not come for any of them.

"You gonna dance with me?" one burly sergeant questioned Clara.

She smiled down and, even though her feet were aching, gave an enthusiastic "You betcha" to the man's request.

She and Jeanine danced and laughed, listened to various stories, and looked at pictures of kids and wives. The Red Cross sent doughnuts by the dozens and coffee by the gallons, but it was the listening ear and friendly female smile that seemed to do the most to nourish these men.

When it was time for the soldiers to depart, Clara and Jeanine switched from dance music to patriotic marches. They took their place at the front of the Clubmobile and waved as the men marched off to board their ship. They were heading off to God only knew where. The prospect of looking at many a man who would never come back alive haunted Clara.

She shivered in the salty harbor breeze. How she wished she could do more to cheer them on, to brighten their spirits. It was so hard to watch them go. She glanced sidelong and saw that Jeanine was crying as she waved. Clara had been fighting back her own tears and seeing Jeanine's caused her to forget her resolve.

Please, God, watch over them. Protect them from the enemy.

When the last soldier was on board the ship, Clara and Jeanine gave one final wave and hurried to pack up the truck, or lorry, as the English called it. The truck, a large, boxy contraption with side panels that lifted up in order to provide access to the coffee and doughnuts, wasn't half the battle that the narrow English streets were. Clara had mastered the bulky machine and had even managed to become fairly familiar with driving on the wrong side of the road, but poor conditions and limited maneuvering space were enough to give her a headache.

"We're going to have to hit it double-time if we're to get another load of food and get to our next assignment," Jeanine called.

"I know. I know. You just make sure you get everything secured back there. I'll get the panels down and we'll be off," Clara replied.

It wasn't long before they were on their way and heading at a maddening pace across the English countryside. They had far more liberty and freedom of travel than most of the English, and still Clara couldn't seem to work it to her advantage. There had to be someone somewhere in England who'd be willing to trade for a wedding dress. Clara had money and even knew that she could get her hands on C-rations if need be. Of course, the latter was all on the sly, but she'd worked it out nevertheless. With the rationing so severe and the English doing without so much, surely someone would see her offer as a compatible solution to their own needs.

Clara could hardly believe her good fortune when she was given the next assignment. They were to take coffee and doughnuts to two area hospitals. One would be Michael's hospital, and Clara could hardly contain her joy. They were slowed only by the long line of army transports and equipment that seemed to take up every inch of roadway. Men seemed to be everywhere, and Clara and Jeanine called out and waved as they were allowed to inch their way through the mess.

"Hi, boys! Where are you from?" Clara called.

"Colorado!"

"Texas!"

"California!"

The chorus went on and on. Jeanine called out in greeting from her side of the truck, and both girls listened as various compliments were thrown their way.

"Are your legs as pretty as your face?" one soldier called up.

Clara laughed. "I wouldn't know. They've been hidden in a uniform for so long, I forgot I even brought them with me."

This brought a roar of laughter from the men, along with a couple of offers to help scout things out. Clara took their teasing goodnaturedly and finally saw an opening in the road ahead.

"See you boys later. Maybe we'll be down your way to bring coffee and doughnuts."

There were cheers and calls of good-bye and once again Clara couldn't help but feel momentarily overwhelmed. The job was getting harder every day.

"Do you suppose Joe will have time to say hi?" Jeanine questioned as she settled back in her seat.

"I should hope so," Clara answered. "I'm sure if he and Michael know we're there, they'll find a way to join us. Besides, we are going to the hospital. Rumor has it there are a lot of new wounded. Where else would they be?"

"Well, with Joe being a dentist and all, he might not be anywhere around."

"He gets his share of work too. Nevertheless, if there are a lot of new wounded, we'll have our work cut out for us."

"Lots of talk and no dancing," Jeanine suggested.

Clara nodded and tried to keep focused on the task at hand. Finally the base came into sight and Clara felt her heart beat a little faster. What a joy it was to think of Michael. Just knowing he was here was enough to bring a peace to her soul. *Thank you, God, for putting us together.* She knew it was no twist of fate that had seen them so closely connected.

Clara pulled up to the building that housed the hospital patients and convalescence center. "Let's get to work."

They had scarcely opened the back in order to gather their supplies, when Joe surprised them both.

"Ladies, it's good to see you again."

Jeanine smiled coyly from beneath her billed uniform cap. "Hi, Joe."

Clara gave a little wave. "Where's Michael? I figured he'd at least see the truck and beat a path over to see if it was me."

Joe frowned. "Well, I've got some news you aren't exactly going to like hearing."

Clara felt her heart drop to her knees. Surely they hadn't shipped Michael out in the night. "What's happened?" she asked, barely able to breathe.

"They've moved the hospital. I can't really give you any information." He looked around to see if anyone might overhear his conversation. "If you look beyond this building you'll see we took some hits the other night. HQ thought it best to get the wounded out of harm's way—at least as much as possible."

"But we were sent up here to deliver coffee and doughnuts," Clara said, her disappointment evident.

"I know," Joe said, nodding. "We're a sort of clearinghouse, if you will. They're receiving the wounded here and shipping them out to other hospitals from this point. I'm leaving tomorrow to join Michael, but he was forced to leave in the night with the most critically wounded." Joe moved closer. "He wanted me to get a message to you."

"Oh?"

Joe smiled. "The paper work came through for you two to get married. He wanted you to know."

Clara frowned. "Fine lot of good that does me now."

"Now, don't be taking that attitude," Jeanine said, coming alongside her friend. "We'll just get you two together at the new hospital, or somewhere in between."

"That's right," Joe concurred. "Mike and I will get leave and come south." He winked, and Clara instantly understood he was trying to give her an idea of Michael's new location. "The general knows how hard Michael's worked to get this marriage arranged. He's even helped in the matter. All leave has been temporarily cancelled, but you know us doctors, we can get away with just about anything— especially Michael. I mean, what with him having a brigadier and a major general in his hip pocket, he's bound to work out the details."

Clara nodded. "It's just hard to have things change all the time." She looked away and noted the damaged building not far from the hospital. The war made life so precariously unsettled.

"Someone's bound to give you directions to the new hospital. After all, you'll no doubt be called upon to bring us some Red Cross cheer. Especially with Christmas only days away."

Clara tried to be encouraged by the idea, but she felt overwhelmed by her worry. For the next few hours she tried to lose herself in her work, but every now and then, something reminded her of the distance now placed between herself and the man she loved.

"You're Captain Shepherd's fiancée, aren't you?" a uniformed nurse questioned as Clara came back to the truck for supplies.

"Yes," she said, looking up. The light was fading in the skies overhead, but Clara recognized something familiar about the woman.

"Captain Shepherd mentioned you were looking for parachute silk or a wedding dress. I heard rumors of a local woman who had a gown among other things for sale. She wanted food supplies."

A sudden flood of energy coursed through Clara's weary body. "Where can I find her?"

The nurse gave Clara directions as best she could. "I wish I could be more sure of the house. It might all be for nothing," the woman reminded Clara. "It was just a rumor."

Clara grabbed up the things she'd come for and made a mad dash into the hospital. "Jeanine," she said, panting, "I've just heard about a wedding dress. The woman lives just off the base in a little village. Can you handle the rest of this?"

Jeanine nodded. "Go! Just go!"

Clara grinned. "I thought you'd see it my way."

Clara knew it was hardly fair to leave Jeanine to take care of matters on her own, but it wasn't like they didn't have to do this on occasion anyway. Whenever they were short on help and long on need, the girls had managed to serve solo. Clara had once played hostess to twenty-five hundred sailors without being any worse for the wear. It was all a matter of attitude, her superior, Anna Nelson, would have said.

Clara went on a dead run through the base. She couldn't take the truck, as Jeanine would need it in order to reload the empty coffee urns and trays. She glanced toward the west and figured she had an hour at best before darkness would make it difficult to find her way back.

God, she prayed, *please help me to find this woman and help me to have whatever it is she needs in order to make this trade.*

Clara darted mindlessly across the road and nearly jumped out of her skin when she heard a blaring horn and looked up to see an army transport bearing down upon her. She narrowly escaped injury by pouring on steam that she really didn't have to spare. Pausing on the side of the road, Clara gasped for breath and waited for her heart to settle to a less-anxious beat before pressing on. *No sense in seeing myself killed*, she chided. *I'm going to have to take it easy and be more watchful.*

Clara managed to settle her nerves and just as she had regained her wind a jeep pulled alongside, and a smiling sergeant offered her a lift. "Where ya headed, doll?"

"Just a little ways into town," Clara replied. She gave the man her directions and thanked him over and over for helping her out.

"Where are you from, Sarge?"

"Baton Rouge, Louisiana," the man replied. "Ever been there?"

"No," Clara admitted. "I'm from Washington state. I've never been that far south."

"Great place," the man told her. He beamed her a smile. "I got me a gal there. She's as pretty as a picture and twice as sweet."

"Do you have her picture?" Clara asked, turning on her Red Cross charm.

"Sure do." The sergeant reached inside his coat and pulled out a well-worn photograph.

Clara smiled. "She is pretty. What's her name?"

"Gert. It's short for Gertrude, which she hates." The man tucked the picture back inside his coat and maneuvered the jeep around a huge mud hole in the road.

Clara rubbed her cold fingers together and realized she'd left her gloves in the Clubmobile. It was too late to worry about it now, but with the weather growing ever colder, Clara knew she'd have to be more careful in the future.

"Never gets this cold in the south," the sergeant told her. His voice held a longing for his home.

Clara sympathized. "You must miss it a lot."

"I do," the man replied. "I had me a nice little mechanic shop. I was just startin' to make me a real living and lo and behold, I get drafted. So here I am and there they are," he said thoughtfully.

"I know what you mean, but the war can't last much longer," Clara tried to encourage.

"I don't know that I'd say that," the sergeant said with a shake of his head. "Seems every time somebody says that, it adds on three months automatically."

"Well, if that's the case, I won't say it again," Clara promised. "But we have to have hope."

The man nodded. "Yeah, a man ain't much good without hope."

He slowed the jeep and came to a stop not ten yards from the address the nurse had given Clara. "If you're going to be heading back to the base, I'll be going back that way in about an hour," the sergeant told her.

"That would be great," Clara replied. "I'll wait right here. Don't forget me," she said, grinning.

The man nodded. "You're the best company I've had in months. I wouldn't dream of forgetting you."

Clara smiled and gave him a wave as he shifted the jeep into gear. She looked at the row of houses and bolstered her courage. *Please let this work. Please let this work.*

She found the address and knocked on the narrow wooden door. The house was little more than a cottage and not a well-maintained one at that.

A very pregnant woman opened the door. She had a baby on her hip and two toddlers hanging on to her skirt.

"Evenin', miss. What can I be doin' for ya?" she questioned. The baby began to cry and the woman, a look of sheer exhaustion on her face, began to jostle him around in hopes of quieting him.

Clara felt bad for her interruption. "I was told . . . that is, someone mentioned . . . that you might have a wedding gown for sale. I've been looking for a gown or at least material to make a gown and hoped you might be able to help me."

The girl looked at Clara in disbelief for a moment. At least, that was what her expression seemed to suggest to Clara. Even the baby went quiet.

"I 'ave no dress, love. Me mum married me off in blue wool when she 'eard I was expectin' little Joe here." She glanced down at the toddler to her right.

"Oh, I'm sorry for having bothered you," Clara said, her disappointment evident in her tone.

"I'm the one who's sorry. Ya might try Flaghtery's, next block down. He carries second-time goods. Ya might find yarself a dress there, but I wouldn't get me 'opes up. Such things aren't too important these days."

Clara nodded and, after apologizing once again, walked away from the house consumed with guilt. *Such things shouldn't be important to me,* she thought. *What am I doing here? Why has this dress become such an obsession to me?* Clara tried to ignore the feeling of guilt. *It's not like I'm taking anything away from anyone. I'm serving my time and doing more than my duty and I just want to get married in a white wedding dress. Is that a crime? Does that make me the world's most selfish woman? I want to keep my promise to Mama and marry in such a way that I don't regret it down the road.* But even while these thoughts coursed through her head, Clara could still see the hollow-eyed stares of the children who clung so possessively to their mother. What horrors had they already lived through? Did they fret and worry at night as Clara did, wondering when the next bomb might come their way?

She tried not to think of the children lying in their beds at night, listening for the inevitable sound of the buzz bombs. It was all right as long as you could still hear the buzzing. That meant it wasn't yet going to explode. But when the sound stopped, then you knew it was only a matter of seconds. You counted them and prayed and pleaded with God for mercy. Then you held on and waited for the explosion. It was terrifying and certainly no good way for a child to grow up. Many of England's children had been sent abroad to wait out the war, but apparently there were still those who would bear the scars of Hitler's aggression. The sad, frightened expressions haunted Clara as she passed through the narrow streets to the heart of town.

Clara pushed their images aside as she glanced at her watch. She kept moving down the street, calculating that she had enough time to get to Flaghtery's and back before the sergeant returned. She picked up her step, but her guilty conscience continued to eat at her. The day had been nothing but disappointing, and yet here she was caught up once again in worries over a material item that held very little significance for anyone but her.

Flaghtery's looked to be an ancient institution for the little town. The window proudly displayed a list of area men who'd given their lives in service to their king and country, right alongside a sign that denoted a strict adherence to rationing.

Clara went inside and noted the poorly stocked shelves. To the far side of the room a long, slender pipe doubled as a display rack for clothes.

"May I help you?" a shabbily dressed man asked in a rather refined tone.

Clara smiled. "I wondered if you had any wedding gowns?"

The man pursed his lips thoughtfully. "There is one gown, but I'm not sure it would suit you. It was made for a much shorter woman."

Clara didn't care. She'd wear it cut to the knee if it meant having an honest to goodness wedding dress. "I'd like to see it, if I might."

The man nodded. "But of course."

He led her through the store and after thumbing through several modest dresses, he pulled out the off-white gown.

It wasn't much to look at, and a pale reddish stain marred the bodice where someone had evidently spilled wine. She could tell by looking at the dress that it would never fit. Not only had the woman been shorter, but she'd probably been at least two sizes smaller as well.

"No, I don't suppose this will work," Clara said, disappointed. "You don't happen to have any material. You know . . . parachute silk or anything like that?"

The man shook his head. "I'm sorry, miss. I can't say I've even seen such things in over two years."

Clara nodded and thanked him. As she made her way through the store, she noted a shelf containing canned milk. Thinking of the young mother she'd just intruded upon, Clara paused and pulled out her British ration card. Every Red Cross girl was assigned a ration card, and while many of their needs were provided for, the card was a necessity of life.

"I wonder," Clara said, eyeing the milk, "do you make deliveries?"

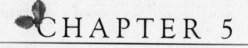

CHAPTER 5

Clara and Jeanine pulled back into their station just after dark. The cold night air was dampening more than Clara's spirits and all she longed for was a warm bath and a hot meal.

"I can't stand the smell of grease anymore," Jeanine said as they headed for their billet. "We aren't even allowed a real bath for two more days. I'll go crazy if something doesn't give soon."

"I doubt anything is going to change our having to ration baths," Clara replied. "We'll just work it out with what we have. Say, I know. Let's put some extra pence in the stove tonight and get the room real toasty. I'll wash your hair in the basin and you can wash mine and we'll make a night of it."

"Sounds like a real party," Jeanine said, rolling her eyes.

"Oh, ladies, I'm so glad I ran into you," Sylvia Clarke said, coming down the steps of the hotel as Clara and Jeanine made their way up. "I came to extend an invitation. Please forgive me for such an impromptu arrangement, but I've put together a little party in my home for some of our officers and wanted to invite you ladies to join us."

"When?" the girls questioned in unison.

"Tonight. I know it's poor manners, but there was little choice in the matter. Can you come?"

Clara felt her feet protest the idea but found her mouth affirming that they would be there. "We'll have to get cleaned up first. What time is the party?"

"If you arrive by eight o'clock you'll be perfectly in order," Sylvia replied.

"All right, then," Clara replied. "Count us in."

"Oh, and bring your other friends. The more the merrier. We want to keep our boys in good spirits."

"Absolutely," Clara replied and cast a weary glance at Jeanine.

When Sylvia was out of earshot, Jeanine leaned over to protest. "I can't stay awake that long."

"I know," Clara said, giving her watch a quick glance. "If we hurry, we can still get our hair washed."

Jeanine sighed. "All right. But I'm only doing this for you."

Two hours later, Clara laughed with as much enthusiasm as she could muster as a navy lieutenant made a joke comparing and contrasting the differences between army and navy personnel. Her head throbbed something fierce as the men joked and guffawed at one another's clever comments.

"Why, Miss Campbell, that is a lovely dress you're wearing," Sylvia Clarke commented as she made her way to where Clara stood.

Clara glanced down at the woolen day dress. The rich plum color suited her dark brown hair and complexion, as she well knew, but its simplicity was hardly suited for a formal gathering of officers and British officials.

"I borrowed it," Clara said in hushed tones for only Sylvia's ears. "I sent my own civilian clothes back home."

"My dear, it's enchanting. You really are a vision tonight," Sylvia replied. "You mustn't be so self-conscious. I'm sure you'd make wonderful company for our gentlemen whether you were dressed in a silk gown or a Red Cross uniform."

Clara knew the truth of her statement. As the party wore on, Clara shared popularity with her girlfriends and was once again struck by the sense of urgency in their gathering. Her mind went back to the poor woman she'd met earlier in the day. The look on her face was so void of hope. Had her husband gone off to play soldier in the war? Or had he been killed?

To Clara, so many of the young boys in uniform had no idea what they were really about. They left their homes with complete enthusiasm and barely restrained energy. Their gait was lively, their conversation bold and boastful, and their eyes nearly shone from the excitement of the moment.

It was, however, a different group of soldiers who returned on the hospital ships. Boys whose limbs had been blown to pieces. Boys who fought to hang on to the slender thread that connected them to the world of the living. Their eyes no longer shone—in fact, they were dull, almost lifeless. They looked up with a pleading suggestion that someone put them out of their misery. They were young men with old eyes.

Clara had seen those expressions over and over and it almost seemed sacrilegious that she should be here in Sylvia's lovely home, safe, warm, and joyous, when they were only minutes away—dying. Her thoughts put a damper on the evening, as if she needed any help to do that. Walking to the fireplace, Clara held out her hands to the flames as if to ward off the chill that had settled in her heart.

Oh, God, so much is changing. Life isn't at all what I expected it to be. She thought of her prideful desire for a wedding gown. In light of remembering everything around her, Clara knew her desire was silly. Yet, like a child hanging on to a most beloved toy, Clara hung on to her dream. Her mother had been so sad about eloping and missing out on a wedding. Clara didn't want to feel that way about her own marriage. She never wanted to regret marrying Michael, no matter the reason.

"I don't believe it. Look who's here," Jeanine whispered in Clara's ear. "Do I look all right?"

Clara looked up to see Joe Wittmer walk through the door with several other officers. He looked nervously around the room as if checking for hidden traps. "You look smashing!" Clara said with an enthusiasm she didn't feel. "But I can't imagine how he got leave to be here."

"I'll bet he went AWOL," Jeanine said, shaking her head. She giggled. "Isn't it romantic?"

Jeanine hurried off to talk with Joe, while Clara contemplated the scene and continued to feel sorry for herself. Something had to give. She knew she was destined to marry Michael. They'd come from clear across the world to find each other again; now the paper work was in order and nothing should be standing in the way of their union.

Clara frowned. "I'm standing in the way."

"No, you're just fine" came the voice of an army colonel.

Clara glanced up and smiled. "I'm sorry. I've taken to talking to myself."

The man grinned and leaned closer. Clara could smell the unmistakable odor of whiskey on his breath. "You can talk to me instead."

"It's a lovely party, don't you think?" Clara tried to keep the conversation impersonal.

"I think you're lovely. How about taking a walk with me. Mrs. Clarke indicated there were some nifty gardens in the back."

Clara noticed the man's wedding band. "I see you're married. Do you have children as well?"

The man's expression grew rather puzzled. "I have two daughters. Why do you ask?"

"I just wondered. It's my job to notice things and draw conversation out of soldiers and sailors," Clara said rather flippantly. She didn't want this man getting any ideas about playing games with her. She'd much rather put him on the defensive than have to fight off his amorous advances.

Unfortunately, her lack of interest was not a deterrent to the man. "My family is back in the States, but you're here. A guy could sure go for a little gal like you." He put his arm around her shoulder and leaned into her rather heavily. Clara couldn't help but wonder how much the man had already had to drink.

"Look, I appreciate the compliment," Clara said, trying to pull away, "but I'm engaged, and while marriage may be a rather casual thing to you, I take my commitment seriously."

He grinned rather lecherously. "A little fun in the garden never hurt anyone. Now, why don't you let me get you a drink and we can just see what develops from there."

Clara shook her head. "Why don't you go have some coffee and sober up?" She turned to walk away, but the man wasn't that easily put off.

"You're sending me into battle without the one kindness you have to offer?" he whispered in her ear.

This stopped Clara in her tracks. She turned and eyed him seriously. "You're leaving? When?"

"Day after tomorrow or the next," the man said, weaving just a bit. He put his finger to Clara's lips. "But that's top secret."

Clara nodded and thought of Michael. "Are there to be a lot of troops heading over?" she asked softly.

"As many as we can send. We have to do our part." He put his arm around her waist this time. "And you need to do your part too."

"Ah, Colonel Adams," Sylvia Clarke said as she came to the

rescue. "I thought I'd lost you. Won't you please come and meet my dear friend Colonel Thomason. He was in India, don't you know."

Sylvia threw Clara a quick glance as she steered the colonel in the direction of her friend. Clara mouthed a thank-you and sighed. Some Christmas. She had hoped against hope to be married, share a romantic leave, and enjoy Christmas all without the interference of the war. Was that too much to ask?

She glanced around the room, almost afraid she'd asked her question aloud. Joe smiled at her from across the room, and when Jeanine left his side for some unknown business, he crossed the distance and greeted Clara.

"You're looking pretty down in the mouth."

"That sounds like a professional assessment," Clara said, trying to sound good-natured. "Really, I'm fine, but I've been hearing so many rumors. Joe, may I ask you something?"

His expression grew very serious. "I don't know much. If you want to know about this latest push, I really can't give you any more information than you probably already have. I know there's a need for more troops. I know we're loading men out nearly as fast as we get transports for them."

"And what about you and Michael?"

"We'll no doubt be headed out sooner or later," Joe replied. "I wish I could say something more positive, but there's a war on, don'tcha know." He smiled in his boyish way. "We've been told it might be anytime this week. Maybe even before Christmas. They're hoping to delay it, but there are no guarantees. Still, we've had it pretty soft, haven't we?"

Clara nodded. "More so than I realized or appreciated. Look, Joe, I have to get to Michael. I have to marry him before they ship him out. Will you help me find the way?"

"Tonight? Now?" he asked in disbelief. "I'm already going to be in hot water. I'm not supposed to be here, you know."

"Yes," Clara replied. "I already figured that. Look, I know it's cold out there, but we could liberate a Red Cross Hillman. I can drive, if you just show me the way. We don't have to be gone long."

Joe looked at his watch. "What will they say if you leave the party?"

"Sylvia will understand. I'll tell her something has come up. Will you go with me? Please? I don't know how to get there—especially in the dark."

"And it will be dark," Joe replied. "You can't be driving with full beams in a blackout."

"The headlamps are covered and shielded. If we hear any planes we'll turn them off and take cover. Please, Joe. I need to see Michael."

Joe sighed and looked heavenward. "I know this is a mistake."

Clara grinned. "Thank you." She leaned up and kissed Joe's cheek.

"Ah, getting cheeky with my date?" Jeanine questioned in her best Cockney imitation.

"Literally," Clara replied. "Look, Joe and I are going to cut out of here. I have to see Michael and Joe's going to help me. I figured I'd take one of the Hillmans."

"Can I go too?" Jeanine asked.

"That's fine by me," Clara replied. "But we'll need to hurry. Joe will have to be back to his base at a decent hour. They're moving you out in the morning, right?"

Joe nodded. "Right, and given my leave status," he said rather conspiratorially, "I'd like to try and get back before I'm missed."

"Well, just consider this a reconnaissance mission," Clara teased. "Come on, let's hurry."

It was easy enough for Clara to get the Hillman, but negotiating the roads in the pitch darkness was another matter. Joe tried his best to offer her directions, but more than once they took a wrong turn and ended up having to backtrack.

"We won't be there till morning at this rate," Joe said rather dejectedly.

"Well, you can just tell everyone you got an early start," Clara replied, her steady gaze affixed to the road. "Then instead of being AWOL, you can just be ahead of schedule."

"Yeah, I'm sure they'd buy that one," Joe replied.

The Hillman, nothing more than a small pickup truck, had four gears and offered them very little power no matter what gear they chose. Bouncing and rattling along the darkened path, Clara could only keep her thoughts on Michael. She had to show him that he was more important to her than anything in the world. Of course, the dress would still be a nice touch, but maybe plum-colored wool wasn't such a bad substitute.

"I think you have to turn just up ahead," Joe told her. He leaned forward as if it might help him to see better. Just then the back of an army transport came into sight, and Clara and Joe both seemed to catch sight of it at the same moment. Reaching across Jeanine, who'd been sandwiched between them, Joe turned the wheel hard to the left.

Clara felt the Hillman lurch but not in time. Before anyone could say a word, the two vehicles met with the unmistakable sound of metal against metal and broken glass.

CHAPTER 6

"Is everyone all right?" a soldier questioned as he peered in at the trio.

"I think we're still in one piece," Joe replied.

"Then what's the big idea?" the man barked, his tone much harsher this time.

"The big idea is that you've chosen to make the middle of the road your personal car park, and we're trying to use it for a road," Clara replied angrily. The accident would go on her record, along with her commandeering the Hillman without permission. The last thing she had patience for was arguing with some ill-tempered sergeant.

She put the Hillman into reverse and tried to disentangle the two vehicles, but instead of moving, the tires simply spun in place.

Joe reached over to pat her arm. "Just give us a chance to assess the damage and get the matter settled. We'll be on our way before you know it." Then with a sigh he leaned back against the seat and muttered, "Please don't let there be any military police."

Clara wasn't at all pacified. She was less than five miles from Michael. It was maddening to have to sit here and kill time when the love of her life was only minutes away.

"Why don't we go talk to the boys?" Jeanine suggested. "They're obviously being shipped out. Maybe we can take their minds off the war for a while."

"It's not like we have any records or doughnuts," Clara protested.

"No," Jeanine agreed, "but we have ourselves. Come on. It'll do you good to get out and talk to them."

Clara shrugged and opened her door. "I guess it might help the time pass at that." She got out and went to the front of the Hillman, where Joe and the sergeant were discussing the best method for disengaging the two vehicles. "We're going to talk to the troops, Joe," Clara offered. "Just give us a holler when you're ready to move out."

"Will do," Joe replied, seeming relieved to find the girls otherwise occupied.

Clara moved down the convoy, grateful for the few flashlights that snapped on from time to time.

"Ha . . . Halt! Who . . . who goes there?" a nervous voice called out before shining a light in Clara's face.

"Hello, I'm Lieutenant Campbell with the American Red Cross." Clara tried to sound cheery in order to calm the nervous soldier. No sense getting shot by some nervous sentry on his first real guard duty.

"Advance and be recognized."

Clara stepped forward and held out her identification. "I managed to plow my wagon into your rear transport, so I figured the least I could do was come and talk to the boys."

The sentry seemed satisfied with her explanation. But then his nervousness seemed directed at the fact that she was a woman. "Gosh, Lieutenant," he said, his voice breaking, "that's pretty lucky for us."

Clara could almost hear the boy blushing in the darkness.

"Hey, Lieutenant Campbell, you can climb up here and talk to any of us, anytime you like," one soldier called down.

Clara glanced up in the dim light to see men packed shoulder to shoulder in the back of the transport. "Where you boys from?" she questioned.

The routine was suddenly no different than when she served doughnuts and coffee on the wharf. She listened to their comments with as much enthusiasm as she could muster.

"I'm from Texas, ma'am."

"I hail from Georgia! Just over here long enough to kick old Hitler in the pants, then I'm headed back home to marry my gal."

"Say, could you mail these letters for me?" another called down.

Clara reached up to take the letters, then suddenly found herself accepting all sorts of things. Packages destined for home, letters, trinkets that the men seemed intent on sharing with a pretty girl. They were excited about leaving England. Excited about getting their first taste of war—but they were scared as well.

Clara could see the fear in their eyes as the man at her side flashed the light upward for her to see the men. *They're children*, she thought. Not one of them even looked as old as she was. They barely looked old enough to shave.

I'm looking at dead men, she thought again. *Dead children.* The idea suddenly ripped at her heart like a knife. Names were thrown out—hometowns, girlfriends, and mothers' names were mentioned. Compliments came in waves of sincerity and desperation.

"You're the best-looking Red Cross girl in all of England."

"Haven't talked to an American gal in ages!"

"How about a kiss for luck!"

Clara laughed with the men and shared stories of home and of her work in England. She forgot about the Hillman and her own problems and for nearly half an hour walked up and down the transports, listening to comments and stories.

Where were they going? Would they ever come back? Would she see them in a few days, ripped and torn apart by the weapons of war?

She looked into the eyes of one freckle-faced, redheaded boy and felt tears come to her eyes. These were mothers' sons. These were brothers and cousins and husbands. And they were soldiers, first and foremost. They were heading off to war, their hopes high and their ambitions fixed on staying alive.

Oh, God, she prayed, *keep them safe. Watch over them. It's nearly Christmas. Don't leave their loved ones to later learn that they died on Christmas.* She felt her heart nearly bursting from the sorrowful thought that as she sat down to turkey and all the trimmings, these men would be lucky to share K-rations. She would be safe, at least relatively so, warm and comfortable, while they would be in foxholes, marching through snow, enduring the relentless nightmare of combat.

She glanced down as if she'd stepped on something and quickly wiped her eyes. There was no sense in letting these men see her crying over them. It would only grieve them, and Clara wanted no part in that. It was her job to encourage and bolster spirits, and *that* she would do.

"So is anybody here from Washington state?"

"I am," a voice called from the back of the truck.

"Me too," Clara announced. "I'm from Longview down on the Columbia River. Where do you call home, soldier?"

"Spokane," he replied.

Jeanine came up and lightly touched Clara's arm. "Joe says it's going to be a few more minutes, but even after that, we can't get around these trucks. We're going to have to go back to our own billet."

"No!" Clara said, knowing she sounded terribly urgent. "We have to get to Michael."

Jeanine was sympathetic. "We can't, Clar. It's nearly midnight now and if we don't get Joe back, he'll be in big trouble. You wouldn't want to see him catch it for something that was your own doing, would you?"

Clara sighed and shook her head. "Of course not."

Jeanine nodded. "I knew you'd feel that way. You'll just have to call Michael when we get back. There's got to be a way to get word through to him."

"I hope so," Clara said softly. "I have to see him before they ship him out."

"I know how you feel," Jeanine replied. "And I'll do whatever I can to help."

Clara nodded as Jeanine called up to the men in greeting. She felt as though the proverbial rock and a hard place had come to be her resting ground. *Why can't things just work out the way I want them to?* Of course, if Clara had her way about it, there wouldn't have been a war going on and she certainly wouldn't be standing here in the bitter cold of an English December, wondering if she'd ever see Michael again.

"Would you mail this letter for me?" a soldier asked, leaning over the side of the truck to hand it to Clara. "It's to my mom," he added as if that might make a difference.

Clara took the letter and smiled. "Sure thing."

"I'm obliged," he said, his voice lacking any enthusiasm.

Clara could read the fear in his expression. "So where is home and Mom?"

"Columbus, Ohio," he replied. "I didn't want to go without making sure this got back home."

Clara nodded. "Mail moves kind of slow over here—even slower where you're headed, I'm sure. It's probably good to get all your Christmas greetings in before heading out."

No one mentioned the war or the combat the men were soon to

face. For all intents and purposes they might have been headed off for a baseball game. Except few people ventured outside for baseball in this kind of cold and they certainly didn't need M1s to play the game. It was like a strained code of silence. They had all agreed without speaking a word to not mention the war or the fact that many of them would probably be dead before Christmas. It was an unspoken pact to temporarily suspend time and reality and instead to live for the moment.

Clara felt her eyes dampen again. She scanned the faces as best she could with the limited light. She forced herself to see each one of them. She tried to memorize their faces and names. Someone needed to remember them—to think of them once they were gone. Oh, there were no doubt folks back home who loved and cared about each one of them, but those folks weren't here now and they didn't know what was about to take place.

Clara wished for just a moment they could break their silent agreement. She wished that she could climb up into the trucks and take each man by the hand and lead them in prayers of encouragement. She wished she could tell them that it was all right, that they could speak of their fears and their worries and she would listen and understand. She longed for nothing more than to be able to assure each one of them that everything would be all right—that they would survive their ordeal—that they would live.

But I can't, she realized just as quickly. *I can take their cards and letters, their packages and gifts. I can promise to pass these on and see them into the mail bags for home, but I can't do anything else.*

In one of the trucks, someone began playing "Silent Night" on a harmonica. The sorrowful tones filled the air and several men began to sing. Soon the few voices were joined by many others and even Clara began to sing.

"'All is calm, all is bright.'" And for the moment it was. But as for tomorrow, no one could tell.

CHAPTER 7

Clara awoke the next morning to Darlene excitedly calling her to the telephone. "It's Michael!" her friend announced.

Clara hurried into her robe and went down the hall to answer the phone. "Michael!" she exclaimed as she picked up the receiver.

"I thought I'd never get through," Michael declared. "Look, I've only got a minute. I'm in General Blevins' office and he's been gracious enough to let me call you. I need to see you. We need to go forward with the ceremony right away. Are you ready?"

Clara thought of the desperation from the night before. "I'm ready, Michael. Dress or no dress, I'll marry you when you give the word."

"Great! I'm arranging leave for tomorrow—day after at the latest. Be ready. I love you."

"I love you too, my darling," Clara countered. "I'll see you hopefully tomorrow."

"Tomorrow!" he replied and then the line went dead.

Clara held the receiver for another few seconds before slowly hanging it up. A part of her rejoiced in knowing that Michael would soon be with her and they would be married. But another part of her began a mourning process that would surely take her through the war. He was leaving. She could hear it in his voice. She could feel it in her heart. There was no doubt about it, especially given the most recent push. They needed more men to repulse the German offensive and get the war back on track for an Allied victory.

Clara immediately turned and knocked on Anna Nelson's door. Her superior opened the door with a rather exhausted expression. "Oh, Clara. You're just the one I wanted to speak with. Come in."

Clara tightened the sash on her robe and stepped into Anna's room. "I need to make a request."

"So do I," Anna said rather sternly. "You go ahead and tell me what you have in mind."

"I'd like leave for tomorrow and maybe even the next day."

"Christmas?"

Clara nodded. "Michael is coming tomorrow and we're to be married." She frowned and bit at her lower lip to keep from crying. The sudden burst of emotion startled Clara. She hadn't anticipated that this would be difficult. "They're shipping out soon," she added in a barely audible voice.

Anna put her arm around Clara's shoulders. "I know. I'm sorry."

Clara let the tears come, and when Anna guided her to a chair, she buried her face in her hands and sobbed. After a couple of minutes, she regained her composure. "I'm sorry," she said, sniffing loudly. "I don't know what came over me."

"I think I do. It's this war and everything about it. I heard what happened last night. I was going to be rather harsh with you for taking the Hillman without permission, but the major in charge of that particular convoy sent a note praising the Red Cross's devotion to sending girls out in the middle of the night to encourage embarking troops. I suppose since things worked out rather well, I shall let it go this time. However, there mustn't be another incident like this one."

"I understand. I just felt desperate to get to Michael and marry him. I've been so silly, fretting over a wedding dress and all the trimmings of a home-style wedding. I just wanted things special," Clara said, looking up at Anna as if to receive absolution for her feelings. "My mother always told me what a regret her elopement had been. She missed out on the parties and the dress and the church. She missed out on the all the fun of the wedding and found herself rather suddenly settled into the marriage. She wanted it better for me, but—"

"But the war came along and changed everything," Anna interrupted.

"Just like it had with the Great War," Clara replied. "That was the very reason my mother missed out, and I promised her I would do whatever I could to keep from having the same thing happen to me. Michael and I were going to marry before he left for duty, but several things conspired against us and we decided to wait. We were going to have a wedding when he came home on leave. I was going to have everything ready and waiting, but then I joined the Red Cross and one thing led to another." She sighed heavily. "I can't wait any longer. Michael is soon to be shipped out. He's coming here tomorrow and whether we have much of a wedding or not, we're getting married."

Anna smiled. "We'll do what we can to make it special, Clara. Of course you may have the day off. However, I need for you to take the trucks out today. There will be no time for breaks. You'll need to leave immediately and you will no doubt be gone until late. There are thousands of men lined up on the docks and in loading sheds. You go with Madeline."

Clara nodded. So much for making any last-minute provisions for her upcoming nuptials. "Would you get word to Sylvia Clarke?" Clara questioned. "I'd like her to be at the wedding. It would mean a lot to me."

Anna smiled. "Why don't you run on over and tell her yourself. I'm sure she'll be just as charmed. We've got things covered for the moment. I think it would do you good to spend a bit of time with her."

Clara got up and wiped her eyes with the sleeves of her robe. "I have a feeling I may be spending a lot of time visiting Sylvia once Michael has shipped out."

"A wedding!" Sylvia exclaimed. "How lovely. Why, it's just the thing to lift your spirits. Why don't you come inside and tell me all about your plans."

Clara shook her head. "I can't stay. Miss Nelson let me come and tell you, but I have to get right back." She smiled at the older woman. "I've really appreciated your friendship. I hope in the time to come that we can become true friends."

Sylvia nodded and reached out to squeeze Clara's hands. "Oh, I would very much like that."

Clara glanced at her watch. "I've got to go. Maybe I can tell you more about the plans tonight. I have a full day and probably won't be back until evening, but Anna promises me I can have tomorrow and the next day off. We have to be ready to go at a moment's notice."

"I completely understand," Sylvia answered. "Until tonight."

Clara worked all day at dispensing doughnuts, coffee, and American charm. Her feet hurt and her back ached, but she worked on faithfully. Driven by sheer willpower and a desire to send the men off to war with a memory of a sweet smile and a kind word, Clara refused to let despair overrun her.

Several times during the day, she and Madeline loaded up and moved to other areas. They stopped only long enough to restock on doughnuts and coffee before moving out to yet another troop of men. By the time evening came, and Clara received the word to return to her billet, the clock was edging toward seven-thirty.

"Clara," Jeanine said conspiratorially, after issuing the word to return, "I have some interesting news."

Clara pulled away from her tasks at hand and went behind the truck with Jeanine. "What is it?"

"Well," Jeanine said, her eyes lit up with excitement. "I found you some parachute silk."

"What! That's wonderful! Where?" Clara could hardly contain her excitement.

"Well, there's a base not too far from here where some of the parachute troops are temporarily being stationed. I have a feeling it's part of this big push we keep hearing about. Anyway, I met up with this one grungy-looking misfit of a sergeant who said he could get you as much parachute silk as you needed."

"What does he want in return?" Clara asked.

"A Christmas feast," Jeanine replied with a shrug. "They're shipping out before Christmas—of course, he isn't supposed to know that. But he's all miffed and they're going to miss out on the planned turkey and dressing. He said if you'll bring him the fixings for any dinner that isn't K-rations or C-rations, he'll give you the parachute."

"Well, we can do that," Clara said, her tone becoming animated. "I mean, I've been promised just about any kind of food I want from those nice navy officers we met a couple of weeks ago. I'll bet if I were to go to them right now and beg for some food, they'd be more than happy to help."

"Sure," Jeanine said, nodding. "You go ahead and I'll tell Anna you and Madeline are still busy with the Clubmobile. It won't take you long to get the food. Then just come back to the hotel and get me. I'll arrange for us to borrow the Hillman."

"Okay," Clara said, licking her lips against the cold. "I'll be as quick as I can." Her heart soared with the anticipation of a gown. It seemed that God had heard her prayers. *Maybe letting go of my needs or demands,* Clara mused, *was necessary before God could work. Maybe my heart still wasn't right.* She fairly danced back to the cab of the truck. Madeline was already seated inside waiting.

"What's going on?"

"We need to take a little detour," Clara said, starting the engine. "I need to see a couple of friends about some food."

Nearly an hour later, Clara lugged a big pillowcase full of food back to the Clubmobile. She had T-bone steaks, potatoes, pie, and all kinds of trimmings carefully loaded in her Santa-style pack. She felt a little like the mythical fat man all bundled against the winter chill, lugging her bag full of goodies back to her sleigh.

"Did you get it?" Madeline questioned.

"Yes," Clara nodded. "They're a good lot, our boys. Gave me everything they could spare."

"So now where?"

"Back to the hotel. Jeanine is borrowing the Hillman and she knows where we're going."

"I want to come too," Madeline said, "but I suppose someone has to remain behind."

"I'll need your help to make the dress when I get back with the parachute silk," Clara said, swinging the truck onto the road. "I know you're probably the best seamstress among us."

"If we all work on a piece," Madeline said, considering the situation, "we can have it ready by morning."

"Yeah, if we work all night," Clara laughed. "I may sleep through my own wedding, but at least I'll have a dress."

She parked the Clubmobile in its regular place, then grabbed up her pack. "I'll be back as soon as I can."

"Will do," Madeline said. "I'll start cutting out a pattern for the dress."

Clara was fairly singing as she jumped from the truck. Jeanine appeared within moments of their arrival, motioning her toward the Hillman.

"Anna said this was a one-time thing. She didn't want us thinking we could use Red Cross property for personal needs on a full-time basis."

"She's got a good heart," Clara said, jumping into the passenger side of the Hillman. Jeanine climbed in the driver's side and fired up the engine. "It's pretty cold, so we're going to have to wait a few minutes."

"It's been terribly cold here lately. Cold and damp," Clara said, hugging the pack protectively. "It reminds me of home."

Jeanine finally eased the Hillman out from behind the hotel and made her way to the main highway. "It's only eight, but it feels like ten or eleven," she said. "At least we should have plenty of time to get there and back, even if they need us for a midnight run."

Clara sighed, feeling a bit nervous. Here she thought she'd let go of her concern about the dress and now her desires were working against her. "Oh, I just hope this works out. Madeline said if we all work on the dress together, we can have it finished by morning."

"Well, there's only one sewing machine. Thank goodness it's foot powered," Jeanine said, grinning. "I'm sure we'd never get clearance to run it otherwise. You know how everyone is about waste."

"Yes, but this isn't waste," Clara replied. "This is important." But in her heart, Clara was gradually beginning to feel guilty. She'd given this matter to God, and now it seemed she was taking it back.

It's not because of the dress, she reasoned. *I just want a nice wedding for Michael's sake, as well as my own. If he has to go off to war, he should at least get to go off with the pleasant memory of a decent wedding.* But even as she thought this, Clara knew the ceremony meant very little to Michael. He simply wanted to be her husband. He didn't care about the gown or the other trappings. He only wanted her.

"Oh, look there," Jeanine said as she crept the Hillman through the narrow streets. "Those children shouldn't be out on such a cold night."

"I wonder what they're doing," Clara questioned, craning her neck to see.

"Probably begging," Jeanine replied. "Sometimes I think they should have sent all of the children away. Children shouldn't have to live like this. I mean, it's nearly Christmas and these kids are out here begging for their very existence."

Clara hugged the sack of food close and felt a lump rise in her throat. "Maybe they're just running an errand for their mother," she suggested. She could see there were at least four children and all looked to be under the age of ten.

Jeanine rolled down her window and leaned out as the Hillman rolled to a stop. "You kids need a lift home?"

The oldest, a ragged-looking little boy, shook his head. "No, ma'am, thank you." His speech suggested a good upbringing, but his appearance betrayed his present poverty.

"What are you doing out on such a cold night?" Jeanine questioned.

"Our mum sent us to see if we could get some extra food," a little girl offered. "We don't have anything to eat. Mum said the Yanks might share a bit." She pulled at her stocking cap and tugged on her brother's sleeve. "Are these Yanks?"

Jeanine looked back at Clara and sighed. She couldn't imagine that any mother in her right mind would send her kids out to beg from total strangers. Why, what if something happened to them?

But something had happened to them. They had been exposed to the harsh realities of war. They had gone hungry and cold. Clara shuddered and thought of other encounters she'd had with the poverty-ridden English. They were a proud people and they were getting by doing the best they could under the circumstances. Clara could smell the aroma of the mince pie in her sack. Suddenly the food seemed to weigh a ton.

"Come on, Jeanine," she said. "Let's get going. We haven't much time."

Jeanine nodded. "You kids be careful and don't stay out too long. It's very cold."

She rolled the window back up and started them back on their way. "I can't stand seeing them like that. I mean what will happen to them? They have nothing to eat and no doubt nothing for Christmas. Oh, it just doesn't seem right."

Clara nodded. She knew it wasn't right, but the things that suggested themselves to her also seemed unfair. She knew she should have Jeanine stop the truck here and now, backtrack the brief distance, and turn over the food pack to the children. But if she did that, there would be no hope of getting her parachute silk.

She let the truck rumble on in silence, all the while haunted by images of the hollow-eyed stares of the children. Now she could smell the stuffing and she even imagined that the uncooked T-bones were putting off a deliciously tempting aroma.

"Inasmuch as ye have done it unto one of the least of these . . ." The words weighed on her soul.

Laughing silently at herself, Clara knew what she had to do. *I'm such a silly woman. Still so caught up in myself. I see what you're trying to show me,* she prayed. *I see that there was still this last stronghold of selfish greed. I can't be that person anymore, Lord. I can't buy myself a wedding dress knowing that little children are going hungry.*

"Stop!" she declared.

Jeanine slammed on the brakes and turned to Clara. "What's wrong?"

"Go back," Clara sighed. "I can't do this."

"Do what?"

"I can't just leave those kids there. I have enough food here for half an army. We'll just go back and give it to them."

"But what about the parachute silk."

Clara shook her head. "It doesn't matter anymore," she said. And with a sigh of relief, she knew it was true. She was finally free from her self-driven desire to have a gown at any cost. She couldn't feed all of England, but she could give this gift of hope to a suffering family. *And after that,* she thought, *I'm going to talk to Sylvia about what else we can do to help.* Her mind was already whirling with possibilities as Jeanine maneuvered the truck.

They reached the little pilgrimage of children without any trouble. In truth, the kids hadn't managed to get far. Their bodies were no doubt slowed by the bitter cold. Jeanine pulled up alongside them once again, and Clara got out of the truck, pulling the pack with her.

"I have a Christmas present here for you and your mother," she said as the children stared up at her rather blankly. "There's enough food in here for a real Christmas feast. Take it home to your mom. She'll know what to do to fix it up right."

Their eyes were as huge as saucers. "Thank you, ma'am," the oldest one said, reaching out to take the pack. The little ones danced around trying to get a peek inside the pack. The older brother was undaunted, however. He took on his new duty almost ceremoniously.

With only a little trouble, he hoisted the food to his back. "Merry Christmas," he said, giving Clara a smile that warmed her clear through.

"Merry Christmas to you too," Clara replied.

She watched them hurry down the road. Their chattering voices could be heard as they scurried along the pavement. Now their feet seemed more sure, their steps lively and determined. Clara felt like laughing at the wonder of the moment. Somewhere tonight a war-worn mother would open up a pillowcase of the finest navy steaks and assorted foods. *Will she feel like I do?* Clara wondered silently. *Will she recognize the gift as being divine?*

"Thank you, God," she whispered and looked overhead into the starry night skies. There might be a war going on, but this was the season of Jesus' birth, and Clara intended to celebrate it in full. The true gift of the season was love. God's love in the form of a baby come to earth. God's love in the form of a pillowcase of food. God's love in the face of hopeful children.

"Come on," Clara said, climbing back into the Hillman. "Let's go home and get me ready for my wedding."

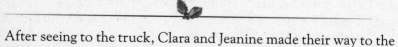

After seeing to the truck, Clara and Jeanine made their way to the old hotel. Clara desired only one thing in the entire world at that moment, and that thing was a hot bath. The only trouble, however, was that it wasn't Clara's night for a real bath.

"Miss Campbell," Sylvia Clarke called as Clara approached the steps.

Mrs. Clarke stood at the top of the staircase and waited for Clara to join her before continuing. "I'd like to help with your wedding plans."

Clara smiled warmly in spite of her exhaustion. "I'm afraid I don't really have any plans." Clara turned to her friend. "You go ahead, Jeanine. Tell Madeline not to worry about the sewing. You can explain everything and I'll be up later."

Her friend nodded. "Good to see you again, Mrs. Clarke. I'm still remembering the wonderful flavor of those hot scones."

Sylvia smiled. "I'm so glad you enjoyed them. Do come again."

"Don't worry. If I can ever get caught up on my sleep, I'll make a special occasion of it."

Clara waited until Jeanine had gone before suggesting Sylvia step back inside. "We can talk in the lobby. At least it's marginally warmer than the front steps."

"I have a better idea. Why don't you gather some of your things and come to my place. You can have a hot soak in the tub and share dinner with me. We can discuss how I might help with the wedding."

Clara sighed. "A hot bath sounds wonderful."

"Then you'll come?"

Nodding her head, Clara ignored her exhaustion. She could sleep anywhere, but she certainly couldn't get a bath just any old place. "I'll be there. In fact, if you'd like to wait, I can just run upstairs and grab my things and walk back with you."

"That would be fine. I'll sit right here," Sylvia said, taking a seat on a well-worn wing-backed chair.

Clara hurried upstairs, gathered her things, and told Jeanine her plans. "I'll be back as soon as I can and we can finish discussing the wedding. Mrs. Clarke wants to help as well."

"I'll talk to the baker and see if I can get us a cake for the wedding," Jeanine said, suddenly encouraged. "Who knows. He just might be able to pull something together with doughnuts."

"Oh, thank you very much," Clara said, letting the sarcasm mark her words. "I thought you were my friend."

Jeanine laughed. "Of course I am. Who else would go out on a night like this just to talk wedding cakes with gruff, sour-dispositioned doughnut friers?"

Clara took up her hairbrush and headed for the door. "That's true friendship, all right." She paused and looked back at her friend. "But don't go to any extra effort. I've learned a very important lesson tonight. I'm only ashamed I didn't learn it sooner. God has done a work in my heart and I know my love for Michael is all that matters. He's all I care about."

Jeanine nodded. "I know that. I've always known that."

"I'm not sure I did," Clara replied, "but I do now."

❦

"You look like a new woman," Sylvia Clarke announced as Clara joined her fresh from her bath.

Attired in her battle dress rather than her Class A uniform,

Clara apologized for the casualness of her clothing. "I thought this might be warmer and rumor has it we might be headed back to the docks at midnight."

"But you've been up and working since six this morning. Surely no one would expect you to wear yourself out in such a manner."

"We're shorthanded and if we don't go, no one goes. I hate to think of all those men leaving for Europe without so much as a cup of coffee or a smile."

Sylvia nodded. "I completely agree. It's a pity we can't be better staffed."

"Maybe after the first of the year," Clara replied. "Then again, maybe the war will be over by then."

"We can only hope and pray," Mrs. Clarke said sadly.

They sat down to a small, very intimate dinner. Clara smiled to find an actual steak on her plate. "You must have connections, Mrs. Clarke."

"Please call me Sylvia," the woman replied with a smile. "The Red Cross and your military have been particularly generous. I can't see any reason not to share it with others. I must say, beefsteak was never a mainstay in this house, but I've grown to enjoy it when it makes its way to my table. I prefer lamb, to tell the truth, but don't tell Admiral Block. He's the one who sent over these particular steaks."

Clara nodded conspiratorially and cut into the meat. She quickly tasted it, almost fearful it would disappear from her plate. The flavor was incredible. The steak was so tender she hardly had need to chew it. "Oh, this is the most marvelous meal I've had in weeks."

"I thought it should be a celebration. Your young man is probably having festivities with his friends, so it seems only proper that you should enjoy a little party of your own."

"You are very kind. I knew from the moment I first met you that we'd be good friends. Of course, if you feed me like this every time I come to your house, I might well become your best friend."

Sylvia chuckled. "Good friends are few and far between. We must take them as they come."

Clara sobered a bit. "Has it been very different? I mean with the war and all?"

"Oh my, yes. The country isn't at all what it used to be. We had such a peacefulness about us. There was never any rush or hurry. We simply let life come at its own pace. My son said that with all the Yanks over here, we're bound to be racing against the clock." She smiled. "You Americans seem to always be in a hurry."

Clara laughed. "Maybe it's our zest for living. Or maybe it's just that we're afraid if we don't keep moving we'll find ourselves bogged down and held fast."

Sylvia nodded knowingly. "I'm sure both have their place in explaining this driving force inside you. I suppose that's why I find it so surprising that you've made so few plans for your wedding."

Clara put down her fork and said rather thoughtfully, "I had a great many thoughts on what I wanted my wedding to be. I wanted flowers and a beautiful church. I wanted a veil and satin slippers, but most of all, I wanted a beautiful white wedding gown."

"And why has that changed?"

"I realized that my heart was on the things and not on the man. Oh, don't get me wrong, I love Michael with all of my heart. I couldn't see myself happy without him, but long ago my mother told me about her own wedding. They had eloped before my father left for service in the Great War. She regretted her hurried marriage and lack of celebration. But most of all, she regretted having no wedding gown. I promised her I would do things differently, and for a time, the gown was all I could think of."

"Did you find a gown?"

Clara shook her head. "I tried to. I raced all over southern England every chance I got. If they sent me one way or another on Red Cross business, I was out there looking for a wedding gown or parachute silk or any white material. I couldn't find anything, though. Every time I thought I had a sure thing, I'd arrive to find that I was either misinformed or ten minutes too late." She ate a forkful of potatoes before continuing. "I have to say my pride nearly ruined my life. I wanted that dress so much and I could hardly see anything else because of that need."

"Often we allow the things of this world to overwhelm us," Sylvia agreed. Her voice sounded sad, almost regretful. "What changed your heart?"

"God did. Tonight I was supposed to trade food for parachute silk."

"What happened?" Sylvia asked softly.

Clara waited for a feeling of regret to come over her and when it didn't, she smiled. "I had the food, but I gave it away. I knew God wanted me to see that there were more important things. I couldn't stand the fact that my dress was more important than starving children. I couldn't believe the way I was acting."

"You sound as though something quite important happened."

"It did. Jeanine and I were headed with our food to one of the local bases. A man there was supposed to trade us. He was shipping out and found out they were going to miss Christmas dinner, so he promised me parachute silk if I would bring him a Christmas feast." Clara smiled at Sylvia's obvious interest. "I had the food donated by a couple of navy lieutenants who felt particularly generous. But then Jeanine and I saw these little children on the way out of town. Not one of them could have been over ten or twelve. They were heading down to the docks to beg food and such from the soldiers who were down there loading or waiting to load. I couldn't stand it. At first I just wanted Jeanine to drive off before I changed my mind. I told her we didn't have much time and I encouraged her to leave them."

Sylvia dabbed her lips with a napkin. "You can't hope to save the world."

"That's what I told myself. In fact, I reminded myself of that over and over, but I knew I could help these hungry children—at least for the time being. I had Jeanine turn back and I gave them the food. Sylvia, I have never felt better about any choice I've ever made. I know it was the right thing to do. I'm only sorry it took me more than a single thought to do it."

"We all have to learn our lessons in life," Sylvia replied. "Some are easy lessons. Some come very hard."

"You sound as if you speak from experience," Clara said, hoping the older woman would talk about herself.

"I do, indeed," Sylvia admitted. "I lost my husband a dozen years ago after a battle with pneumonia. He was very important to me, but I didn't realize it until after he was gone. I was too caught up in the society of good company and the things of this world. When my son joined the army and was later appointed a position of some importance in India, I suddenly realized how little time I'd spent with my children. He was gone and it was understood that visits would be few and far between. I was left here with my daughter, Meredith, and I realized that I could spend the time doing for myself or doing for her. I chose the latter. I wish I had chosen that path much earlier in life."

"I know what you mean," Clara said, wishing now that she and Michael would have married while still in the States. "I don't mean to pry, but it was said that your daughter had died. Can you talk about it?"

Sylvia gave her a sad little smile. "It hurts so much to think of her passing, yet talking about her is a joy. Meredith was much like you. She was happy and in love and planning a beautiful wedding to a man I completely approved of. I had taken her to London in order to gather a trousseau. We had a marvelous time shopping in spite of the war. You must remember, it was still fairly early and the heavy bombing of London and other cities had not yet come. Our last evening in London, I sent Meredith back to our flat while I went to dinner with friends. While at dinner, bombs began falling on London. The explosions were terrible and the fires and destruction were such as to leave us all quite stunned." She fell silent for several moments.

"I don't even remember how I made it back to the flat that night. I do remember the sight of the rubble that had once been my home. Meredith had died when bombs destroyed the entire block of flats."

"I'm terribly sorry," Clara said, not able to comprehend the horror of returning home to find your child dead.

Sylvia nodded. "It was a bleak time, to be certain. God was my only sustaining element. He kept me going when I had no will of my own."

"He's like that," Clara said softly. "I know I've not had to suffer anywhere near your loss, but His love has seen me through many bad times. I know that after Michael is sent to Europe, God will still be my rock of support."

"It is a fearsome time to endure," Sylvia replied.

"There's such a feeling of desperation among both soldiers and civilians. I see it whenever I'm out on the town or among the troops. I hear it in their voices and see it in their eyes. I wish I could share something more than doughnuts and coffee. I wish I could give them peace of heart and mind."

"It would be wonderful if such things as peace and love could be handed out like doughnuts," Sylvia agreed.

"If they could," Clara replied, "we'd never see an end to our day."

CHAPTER 8

"This message came for you while you were at Sylvia's," Jeanine said as Clara came into the room.

Exhausted but feeling marvelous from her respite with the older Englishwoman, Clara took up the note, read it, then relayed the message to Jeanine. "Michael says we're to be married tomorrow evening. He can't get here before then. He wants me to pick the place and be ready. He's bringing the base chaplain with him." She grinned over the note at Jeanine. "Sounds like an army sergeant giving out orders instead of a sweet-tempered doctor."

"Just think, after tomorrow you'll be Mrs. Michael Shepherd," Jeanine said romantically. "Oh, that reminds me. We're going to have a cake. It won't be big, but we're going to have one."

Clara felt blessed by her friend's concern and attentiveness. "Jeanine, you are so sweet to arrange a cake."

"That's not all. Madeline wants to arrange your hair, and Darlene said you may borrow her cream-colored suit. It isn't a wedding gown, but it's as close as we could come. Darlene is also going to try to find some hothouse flowers for the ceremony."

Clara felt her eyes dampen. "You are all so kind to me."

Jeanine smiled and put her arm around Clara. "So where are we having this soirée?"

"Mrs. Clarke has offered her home," Clara said. "I hadn't really given any thought as to where we might marry, but tonight over dinner she suggested we come there. She wants to throw us a party afterward. She told me to invite everyone."

"Wonderful! What a grand time. We'll party all night."

"Not me," Clara said, her thoughts drifting to a night spent in Michael's arms. "I have plans."

Christmas Eve dawned cloudy and cold. The gloomy overcast might have dimmed the spirits of a less-determined woman, but Clara didn't care. She felt overwhelmed with joy at the prospect of marrying the man she loved. How good God had been to work through all the details for her.

Humming Christmas carols and thinking of how it might be back home, Clara was unprepared when Jeanine burst into the room. "Look what I found downstairs."

"What is it?" Clara questioned, seeing several small boxes and envelopes atop a larger box. "Oh!" she squealed in recognition. "It's mail!" For weeks Clara had received no mail at all. Anna Nelson had told her this was typical, but it certainly did nothing to bolster Clara's spirits.

"These are all for you," Jeanine declared. "I'll bet there are Christmas presents in the boxes."

Clara laughed and pointed her friend to the bed. "Let's open them and see."

The two young women giggled like schoolgirls as Clara tore into the largest box. "Oh, look! My mother remembered! Peanut butter and crackers. Oh, how marvelous." Clara pulled the items from the box and continued the search. "And cookies and look, Jeanine!" She held up a box of candy. "Chocolates!"

"I've died and gone to heaven," Jeanine replied.

"She has three presents in here that she says I should wait until Christmas morning to open," Clara said, looking at a brief note that had accompanied the box. "But I can't wait." She grinned mischievously at Jeanine. "Besides, it says, I *should* wait. Not that I have to wait."

Jeanine giggled. "Open them!"

Clara ripped at the paper covering the largest of the three gifts. Inside, Clara found a white box and opened it to reveal a hand-embroidered white nightgown. "Oh, would you look at this!" Clara held it up against her and gently touched the delicate embroidery. "My mother made this. I just know it."

"It's wonderful and perfect timing too," Jeanine said, grinning. "You can use this for your honeymoon."

"Not that there's going to be much time for one," Clara said wistfully. "I wish I could wake up and find that we're all safe back home in Longview. I wish this war was nothing more than a bad dream, but I know it can't be so."

Jeanine patted her arm reassuringly. "I can't help but believe everything will be all right. It just has that feel to it."

Clara hoped her friend was right. She wanted to believe that Michael would be safe and that even if he left as planned, he would soon rejoin her.

Jeanine eyed the nightgown thoughtfully and lightly fingered the material. "Too bad it's so thin or you could just get married in this."

Clara laughed. "Oh, and wouldn't my mother be delighted at that prospect."

Jeanine shrugged. "It was just a thought. So open the next package."

Clara put aside the gown and nodded. The next package contained soft white slippers. "These will help to ward off the cold," she said, holding them up.

"Did your mother make those as well?"

"Looks like it," Clara said, noting the duplicated embroidery on the footwear.

"So what's in the next one?"

Clara opened the next package and found a bottle of her favorite perfume. "Well, my Christmas is complete. I got everything I wanted."

"Including Michael," Jeanine teased.

Clara smiled. "Especially Michael."

Clara went through the other mail. There were odds and ends of notes and Christmas wishes from home. Her grandparents had sent lace-edged handkerchiefs, and her sister Natalie had sent her a photograph of her family and a stationery set. There was film for the camera from her aunt and uncle who lived in California and a book of poetry from an old girlfriend back home who figured Clara was probably bored to tears being stuck in war-torn England. Clara smiled at the thought of boredom. There was never much time to be anything but tired and overwhelmed.

"I have the dress," Darlene said, popping into the room carrying a cream-colored suit.

Clara put her mail aside and eyed the outfit. It was a simple wool suit with a snug bodice that flared out at the waist. The skirt was straight and would be just a bit short, as Clara had at least two inches on Darlene. It wasn't what she had hoped for, but it would suffice.

"Thank you, Darlene. I appreciate having something to wear other than my Class A's."

"And look what she has for the wedding night," Jeanine teased, holding up the white gown.

"Oooh," Darlene exclaimed. "That's beautiful. Wherever did you get it?"

"My mother sent it for Christmas. I'm pretty sure she made it."

"Tell her to make me one too," Darlene said, hanging the suit in Clara's closet before coming over for a closer inspection.

"Oh, good, you're all in here," Madeline said, coming through the door. "I have this picture of Rita Hayworth. I think we should fix your hair like this for the wedding."

After that, the focus was clearly on getting Clara ready for the event of her life. Anna Nelson appeared only briefly to offer her blessing and to release all four girls to spend the day with Mrs. Clarke. They thanked her profusely, and Clara even received a small gift of sonnets from her supervisor.

"It's just a little gift for your wedding," Anna said, trying hard not to become overly sentimental. "Now, go on with you. All of you."

The girls gathered up their things and hurried over to Mrs. Clarke's with such abandonment and joy that the war was nearly forgotten.

"Oh, ladies, do come inside. You'll catch your death of cold out here," Sylvia said as she opened the door for them. It was unusual to find Sylvia answering her own door. "I just happened to see you coming down the lane. What a merry group of maids you make."

"We've come to prepare Clara for her wedding," Jeanine announced.

"Well, I have a room in the west wing set up for just such an occasion," Sylvia said, smiling. "I hope you and Dr. Shepherd will allow me to extend you an invitation to be my houseguest tonight. I didn't want you to feel the need to hurry off and find some pitiful lodging house for your honeymoon. The west wing is quite secluded. I can assure you all the privacy a young married couple should have. Will you stay?"

Clara felt her cheeks grow hot. "If Michael has no other plans, I would love to take you up on your offer. I know we won't have much time together and I certainly don't want to waste any of it traveling from one place to another."

"Wonderful. I shall see to it that your young man is completely convinced of the advantages. Now, if you ladies will just follow me, I will show you to the room in question."

Clara drew a deep breath and nodded. "I'm ready."

Sylvia led them up the long oak staircase. She had trimmed the banister with holly and ivy and red bows that looked slightly worn from years of use. Clara could picture herself coming down the stairs for her wedding. Suddenly the prospect of her rather rushed ceremony began to take on a new light. Sylvia had a beautiful home. The furnishings and decorations were refined and elegant. Who could want for a more perfect setting in which to marry?

"I had the maid air out the room this morning and give it an extra cleaning. I don't want you choking on dust while you're preparing for your special day."

"I'm sure it would be just fine, no matter," Clara replied.

Sylvia took them down a long hallway on the second floor and paused at the last door on the right. She sobered slightly. "This room once belonged to Meredith. I thought it would be the perfect place to put you."

Clara met the woman's thoughtful expression and nodded. "I'm so very touched, Sylvia. I know you understand what this means to me."

"I think I do," Sylvia replied. She opened the double doors and pushed them back. Clara and her entourage stood in gaping surprise at the suite. A fireplace decorated the wall to the left and a cheery blaze rose up from the hearth in welcome. On the mantel above, pictures of a smiling young woman and handsome man graced the oak surface. Clara knew it must be Meredith and her young beau. For a moment, Clara couldn't help but wonder what had happened to the young man after Meredith had died. Perhaps the time would present itself when she could ask.

To the right, a huge wood canopy bed dominated the remaining room. The dark walnut wood of the bed was further enriched by the burgundy and navy brocade that trimmed the posts.

"Oh, it's so . . . so . . ." Clara had no words. The bed was something out of a fairy tale. At least eight feet long and six feet across, the bed commanded their undivided attention.

"Now, that's a bed!" Jeanine said, marveling.

Sylvia chuckled. "The bed once belonged to my great-great-grandmother and has been handed down throughout the generations. Meredith thought it the most glorious creation she'd ever seen. When my mother died and left it to me, Meredith instantly claimed it for her own."

"I can understand why," Clara said in complete awe. "It's a marvelous bed." She turned to take in the armoire and Chinese rugs. "The entire room is like nothing I've ever known. I hope Michael has no other plans, because I want my honeymoon to start in a room like this."

"Me too," Darlene said, nodding. "If I can find me a guy to marry in the next week, can we stay here as well?"

Sylvia laughed. "There's no rush, dear. If you find a young man to marry, make certain it is for love and not the room in which you'll stay. Now, while Clara settles in, why don't you ladies go downstairs and see the cook. His sister owns a hothouse, and he is going to take you around to see about some flowers for the wedding."

"Wonderful!" Darlene exclaimed. "That was my job."

Sensing that Sylvia wanted a few moments alone with Clara, the girls quickly departed. Clara turned and surprised Sylvia with a hug.

"I don't know what to say. This is all too marvelous. I was just imagining descending the stairs to marry Michael, and then you give me this wonderful room for my wedding night. Sylvia, no one could have blessed me more than you have."

"Well, if you think you can handle one more surprise," the older woman said, "open the wardrobe." She pointed to the tall armoire in the corner.

Clara hesitated only a moment. Crossing the room, walking gingerly on the Chinese carpets as though she might damage them with her heels, Clara reached for the handles of the wardrobe. They creaked from lack of use, but Clara gave it no real consideration, for once the doors were open and the light of day had touched the contents inside, Clara knew why Sylvia had sent the girls away.

"A wedding gown!" she gasped. And without even trying it on, Clara knew it would fit. She touched the ivory satin and shook her head. With tears in her eyes she looked at Sylvia. "Was this Meredith's gown?"

Sylvia nodded. "I had no idea you were even looking for a gown. When you mentioned it at dinner, I suddenly knew why I'd held on to the dress for all these years. God knew you were coming and He wouldn't let me part with the gown you would need."

Clara could hardly believe it. She turned her attention to the gown. The Juliet sleeves, inset with lace, begged her touch. "I've never seen anything so lovely."

"We were a family of some means," Sylvia said, coming to stand beside her. "The gown was made nearly as soon as Meredith was engaged to be married. She had dreamed all her life of such a dress, and when Bryce finally asked for her hand, she couldn't wait to have the gown designed."

Clara traced the lace-edged neckline and felt tears slide down her cheeks. Just when she had given up her prideful ideas and handed the matter back over to God, her prayers had been answered and then some. She was to have a beautiful setting for her wedding—flowers, a party, and now a beautiful gown and honeymoon suite. She looked away from the dress and settled her gaze on Sylvia's face.

"I am completely amazed by all of this. You've made my dreams come true."

Sylvia shook her head. "No, love. God arranged it all. I was simply a tool for Him to use."

Clara flung her arms around Sylvia's neck. "Thank you. Thank you so very much for letting Him use you. And thank you for your kindness to a stranger."

Sylvia hugged Clara tightly, then pulled back. "No more tears now. You don't want to have your eyes all red and puffy for the wedding. I suggest instead that you unpack while I send up some lunch and arrange a hot bath. We must have you at your best when the groom shows up."

Clara nodded and dried her eyes with one of the lace handkerchiefs she'd been given for Christmas. "I'll try not to cry anymore, but I know it won't be easy. I'm just so happy." She smiled, unable to hide her joy.

"That's just as it should be," Sylvia replied. She glanced around the room and nodded. "Yes. Just as it should be."

"No, put some more lilies of the valley in her hair," Jeanine suggested. "Right up front where the veil is pinned. That way you can hide the pins."

Darlene did as she was instructed and then stood back. "Perfect!"

Clara bit at her lower lip nervously. "Are you sure? I want to make sure everything is just right." She strained to see the mirror, but the girls hadn't allowed her that liberty yet.

"Just sit still now," Madeline commanded. "Do you have something old?"

Clara nodded. "My necklace," she said seriously, then added with a grin, "and my undergarments."

The girls laughed as Madeline continued. "Something new?"

"Yes. I'm wearing the slippers my mother made for Christmas." She pulled up the skirt of the gown and displayed her feet. The white was a little brighter than that of the ivory gown, but no one seemed to think it a problem.

"Good. What about something borrowed?"

"The gown," Clara said, running her hands lovingly over the bodice. It fit as though it had been created for her, with exception to the fact that it was a tad short.

"That just leaves blue," Madeline replied. "Do you have something blue?"

Clara started to panic. "No! I have nothing blue. Oh no. What do I do?"

"Calm down," Jeanine laughed. "We'll figure it out."

"You could wear your battle dress pants under the gown," Darlene teased.

"Or the cap instead of this veil," Jeanine threw in.

"This is serious!" Clara nearly shouted. Her nerves were raw from the entire experience. Maybe she should tell her mother that eloping was the better choice and that she should stop bemoaning her own simple wedding. Worrying over the details was about to send Clara scrambling for the nearest window.

"Here," Madeline said, reaching into her pocketbook. "I have this." She pulled out a handkerchief with blue bells embroidered in one corner. "This will work."

Clara breathed a sigh of relief and leaned back against the wall. "I may not live through all of this."

The girls laughed and turned her for one final inspection. The knock on the door nearly sent all of them into a panic.

"It's time!" Darlene declared.

"Don't let anyone in!" Madeline exclaimed.

"Hurry up and let me see what I look like," Clara demanded. "I'm not even going downstairs if I look silly."

"You would go down there even if you looked like a circus clown," Jeanine said, laughing. "But have it your way." She stepped back and unveiled the cheval mirror.

Clara caught her reflection for the first time that evening. *Radiant* was the only word that came to mind. Her face radiated the joy she felt, and the gown and trimmings that her friends had so thoughtfully arranged only magnified the happiness that came from within.

"Oh!" was all she could say.

"He won't be disappointed when he sees you," Jeanine whispered. "But I doubt he would have been under any circumstances. So are you ready?"

Clara nodded. "I'm ready, but I'm also suddenly terrified."

"Wedding jitters," Madeline whispered. "That's all. You'll be fine once the ring is on your finger."

"Ring?" Clara said. "Oh no. I wonder if Michael thought to get a ring."

"Calm down," the ladies said in chorus.

"You'll still be married even if there's no ring," Darlene reminded her.

Clara nodded. "Yes. I suppose you're right." She took a deep breath and prayed silently. *Thank you, Father, for the miracles you've arranged tonight. Thank you for bringing Michael here safely and for the minister being available and for the gown and the room and everything! Thank you for hearing a young woman's dreams and making them come true.*

CHAPTER 9

Michael stood in his Class A uniform, shifting nervously from one foot to the other. When he saw Darlene appear at the top of the staircase, he realized the time had come. His waiting would soon be over and he and Clara would finally be married. He felt regret only for the fact that he hadn't been able to get her a wedding gown. It seemed like such a small request, even if there was a war going on.

Darlene beamed him a smile and stepped to one side as Madeline descended the steps behind her. Next came Jeanine, who seemed particularly joyous over the occasion. Michael felt Joe nudge him and turned to see his best man eyeing Jeanine with an appreciative stare.

"Isn't she beautiful?" Joe whispered. Then his eyes caught sight of something else and he poked Michael hard in the ribs. "Well, would you look at that."

Michael turned back to the staircase and felt his heart nearly stop. Clara stood at the top, a vision in satin and lace. Michael moved forward as she descended the stairs slowly and cautiously. Her right hand clung to the banister, while her left hand held a bouquet of roses and lilies of the valley.

She smiled at him, and Michael felt his knees turn rubbery. He'd known for a long time that he would marry this woman, but somehow he had never imagined the wonder of this moment.

Clara reached the bottom step and took hold of Michael's arm. Leaning close, she whispered, "You should probably close your mouth, Michael. Joe's going to think you're here for a dental exam instead of a wedding."

Michael looked around, rather embarrassed, then grinned. "You shouldn't shock a man like this, you know." He gripped her possessively. "Come on, let's get this wedding on the road. The chaplain has to be back before midnight."

The ceremony itself was quick and orderly. Clara had her own pleasant surprise when Michael slipped a gold band onto her finger. He hadn't forgotten the ring! Sylvia was the first to congratulate them before leading them both into the dining hall, where she had set up the reception. Clara and Michael greeted their guests, laughing and commenting on each person's reaction.

"After running all over England looking for a dress," Anna Nelson teased, "you must have felt rather silly to find one right under your nose."

Clara exchanged a glance with Sylvia, who was standing not a foot away serving tea to her guests. "I don't feel silly at all," Clara replied. "I feel only blessed and very fortunate to have such good friends."

The evening wore on and the party intensified. Most everyone in the room knew that the men would soon be heading across the Channel. No one knew how long the war would continue. What had once been thought to be a simple matter of tying up loose ends and forcing the Germans to surrender had changed overnight to leave them all discouraged and baffled. The war showed little sign of being over, and that would mean more soldiers, more wounded, more dead.

"Sylvia suggests we make a break for it," Michael whispered in Clara's ear. "It's nearly eleven-thirty."

Clara nodded. "Did she tell you about our suite?"

He grinned. "She did. It came as welcome news. General Blevins managed to get me here, but he can't work miracles. I didn't want to spend our first night together in the back of the Clubmobile."

Clara laughed. "Me neither. I've spent enough time there as it is." She took hold of his hand and lead him toward the stairs. "Hurry before someone sees us."

They raced up the stairs, barely containing their laughter. When they reached the top, they slowed and walked leisurely down the hall, arm in arm. Clara looked up at Michael with such adoration and love that he could hardly breathe. They paused at the doors, and Clara opened them without ceremony.

"It's the most beautiful room in the world," she declared.

"Perfect," he said, lifting her into his arms. "For the most beautiful bride in the world."

She looped her arms around his neck and smiled. "We finally managed to see this thing through."

"Any regrets?" he questioned seriously.

Clara shook her head. "Not a one."

He crossed the threshold with her and, before he put her down, pressed his lips to Clara's in a passionate kiss. As she wrapped her arms around him tightly, Michael slowly allowed her to stand. He embraced her tightly, pulling her against him. "I love you, Mrs. Shepherd," he whispered.

"And I love you," she replied, her gaze meeting his.

He set her away from him, then turned to close and lock the doors. Sliding the top bolt into place, he suddenly felt very nervous. He turned to find her pulling the pins from her hair in order to remove the veil.

Suddenly the future seemed very uncertain. He knew he'd been advised not to have a true wedding night with his bride. The danger of leaving a widow carrying his child was great, especially if things in Europe were as intense as rumor had it. Swallowing hard, he broached the subject.

"Clar," he said softly.

She looked up at him and smiled. "You'll have to help me with the buttons. I can't reach them."

Michael stepped forward as she turned to show him her back. He reached out hesitantly, his hands shaking slightly as he unfastened the first of many satin-covered buttons.

"We need to talk," he began again.

Clara turned around as soon as he finished with the buttons. "What's wrong?"

He put his hands on her shoulders. "Nothing is wrong. I just want you to think about our night together. I'm leaving tomorrow—at least that's the way they're telling it right now. And whether this is the real thing or just another false alarm, the reality of it is simple. The future is very uncertain. We have no way of knowing whether I'll stay or go. And if I go, we have no way of knowing if I'll make it back alive. We have to face facts."

Clara nodded, although he could see that a little of the color in her cheeks had waned. "I know all of this."

"It might be better if we put off having a real wedding night," he said. "I would hate to leave you a widow, but I would hate even more to leave you as a pregnant widow."

Clara's expression soften as she reached up to touch his face with her hand. "Michael, there's no way to predict the future. We have to trust God for what will come. Whether you head off to war or off to a regular day of performing a physician's tasks, we have no guarantees."

"I know, but you have to admit this is different. I don't want to leave you and I'm going to do everything in my power to stay alive, but—"

She put a finger to his lips and shook her head. "'Take therefore no thought for the morrow: for the morrow shall take thought for the things of itself. Sufficient unto the day is the evil thereof.'" She gently moved her finger over his lips and down the line of his jaw. "I would not have married you if I didn't intend to be a wife to you in every way. If God chooses to bless us with a child, then that is His will and I will gladly accept it."

Michael pulled her close and buried his face in her hair. She smelled of lilies of the valley and the same sweet scent she always wore. "I just wanted you to be sure," he said, gently touching his lips to her earlobe. "I didn't want you to regret tonight."

She shook her head. "No regrets, Michael. Only hope. Hope for the future and time to grow the love we have for each other."

From somewhere down the hall, the clock began to chime. "It's midnight!" Michael said. "It's Christmas! Christmas, Clara!"

Clara laughed. "You sound like a little boy who's been waiting to unwrap his presents."

Michael raised a brow and gave Clara a look that caused her to blush. "I *have* been waiting to unwrap my present," he said, reaching for her hand. *Let the war rage,* he thought. *Take no thought of the morrow—tonight is ours.* God had brought them together and worked more than one miracle to see them married. How could Michael doubt that He must also have great plans for them both?

He pulled her close. "Merry Christmas, my sweet wife."

She met his eyes and he felt her tremble in his arms. "Merry Christmas, my love."